Other Books by
Jess E. Owen

Song of the Summer King

Skyfire

A Shard of Sun

By the Silver Wind

BY THE SILVER WIND

JESS E. OWEN

five elements press

Five Elements Press
Suite 305
500 Depot Street
Whitefish, MT 59937
www.fiveelementspress.com

PUBLISHER'S NOTE
This is a work of fiction. Any references to historical events, real people, or real locales are used fictitiously. Other names, characters, places, or incidents are the product of the author's imagination, and any resemblance to actual events, locales, or persons, living or dead, are purely coincidental.

Cover art by Jennifer Miller © 2015
Cover typography and interior formatting by Terry Roy
Author photo by Jessica Lowry
Edited by Joshua Essoe
Copy Editor: AnthroAquatic Literary Services

ISBN-10: 0-9967676-3-0
ISBN-13: 978-0-9967676-3-7

First Paperback Edition

This one is for the Pride.

TABLE OF CONTENTS

By the Silver Wind

Jess E. Owen

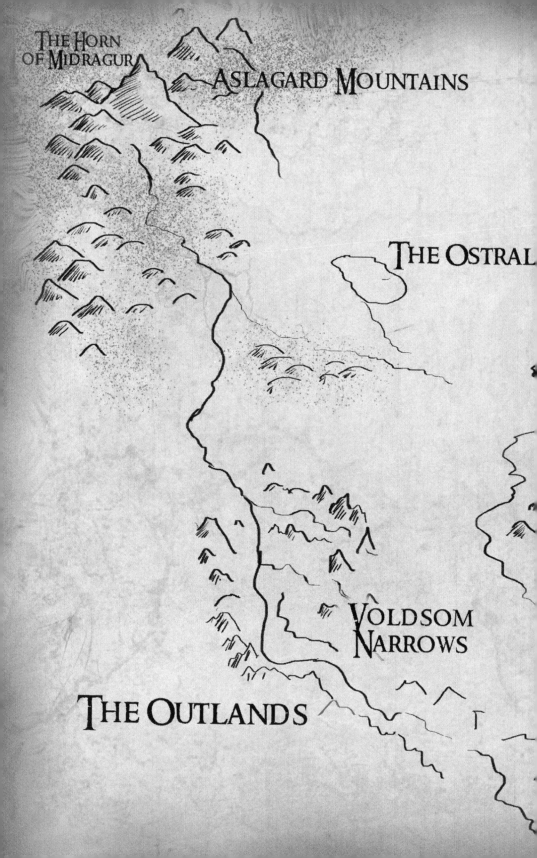

Starward

Nightward

Dawnward

Windward

HORES THE WINDEROST

DAWN SPIRE

THE DAWN REACH

THE VANHEIM
SHORE

S HE HAD ONCE BEEN AS beautiful as the mountains. Her eyes once fierce as stars, her claws like shards of shell, her hide as strong as stone. Like a new mountain having just broken from the flat of the earth, she had been rugged, sharp, and mighty.

Now, like the oldest mountains, she had worn down. Her hide was dull, and scored by the little talons of the unworthy. Her eyes dimmed, weaker and weaker in the dark and in the rain, and from a great distance, things were never what they seemed to be.

The cords of muscle between her wings ached from the assault of the unworthy's attack. Her claws flexed. Those blasphemous progeny of Tyr and Tor. How they nettled her, and strutted, and babbled, and shrieked, while she and her family—graceful, powerful, as ancient and pure as the stones and the sea—floundered in Nameless servitude.

Her wounds had scarred, but they burned. They burned, because she had fled with her sons and her mates, and her daughters. She had fled, and her wounds festered with malice.

The great wyrm shifted, edging deeper into the murky den that they all called home when the sun was high. Her family coiled around her protectively as they slumbered, sprawling across the rough, digging rocks.

She remembered a nest of firm, warm gold, lined with sweet-smelling waves of raw silver, and tumbling gems that massaged her hard hide. The bright ones had come and envied her gold, and offered a trade. But that was so long ago, and in another place.

She remembered the rich, heady scent of fallow earth and tender spring grass, green as a new hatchling before its hide hardened and turned dull. She remembered being that young.

A low, experimental rumble rolled from her chest.

Rhydda.

Rhydda.

She couldn't form the noise as he had. Her jaws were too primitive, wide and limited in shape, her tongue too scaled and thick. The low, steady growl began to disturb her family, and they grumbled in complaint. Outside, the pale light of afternoon deepened to gold, then orange, and finally red through the haze. Sunset.

Rhydda. Are you she?

Over and over she turned the word, his voice, his voice. It was not like the rest of the unworthy, for he changed his tone again and again to speak to her, until she realized he was speaking after all, not just squeaking at her. Like a quick, cool, spring wind, his voice soothed the malice in her muscles, cooled the burning in her wounds. It had been a trick, though, a trick while he gathered his fire, and attacked.

She should have known.

Rhydda. Did you fly to the Sunland?

The Sunland.

The sun.

Did you fly under the sun?

She closed her eyes. Stretched a hind leg. There was no hurry. She mulled over his voice and why it no longer irritated her into blind anger.

Did you fly in the sun? Is that your home?

Home. It was not this place, though she had been here a long time. Enough to hatch two broods.

Is that your home?

Waves of chilly gray ocean and the boggy scent of wet peat and crawling vetch seemed to fill her senses with each breath. He flew with her, the little slip of wind and his silver voice, in her dreams now. Every night since the fires defeated them, she had flown, in her dreams, to the green land. And he had been there. Then he showed her another place. Another place like hers, but less green. Six islands in an icy sea, mountains, woods, a rich and wild place. His home.

She opened an eye to check the sunmark, then closed it again. Red light touched the entrance of the dark cave. They would wait until night to hunt, for they were never to go out in the day.

You are not worthy of Tyr's light. Your kind is bred for the night, for the dark. You must always remain in the dark until you are enlightened, as we are.

It had been so long ago. She could not remember how they learned their proper place, if it wasn't the bright voice of Tyr himself, or thundering Tor, or the terrifying, stark voice of Midragur, the First.

Rhydda. Rhydda.

He was trying to find her. To give her another dream.

Did you once fly under the sun?

She thought of nothing. She thought of blood and stone, until his voice slipped away.

A long time ago, she dreamed she had flown over the largest water, flown to the masters, the bright ones, so that they might return and bring gems and give names to her new brood. But then . . .

But then . . .

One of her sons shifted and she stretched her wing to cover him.

Rhydda. Are you Rhydda? Did you fly under the sun?

In her dream, the sky welled around her, blue-bird bright, and the ocean rolled cobalt under her wings, dazzling her eyes with a wash of sparkles like diamonds blazing under the sun.

The sun?

He'd found her. He glided beside her, and with her, beheld the vision.

The sun! His voice, surprised, knowing, exhilarated, gusted around her and under her wings, lifting her high like a sudden, hot wind. *Don't you see? You once flew under the sun!*

It was not a dream.

It was a memory.

Rhydda's eyes snapped open.

1
THE SALT LAKE SHORE

SHARD HIT THE SALT WAVES with a hard splash after a flailing, spiral dive. Turning about, he kicked hard to break the surface again and gasped before hacking up bitter water. Wind buffeted around him and white-capped waves slapped his face. All around him, gryfons dove and struck the water, and he watched them with a critical eye. He had purposefully illustrated a poor crash landing, and how to correct.

The salty waters of the landlocked lake claimed by the gryfon clans of the Ostral Shores proved to be the perfect training grounds for young, exiled Vanir. Shard knew they would need both strong swimming skills and the ability to save themselves and fly out of the water during their long flight home.

Thinking of home, Shard recalled his dream. The lake seemed to disappear from around him, and the memory of the she-wyrm's mind and memories held him fast.

Rhydda, he thought with bright surprise, *did we dream together?*

"Good!" hollered Stigr from the shore, snapping Shard from his thoughts. Alert, he paced as Vanir pelted the water like gulls. The old warrior gryfon might have been missing both his left wing and his

left eye, but he still knew flying and swimming better than any gryfon
Shard knew, and he was grateful for the assistance. He would tell Stigr
about the dream later. "Well done, Keta!"

A high keen answered Stigr, triumphant, and the young gryfess
he'd addressed not only dived with ease, but flapped hard from the
water and took to the air again as easily as a tern.

A born Vanir, Shard thought. Many of them, so desperate to return
home and hungry for their birthright, had learned the skills faster than
Shard ever had. For the last days they'd swiftly learned and rediscov-
ered fishing, swimming, and their own lore.

Chilly in winter, though the sun remained warm in the day, the
conditions were the perfect proving ground for any who meant to
make the flight over the sea. A high wind had risen at dawn and white-
capped the lake all day. For nearly a moon the entire Winderost had
been obscured and buried under the falling ash of a volcano called
the Horn of Midragur, but within the last couple of days the air had
settled and cleared. Now, everything seemed extra sharp, bright and
hopeful in contrast. It was a perfect day to fly and practice and Shard
wished he could focus on it.

"Toskil," he called to a gray and brown gryfon, who floundered
to right himself and sort out his wings. "Use your wings like fins.
Try to spread them and just float." He swam toward Toskil, a Vanir
his own age just recently rescued from the wasteland that gryfons of
the Winderost only called the Outlands. "And I know it's frightening,
but try to dive head first. You're less likely to strain a wing or break a
bone. Watch the gulls and terns."

"Yes, sire," Toskil said, shaking his head and flinging droplets of
water everywhere.

Shard almost corrected him to use his name, but stopped himself.
Stigr insisted that the Vanir needed a prince, needed a king, though he
knew Shard preferred informality.

Let them serve you. Let them respect and honor you. For one thing, the gruff
warrior had said more than once, *you blazing well deserve it.*

So Shard merely dipped his head as Toskil sorted himself and corrected into a respectable floating position. Stroking the water slowly, he watched as Toskil paddled noisily away from him to try flying out. He looked around for any struggling Vanir, and was pleased to see them helping each other, the older ones remembering their skills, the younger calling advice to their peers. As they learned fishing and swimming, they also strengthened, grew healthier, shed any lingering sickness or weakness from the Outlands.

They were beginning to look like Vanir again. They were almost ready to fly home, once Shard's business in the Winderost was done.

Water swirled around him, alerting him to movement just before a gryfess face popped out of the waves in front of him.

He had a flashing second to see fierce gold eyes and red-flecked cheeks before hearing a war cry of, "Sea wolf attack!" The gryfess surged forward and shoved him under the water.

Shard shrieked out a shower of silver bubbles and wrestled away, more wiry and agile than she in the water, though her grip was strong. He twisted and stroked his wings hard, breaking the surface again two leaps away. Talons caught his tail just as he gasped a breath, grabbed his wing joint and his shoulder, and dragged him under as she used him to climb up and emerge from the water.

Shard grasped her foreleg and thrust his head from the waves again, shaking his head to shower her. "I submit!"

"Then you're sea wolf food." Brynja flicked water from her ears. The joke was a weak one. It hadn't been so long ago that Shard had nearly been killed by whales in the arctic ocean. "How was that, my prince?"

"Just fine," Shard said, laughing, still gripping her foreleg gently. "If we see battle in the waves, I know you'll hold your own. But I knew that anyway."

Stockier than he, with russet feathers and the broad, strong wings of an Aesir, Brynja displayed a very different picture than the rest of the diving gryfons. Her voice lowered. "Well done enough for a Vanir, or just for an Aesir, pretending?"

"As well done as any of us," Shard said, ignoring the eyes on them from the shore and the air. "Even Stigr approves."

He meant it in more ways than one. He thought of telling her about his dream right then, but decided against it, for she seemed worried about other things and he only wanted to reassure her. She searched his face, then nodded once at his encouraging look, nipped his ear, and dove under the water again. Just like the younger Vanir, she was anxious to prove herself, though for different reasons.

Shard let out a slow breath, and before he could pursue, heard his name called.

"My lord! Rashard, a moment, sire!"

He closed his eyes briefly at Ketil's voice, gathering his strength. The older Vanir gryfess was invaluable, strong, a great huntress, and a member of his pride who had suffered long years in the Outlands. He had the utmost respect for her, but she was ever after him for something. Rather than fly, for his wings ached from repeated diving exercise, he swam back to shore and shook himself, ruffling and settling his feathers in the late afternoon light.

Ketil trotted up to him on the pebbled beach, mantled briefly, and looked out over the water.

For most of the time Shard had been a prince, there was only his uncle, or he'd been alone. Being a prince was much different once he was actually surrounded by subjects.

"Frar is insisting that the Aesir conqueror means to send us into battle against the wyrms again, though this time for his glory, and not your aide."

"Kjorn," Shard said tightly. "His name is Kjorn. *Prince* Kjorn, and I doubt Frar heard correctly. Kjorn wouldn't do that."

Ketil didn't seem to hear, her gaze roving out and ears perked toward the water instead. "I've tried to assure him you won't let this happen, but he goes on."

"I'll speak to him, thank you for telling me." He stretched a wing toward the water. "Keta is doing well." The young gryfess circled, preparing for another dive. He'd changed the topic purposefully, and quickly realized he should've chosen a different one.

"You think so? I agree." Ketil's gaze grew keen, and she paced into the water, tail flicking like a stalking huntress. "Very well indeed. As if she'd been raised on the Copper Cliffs of home like any Vanir." She looked over her wing at Shard. "She's learning fishing. A fine huntress on land too, though we won't need to worry about that when we arrive home."

"I'm sure she is," Shard said, keeping his voice neutral. "She's endured much."

"Yes, but see how she rebounds now." Ketil's voice nearly shivered with pride. And calculation. "See, there, how she teaches the others, and leads them."

There it was, the hinting. Shard flexed his wings, hoping they would dry before night fell again. "I'm very proud and pleased for her, and glad to have her in my pride."

Keta prowled out of the water, and shook her talons daintily. "As you should be. If you'll permit me to say so," she used that phrase often, and always said whatever it was with or without permission, "you might come to know her better."

Shard inclined his head. "I'll come to know all of you better as we go on."

"You are the very image of Baldr." The older huntress's gaze traveled over him, respectfully. "I know you'll do all you can to honor his memory." She always appeared to approve of everything about him, save one thing.

"Shard," Brynja called as she trotted out of the water, pausing to shake and fold her wings. Ketil looked firmly away, watching the Vanir dive. "We should start the fires now, before dark."

"Agreed. Ketil, fair winds." Shard inclined his head to say goodbye.

"Sire." Her gaze was locked on the lake and her own daughter.

Shard's feathers prickled in irritation. At one time in his life, not so long ago, he would usually let slights pass. He'd rarely been in a position to defend himself or to demand respect from others. Sometimes, he still counted it not worth his time to argue over matters of simple pride.

But a slight to Brynja, he would not let stand.

"Ketil." She looked at him, and his tail lashed. "You will acknowledge a fellow member of your pride, and your future queen."

Brynja drew herself up, ears perking. They had not formally mated yet, but all who watched them could see their intention, and it was one of few times Shard had said it out loud.

Ketil turned slowly, lowering her head not in respect, but in the manner of a wolf, defensive, challenging. "As a huntress, you have my respect. As a warrior who faced the enemy and flew with fire, I honor you. But I did not spend ten years in exile to acknowledge an Aesir as my queen, and I will not, until you have locked talons and vowed under the light of Tyr and Tor." She looked between them. "And I still hold hope you will both come to your senses and see the folly of this. My lord." She dipped her head. "Brynja."

With that, she stalked away.

Shard growled low and moved to follow.

"No," Brynja murmured. He turned to her, expecting to see doubt. But her ears lay flat, her eyes narrowed in determination. "Don't bother. If she wants to wait until we've made our vow, so be it. Who knows, maybe you will come to your senses." She was teasing, but Shard only prickled.

"That's not funny." He walked to her and butted his head against her wing, then preened lightly on her neck. "I'll make my vow right here," he murmured into her feathers, "on this shore, under this sun."

Brynja laughed, wincing away as if he'd tickled her. "No, my prince. It must be right. It must be at your—at *our* home. In the Silver Isles, on the Daynight as you have watched others vow before you. I want no more reason for anyone to call our decision to mate a cursed one."

Shard stepped back, feeling warm, feeling grateful for her honesty and for wanting to honor his traditions. "If that's what you want."

"It is." She studied his face with a warm expression. In the sunlight her feathers looked aflame, and Shard's thoughts flashed on the Battle of Torches, when he'd first seen her again. Fire, smoke, and hulking, roaring wyrms clustered in his thoughts, and with apprehension, he thought of his dream.

Brynja tilted her head. "What's wrong, Shard?"

He glanced toward the Vanir swooping and diving across the lake. "The most vivid dream of Rhydda that I've had. I think, maybe, I communicated with her."

Her eyes widened. "As Groa said you could?"

She spoke of the spirit of a gryfon priestess who had appeared to Shard, and taught him about dreaming. He ducked his head, lowering his voice. He didn't want everyone to hear, just yet. "I'll tell you more after supper."

"I hope you do," she said quietly, following his cue. "And Kjorn."

"Of course," Shard said softly, and leaned in to touch his beak to Brynja's cheek. "I must see to the fires now."

He backed away and mantled to her, and she to him with a concerned look. Then she slipped away to help with the division of fish for supper, and as the last of the Vanir swam or flew from the water, Shard left to light the evening fires. Since Shard had acquired fire stones in the Sunland, they didn't have to keep fires burning all night and all day as they once had at the Dawn Spire—Brynja's home, and where Shard had first seen gryfons using fire at all. Now they rebuilt the fires every night, to give themselves warmth, and more time in the evening to see and to plan.

Remembering Ketil's original purpose in speaking to him, Shard reminded himself to seek out Frar, the first and oldest of the exiled Vanir who had come to his beacon in the Outlands nearly a month ago, and reassure him that they would not send any unwilling Vanir into battle again.

Stigr found him as he struck sparks onto the last of the brush piles.

"Well Ketil's in a crosswind," Stigr said, sounding more amused than anything. "And she's complaining to everyone but me. What did you do this time?"

"The same as every time." Of course Ketil wouldn't go to Stigr. Though he was Shard's closest friend and relative present, a leader among the Vanir, he too had inadvertently bonded with an Aesir huntress. This must have disqualified him, in Ketil's estimation, from offering any help to sort out Shard's affairs.

"She still wants you to mate with that daughter of hers?"

"Or any Vanir, but I'm sure Keta is her first choice." They backed away as the tinder caught and the blaze crawled over the dry wood.

Stigr watched the fire with his single eye, pale moss-green like Shard's eyes, though Shard didn't resemble his uncle in any other way. Half a head shorter, slighter, and gray of feather rather than black, Shard could only really claim his uncle's teachings to give them similarity. "Best of luck. I know you won't let them bully you."

Grateful for his uncle's simple, uncomplicated assessment, Shard nodded once. It was beyond the scope of any gryfon to meddle in another's mating decision, and while Shard wished his decision was less complicated, he would choose no other.

"Thank you, Uncle." He was about to tell Stigr about the dream when the old Vanir spoke again.

"Meanwhile," he said, turning from the fire, "Kjorn needs you. Come with me."

2

PRIDE OF THE LAKE

THE GRYFON TERRITORY CALLED THE OSTRAL Shores was a series of blunt hills and hollows around the shore of the great lake. Beyond that, the land stretched away again into long, grassy plains and more unforgiving desert. In the hollows on the starward shore of the lake, gryfons had dug their dens. Usually by the dark of night they'd all gone in to sleep, but now they gathered around fires to eat and talk.

One bluff rose above the rest, stretching at least twenty leaps in length and just as much in height. It was there that the leaders of the Ostral Shore pride had gathered, in the light of a bonfire. A few dens were dug into the side of that bluff near its extremities, but the main and highest crown served as a meeting place, much like the King's Rocks in the Silver Isles. During the day, they met on top, but now in the windy night, they relished the fire in the protected embrace of the bluff.

Kjorn stood in a ring of gryfons around the fire, listening to gryfons argue about why they would not join him, or why they should, and whether or not they trusted him.

Five clans who called themselves Lakelanders made their home at the Ostral Shore, with two gryfons representing each clan. Kjorn had learned these were not necessarily the wisest of their number, but the largest and the loudest.

"You've heard my plan," Kjorn said, quietly so they were forced to quiet as well. "My wingbrother and I will visit each gryfon clan, as well as the painted dogs, the lions, and the eagles, gain their alliance, and rid the Winderost of the wyrm scourge. Then I shall return to the Dawn Spire, as is my birthright."

A burly, heavily-muscled and pale gryfon with a bit of middle-aged gut paced before the bluff, the fire casting his shadow five times as large behind him.

"And if you fail?" he demanded. His words slurred a bit with extra breath, for the tip of his beak was chipped. Fresh injury, Kjorn thought, and realized this gryfon fought at the Battle of Torches. "Why should we bow again to a king of the Dawn Spire? Not even a king, an exile. All these pretty promises you make, with not a talon to back you."

"He'd like *our* talons, Lofgar," growled a female. Just as tall, silver-gray in color with an entirely black head, she cut a haunting shape against the fire. "You leaped into battle quick enough before."

"Are you afraid?" a familiar voice asked Lofgar.

Kjorn looked along their number for that voice, and saw a friend. All assembled were seasoned, hearty, large warriors, but Asvander stood out among them. He was not a leader of the Ostral Shore yet, but his father was, and Kjorn saw how he was at odds with them. Asvander had chosen to serve as a warrior of the Dawn Spire where a different king ruled, a king who had taken over when Kjorn's grand-father fled to the Silver Isles. "Your beak will grow back, but withered courage is a cursed vine."

"Say that again, whelp," roared Lofgar, turning to face Asvander, his tail whipping the flames. "I fear nothing. I'll fight tonight if you like. But whether I do so in the name of the Ostral Shores or in the name of Kjorn and the Dawn Spire is the question, here."

"I say it is time for us to reunite," Asvander said, his voice like iron. "The line of Kajar has returned."

Though they had once been allies, most of the Lakelander clans had abandoned the Dawn Spire when Kjorn's grandfather left the Winderost. Shard told Kjorn that Asvander had been a rival, then a friend to him at the Dawn Spire, brazen and steadfast. He stood as strong as any among them, with iron-gray, falcon coloring and a black mask running over his eyes.

"Quiet your kit, Asrik," Lofgar growled to an older yet mirror-version gryfon who stood beside Asvander. "He speaks out of turn."

"Mind your own nest," Asrik said, but didn't look at Asvander. Kjorn noted the tension. Shard had told him they'd been estranged when Asvander left for the Dawn Spire, but with Kjorn's return there seemed hope to unite the Ostral Shores and the Dawn Spire again. Still Asrik seemed disappointed in his son's decisions, among other things.

Lofgar huffed. "Asvander will follow anyone on their way to the Dawn Spire."

"Blind loyalty is worse than caution," warned the black-headed female. Scars lined her face and flanks with near artistry, Kjorn thought, countless tokens of skirmishes and battles won. He hoped not to cross or insult any of these gryfons. They were generous hosts, and would be even more powerful enemies. "Lofgar is right. The question at stake is who we are serving."

"Did you not leave the Dawn Spire as a show of loyalty to Per the Red?" Asvander demanded. The others remained quiet as he spoke. "To show all that we follow only the true king of the Winderost?"

Kjorn remained quiet. Though Asvander was in disfavor with some of the gryfons there, he knew it was better to let one of their own make the argument, rather than himself, a near stranger. He admired

Asvander, knowing how painful it was to make a stand against friends and family.

Asvander turned in a circle, as if to encompass them and all that had happened, and faced the fire again. "And now his grandson has returned and offers us a chance for glory, a chance to renew our oaths, and we stand here nattering like old gulls?"

At his words, all eyes turned at last to Kjorn again. He lifted his head a fraction, knowing who he was to them, knowing his own legacy. Son of red Sverin, Prince of the Aesir in the Silver Isles, he stood tall among them, more leanly-muscled than Asvander but taller. His feathers gleamed like gold, his eyes summer blue like his mother's, a rare trait that identified him for all. A trickle of true gold glinted from his feathers, a thin chain that had belonged to his father.

Lofgar shuffled, ruffling his feathers. "I won't serve an untested exile."

"He's not untested."

Shard's voice filled Kjorn with relief, and all turned to see where he approached, with his uncle.

Stigr dipped his head to all, and Shard murmured a greeting. The changes in Shard still surprised Kjorn, and he wondered if he looked the same. Older, a bit haggard, lean, but Shard's eyes always shone now with the prospect of going home, of returning his lost Vanir to the Silver Isles and making things right. Before, his fine features and green eyes had always been a friendly sight for Kjorn, now they were something more. Now he was grown up, a fellow prince, a strong ally.

The Summer King, Kjorn thought, with a touch of chagrin.

"And these," the scarred female said warily. "How much longer is your pride to enjoy our hospitality, son of Baldr?"

"Not more than a moon," Shard said, moving to Kjorn's side. Kjorn drew in a large breath, hoping to gain some resolve. "Once they've fully recovered, once they've learned swimming and sea flight, and once the enemy is overthrown. I will stay to support Kjorn, with any of my number who are willing. Some of them will travel when

Kjorn and I leave in two days. We will help him to reunite the gryfon clans who splintered when Per left, and we'll help to rid the Winderost of the enemy wyrms."

His announcement had the desired effect, and Kjorn heard Stigr's soft rumble of approval. There Shard stood, nearly two heads shorter than Kjorn, dull gray and wiry, with a single thick scar on a hind leg to hint that he'd ever survived any real battle. They'd all seen him fight at the Battle of Torches, seen him face and challenge the wyrms alone, and knew his appearance was deceptive.

Kjorn certainly knew that his appearance was deceptive.

Still, his announcement was a challenge. The Lakelanders shifted, casting glances over the fire to each other uneasily.

"Here now," said Asvander loudly. "That's more like it. If this foreign prince has pledged his lot in, and he with no more to gain here, how can we do less? He could flee, yet he stays. He stays out of love for his wingbrother, he stays to right the wrong in this land—"

"He stays to court," said an older male near Lofgar, badly scarred along his flanks as if he'd been burned. "Or so I heard. Isn't that right, Asvander?"

"Shut your beak," Asrik said, as Asvander's ears slicked back.

Kjorn's feathers prickled and he tried to catch Asvander's gaze, but Asvander didn't look his way again. The argument had to do with Brynja, and a former arrangement the current king of the Dawn Spire had for her and Asvander to mate, though neither of them particularly wanted to. Then, Shard and Brynja had met, and Kjorn returned, giving the possibility that any bad promises made under the old king might not have to be kept. Apparently, to the Lakelanders, this cast Asvander in further dishonor.

Meanwhile, Kjorn couldn't afford to go so far off topic.

"More to the point," he said, raising his voice before the rest of the Lakelanders could resume their quarreling, "he stays. Several of you fought beside us at the Battle of Torches, and boldly. Your own pride joined us. Why is the next fight even a question? Families are separated between the Ostral Shores, the Dawn Spire, and exiles who've sickened of our bickering and left to roam free. Shall we continue this way? Or shall we band together again, oust the great wyrms and reclaim our land and our peace and freedom?"

"And under your name?" Lofgar asked, slyly.

Kjorn looked at him, perking his ears at the challenge. "Yes. As united gryfons of the Winderost. Under my name and in the name of the Dawn Spire, but for each other, in brotherhood."

The fire shivered and sparks popped high into the night. Kjorn saw the light of Tyr in their faces, the thought of fierce battle and glory. To be among the gryfons who drove the scourge from the Winderost...

Kjorn latched on to the glimmer of interest. "Are the Lakelanders not the most famed warrior pride in the Winderost?" he demanded, when no one spoke again. "For what reason do you shrink from battle now? In two days I will leave to speak with others in the Winderost, and what shall I tell them of you?"

The scarred female spoke. "How do we know you won't flee again, like Per, and Sverin?"

The names sent a prickle of frustration under his feathers, but he managed to keep them smooth, calm. "Because I've come home, of my own accord. I will not abandon the Winderost, no matter the enemy."

"How do we know you'll win the Dawn Spire?" asked Asrik, quietly.

"You don't," Kjorn said, turning to him as he felt the tide turning. "But I intend to, and when I do, all loyalty will be rewarded."

"Is that why you fight?" Stigr asked Asrik and the others mildly, and his low voice drew several stern glares. "For reward?"

"Silence, Outlander," Lofgar growled. "This isn't your affair."

Stigr drew himself up, wiry and shorter than the average Lakelander, but in the orange light his presence seemed as large as any of them. "It is now. I am a warrior of the Dawn Spire. I'll fight the cursed wyrms, *again*, and I'll see my nephew's wingbrother retake the highest tier. I'll do it one-winged, half blind, and with no assurance that we'll win. What will you do? Wait 'til you have promises and treaties and assurance from all other gryfons that they'll bow to Kjorn before he stands again as king?"

As if skyfire struck the group, they fell silent again, checking each other with their gazes.

"There you are," Kjorn said, flushed with gratitude and pride. Not so long ago, Stigr had not been such a friend, not until Kjorn had proven himself to the exiled Vanir. "Will you do less than this warrior of the Silver Isles? Show me the descendants of Oster. Show me the pride of the lake, my friends, the might of the Ostral clans. I am not here to bribe and beg, but to offer you a new age."

He opened his golden wings to blazing effect in the light of the fire, and a couple of gryfons stepped back from the brightness of him. "The greatest battle of our time is upon us, and you argue whether or not you'll partake? We should not be arguing if, but *when*, and having to fight off every eager fledge from begging to join us! I don't ask for you to grovel and call me king, I ask for you to join me in glorious battle. And yes, maybe die, and join Tyr in the Sunlit Land, to be remembered forever in new songs from the end of this age."

He tilted his head, eyeing each gryfon who stood around the fire as the words rushed to him. "And those who do not die, I ask to stand victorious with me in a place of honor. Stand in Tyr's light, at the end of our longer lives, and say *I defeated the great enemy. I was there.*"

Hard light angled their faces as they stared, as the fire shifted the light over them, and Kjorn saw them caving. All around them, other gryfons had fallen quiet, ears turned to him. Stigr watched him with gruff, keen admiration. Even Shard, who Kjorn knew had little stomach left for war, seemed caught up in the vision.

"You," muttered the scarred female, "will be called a poet king."

Kjorn gave a harsh laugh, and folded his wings. "But will I also be called friend, brother, and lord of the Ostral Shores?"

A collective breath. Eyes drifted, and landed on Asrik. Heads dipped, acknowledging he would speak for the group.

Kjorn let his gaze flick around the faces as Asvander's father gathered his thoughts. He knew that they wouldn't be won over by mere words, even if their hearts had pounded at his statement. Maybe it was poetic, he thought wryly, but it was also true. He hoped they saw that.

"You have the lake," Asrik murmured, and most looked heartily in agreement. Kjorn began to speak, warming with triumph, but Asrik arched his head up, lifting his wings. "You have us for battle, every able talon. You have us to route the enemy. After that, *after*… if you're still alive, we'll discuss our relations with the Dawn Spire."

So much was implied in that simple statement, Kjorn thought, that nothing more needed to be said. But he had them for the moment. He had them for the battle. And surely, after they had seen him unite the Winderost and win in battle, they would wish to pledge to him.

After. If Kjorn was still alive. If any of them were. Kjorn bowed his head to all of them. "Then our victory is assured."

"Come," Asrik said, "it's time for supper."

That was met with loud and boisterous agreement. Some brushed Kjorn as they passed, wishing fair winds, looking aflame and ready to fight.

Lofgar thunked a wing against Kjorn's chest in a not-unfriendly way. "Pretty words, son of Sverin, but I hope you won't be making many long speeches."

"I hope so too, son of Ofgar, and I'm glad to have your strength."

Lofgar paused, as if surprised that Kjorn knew him so well, then ruffled his feathers. "Aye, you should be." He turned and roared for someone to bring him meat—Kjorn flicked his ears back from the volume of it—and the Lakelander strode off to find his fellows.

Kjorn stood still as the rest dispersed, and when enough had left, sagged against Shard.

"Thank you," he whispered.

Shard chuckled, nudging a wing. "I hardly did anything."

"You came to my side," Kjorn said quietly, watching the orange flames, letting his pounding heart settle. "You make my words stronger."

Kjorn sensed Stigr watching them, then the black gryfon slipped away with the rest. He was relieved they had become allies, for a rift between Shard's mentor and himself would've made Shard's tasks that much harder, and weighed on his heart. Now he seemed optimistic, strong and hopeful, which helped Kjorn to feel all those things too.

"Let's eat," Shard said, drawing him from his thoughts. "Even you won't be having any glorious battles on an empty stomach."

3

THE BALLAD OF OSTER AND EN

A THRONG OF GRYFONS GATHERED AROUND the dancing fires nearer the lake, telling stories. To Shard, it felt strange to be in the stormy season in between, the wind and rain and half-hearted days of sun seeming to drive winter away but not quite readying for spring. Night settled still over the lake, and Shard heard the voice of a singer.

News spread fast—the Lakelanders would go to war. They would follow Kjorn, they would assure victory over the wyrms. Blazing exuberance swelled loudly through the lakeshore in boasting, singing, over-eating, and spontaneous sparring.

"There they are," Shard murmured, pointing with a wingtip where Stigr, Asvander and their friends sat gathered near the largest fire.

Brynja was there, warm and ruddy in the orange light. She caught Shard's gaze and called them over. Beside her sat her wingsister Dagny, lean and rich brown all over, with Asvander beside her, looking more gloomy than Shard would have thought, after their success. Stigr sat with Brynja's aunt, Valdis.

Shard and Kjorn stepped forward, slipping around gryfons who were lounging, eating and dozing, all with at least one ear perked to whomever was singing. After a winter-rain song came a speaker, her fine, rich voice re-telling the most recent Battle of Torches when Shard, Kjorn, and a mingled band of gryfons had driven off the wyrms from the Outlands.

"Fair winds, my lord," purred Valdis as they approached. The gryfess, very like Brynja in bearing and color, but older, stretched out on her belly before the fire, her tail ticking off beats in the speaker's tale. "Stigr tells me your meeting went well."

"Very well," Kjorn agreed.

"Well enough," Stigr said. "These Lakelanders are stubborn."

"But honorable," Kjorn murmured.

"And loyal," said Shard, looking to Asvander, who inclined his head a degree in acknowledgement. Shard wondered if Lofgar's comments still bothered him, and knew they should probably talk. Neither Asvander nor Brynja wanted a forced mating, but perhaps from his family's point of view it looked weak or dishonorable that Brynja had chosen Shard over Asvander.

"Hm, stubborn and loyal." Valdis nibbled at Stigr's neck feathers. "I don't know any gryfons like that."

"You fly the same wind," Stigr said, stretching his good wing to cover her.

Mild embarrassment at their fluffing and flirting flushed Shard's neck, but it faded in the face of seeing his uncle happy. Stigr had lived ten years in lonely exile, counseled by ravens and the occasional wolf about the goings-on of his own pride. To be surrounded now by admiring warriors and a soon-to-be mate was just barely enough, Shard thought, to repay what he'd lost.

"Tyr's wings," Valdis said. "Then we should fly together." She sighed gustily, lifting her talons to run down Stigr's back.

"Sit down," Dagny said to Shard and Kjorn. "You two make me nervous, standing there looking ready to fight."

"Ready to eat, more like." Brynja pushed a fish toward Shard, and Asvander motioned Kjorn toward a piece of back strap—a choice meat saved for the prince.

They all shifted to make room for Shard between Brynja and Valdis, and room for Kjorn on Shard's other side, near Asvander. They settled in to eat, and Shard planned to tell Stigr about his dream after he finished.

"Shard," Kjorn said quietly as the speaker finished her recounting of the battle to enthusiastic calls and happy, rumbling purrs. Shard looked over at him, ears perked. "Will you still be ready to leave in two mornings? Now that we have the Ostral Shores, we should move on, speak to the painted dogs, then the Vanhar as we planned."

"I will." Shard picked at his fish. "I'll need to find someone to guide my Vanir to meet us at the Voldsom."

"I will lead them," Stigr began. "I'm slow but I know the way. By the time you two make your rounds we'll be there—"

"And now," boomed Asrik's voice. Shard and the others looked up, and Asvander shifted, looking wary.

"A favorite song, the last of the winter songs. Let it remind us of our ties, our loyalties, and our love."

Though Kjorn sat between them, Shard sensed Asvander tensing, and beside him, Brynja. "What is it?" he whispered as two gryfons stepped up, a leaner, pale male and gull-gray huntress, both of the Ostral Shore.

But Brynja looked around him to catch Asvander's eye, and he shook his head once, as if refusing an accusation. "I had nothing to do with it."

"Brynja," Shard began.

"Listen," she said, shifting her feet and narrowing her eyes.

"Warriors," said the pale male from the little knoll on which all the singers and tale speakers had stood.

"Huntresses," said the female, her face glowing in the firelight. "For our honored guests, and our new allies, the Vanir, and Prince Kjorn, the long lost heir of Kajar, we offer a song of the Second Age."

The male's gaze slid across the fires. "When gryfons, like eagles, hawks, and witless birds still mated only with others of their clan."

"When all bloodlines ran pure," said the female. Anticipation grew in the pride, Shard sensed it like wind fanning an ember.

"When enmities ran even purer," barked the male.

"Tyr shone his light on the hearts of two warriors."

"If it pleases my lords," the male said, dipping his head, "we give you the Ballad of Oster and En."

So beloved, apparently, was the song, that Shard heard others whisper the title with relish along with the singer. Brynja, however, let out a slow hiss of air through her beak, and glared once again at Asvander.

"If you—"

"I didn't," he growled, and Dagny made an unhappy noise at the tension. "This is all *him*."

By *him*, Shard supposed he meant his father. He would have to wait for enlightenment, for when the song began, all fell quiet to listen, even Brynja and Asvander. The male sang first, his voice as long and pure as the tenor howl of a wolf, so surprising that Shard's feathers prickled.

> *"Long ago and far away*
> *In the time when all legends began,*
> *There lived bold Oster of the saltwater shores*
> *And a beautiful huntress called En."*

The gryfess sang the next verse in rich alto, her voice like thunder to the male singer's skyfire, the song a haunting storm.

> *"Their clans made war on the saltwater shore*
> *And stained the blue lake red.*

But when bold Oster met the beautiful huntress
He vowed never to fight again."

Brynja fluffed her feathers, then shook herself and sleeked again, and Shard preened hesitantly at her wing, trying to calm her. She shook her head, and with the next verse, he began to understand her tension.

"Let's flee the war and the saltwater shore,"
He said to the huntress called En
She agreed, and away they winged
Together, forever, they pledged."

All around, gryfons whispered along, hummed in their chests, cast fond glances to the singers and to each other. Shard peeked around and noticed some of his Vanir listening, rapt. Taking up the refrain together, the singers' voices mingled and soared in sharp harmony.

"We will fly beyond the Dawnward Sea
Where the sun rises eternally.
My love will be safe
And I will be free
Beyond the Dawnward Sea."

A song of the first gryfons to mate outside their own clans. *And not just any gryfons,* Shard thought with irritation as he understood the tension between Brynja and Asvander. Oster, a founder of the Ostral Shore, and En, whose bloodline, most claimed, could stretch down through the centuries to Kjorn himself, Sverin, and all their cousins, including Brynja's family.

Shard sought a glimpse of Asvander's father around the fire. He sat with his mate and Asvander's younger sister, watching the singers attentively. His tail twitched lightly in time with the song.

"Asvander," Shard whispered, and Dagny hushed him sharply. Surprised, Shard sat back, listening to the next verse.

"But word of the plan went along in the wind
And reached the father of En.
He sent her sisters out across the land
To bring her home to him."

Shard watched as Asrik glanced casually toward his son, and Asvander glared back at him, then looked resolutely away. Dagny shifted uneasily.

"They found them there, on the shore of the sea
Together, Oster and En.
They made their stand, with the waves at their feet
And made their vow again."
"We will fly beyond the Dawnward Sea . . .

Asvander stood slowly, politely, as subtly as his large frame would allow, and left the fire. Dagny blinked, stood, and with one look over her wing, followed him. Shard looked at Brynja and she gave her head the slightest shake.

"It's enough that he left," she said under her breath. "If we all do, it'll insult the singers."

"Is his father trying to prove some point to shame Asvander?" Shard muttered darkly. "To remind you of your glorious history?"

"It *is* a glorious history," Valdis said from her spot, and Shard looked to her in surprise, unaware she'd been listening. "Oster and En were the first gryfons to ever break the barriers of clan bloodlines. The unity of the Ostral Shore and the gryfons of the Dawn Spire stretches back to the Second Age, sundered only when Per left."

"Fled," Stigr reminded her, and she rustled her wings in a shrug. Nearby gryfons glared at them for talking as the song wove on through verses of fighting by the sea, En admitting she already carried Oster's kit, and pleas for peace.

Valdis continued, "Asvander and Brynja's mating was to remind both the Dawn Spire and the Ostral Shore of that glorious history, to reflect that first union between Oster and En."

"But Kjorn is back now," Brynja said stiffly. "So the line of En and Kajar will be restored, and any promises that King Orn made on behalf of other gryfons made irrelevant. Unless Kjorn plans to honor arranged matings and other such things."

Challenging, she looked around Shard to Kjorn, who'd been listening to them and to the song in thoughtful silence.

"I would never force a mating," he said quietly. "I'd never heard of such a thing until coming here. Perhaps that, at least, is a change Per and my father made for the better in our pride in the Silver Isles."

Stigr snorted. "But the killing and the stealing remained—"

Valdis nipped his ear sternly, before Shard could say anything. "You speak to your future king," she reminded. "Unless you've decided not to remain at the Dawn Spire, after all, and force me to live as a rogue."

Stigr stared at her a moment. "He doesn't mind. He's heard how I speak to Shard." He looked over at Kjorn and Shard saw a challenging, but friendly gleam in his eye. "You should've heard how I spoke to Baldr. It would've shocked you, my lord."

Despite themselves, they chuckled, and Shard was relieved that Kjorn didn't seem offended one way or the other. Stigr had earned a place at the Dawn Spire and meant to keep it. Which meant, Shard reflected with an odd pang, that he would bow to an Aesir king after all. But then, it was not Kjorn or Sverin who'd conquered Stigr, but his own heart.

"Anyway," Valdis said, "I wouldn't worry too much. It's mostly hot wind, and what will he do anyway? Lash them together and force them to make vows?"

That image was so ridiculous that even Brynja huffed a short laugh. Shard felt uneasy, and looked into the dark where Asvander had gone.

Brynja said softly to Shard, "It would be nice if a few gryfons actually wanted us to mate and be happy."

He knew she was thinking of Ketil and the Vanir. Now Asvander's family, and clearly other members of the Ostral Shore pride, were disappointed that her union with Asvander was not to be. As much as it irritated him that even though he was a prince, his choices were still questioned, it bothered him still more that it caused problems for Asvander.

"Well you've got our support," Stigr said, speaking for himself and Valdis.

"And mine," Kjorn said drily. "If I count."

Brynja dipped her head, looking chagrined. "I know. You understand what I meant."

The song finished in haunting tones, Shard was dismayed to find out, with the death of En's father in the final fight between their clans. Only after the battle did En and Oster tell their parents that she carried his heir. Their clans were already united, despite themselves. With that heir came peace, the blending of clan and bloodlines and unity ever after—at least, until Kajar, an Age later.

Shard looked over to see Asrik watching them, and Shard narrowed his eyes, perking his ears in challenge. Asrik looked away, dipping his head to speak to his young daughter.

"I'll go speak to Asvander," Brynja said, standing as cheers and calls and stamping feet announced the pride's pleasure in the song. Even the Vanir had been swept away, Shard saw, and that made him feel a little better. Anything that could make the gryfons of the Winderost seem less of an enemy to his Vanir, anything that would encourage them toward the idea of lasting peace, was good.

Still. He looked around the fire and caught sight of Asrik again, now watching Brynja. Shard's feathers prickled and he stood, stepping in front of her to stare down Asrik himself. Brynja made a low noise. "Shard, don't."

"No, I've had enough of this. He insults you, he insults me, and he insults his own son. We are grown gryfons and can choose our own mates. They act as if I stole you, as if you're a pelt to be won, and Asvander let me steal you. This is foolish."

Bustling feathers and bodies filled the silent space after the song as gryfons rose to find their dens. Stigr pushed himself up, tilting slightly to one side as he adjusted his balance to his missing wing. Resisting the urge to help him, Shard watched instead as Valdis slid up beside the black gryfon and pressed to him in an apparent show of affection, but one that helped to steady the old Vanir.

"Nephew," Stigr said warily, for they both knew Shard had a habit of impulsiveness. "What are you going to do?"

Kjorn stood as well. "Shard, I agree with you, but I ask you not to risk our new alliance."

Shard looked at him sharply. "They disrespect their own, and me. How strong can our alliance be with Asrik making petty nips at his son all the while? I'm going to settle this."

"Shard," Brynja began, but before any could argue further, he dipped his head to all of them and trotted away toward the rise where they'd met with the clan leaders.

Kjorn followed him. "How do you plan to settle it? Shard, don't risk their allegiance for your mating. I can't afford it. We can settle everything after, and we will, I promise."

"No, Kjorn." He negotiated through departing gryfons to the slope leading up to the bluff and began to walk up it. "They'll have no respect for me, and they'll keep whispering about Brynja and Asvander. The only reason he's not doing anything is because he's my friend. I'm settling this, and I'm doing it now. Support me, brother."

Kjorn's feathers ruffed. Once, he had not just been Shard's wing-brother, but his lord and prince. Now they were equals, and Shard saw how, despite their friendship, Kjorn was not used to the idea. Shard still wasn't, either, and he didn't meet Kjorn's gaze.

"How?" Kjorn demanded again, stopping halfway up the rise while Shard continued on. "You don't even know what they want you to do."

Shard opened his wings, looking down at the gathering. He could see everyone, and all would be able to see him. He glanced over his wing at Kjorn, dim gold in the last of the firelight.

"You forget, I was raised by a Lakelander." Shard returned his gaze to the scene below him. "I have a decent idea what they want, and I'll get at least one clan of gryfons to stop whispering behind our backs and shaming their own."

"Shard, I beg you—"

"Let it be known!" Shard bellowed, flaring his wings. Departing gryfons stopped, looking for the source of the shout. Shard waited until they found him, staring up, eyes wide and surprised in the firelight. No one spoke. He caught sight of Asvander and Brynja, their gazes bewildered. "I, Rashard, son-of-Baldr, prince of the Silver Isles in the Starland Sea, challenge Asvander, son-of-Asrik, for his claim on Brynja, daughter-of-Mar. He will choose the ground, and the day."

Fire popped somewhere.

The gathered gryfons gazed at him, bemused, then bent their heads to whisper, or hurried on, perhaps thinking a fight was about to break out right then. Shard discerned a muffled sound of rage from somewhere, most likely Brynja. He didn't want to do it, of course he didn't. But for the sake of Asvander's honor in the eyes of his family, his own, and Brynja's, he would.

A gryfon moved in the gathering, Asvander, striding forward. His expression had hardened from bewilderment to determination. "I accept your challenge, son of Baldr. We fight at dawn."

Shard dipped his head, eyes locked on his friend, in whose eyes shone the tiniest spark of gratitude. With that, not even looking at the leaders of the clan or particularly at Asrik himself, Shard strode down past Kjorn and left the gathering, walking proudly into the dark. He didn't want to insult his wingbrother, but he couldn't show hesitation. Kjorn grimly wished him good luck in passing.

Brynja and Stigr were not far behind.

"That was foolish," Brynja admonished. "Shard, it was unnecessary."

"No, it wasn't." Shard kept walking, toward the scent of water and the lake. "When you and I are happily away in the Silver Isles, Asvander will be here, with his family, enduring their remarks and their judgment for me *stealing* you from him."

"Barbaric," Stigr muttered, and Shard stopped at last when his feet touched pebbly shoreline. "Trading gryfons about like rabbit pelts. It's Brynja's decision, not theirs."

"It is," Shard said, looking not at Stigr, but Brynja. "But this is their way. I'll respect it, because we're in their home. If we were in the Silver Isles, everything would be different."

Brynja growled low in her throat. "I should have challenged him myself."

Shard chuckled despite himself, and Brynja gave him a half-hearted glare. He smoothed his expression. "Maybe, but you were too slow."

"I can hardly keep up with you," she said, with tart fondness. "If you aren't flying across the world then you're picking fights with marauding wyrms and gryfons near twice your size." She butted her head against his shoulder, then glanced toward the fires and the gryfons who had stayed to gossip. "And Shard, they'll know if he lets you win. It will be a real fight. Not a spar, a fight."

"To the death, I suppose," Stigr said wryly.

"To yield," said Valdis, coming up on them. "Only to yield. But he won't yield easily, or what's the point?"

"Well that's encouraging," Stigr said, eyeing Valdis fondly.

"We can't afford to be killing princes over things like this," she said. "Even these big rock-heads know that."

Stigr paced around in front of Shard, tail lashing. "I'd like to remind you, my prince, that we're on the verge of battle with the wyrms, and you could be injured. This was no small thing you've done."

Shard's feathers prickled with irritation as he looked around at the faces of his friends. "Asvander could be seriously injured too, you know."

Stigr inclined his head, but, ever blunt, added, "The last time you fought Asvander, you lost, and not by a near thing."

"Thank you," Shard muttered, ears slicking back. "But you didn't lose." He lifted his gaze, watching Asvander walk down from the fire to speak with his father, who looked entirely too pleased. "And you have until dawn to advise me."

Stigr huffed, then tilted his head. "Walk with me."

"Good luck," Brynja said, and she and Valdis stood aside to let them pass.

They left the fire together, and Stigr began. "Now, Asvander doesn't have any great tells to show you when he's going to make a move, but I noticed he'll *look* where he's planning to strike . . ."

4
PRISONER OF WAR

DUSK BROUGHT A DRY, COLD wind from the starward quarter to
buffet the nesting cliffs of the Sun Isle.

Ragna had taken to her den early after the day's fishing and she
pulled at her nesting material, fluffing it up to prepare for what would be
another freezing night. Spring would be long in coming, she feared, as if
it held off, holding its warm breath in wait for the return of their king.

"Shard," she whispered as a draft bustled into her den, chilling it.
"Rashard, my son. We wait for you." Perhaps, on the wind, it might
reach him, and he would know she thought of him.

With a huff, she settled, then re-settled, then growled and shifted,
kicking against the deer furs that usually warmed her. They had been
a gift, long ago, from the wolves of the Star Isle, a mating gift when
she and Baldr made their vow. Now, their scent only reminded her of
the long years of living under the talons of the Red Kings, the long,
hungry winters and being forced to hunt on land and eat red meat.

Still damp from fishing and not at all sleepy, Ragna sat up to preen,
and considered throwing the deer hides into the sea. But that would
be foolish and leave her with a cold nest.

"Rashard," she whispered, closing her eyes briefly. No sooner had she at last been able to finally gaze upon her son and have him know she was his mother, know that he was a prince, than he'd spirited away to foreign lands on some greater purpose.

I know it's what you wanted, Baldr. I know he is the Summer King. But we need him home.

Her wings ached from the day's fishing, her muscles chilled and cramped. Ten years ago she wouldn't have felt it at all, would have stayed up late under the moonlight, laughing with Sigrun, her brother Stigr, and Baldr, watching the frost collect on the grass until dawn. Now, like an old thing, she burrowed into her den each night and pretended, in the morning, that the cold and the work only made her stronger.

She must be a queen. She must show them what it was to be Vanir.

With a sigh, she settled her feathers and crawled back into the nest. The wind sang against the rocks and grass on the cliff tops high above.

Her tail ticked back and forth.

The scent of the deer hides hung thick, heavy, smothering.

"White Tor," she growled, and sank her talons into the leather of one hide, flinging it from the nest.

It smacked into a young Aesir gryfon who landed just inside her den at the same moment. Ragna flattened her ears at his surprised noise, chagrined. His feathers blazed the wild orange of sunset, wings flaring awkwardly as he grasped at the hide to keep it from falling out of the den.

"My lady," he stammered, twisting the fur in his talons. "Forgive my intrusion."

"Vald," she said evenly. "What can I do for you?"

"Forgive me. They said to fetch you." Looking uncertain, he tucked the deer hide against the stone wall. "He won't eat."

Ragna perked her ears, then shook her head and forced her feathers to sleek down, calm. "I'll go. Fetch Caj as well."

"My lady." He inclined his head, glanced once more from the deer hide to Ragna, then leaped from the den and flapped away.

Grudgingly grateful to have something to do other than not fall asleep, Ragna trotted to the entryway, tossed the hide back onto her nest, and leaped into the frosty wind, opening her wings in the last light of evening.

The den of the fallen king stretched the widest of all those in the nesting cliffs, a yawning maw of rock in the cliff face, large enough for a fully-grown Aesir to flare broad wings and land inside. Ragna swooped to land easily, being much shorter and narrower of frame than even the smallest Aesir, with streamlined, angled wings besides.

She made a stark contrast to the two hulking warriors who guarded the entrance, they being half-bloods—one vivid green, the other near black, flashing blue like a crow. Sons of the Conquering. Ragna noticed since Sverin's penitent return that all but the most stubborn of pure-blooded Aesir had ceased wearing their dragon treasures, chains, collars, gauntlets of gold and gems, and other ornaments. It satisfied her, probably more than it should have.

"My lady," they murmured.

The green warrior stepped forward, though he didn't mantle to her. Ragna was used to it. He recognized Thyra as his queen, not her. "Vald told you?"

"Yes. Stand aside, Halvden, let me speak to him."

Halvden complied, looking doubtful. Ragna stood two full heads shorter than he and her feathers were quiet, pale white like sea foam, like a gull, with no outlandish hues from some mysterious ancestral curse.

She walked between Halvden and the other sentry, Andor, drawing herself up, imagining shining white Tor to cool her heat.

I am queen of the Vanir. My son lives, and he will be king. I have strength. Strength as unending as the sea.

The king's nest sat near the back of the cave, a huge, compact construction of stick and stone atop a rock platform that overflowed with dragon treasure. The stone cave glowed with odd warmth.

"My lord," she said firmly to the nest.

Golden baubles tumbled loose, bracers of bronze, jeweled collars and bands that caught the fading light and cast the entire rock den in sunrise colors.

A mound of red feathers stirred within the nest. Ragna twitched her tail, eyeing the fish that lay untouched near the foot of the nest platform, and moved forward three more paces.

"Sverin. Stand and address me. They tell me you will not eat?"

The great mound of feathers shifted, becoming red wings, broad shoulders, a severe, weary eagle head rising from the gold. Seeing Ragna, he pushed to his feet and climbed out. The largest of the pride, the son of Per strode down, head low, until he stood a respectful distance from her, and inclined his head. She pressed her talons hard to the rock to keep from backing away from him, and forced her feathers to remain sleek. She was a huntress herself, a warrior, a queen. Two young, healthy warriors stood at her back. She had nothing to fear and she would not back down.

Forcing her ears forward, she watched him expectantly. She would not repeat her question.

"At least," he said at length, "I will not eat *that*."

"Our fish isn't good enough for you?"

"I am sorry for the trouble, only I cannot bear the taste of the sea. You know why."

She did know. It reminded him of his mate, who had drowned ten years before. "What am I to do, then, with your little rebellion?"

A strange, pained look flickered across his face. "It isn't rebellion. Allow me to hunt."

Ragna could have laughed, but realized he was in earnest. "No."

He watched her, as if deciding what to say. His wicked, black talons also flexed against the rock, though what urge he suppressed, Ragna didn't know. Once, he'd been magnificent. Even in her anger and imprisonment, she had to admire that the Aesir were impressive examples of gryfon kind. Tall, strapping and muscular, decked in golden collars and dragon jewels, Sverin had once been a sight to behold, fearless and proud.

Or so he had appeared. After nearly ruining the pride that winter, he'd fled, Nameless, into the wilds of the Silver Isles. Only his wing-brother had pursued, to find and restore him. Now the shame of his lies and his failures crushed down on his bearing, shadowed his eyes, hollowed his voice. Now the golden chains that had once adorned his crimson feathers in kingly fashion were wrapped around and around his wings, binding them.

His ears turned slowly, his gaze darting to the entrance, where the younger warriors watched, nearly unblinking, for any sign of aggression. "Then I will starve."

Andor made a quiet noise of disgust and Ragna silenced him with a twitch of her tail.

"Then you will never see Kjorn again," Ragna said, firm and cool, but not cruelly.

He watched her. Silent. The fallen Red King. Ragna had to admit to herself that now, now that he'd confessed his failures and stopped masquerading as a fearless tyrant, he didn't look paranoid at all.

From the entrance, Halvden spoke, his voice low. "My lord, you must eat. The fish isn't so bad, once you get used to—"

Sverin's head flew up. "Silence, deceiver."

Ragna looked between them. Halvden ducked his head, ears flat. Though he'd redeemed himself a little in helping Caj to hunt Sverin down, the young warrior had done all he could to undermine peace in the pride, and Kjorn, and to drive Sverin's madness further. Caj had helped him see his errors, and still his loyalty to Sverin didn't waiver. Ragna had to admire that, at least, had to respect that he was trying.

"He is right," she said. She glanced at the fish, resisting the urge to step back from Sverin, holding her ground. "You must eat. This martyrdom is pointless."

"I would choke on it. It represents my most evil act of cowardice."

"It's a fish," Ragna growled.

Sverin measured her, and the fish lie between them, smelling of wet meat and the sea. "To you it means freedom, my lady, to practice your ways. To me it means the first step back into Nameless madness."

Ragna stared at him, then at the fish, and for a moment, almost laughed again, but more in consternation. "That's a long leap even for you, Sverin. I don't think a fish will drive you mad."

"Don't you? I'm not so sure. Unless you're doing it to punish me, or ensure that I won't eat."

Ragna growled, and almost stepped toward him. Sheer instinct and wariness of his size held her back. "Don't be foolish. I wish you to live, to suffer for what you've done. You will face my son, and justice."

"I'm not arguing the point, my lady. I'm asking you to see mine. To you, fish is freedom," Sverin repeated quietly, eyes locked on hers. He didn't move. He wasted no energy, like a mountain cat, standing, staring at Ragna. "To you it represents your peace. To me, it is something else."

Ragna knew it. The conquering Aesir had forbidden the entire pride from fishing when an Aesir huntress died in the attempt. One huntress. Sverin's mate.

He spoke quietly. "When you tasted fish again, did you think happily of your son, brother, perhaps even your mate—?"

"I see your point," Ragna cut in sharply.

He inclined his head. His silent, sane expression—at last sane, at last grieving and accepting and humbled—gave her pause, and she found herself on the absurd edge of apologizing for giving him fish when she knew what it meant to him.

Scuffling talons and paws drew their gazes to the entryway. Caj, Sverin's burly, cobalt blue wingbrother, had climbed into the den between the two sentries with a dark expression on his face, striding forward without asking permission. Both wings closed, one still packed in a mud cast.

Sverin's expression cleared somewhat. "Caj. How fares the wing?" His gaze slid to green Halvden, who bowed his head. During the dark winter, it was Halvden who had tried to murder Caj in a wild effort to take his place at Sverin's side, Halvden who had broken Caj's wing. It was also Halvden who had helped to find Sverin and bring him back to the nesting cliffs.

What a merry band we are, Ragna thought wearily.

Caj lifted his good wing. "They've told me you won't eat. Sverin, it's unacceptable. Don't you want to see Kjorn?"

Sverin dipped his head, gaze switching to Ragna.

"The meat . . ." She shook her head. "He won't eat the fish."

Caj looked at Sverin, measuring, then the fish, then Ragna. "My lady. Is there nothing we can do?"

She had been the one to summon Caj to Sverin's den. He was not an unreasonable gryfon, he was her wingsister's mate, but he was still Sverin's wingbrother. Of course he would be loyal. And in the face of both of them, she couldn't remain blindly obstinate.

"I'll find you red meat," Ragna said shortly. "If anyone will hunt with me on your behalf, now."

There was a part of her, a small, ugly creature within her that enjoyed seeing Sverin brought low, that enjoyed being able to say whatever she was thinking without fear of death or banishment. She had to rise above that petty urge.

Sverin ducked his head in acknowledgement, almost humble, but that Ragna spied the slow twitch of his tail. "Thank you for your concern, my lady."

"It isn't concern for you." She grasped the fish firmly in her talons. "Rest assured that I will do all in my power to keep you whole and healthy until you have faced Rashard again."

Both Sverin and Caj murmured low, in thanks, though she saw their tension. She took the fish from the den and winged out into the dark, intending to take the meal to Sigrun in case any of her pregnant charges were hungry. In the morning, she would see if there was any gryfon left in the pride willing to help her hunt for the disgraced War King.

5
THE DUEL

FIRST LIGHT SAW GRYFONS OF the Ostral Shore gathered on a flat expanse some leaps away from the nesting area, just before the landscape changed to hills.

Shard's challenge had become a subject of gossip and great interest. Especially when word was passed around that he and Asvander were friends, that they had not always been, that Asvander had beaten Shard in a contest at the Dawn Spire when Shard first arrived in the Winderost. Even more of interest was Brynja's dignified silence, and her refusal to tell anyone whom she hoped would win.

Shard stood with Stigr at the edge of what had become a large ring of spectators, warming his wings and muscles in the dawn light and wishing they'd opted for a later time. Peering around, he saw Brynja, who lifted her beak and perked her ears in encouragement. She hadn't liked the idea of the duel, but understood Shard's principle of the thing. They were both Asvander's friend, and settling the matter would be best.

To Shard's surprise, he saw Vanir threading through the growing crowd of onlookers. Ketil, Keta, and her nest-sister Ilse filtered to the front to watch. Toskil and another, old Vanir named Frar sat further back, and when he caught their gazes, they called encouragement.

More gathered, and amused Lakelanders let them to the front to see, as the Vanir were almost all shorter.

"You look surprised that your pride is here to support you," Stigr said as he came up beside Shard.

"I suppose I am. They know I fight to win Brynja, in a way."

"They support you, Shard. You." Stigr eyed him up and down, as if assessing his readiness. "You're their prince."

"Ketil doesn't look happy."

"That doesn't mean she hopes you'll lose, Shard. You represent the Silver Isles and all the Vanir and you have a reputation to uphold now."

Shard had felt relaxed and ready, but his muscles tightened at those words. "Oh, thank you. That doesn't make me nervous at all."

Stigr laughed, causing Shard's feathers to prickle in irritation. "Have faith. All of us do." He jerked his head to make Shard look back toward the Vanir. Standing there too was Kjorn, bright in the morning, with his head high. He hadn't wanted Shard to fight, to cause ripples, but there he stood in support. Shard drew in a long breath.

"Fight well my prince," Stigr said, mantled quickly, and drew away.

"Fair morning winds, clans of the lake!" roared Asrik, gliding overhead. He landed hard in the middle of the ring of spectators, looking pleased that the entire pride appeared to be there, gawking and ready for a fight. "You have come to witness the challenge between Shard, son-of-Baldr, and Asvander, my son, who has until this morn been promised in *mutual* agreement to Brynja, daughter-of-Mar, of the Dawn Spire. This promise hearkened back to the days of Oster and En . . ."

He recited the history, as if they hadn't just heard the song the night before. At last Shard spied Asvander, striding determinedly forward through the other big, rough gryfons. He met Shard's gaze and dipped his head, resolved, but not unfriendly, Shard thought.

At least no one expected a fight to the death. It only then occurred to Shard what would happen if he lost. Brynja would be expected to keep her promise to Asvander, or risk shaming him all over again by choosing Shard anyway.

Shard flexed his talons against the earth and stretched his wings. He would not lose.

Asrik finished his introductions with, "And when the fight is done, let no gryfon, common or royal, contest the fair results." His fierce gaze passed from Asvander to Shard himself, and he opened his wings. "You do not stop for pain, blood, or broken bone. You fight until one yields."

Folding his wings, he bowed out of the ring. Some gryfons shuffled back as Shard and Asvander stepped forward. Shard looked across the expanse at his friend, and a sense of foolishness washed over him. With a glance behind him, he saw Brynja, watching with perked ears and an entirely neutral, huntress's look of observation.

As Shard forced his muscles forward to circle the ring and Asvander did the same, Shard distantly recalled Kenna, a Vanir from his home pride. He'd thought they might have become something more, for she was half Vanir, but she had tripped away with Halvden, a larger, stronger, louder gryfon.

As his talons crunched the frost, Shard recalled with irony how he'd wished for a female who didn't want him to win a contest of strength in order to win her. With a final look at Brynja, he realized with mingled shame and happiness that he'd found one, and there he was, fighting anyway.

Beside Brynja, tall and shining in the light, was Kjorn. He met Shard's gaze with firm encouragement, but Shard noticed the undertone of worry. Shard wasn't sure if the worry was over losing clan loyalty at the challenge, or worry for Shard being injured, but either way the look didn't inspire confidence.

His gaze flicked to the Vanir. Ketil watched him, her gaze keen, hard, and hopeful. Toskil and Ilse murmured to each other, while Keta watched Shard with bright optimism. Shard found Stigr, who nodded, and beside him, old Frar, staring at Shard as he might stare at the rising sun. Frar believed he would win. A spark flicked up in Shard's heart.

Someone shouted for them to start fighting, they couldn't wait all day. Shard shook himself and raised his head, looking again to his opponent, who had been waiting.

In that moment he saw Asvander's gaze flick to the side, and remembered Stigr's first tip. As the big Lakelander leaped forward, talons raking toward Shard's right shoulder, Shard ducked and slid away. The match was on. Stigr's next advice had been for Shard to do something Asvander had never seen before. Shard had confessed to observing and learning from the warrior dragons of the Sunland.

Do that, then, was all Stigr had said.

Air, Shard thought, thinking of the stone rings the dragons used to train, mimicking the elements. *I am air.*

Asvander spun, and Shard had to admire his speed relative to his size as he dodged away. But Shard had fought gryfons, wyrms, and Sunland dragons.

Once, he would have had to plan every move and attack and defense. Now his body fell into fighting rhythm, one especially that he had learned in the Sunland that Asvander wouldn't have seen before. Based on qualities of the elements of wind, earth, water, and fire, it dictated his responses to Asvander's attacks.

The Lakelanders grumbled and shouted for blood, for Shard to stand and fight.

I am the Vanir, Shard thought, *and I will fight on my terms, not theirs.*

Asvander whipped in with a flurry of frustrated swipes and his snapping beak, and Shard fell back. And back, circling backwards as Asvander advanced. He didn't scramble or hurry, but dipped, dodged and planted his hind paws firmly with each evasion. *Air, air, earth*—he blocked Asvander's slashing talons—*air*—he slid away.

Hearty cheers and shouts from the Vanir of, "Shard! Shard, the prince!" sent strength to his heart. *I am the Silver Isles, the Vanir. And we are as strong and unending as the sea.*

It came to him like a bright wind. He would win the fight not by forcing a yield, but by outlasting Asvander.

Water . . . use his strength.

Asvander shoved forward again, and Shard dropped to his belly and rolled forward into the charge, causing Asvander to all but trip over him and skid face-first in the dirt.

The Vanir roared their approval. Stigr shouted, "Ha, fast as a falcon!"

Unable to catch Shard on the ground, Asvander roared his frustration and shoved up to leap at Shard from the air.

As Asvander dove, Shard held his ground, facing down the open beak and big, curved talons. Just when Asvander's expression changed to panic that Shard had not moved, Shard dropped to his belly and darted forward under the dive. *Air. I am wind, which does not tire or yield.*

With no time to correct, Asvander crashed hard in the dirt again and rolled.

Ketil shouted for Shard to attack while he was down. In the Sunland, Shard might have attacked. But that was for a different goal—to drive an opponent from the ring. Here, he had to follow his new plan.

He circled, flexing his wings. Asvander lurched up and around and watched Shard with renewed, wary calculation. With a sharp battle cry, Shard leaped forward, talons splayed, and Asvander ramped to his hind legs to meet him.

The Lakelanders bellowed approval—at last, there might be blood—but Shard feinted to one side, then when Asvander turned, changed course and darted around behind him. Asvander twisted to follow, falling to all fours and swiping blindly. Shard scampered a quick ring around him, causing Asvander to spin almost comically after him, as if he was chasing his own tail.

I am wind, he can't touch me.

If the fight was to first blood, Shard would have fought differently. But it was to yield.

"Stop and fight!" roared Asrik from the crowd. Shard ignored him. It wasn't as if dodging Asvander didn't take skill, or if his repeated attempts to pin Shard down or leap at him weren't earning the Lakelander a scrape or two.

"Why?" laughed Stigr, from the group of Vanir. "Your son's bruising himself enough!"

Again, Shard made it look as if he planned a grand attack. As Asvander crouched, looking wary, Shard gathered himself and lunged, but as Asvander flung up his talons to meet the charge, Shard shoved from the ground and leaped straight over his head, flapping hard to circle. Asvander followed with a ringing shout.

Shard, being smaller, leaner, with the shaped wings of a sea eagle, spun loops around Asvander, and his tail-feathers were always just out of reach of the bigger gryfon's talons.

He heard cheers from below and flushed with pleasure that his plan seemed to be working, and that his pride would see him succeed on his own terms.

He heard Brynja cheer for him at last, and sheer delight filled him. His flying had been one of the first things to attract her interest, and it filled him with pride now. Shard flew high, into the wind, and Asvander followed stubbornly, until they were out of earshot of the spectators.

"This was your idea," Asvander snarled at him, flapping hard to hover, though respect softened the harsh words. "Fight! I can't do this all day. "

"No?" Shard angled to glide a sharp circle around his friend. "Do you yield then?"

Asvander's eyes lit as he at last understood Shard's plan. Rather than yield, he bellowed a lion's roar from his chest and swooped in to try and catch Shard's tail. Shutting his wings, Shard dropped easily out of reach. Diving fast, he laughed at Asvander's half chuckle, half growl behind him.

The Lakelander, realizing he was no match for Shard in the air, swooped down to land. He hit hard on all fours in a cloud of dust and frost. Shard landed lightly, and when Asvander leaped after him, left his wings open to propel himself backwards. He slapped his wings together to smack Asvander's head, and circled away.

Asvander backtracked, growling in frustration, and Shard saw one eye winked closed as if one of his feathers had scraped it.

He feinted in to Asvander's left, ready to make him spin, but the Lakelander shouted and caught his tail feathers as he darted away. Catching hold, Asvander surged up and thrust his body against Shard's to knock him to the ground.

A flare of worry gave Shard strength and clarity, for Asvander had lost himself in frustration the last time they'd dueled, and he'd nearly broken Shard's wing. Rather than scramble away or try to gain his feet, he went still, as if he'd struck his head.

Asvander lunged up to him and ramped, wings flared, talons raised, then hesitated. "Shard? Are you—"

Shard threw his body into a roll, knocking into Asvander's hind legs. The bigger gryfon tumbled forward with a shout and Shard clawed up to his own four feet, darting away. A half laugh, half snarl came from his opponent, who whirled and leaped at him. Shard dodged back.

Asvander trotted forward, more hesitantly, seeking an opening. Shard weaved one direction and when Asvander moved, he leaped the opposite way and scored a light scrape on his friend's flank. Then he withdrew. Asvander followed, circling, but slowing.

Shard darted in and out and around, taking a hit here and there but nothing serious. He watched as Asvander's frustration mounted, then ebbed toward weariness.

When Shard leaped forward the next time, it was Asvander who fell back, stumbling slightly. Then he took to the air again. The nimble, constant movement took all Shard's focus and energy, but he could see it took even more from the Lakelander, who was used to fighting head-on, to blood or the death.

They circled in the air, Asvander swiping for Shard's tail and wing-tips to try and throw him off balance, and hard swooping under and around to avoid and dizzy him.

Shard swept talons in to drive Asvander back, but he caught Shard's foot in his own and folded his wings, dragging Shard in a dive.

"Yield!" Asvander shouted, as they both plummeted toward the ground.

Shard wrenched and twisted but couldn't break Asvander's grasp. *Water, water*...he tucked one wing and fell to that side, which yanked Asvander along with him. Flapping hard, Shard steered their fall toward the onlookers.

"Shard—"

"Better let go!"

When gryfons realized they were about to be smashed, they scattered with shouts and cries, some flying, some shoving into each other to get out of Shard and Asvander's path.

At the last moment Asvander swore and unlocked his grip. He was too late to correct, too big and broad.

Shard flipped his wings open and managed to flap back into the fighting ring. Asvander tumbled on the ground, smacking into gryfons who were not fast enough, who growled and herded him back into the ring.

He hobbled forward, some feathers out of place and perhaps a sprain, Shard thought, looking with a healer's eye. Shard lunged forward, running a circle around his friend and suppressing a triumphant laugh. Asvander turned in place, swiping talons, but did not leap again.

After a moment of this, Shard turned and butted into him head-on, and to his surprise and everyone else's, Asvander fell with a grunt. Shard waited for him to rise. He did not, but lay there, panting against the dirt. Shard placed talons firmly on the feathers of his neck and squeezed lightly.

"Do you yield?"

Asvander growled.

"We can keep fighting."

A single, choked laugh. "No. No, we can't. I yield, son of Baldr."

The ring of onlookers' gazes darted from Shard to Asvander. Shard caught Brynja's bright gaze, and near her, Kjorn, a fierce look of surprise and approval.

"I yield," Asvander said again, low but clear. He shifted and stood, favoring a hind paw as he addressed the spectators. "I cannot defeat him."

The Vanir broke into cheers and roars, and Shard heard Stigr shouting and calling him the Stormwing once again. He allowed himself to feel a moment of kit-like, ridiculous pride.

"Impossible!" Asrik marched forward, wings raised, his feathers ruffed as if the wind blew the wrong way. "That's no way to fight!" Before Asvander could defend them both, Shard stepped forward, opening his wings in challenge.

"Fight me yourself then. See that my win was genuine."

Asrik gazed at him, eyes narrowing. Then he looked at his son, taking in his battered feathers, his short breath, the injury to his paw. "Asvander, you can't possibly—"

"I cannot defeat him," he said again. "I yield the match, and my claim on a pairing with Brynja."

Before Asrik's feathers could lift any higher, Stigr came forward as well. "No one can say Shard didn't use skill to fight the way he did. Blood and bruises isn't the only way to win a battle."

Asrik looked doubtful. A tense, quiet moment lingered, then he inclined his head. "It was ... unexpected. I see it was truly won. I know my son to be honest, and I could see he gave his best. I concede."

"Good," Shard said, and found himself mobbed by Brynja, Dagny, and the younger of the admiring Vanir.

"All right, all right," Stigr said, pushing through the Vanir. "Off with you. To your fishing, to your lessons. Ketil, lead them?"

She eyed Stigr, then called the group away. When at last they cleared, Shard's friends remained. Stigr sat down, preening his wing. Brynja stood at Shard's side, head high and proud, Asvander remained, and Dagny romped forward to butt her head against Asvander's shoulder and murmur an encouraging word.

Kjorn approached and ducked his head. "Well fought, Shard. You'll have to show me where you learned some of those moves."

Shard felt it would be too much showing off to say, *from the dragons,* so he simply lifted his wings. "Of course. And see, I didn't lose you any allies."

Asvander flicked his tail. "Hardly. If anything, you impressed them further." He shifted his weight, still favoring one hind paw.

"You should see a healer," Dagny said, eyeing Asvander's feet, then looked at Shard. "Both of you."

"I think Shard's fine," Asvander said dryly. "I barely recall laying a talon on him."

Kjorn lifted his wings. "If you please, we need to discuss our departure."

"Yes," Shard said. "Of course."

They remained where they were as they reviewed the plan. They would secure an alliance with the painted wolves that roamed the lands bordering the Ostral Shores, then move on to the Vanhar on the windward coast.

Kjorn eyed the windy sky. "When Nilsine parted from us, she promised she would speak to the elders on my behalf, but that they would still like to meet in the flesh."

"Naturally," said Stigr. "While you lot are traveling that way, I'll lead the Vanir to the Voldsom Narrows. Any who wish to join the fight can, and any unable or unwilling can take shelter in the canyons, provided the eagles are still friendly."

"They are," said Brynja.

Kjorn looked pleased. "On our way to the Vanheim, we'll also seek out the painted wolves. Ilesh and his pack, and see if they'll fight with us."

Shard looked proudly at Kjorn, still impressed that he was now so willing to seek help and alliance with creatures other than gryfons. "After the Vanheim, the lions?" he asked. He thought of Ajia, the lioness singer and healer who had first shown him the wyrms of the Winderost. He thought perhaps she could help him with the dreams.

"The lions," Kjorn confirmed. "Then the Voldsom and the eagles, then . . ."

"The wyrms," Asvander said, with relish, as if he looked forward to battle.

A battle Shard hoped not to fight.

"Kjorn," Shard began quietly. "I meant to tell you sooner, to tell all of you sooner, that I had a dream of the she-wyrm, Rhydda." They looked at him, ears perked. Stigr shifted, his eye narrowing. "But not a normal dream. It was more like a vision, I knew it was real. I was with her, in a memory. We flew together and I felt almost as if I could speak with her."

Kjorn's face lit. "Truly? Do you think you could do it again?"

"I'm going to try," Shard said, letting his tail sweep the dirt in determination. "When I was in the Sunland and the spirit, Groa, spoke to me, she said I could talk to others in their dreams. She showed me how, though I haven't tried since. Maybe I still can. Maybe I can even speak to Rhydda." He looked around at the faces of his friends—Kjorn, fierce and hopeful, Stigr, pensive, Dagny and Asvander doubtful, and Brynja, her quiet look of observation.

Kjorn spoke. "If that's so, do you think you could speak to her before we come to battle?"

Shard raised his head, trying to look strong and sure. "I hope, if I can talk to her, that you won't need a battle at all."

6

HUNTRESS

S NOW FELL LIKE OWL DOWN as Ragna paced before a group of hunt-resses who'd answered her summon. Only six had come, and those were near her own age. The rest were too old, too young, pregnant, or, once they heard her briefest reason, refused to come at all.

"I hold Sverin captive until my son and Kjorn's return," Ragna said. She caught the gaze of Asfrid, a full-blooded Vanir who was the mother of Astri—Astri, whose mate Einarr was slain by Sverin's own talons. She tried to think how to say any of it so they would understand, and had to remind herself why she had understood, when Sverin told her. "He refuses to eat fish, in honor of his drowned mate. I have chosen to recognize this grief. Who will help to hunt for him?"

The gryfesses exchanged looks. Asfrid met Ragna's gaze, though her head was low. "I will not," she said quietly. "My daughter still grieves Einarr. Forgive me, my queen."

At Ragna's nod, she turned and walked back toward the nesting cliffs. Ragna's chest constricted, both in frustration and sadness.

"Well?" She looked at the five remaining, and saw only anger and pain. A chorus of, "I cannot," and a quiet, "Are you mad?" forced

Ragna to dismiss them. She would not punish them. If not for her sense of duty to keep him well, she wouldn't have been there herself. She looked to the last gryfess remaining, a strapping, broad-shouldered Aesir of ruddy color with copper highlights.

"Eyvin. You are his father's cousin—"

"This did not stop him from killing my son."

Ragna ducked her head, hunching her wings slightly in acknowledgement. Einarr's death pressed talons against her own heart. Still, Eyvin had come. There must be some shred of pity in her. "Einarr flies at Tyr's right side, the most courageous of all of us—"

"Why him?" asked Eyvin sharply.

"In the height of Sverin's madness—"

"No," snarled the gryfess, her wings tensing as if she meant to fly at Ragna. "I mean, why was he the only one to stand against Sverin? Why not the Vanir? Why not you? Why did he stand alone?"

Snow dusted down, the quiet between them so fierce Ragna could hear the flakes hitting her own wings. "I have no answer for you."

"Then I cannot hunt with you."

"Have mercy, Eyvin—"

She tossed her head, feathers prickling against the snow. "As Sverin had mercy on Vidar, for flying at night? As he did when he exiled Dagr? As he had mercy on Einarr, my youngest, the only gryfon left of my nest? He severed our family bond, not I. I tell you I was glad to see Shard fight Sverin, glad to see the Vanir have some courage. My lady, I hope when your son returns, he will repair the damage from all these years, the damage of cowardice and silence."

Ragna gazed at her, long, until she realized Eyvin was waiting for an answer. "I hope that too," she said, and nodded in dismissal.

"Tyr have mercy on us all," Eyvin said, turned, gained a running start and flew back to the nesting cliffs.

For a moment Ragna stood in the falling snow, her gaze drifting to movement that was gryfons traveling to and from the Nightrun River, wandering the nesting cliffs, flying out over the ocean. Her eye settled on the horizon, as it always did, checking each point for sign of gryfon wings.

Last summer, two gryfons had flown for Shard to seek the exiled Vanir. Eyvin's first son, Dagr, had flown nightward, seeking his father and any others he could find. A Vanir gryfess, Maja, Halvden's mother, had flown starward. They had promised to return in spring. There had been no sign, no word in the wind, not a gull or a hint of their return.

Ragna muttered a curse that was a favorite of Stigr's, and loped back to the nesting cliffs.

Sᴠᴇʀɪɴ's ᴅᴇɴ ᴡᴀs ɢʟᴏᴏᴍʏ, though the curtain of snow lent more of a peaceful quality than a grim one, at odds with Ragna's fierce mood. She landed between Halvden and Vald and trotted forward. "Sverin! I hope you're pleased. Not one gryfon in this pride will hunt for you."

In the corner of her eye Halvden shifted, an ear ticking toward her, but other than that he didn't move from his post.

Sverin was in the nest, and shifted to raise his head and look at her for a long, quiet moment. "Nor did I think they would. I'm surprised you did."

"I thought perhaps mercy would overcome them."

"As it did you? You are a singular gryfess and a queen, daughter of Ragr. Not all are as honor-bound as you."

Ragna shook herself of snow and folded her wings, ignoring what might have been a compliment. She didn't need compliments from him. "Not even your own family? Eyvin herself turned me down."

Something flashed in Sverin's eyes. Whether anger or regret, Ragna couldn't tell, so severe and tired was his face. "That surprises you?"

"No. Though she did surprise me by laying some blame on me for not fighting you."

Sverin perked his ears. "Now this is something. I wondered too, once. Could you not have raised a rebellion without your son?"

He appeared honestly curious, but Ragna suspected him of baiting her, of distracting himself from the fact that his own kin wouldn't take pity on him. She forced her feathers to remain smooth, thinking of all the Vanir whom he'd sent into exile, or those his father had killed. Raise a rebellion indeed. But she would not snap back, she would not argue with him. She would not rise—or sink, rather—to his level.

"If I could have, the question is long past. I will not dwell on it."

He tilted his head just slightly, and she flattened her ears. "Not dwell? How very not-Vanir of you."

"You are one to speak of dwelling, Sverin. You won't even eat a *fish*."

At the entrance, Halvden and Vald shifted, stepping out as far as the ledge would let them, Ragna thought, to give them privacy.

Slowly Sverin pushed to his feet, and climbed down from the nest to stand in front of her. He had lost significant weight over the winter, and more in the last days. Looking at him, she felt the inverse suffering of the pride—as he diminished, they prospered, even if grief remained.

"You may have forgotten," he rumbled, watching her, "but I didn't kill Baldr."

The breath flitted from her chest. Baldr's laugh, his quick, swooping wings, and his measured voice crowded her memory. Grief and longing and fierce anger thrashed up like a skewered fish in her chest, and she breathed it away. "No, you didn't. My wrath for you is over other things. As for Baldr, you did nothing at all."

"It was war. We were conquering. You expected me to tell my father to stand down, to accept friendship and simply live in peace?"

Ragna could only watch him with a long, quiet look. "Yes." Having looked ready to laugh at the very idea, instead he ground his beak and turned away, pacing back up to his nest as if to avoid her simple answer.

Ragna took one step forward. "Yes, that is what I expected. You didn't come here to conquer. By your own admission, you fled a nightmare in your own land. Baldr offered you friendship, a new home, sanctuary. But . . ." She stopped. But, everyone knew what happened after that.

Sverin didn't look away, and his eyes searched her, critically. "I cannot change what my father did, what I did. I cannot change Baldr's death, Elena's death, nor the regret, the pain and the wrongs I brought on this pride to protect myself. But I have confessed, and that has cleared my mind. I will confess to Rashard, to Kjorn, and ask their forgiveness. I grieve. I regret, and to an extent you cannot understand. What more do you want from me? All I ask is food to sustain me."

Where was this sense of reason ten years ago? Or five? Or this winter, in those last moments before Einarr had to die? She wanted to slash his eyes and ask him, to scream eagle's fury and run the sun back so they could relive those horrible days with this new, quiet, sane red gryfon as king.

When she said no more, his eyes narrowed, and she knew he was trying to read her expression. Then he turned away, tail flicking once. "What will you do, if no one will hunt with you?"

"That's none of your concern."

"You haven't decided, then. Well enough."

"Self-pity doesn't become you, son of Per. Rest assured we will provide for you."

He paused, eyed her over his shoulder, then turned twice in his nest, clawing up furs and sticks and discarding golden bracers and chains, then settled heavily. Lying that way, where it was hard to see that his wings were bound, he still managed a trace of majesty, with his feathers that matched his rubies, his eyes that matched his gold.

Ragna tilted her head, thinking of how young he'd looked when he'd first arrived with his pride. Thinking how much older, brittle and lost she'd felt, watching Baldr fall to his death in the sea. The Conquering had aged all of them.

Sverin returned her gaze, measuring, and Ragna said the next thing on her mind. "Elena brought out the best in you. Even I saw that. I sometimes wonder," she said thoughtfully, "what sort of king you might have been, if only you had stood up to your father and followed your own heart, if only it hadn't drowned in the sea with Elena."

If the observation stung, he didn't show it. He inclined his head. Ragna turned to leave.

"Funny," his voice carried only to her, not the sentries at the entrance. "I sometimes wonder what sort of gryfess you might have been, if only you hadn't died with Baldr."

Ragna stopped, feeling as though her backbone locked, and with every muscle she resisted the urge to look back at him. She kept walking, and had just opened her wings to take off when Halvden's voice made her pause.

"My lady."

The address, from one who didn't truly recognize her as a queen, made her look at him. He stood stiffly, with his head low in forced respect. "I have no great skill, but I did learn this autumn. If you wish, I will hunt with you."

Ragna gazed at him, wings still open. Perhaps some of Caj's tutelage had sunk in at last. This gryfon, who'd sworn a wingbrother vow to Sverin, look determined to honor it even though Sverin no longer acknowledged him.

"I accept," Ragna said, though she wondered how well they would work together. "Find Tollack to take your place here, and meet me in half a mark on the Star Cliff."

"My lady," Vald said from his place, several paces away. His feathers looked like true fire against the snow. "I don't think he'll try to escape."

Ragna managed not to laugh. "I know."

He looked surprised, then dipped his head.

She didn't explain her reason to these young warriors, her petty reason that she wanted Sverin to feel guarded, imprisoned, his every movement watched and judged, as the Vanir had been the last ten years.

Tor light my heart, she thought desperately as she and Halvden flew from the den.

She hoped that seeing her own son again would drive away some of her resentment. She hoped seeing Shard take his rightful place as king would correct the sorrow in her heart. Her desperate hope was that he would be a balm to all the pride, his love and acceptance of both Aesir and Vanir enough to balance against all the wrongs of the Conquering. But part of her feared she would never know balance again.

7

LEAVING THE LAKE

A SWEET BREEZE TRICKLED THROUGH THE morning over the lake, smelling of water, fish, and just a breath of warmth. The longest winter of Shard's life was coming to an end.

"Don't let him bear over you," Stigr instructed firmly, as he and Shard walked through the nesting hollows where the Vanir were given quarters. "I don't care if he becomes king of the whole blazing windward quarter of the world. You are a prince too, and you do as you see fit."

Shard stopped walking, turning to face Stigr. They stood between hillocks, and dawn light touched the highest tips of the grass and shone off the nearby lake. "I wish you could come too, Uncle."

"If wishes were wings, wolves would fly," his uncle intoned.

Shard knew what truly bothered Stigr, and it was no longer his friendship with Kjorn. During the Battle of Torches, he'd at last gotten to see the courageous, noble side of Kjorn that Shard loved. Stigr was no longer blinded by him simply being a brightly colored Aesir, and the only son of Sverin, the War King. No, it was that no matter how fast he might run, he couldn't keep up on the journey, could not accompany and advise Shard as he'd once done.

"I'm sorry you have to stay, but I'm even more grateful that you'll be here for the Vanir."

Stigr grumbled. "I'd send Valdis to keep an eye on you, but—"

Shard laughed, imagining Valdis along, a sort of nest-aunt now. "No. I think she needs to keep an eye on *you*. I'll have plenty of eyes on me, between Kjorn, Brynja, Asvander, Dagny, and the others . . ."

"You'll need every single one of them." Stigr watched him, appraising. "And this dream weaving, this wyrm . . ."

Shard perked his ears, attentive. It was Stigr who'd first taught Shard about Vanir visions, that Tor granted them, that Shard's father Baldr had also been a seer. But they both knew Shard had surpassed his father by far. "Yes? What do you think?"

The old Vanir's single, keen eye seemed to look through Shard, and he slanted one ear thoughtfully. "Mind how you put things to her. If you truly are dreaming to her, remember we don't know how she thinks. She isn't using words. Everything you say to her could be misunderstood."

Shard hadn't thought of that. "I will, Uncle. Kjorn thinks the priestess of the Vanhar might be able to help me."

"Good. Yes, that's good." Stigr was gazing at him oddly and Shard shifted his talons in the grass. Around them, sleepy Vanir emerged from their dens, stretched, and climbed to the tops of their hills to watch the sun rise, respecting bright Tyr. "You've become so much more than any of us thought, Shard. Well, maybe Baldr knew. Who can say now."

"I'm just following the wind," Shard said quietly.

"But what wind?" Stigr mused. "I only hope it never carries you too far from us. I thought I waited ten years to help guide you to your kingship."

"You did," Shard said, firmly, "I am."

"But it's more now, and even I can't pretend it's not. You've traveled and had such visions . . . Ah, well. Let the others care for you, Shard. Don't shut them out. There's no reason for it now. We're all in this storm together. There's no reason to go through any of this alone." He stepped forward, locking Shard in his gaze. "Let them help you, love you, and be there for you, now that . . . now that I can't."

Shard's throat tightened. At those words he realized he was really leaving Stigr again, that with Kjorn's plan to treat with the creatures of the Winderost again, this time as a conquering prince. He wouldn't see his uncle again for nearly a moon, when, if all went according to Kjorn's plan, their forces would meet at the Voldsom to confront the wyrms once and for all.

"Take your own advice," Shard finally said, and butted his head against Stigr's good wing. The older gryfon laughed and nipped Shard's feathers before backing away, and bowing down to give a one-winged mantle.

"Now let's go reassure your pride they'll see you again in short order."

SUNLIGHT WARMED THE HILLTOPS as Shard walked among his pride, reassuring them that all he did was for them. It had been his idea, after all, to return Kjorn to his birthright as king of the Dawn Spire, in order that Shard himself would take up his rightful place in the Silver Isles and avoid another war between Vanir and Aesir. It was the best solution, but not the easiest one.

Shard approached Frar, who laid on his belly in the grass with his face toward the dawn light. The air was clear and sweet, and the sky clear of clouds, paling to daylight blue.

Shard sat beside the old gryfon, the last he would speak to. He hadn't wanted to gather them all and make a speech, but simply wanted see each of his fifty assorted exiles, reassure them and share a moment so he would stay real in their minds.

"Frar," he murmured.

"My king," he said, not opening his eyes. Rather than seem healthier by his days of eating well and the better comforts around the lake, the old exile seemed more weary, as if he'd been clinging to the edge of a cliff and was gradually relaxing his grip. Shard was determined to see that he made it home.

"Our plan to leave, to fly and be home by the Halflight is still in place. I hope you understand why I'm going with Kjorn."

"I do now. I didn't at first, but Stigr and I had a good long chat."

Shard tried to picture what that chat would've looked like, and chuckled quietly. "I'm glad you have a friend in him. Frar, trust that I will return, and trust that everything I do is for the Vanir. I will return, and take you home."

Slowly the old Vanir turned his head to gaze up at Shard, then made an abortive movement to stand and bow.

Shard shook his head. "Rest. Ketil told me you're concerned about being sent into battle."

"Ketil has a wide beak. I don't complain. I will do whatever you ask of me."

Shard ducked his head to hide his amused expression. "She cares. I admire and need her strength. But know this, I will send no Vanir against the wyrms who doesn't wish to fight. Only *I* owe Kjorn my loyalty."

The old gryfon looked doubtful. Shard stood, lifting his wings a little in the morning light.

"Frar, son-of-Eyvar, you who were first to come to my beacon, I *pledge* to you that your days of struggle are over. When my business is done here, all I ask of you is the flight home."

Frar gazed at him, and Shard wondered if he was thinking of Baldr. Then he did push with some struggle to his feet, and bow. "Thank you, my lord. Anything else I can do in your service, I will."

"Watch over the Vanir while I'm gone. With Stigr, teach them the old ways. Assure them I'll return."

"I will do it."

Shard inclined his head. For a moment, they stood together to watch the sunrise, then Shard heard the commotion of others at the edge of the Vanir nests, and left him.

Closer to the water, Shard found Vanir gathering on the wet beach. Ketil spotted him and loped over, opening her wings in greeting. She looked preened and refreshed and determined.

"My lord. I understand that you said any Vanir who wish to accompany you, may do so."

His stomach twisted. "Yes, I did say that."

"Excellent." She called two names over her wing, and looked back to Shard, eyes glittering as two huntresses his own age walked self-consciously forward. "Ilse, Keta, and I offer our talons to you and the conqu—prince Kjorn's mission."

Shard looked at Keta, a shorter and more compact version of her mother, still filling out from her days of exile in the Outlands. Truly a lovely Vanir overall, with feathers of gray, touched at the wings and face with a hint of pearly rose. Ilse, her nest-sister, had been adopted by Ketil in the Outlands, though she was an Aesir whose family was exiled from the Dawn Spire. She stood taller than both, rich dun and russet in coloring, with hints of iridescent orange.

"My lord," Keta murmured, dipping her head and not quite meeting his eyes. Whatever she thought about her mother's meddling, she'd never said, and Shard didn't want to put her on point by asking. "I'm happy to help you."

"And I," Ilse said, "am happy to help the Vanir prince, and the heir of Kajar."

Together, they bowed, and Shard could only say, eyes narrowed at Ketil, that he was glad to have them.

THE SUN STOOD AT first quarter, and Shard gathered at the sloping council bluff with those who had volunteered to accompany him and Kjorn as they treated with the creatures of the Winderost.

In all, their traveling party had swelled to nearly fifty. Ketil and her daughters, Toskil, and two other, older exiles who had been friends to Shard's father. Brynja and nine of her huntresses who'd been exiled from the Dawn Spire, twenty exiles from the Dawn Reach who answered to Valdis and went for Brynja's sake, Dagny, Asvander and ten of the Lakelanders who felt an unwavering loyalty to Asvander and to Kjorn's bloodline all waited to depart.

All in all, Shard thought they made a respectable company, a good escort for the future king of the Winderost, and large enough to handle almost any trouble. He took a moment to thank the other Vanir who had chosen to come, though he wondered, in the bottom of his heart, if Stigr and Frar had not insisted they go just to watch over Shard.

Given all he'd been through, he almost didn't mind, though it still took him off guard to be bowed to, and addressed as 'my lord'.

"Shard." Stigr approached and mantled. He eyed the company of gryfons and nodded once, looking satisfied. "Fair winds. We'll see you again at the Narrows."

"Take care of yourself, Uncle."

"Don't worry about me. And Shard…"

"Yes?"

He looked thoughtful, then fluffed his wing. "Be careful."

It was so simple, Shard laughed, then took a deep breath against the pang of regret that Stigr would not be at his side on the journey. "I will."

"Good. Then I'll see you soon." He stepped back and mantled his good wing, fanning the end of his long tail. Shard dipped his head.

Brynja approached them, and Shard realized she'd been standing off, waiting for them to finish speaking. "All stand ready, my lord. My huntresses, those of the Reach, and the Vanir. Asvander and Kjorn are speaking to the clan leaders of the Ostral Shore, arranging our meeting at the Narrows."

"If they actually show up," Stigr muttered.

"I have no doubt," Brynja said, "that they will honor their oath."

Shard nodded once, and Brynja cast him a reassuring glance as Asvander and Kjorn approached.

Kjorn caught Shard's eye, looking encouraged at the site of their traveling band, and nodded once. "All stand ready?"

"All ready," Shard and Brynja chorused.

Kjorn opened his great, golden wings to the sun. "Then we fly."

8
RETURN TO STAR ISLE

RAGNA FLEW WITH HALVDEN TO a long cliff on the coast, where last summer the pride had attempted to begin a colony of gryfons on the Star Island. She recalled being bitter when Sverin had put Shard in charge of it, for it was practically exile from the nesting cliffs. Now, she thought Sverin had inadvertently granted Shard the opportunity to learn some leadership.

Ragna hoped it was serving him now, wherever he was, whatever he was doing.

"Fresh snow," Halvden remarked as they landed. "This will be good for spotting tracks."

Ragna said nothing. She had never hunted on land, always in the sea. After the Aesir forbade fishing, others had brought her red meat so that she wouldn't have to. She let Halvden show off his knowledge, and tried to look thoughtful.

"Hopefully the deer will be less skittish, since we've been gone from the isle for so many days." Halvden didn't appear to notice her silence, and trotted toward the tree line. A long swath of snow stood between them and the trees, soft on top and crunchy with ice below. The first indication of spring, Ragna thought, the melting and refreezing of the snow. It would be a grueling trek through the forest.

"Wait."

Halvden stopped at her voice, looking back. Snow still fell, speckling his emerald feathers.

Ragna lifted her beak and mimicked a raven's call, then, the best she could manage, a wolf's howl. Halvden's feathers puffed and he laid his ears back, looking disturbed.

"What are you doing?"

"This isn't our land." Ragna scanned the tree line. "Did you think I would hunt here without speaking to the wolves?"

Halvden didn't answer, but looked warily toward the trees. Though he had worked together with Caj and a young wolf to track down Sverin less than a moon ago, he was no friend to wolves.

Ragna made her calls again. A black shape flapped up from the trees, chortled, and dove again. A raven had heard her. She sat in the snow, closed her eyes, and waited. Slowly, Halvden followed her example.

A light wind licked up as they waited, and Ragna breathed in the mingled scent of pine forest and ocean. She glanced toward the horizon, but there was nothing to see but endless gray ocean. She heard Halvden shifting impatiently in the snow.

"We usually hunt in threes," he said.

Ragna didn't open her eyes. "As I said, no one else would hunt with me. We'll have to make do."

"You should have ordered them. You should have told Thyra to order them. Are you not queens?"

At those words, her temper flared, but she would not give him the pleasure of seeing her baited. She held still, eyes closed, and spoke softly. "Tell me who in this pride, who is actually able, should I force to hunt for Sverin anymore? Males of your year, driven so hard to hunt and kill wolves this winter they turned on each other and neglected their own mates?"

She sat still, but opened her eyes to stare at him, ice closing over her heart again. "My wingsister, the healer, who treated all the wounds caused by his tyranny? His own Aesir, driven here by his cowardice? Eyvin, whose son died at Sverin's talons? Who, Halvden, shall I order to hunt for this warmonger? I will not become a tyrant to feed one."

Halvden ducked his head, ears slicking back, and didn't answer.

It was just as well, for Ragna caught sight of movement in the trees.

She stood, lifting her ears, though she couldn't yet see who stalked close. "Hail, wolves of Star Island! I am Ragna, daughter-of-Ragr, and I come to ask a great boon."

A cluster of ravens shifted in the trees and Ragna's gaze snapped to them. She hadn't noticed them before. Halvden stood, feathers prickling up with unease.

"Stand proud," Ragna told him. "Show respect. These are friends."

"Forgive me," Halvden rumbled. "From the time I was whelped to just this winter, I've been taught they are enemies."

"Learn quickly," Ragna said, feeling cool and not at all sorry for him. He was more cunning and ruthless than most gryfons of his year. "I trust you can."

From the woods fluted a rich female voice. "Hail Ragna, queen of the Vanir. Welcome back to the Star Isle."

It was with relief Ragna saw a red she-wolf step from the trees, her paws making little sound even in the deep snow. Two long, black feathers flicked at her neck, braided into the thick fur there. Ragna knew them to be Stigr's. Another wolf moved behind her, and Ragna recognized him as Tocho, who had helped Caj in his hunt for Sverin. A quick flash of blue at his neck confirmed this—a small, cobalt feather given as a sign of trust.

"Catori," Ragna said. "You are a good friend to the Vanir, and to my son, and my brother. I wish your brother was here for me to ask a favor. Might I see him?"

Catori stood still as a reed in ice, having grown a bit taller over the winter, Ragna thought, filling out long legs and a graceful neck. She stood out like a fox against the snow, her amber eyes impeccably peaceful. "He sent me, and I can grant you what you wish. He means you no disrespect."

"None is taken," Ragna said.

Halvden shifted and Ragna glanced at him sidelong, relieved and surprised to see him maintaining a pose of respect, his tail low and ears lifted.

"Fair winds," he said, very quietly, when the wolves looked his way.

"Halvden," greeted the gold wolf from the tree line.

"Tocho."

Ragna looked back to Catori, feeling marginally better. "The ravens brought you my word? We seek red meat to sustain Sverin until his son and my son return, and he can face justice."

Catori canted her head, watching for a long moment while falling snow frosted her blazing fur. "Ahanu wishes to know if the War King will face any justice *before* Shard returns, or if that whole duty falls to him, to the Summer King."

Ragna shifted, surprised, and managed to keep her tail from twitching. "Sverin is imprisoned, bound. There is little else I can do to make him face his crimes yet."

"If the chance comes, Ahanu hopes you will take it. Spring is in the wind, but winter is still in his heart. I fear, without justice, there will be no thaw." Catori dipped her head and sniffed lightly at the snow.

Ragna lowered her head in acknowledgement. She hadn't expected a request in return, but perhaps she should have. Halvden remained mercifully silent.

"I will consider what punishments I can offer," Ragna said quietly. "But starvation and mockery of his grief is not one I consider honorable. Will you permit me to hunt here? Oaths older than I prevent me from hunting on our home island."

Catori lifted her head again, and now Tocho emerged fully from the trees to stand beside her. A handsome pair, Ragna thought, unable to avoid motherish thoughts. She wondered if Catori would have pups of her own, or if that duty fell only to Ahanu's mate. It seemed impossible that such a huge pack would have a single mating pair. All very nosy questions for another time.

"You have our permission to hunt here," Catori said. "We recommend you range along the dawnward quarter of the woods, remaining close to the river. Though the deer remain secretive, the snow draws them out, and we have had luck there."

"Thank you." Ragna let out a slow breath, and bowed her head. Halvden followed her lead.

"Good hunting," Catori murmured, then held very still, sniffing the wind. "Also, you should know . . . while I have not had dreams of Shard, I do hear him in the wind. I know he is well. I know he will return before the spring."

Ragna's heart quickened and she stepped forward, lifting her wings. "How do you know this? Please, tell me anything you can of Shard."

"I did." Catori looked regretful, as much as a severe wolf face could, and flicked her ears as if to banish nagging thoughts. "I do wish I could tell you more. I miss him too, and Stigr, who was a good friend to me. I hope for their return, and for Shard to bring harmony to all of us."

Halvden made a low noise that Ragna thought was a derisive snort, but when she look over, his head was bowed in apparent respect.

She looked back to Catori. "I hope for this too."

"I wish we could stay to help, but we have our own hunting to do for a hungry pack." She crinkled her nose, showing the points of her teeth. "We won't interfere with your hunt."

"Thank you," Ragna said. "Good hunting."

Catori turned to go, then paused and circled around to step toward them, looking solely, deeply at Ragna. "Know that I miss Shard, and I believe he is the Summer King, and he will help us to achieve peace.

Ahanu believes this too." She seemed to hold a breath, watching Ragna, and Ragna's heart quickened. "But he allows you to hunt here because he believes we should not wait for Shard to begin."

With a glance at Tocho, she bowed to Ragna, and so did he. Before Ragna could answer, they loped and disappeared into the trees.

"What did she mean by that?" Halvden demanded, speaking in a full voice again and fluffing his feathers.

"She was clear." Ragna turned to walk toward the tree line, dawn-ward as Catori had suggested. "Let us treat each other well now, and make peace now, before Shard even returns."

"Have you thought what will happen if Shard doesn't return?"

Ragna managed to keep walking, and said quietly, "No."

"You should."

She paused, only glancing back at him for a long moment, until he looked away with narrowed eyes. Ragna resumed walking, and didn't speak again.

Once they entered the trees and began carefully scenting and searching, it was Halvden who picked up the first deer trail. He alerted Ragna with a flick of his bright tail, and they followed the tracks easily through fresh powder. At the sight of new droppings, Ragna's blood leaped. It felt almost the same as seeing a flash of silver under the water. She wrestled with a squirm of shame at hunting on land, but hoped that bright Tor knew her heart.

Halvden's movement caught her eye and he jerked his beak up to indicate a meadow three leaps ahead of them. Through the falling snow, Ragna made out the rough shape of a deer. She thought it was a young buck, though its antlers were long since shed.

"Go around," Halvden breathed. "I'll signal you with a crow call. You leap out and frighten it, get its attention, and I'll come from above before it can run."

Ragna nodded once, though she wanted to correct him on what to call the buck. *He,* she thought. *He probably has a name. A father. A mother.*

But so did the fish in the sea, though she didn't know them to speak or act beyond instinct. *I eat meat,* she thought, prowling through the snow as she waited for Halvden's signal. *I must always respect the life I take.*

She found a patch of shallow snow under a sprawling pine and huddled beneath a bough. The buck, unaware, stripped at bark on trees at the edge of the meadow. Ragna realized if she leaped out from where she was, he would bolt immediately into the tree line. Rising slowly, she slunk through the snow. Every touch of her talons made her wince, though the deer didn't seem to hear.

A crow called in the woods. Ragna froze, ears flicking, and looked up. She didn't see Halvden in the air. Perhaps it was a true crow. Creeping forward, she tried to slide her talons and hind paws in silence. The call came again, louder, from the air that time, but it held the rasp of a gryfon voice.

The buck's head flew up, his body stiff and straight and ready to leap. Ragna knew she was in a poor position, so rather than leap from where she was, she bolted forward around the trees, skirting the clearing. The buck would be alert for scent and sound. He didn't catch sight of her at first, her white feathers against the woods and snow, but he heard her.

He sprang, sprinting not to the middle of the meadow, but around the line of trees, probably trying to catch sight of what he'd heard. Ragna sprang from her spot with a shriek, trying to force him to the middle where Halvden could dive at him.

"No!" Halvden shouted from the air. Now Ragna saw him, green and diving fast through the flurries of snow. The buck dodged, swerving toward the trees. Halvden swore from the sky.

Ragna leaped straight up and flapped hard, hoping to land on the other side of the panicked buck. She would be too slow. She swooped forward, swiping talons, as he leaped between two pines and was gone into the trees.

"Curse it!" Halvden swung an angry circle above her. "I called twice! You didn't trust—"

"I was in a bad position." Ragna dropped to the ground, shaking snow from her wings. "We'll get the next one."

"The next one?" Halvden shrieked. "You don't have any idea how hard it is to find one in the open! This was a gift from Tyr himself, a grown buck in a clearing, and you ruined it!"

"I?" Ragna shook herself, containing her temper, for she had ruined it. Halvden was right and she knew it. She knew nothing of hunting in the woods, hunting running game through the snow.

"You did it on purpose," Halvden snarled, landing hard in the snow. "You never wanted to feed the king."

Ragna looked at him coldly. "That isn't true—"

Just then, the buck burst back into the meadow as if driven by demons. Ragna stumbled back in the snow, amazed. The buck saw them just before it ran them over and shied up, flashing his hooves in threat.

Before Ragna could blink, Halvden pivoted and leaped like skyfire. He swiped to block the flailing hooves and slashed the deer's throat with his beak, knocking the big body to the snow.

A swift, clean kill.

Ragna stared at him. Her blood slammed through her body and she flattened her ears, embarrassed, amazed. Then she shook herself and jumped forward to the buck's head.

"Thank you," she whispered, though certain she was too late. Perhaps his spirit would hear. Halvden watched her, but said nothing. Flashing, copper movement caught her eye and she saw a gryfess loping toward them from the woods.

"I thought you might need a third," Eyvin said as she trotted into the meadow.

Ragna ducked her head in gratitude. "We did. Thank you."

"I did it for my own honor," she said, then eyed Halvden. "You've come far, son of Hallr. Very far. A good kill."

Halvden looked pleased, and dipped his head.

"This will see Sverin through some time," Eyvin said to Ragna, though she looked at the meat longingly. All of the pride, Aesir and Vanir alike, had vowed not to hunt on land again unless granted permission.

"Why did you change your mind?" Ragna asked, still feeling numb with surprise. The whole ordeal was very different than fishing. Blood stained the snow, making her think less of food, and more of battle.

"I could not accuse you of cowardice and then withhold my help." Eyvin held her head at a proud angle. "The Aesir don't dwell in the past. I'm not loyal to Sverin, but to Kjorn now, who I'm sure wouldn't wish for his father to starve."

Ragna nodded once. Halvden began quartering the meat, butchering limbs with quick, violent jerks of his beak and talons.

"Thank you." Ragna watched Eyvin's cool, hard face, and thought of Catori's words. *Let us begin now.* "I had spoiled the hunt. I haven't the skill and I know we couldn't have done it without you. I'm grateful."

Eyvin eyed her, perhaps deciding if she meant it. After a moment, she nodded once, satisfied, and set to help Halvden with his work. Ragna moved in to help where she could, and Eyvin quietly instructed her in where to separate the joints, and how best to use one's talons to slice the meat cleanly.

Halvden spoke, green feathers nearly white with snow, except for his red beak and talons. "With three of us, we should be able to carry it all in one flight."

"Yes, true." Eyvin looked at Ragna doubtfully, as Ragna was nearly two heads shorter than both of them. "If the queen is feeling strong."

Ragna lifted her wings, feeling more fierce than strong. "I am. If you can pull a fish from the sea, I can fly meat between the islands."

"Well enough. Gather your pieces, then."

"I wonder," Halvden said as he sank his talons into the heaviest quarters.

Ragna, gathering slender strips and the heart, paused, watching him. "Yes?"

"I just wonder what everyone will say when they see that Sverin is getting red meat while they're still reduced to eating fish."

"Reduced?" Ragna asked. "It isn't a punishment. It's our agreement with all the creatures of the islands."

Halvden tilted his head, peering through the snow flakes. "Forced, then. I just wonder."

Ragna narrowed her eyes. "We'll soon find out."

Without further comment she crouched and sprang, and the other two followed, all dragging their share of the kill.

9

PAINTED HUNTERS

A S EARLY MORNING WORE INTO blue day and then cool, late afternoon, they reached the plains between the Ostral Shores and the Dawn Reach. Kjorn counted a few trees and some scattered boulders.

"This might make a good camp," he said to Shard, who flew beside him.

"Tired already?" Shard asked.

Kjorn laughed. "Not a bit. I'm hoping Ilesh is still hunting here. If we speak to them now and they decide to join us, they can travel with Stigr and the Vanir to the Voldsom and meet us with everyone else."

Toskil, one of Shard's Vanir, flew back from scouting and turned, gliding alongside Kjorn and Shard. "We spotted painted wolves. They look to be hunting, but they know we're here now."

"We shouldn't approach when they're hunting," Shard said over the wind.

"No," Kjorn agreed, studying the landscape below. "And especially not with this many gryfons. Let's settle, make fires, and send scouts. They'll either come to the fires, or we'll find them."

Kjorn noted with approval that Toskil looked to Shard, his own prince, for the final word, and Shard nodded him along.

They chose a place to land where they might have some boulders at their backs, and a view of the sweep of grass and stunted trees windward. Kjorn and Shard called the order to land, and it rippled back through the flight until the rustle of folding wings and paws hitting the earth was all Kjorn could hear.

"Gather kindling!" Shard called.

"Post sentries!" Kjorn said, trotting in a circle to gain attention. Others echoed them and Kjorn watched their band fall into order.

"Shall I go scout?" Shard asked. "I get along with the painted wolves."

"No, Shard. You stay here. I know it's hard," he added quickly, to cut off argument. "Believe me, I do. But you must. You're a prince. You need to remain where they can find, see, and hear you."

Shard hesitated, then his gaze traveled over the gryfons as they moved about, falling into their own patterns. The Vanir gathered kindling. Gryfons of the Ostral Shores asserted themselves as sentries and defined a perimeter, and Kjorn saw Brynja, Dagny, and Ketil talking to the huntresses.

"I know it," Shard said quietly at last. "Stigr said much the same thing."

"Good. Asvander!"

The big Lakelander left a group to trot over to Kjorn, and mantled. "My lord?"

"Choose scouts who you believe will make a good appearance to the painted wolves. By that I mean—"

"Someone who won't pick a fight?" Shard cut in. "That's why you should send me."

Kjorn flicked Shard with his tail. "There are other capable gryfons, your Highness. I know it's difficult to believe."

"I'll see to it," Asvander said, looking amused.

"And what do we do?" Shard asked. "Sit and look handsome?"

"Well I'll do that," Kjorn said. "I don't know about you."

Shard snarled playfully, then Brynja trotted up to them. Now that she and Asvander's arrangement was officially null, Kjorn watched as she enjoyed showing Shard her affection more openly. She nipped his ear, then stood back as Ketil and Dagny trotted up behind her.

"Shall we hunt?" Ketil asked Shard, though Dagny looked to Kjorn.

Kjorn was glad Shard didn't check with him for approval, but nodded. "But Toskil spied painted wolves nightward of us. Go in the other direction, so they don't mistake our purpose here."

"We'll do it," Dagny said brightly. "I used to know this land fairly well."

"Good." Kjorn lifted his wings. "Plenty of time before dark. Know that there might be painted wolves in our camp by the time you return. If you don't find game before dark, come back."

"We won't fly at night," Brynja assured him, though with a hesitant look to Shard, who dipped his head. Only in the Winderost, when the wyrms hunted by night, did the Vanir prince hesitate to fly under the stars. Kjorn understood why his own father had abolished the Vanir practice, but still saw how it nettled Shard not to have the freedom.

"Off with you then," Shard said, commanding with false sternness. "We'll see you by sunset."

"Miss us," Dagny said, mostly to Asvander, who ruffled his feathers and stretched a wing to brush against hers. Kjorn thought she might burst with glee, and she bounded off, leading the other huntresses away.

Kjorn watched Asvander curiously. The big Lakelander flicked his tail nonchalantly. "Oh, you know. When we were fledges, we . . . well. Before Orn and others decided Brynja and I should mate, Dagny and I had big plans to mate, have a whole pride of kits and take over the Dawn Spire and conquer the wyrms."

Shard laughed. "I had big plans when I was a fledge too. I'm happy for you," he said to Asvander. "And Dagny."

Kjorn watched them, and couldn't help but add, "I wonder what we as fledges would think to look at us now."

"That we're not as tall as we wanted to be," Shard said.

Kjorn shook himself, amused. "The day grows late. Asvander, if you're ready?"

"Yes." He mantled. "I'll gather scouts. Shard, all right if I want to take a few Vanir?"

"Of course."

Kjorn thought Shard looked pleased, and secretly Kjorn was grateful. He thought the Vanir would do well treating with the painted wolves. He wasn't sure about the Lakelanders.

A MARK OF THE sun later, when the huntresses were still out and when Kjorn thought Shard might lose his mind from boredom, Toskil returned to them.

"Shard! Your Highness!" He landed where Kjorn and Shard sat with others, discussing battle strategy.

Shard stood, and Kjorn alongside him. "What's happened?"

Toskil's beak was open, panting. "A fight. I tried to stop them. One of the Lakelanders didn't understand what the wolves were saying—"

"How far?" Kjorn asked, opening his wings.

"Not far. Just nightward."

Shard looked at Kjorn. "Now can we go?"

"Lead the way," Kjorn said to Toskil, and the three of them took to the air, with a group of surprised Lakelanders and huntresses following after.

Beyond their camp, nightward, the land unfurled in long, uneven plains like a gryfon wing, rolling, then flat, with sparse trees. Ash had turned the ground gray. Swirling wind mixed the ash with frost and stunted grass, painted odd swirls to Kjorn's eye from above.

"There!" Toskil called over the wind.

Ahead, a dangerous stand-off laid itself before Kjorn's eyes. A massive pack of painted wolves circled not one but two pronghorn carcasses. He counted at least thirty, abnormally large for a hunting pack. The gryfons had done the stupidest possible thing, to ring around the entire pack as if they meant to steal the kill.

All had dissolved in to shouting, growling, snapping beaks and fanged jaws. From above, it was clear to Kjorn that no one understood each other and it was only moments before it broke into real violence.

"Tyr's beak," Shard muttered, sounding like Stigr.

"I told them not to approach while the wolves hunted..."

"Oh no," Toskil said, just as a painted wolf broke the defensive circle and lunged for one of the Lakelanders. Three wolves followed.

Kjorn dove, knowing Shard and the others would be right behind him.

"Stop this!" he bellow, flaring hard so all would see his gold wings and know him. He jumped toward the fighting wolf and gryfon, slashing talons and snapping his beak. "Stop this now!"

Barking wolves either echoed his sentiment or cheered on the fight. The wolf and gryfon wrestled and tore at each other, falling to the ground in a tangle, snarling heap.

Wolves snapped and shouted, but Kjorn couldn't listen properly with all the tension and the growling. Around him, Shard and the others fanned out to begin talking both groups down.

A mottled blur surged past Kjorn, a painted wolf joining the fight. "Help me, son of Sverin!"

Kjorn ramped in surprise, and realized he knew the speaker, and that he wasn't going to help the fight, but break it up. While the painted wolf smashed into his fellow, Kjorn went for the gryfon, grabbing for his hindquarters.

"Enough!"

"They started it!" wailed the warrior, who was one of the younger Lakelanders, named Norri.

"You sound like a mewling kit," Kjorn growled, shoving him back. It didn't work to treat gryfons of the Ostral Shores with any tenderness. Kjorn thought of Caj, his upbringing, and his warrior training, and brought all that cold sternness to his demeanor. "I thought I had grown warriors at my side, not immature fledges. I told you not to approach when they were hunting."

"They weren't hunting," Norri said, lifting his beak smugly. "They'd started eating."

Kjorn hissed and slapped talons across his face, not scratching, but warning, and Norri hunched down in surprise. "What's that again?" Kjorn demanded

Norri lowered his head. "Forgive me. We were rash."

"You were. Shard?" Kjorn turned from him and peered through the dust and the gathered wolves and gryfons. A painted wolf leaped into his face, panting happily. Kjorn fell back, then laughed. "Mayka! I'm glad to see a friend."

The wolf, who had once traveled with a small band of rogue gryfons and helped Kjorn, sat down in front of him. "I'm glad to see you too. I did not think these gryfons meant ill, but then it became hard to tell, and then no one was listening. The Star-sent is speaking to Ilesh."

Kjorn took a moment to understand him, then followed his gaze. Shard, whom the painted wolves called the Star-sent, had found and was speaking to the leader of the wolf pack. Grateful for his wing-brother, Kjorn walked through the tense gryfons and wolves, and mantled.

"Great Hunter." He used the title of the wolves in the Silver Isles, hoping Ilesh took it as a sign of respect.

"Son of Sverin," Ilesh acknowledged. "The Star-sent has told me the tidings."

"And I told him of our fire," Shard said, watching Kjorn's face. "And that if they aren't too offended by our rash allies, they might join us tonight to talk more."

"We have hunted together," Ilesh said to Kjorn. "And the Star-sent was a friend to my sister, so we will trust what you say. But these other gryfons..."

"Will make amends," Kjorn said firmly. "And Shard is right. We would be glad to have you at our fire, to speak of tidings, and perhaps to hear of this great hunt." He nodded toward the two pronghorn carcasses, thinking it couldn't hurt to flatter a little.

Ilesh bared his long teeth. "Yes, we would be glad to tell this tale. But if you mean well, then leave us now to our feast, and we will find you after dark."

"I will go with the gryfons," Mayka said, stepping forward though his head was low and tail tucked. "Great leader, I will go? And lead you back when the stars shine?"

"Yes." Ilesh regarded him with approval, then met Kjorn's gaze, lifting his dark, round ears. "This will do."

"Thank you," Kjorn said. "Shard? Shall we? All of you!" He raised his voice to the rest of the gryfons and opened his wings, but didn't fly. Out of respect for the painted wolves, they walked, backing away from the meal, walking along the plain until it seemed polite to take to the air again.

Shard winged up beside him. "This should be a merry gathering."

"I should skin them," Kjorn growled.

"They'll behave better with Asvander close."

"They'll behave better or I'll see to them myself," Kjorn muttered, and that was the end of it until nightfall.

TWO MODEST FIRES BURNED in the dark, and Kjorn supposed the wolves would've had no trouble finding them even without Mayka leaving to lead them back.

Brynja and the huntresses had found the same pronghorn herd of Ilesh and his pack, and managed to fell three of them—plenty to feed their company and offer leftover bones to the painted wolves when they arrived. Kjorn insisted that the Lakelanders settle away from the fire so Ilesh and his pack would feel honored.

The painted wolf chief laid on his belly before the flames, happily cracking open a bone and licking the marrow from inside. Kjorn and Shard sat with him, with Brynja, Ketil, Asvander, and Dagny ringed around the fire. Most of the gryfons already slumbered, some spoke quietly at the second fire and others eavesdropped from the dark.

The big chief, his fur a dazzling array of swirling brown and white spots that seemed to dance in the shadows of the fire, finished his bone, cleaned his paws, and sat up.

"I am not opposed to alliance with gryfons, if they are led by you," he said to Kjorn.

Shard nudged him, and Kjorn knew his wingbrother's thought—how quickly the wolf chief had gotten to the point. He appreciated that, as he felt they had very little time, and inclined his head. "I understand your boundaries have not been respected under the rule of Orn."

"Nor under your father, or his, or Kajar," Ilesh said, tilting his head. "Gryfons have pecked and pushed at us since the Second Age, and all of us have failed to repair our broken boundaries. You and the Star-sent are the first to even hear our words, and this is good. If we drive out the great enemy together, perhaps we can have new respect, new understanding, new laws."

Mayka bellied forward through the dark and stretched out discreetly by Kjorn, showing his support.

"I have respect for you," Kjorn said quietly.

Beside him, Asvander shifted, nodding slowly. "I make no excuses for Lakelanders who disrespected your hunt today, but know that I have seen the painted wolves fight, and we would be glad to have you as allies."

"Allies? This is a cold word."

"Friends," Asvander said, and gratitude warmed Kjorn's chest. It was not easy for Asvander to change his ways. But, like Brynja and the other Aesir, they were beginning to see as Kjorn saw, as Shard had taught him. Respect and honor for all creatures, Named and Nameless.

"Friends," Ilesh said, and licked his chops as if tasting the word. "Yes. We like this. Know that what I do here, I do for my pups, and their pups. And for your kits, so they will know peace and understanding, not war. I will fight the great enemy with my pack so my pups never have to fight, and I will do so alongside gryfons, lions, and eagles, so my pups never know the prejudice we must overcome."

"Yes," Kjorn said quietly, with a glance at Shard, who looked just as pleased as he could, wings fluffed and ears twitching to soft sounds in the dark. "That's our hope as well. Tell me what lands, what borders you hope to claim at the end of this."

Ilesh raised his dark muzzle and opened his mouth to a panting grin. "The time for that will come. First…" He looked between Shard, Asvander, and Kjorn, and said, "Tell me what plan you have for we creatures of the earth to be of use against the winged enemy."

Kjorn and Asvander looked at each other, and Kjorn deferred to the Lakelander, who was swiftly becoming the head of Kjorn's small war council.

"Well," Asvander began, leaning forward. "Unfortunately the best way I have to describe what you and the lions will do is … distraction. I hope that isn't insulting to you."

Ilesh bared his fangs, his plumed tail dusting the ground. "I have seen tiny fleas bring down even the mightiest hunter. Tell me your plan."

They spoke of war until the fires burned low, and Kjorn invited the wolves to stay the evening near them, but Ilesh stretched and summoned his hunters with a warbling growl.

"No. We will travel back to the red lake, find Stigr, and travel with him back to the Serpent River and meet the eagles."

"Tell him we fare well," Shard said. "If you will."

"I will."

"We'll see all of you at the Voldsom Narrows then," Kjorn said. Weariness clawed at the back of his eyes, but the wolves seemed to be perking back up, ready for a long run in the night.

"You will, you will indeed!" Ilesh trotted around the fire, stepping into Kjorn's space. Familiar with rituals of the wolves in the Silver Isles, Kjorn lifted his head and leaned forward. Ilesh touched the side of his muzzle to Kjorn's beak and they shared a breath, and the heavy scents of meat, blood and muscle washed over him. Then Ilesh bounded away almost like a pup, invigorated, and nipped and barked at his fellows until they all streamed away in the night. Kjorn heard Mayka barking farewell.

"That went well," he said as Shard slipped up on his right.

"Yes. Now we just have the Vanhar, lions, eagles, and the Dawn Spire."

"Breezy," Kjorn said, taking Dagny's favorite expression.

"Breezy," Shard agreed softly, and though they both settled down, Kjorn was certain that every time he woke in night, Shard was awake, staring into the dark at something the rest of them couldn't see.

10

AT THE DAWN REACH

TWO MORE DAYS OF HARD flying brought them to the Dawn Reach—a broad swath of hills, chalky bluffs and long draws. Shard felt good with the alliance of the painted wolves secured, knowing they would take word to Stigr and the others.

As they glided down to land, Brynja told Shard that her bloodline laid particular claim to that territory. It was the ancestral home of the line of En, the legendary huntress from the ballad they'd heard at the Ostral Shore. Shard inquired about the early kings of the Winderost, but Brynja told him that little was known about them.

"Many of those tales are lost," Brynja said as she set her hind feet on the ground, flapped once, and folded her wings. "But any who claim noble blood must at least be able to trace their kin back to En, Maj, Ingmar, or Oster."

"I remember those names," Shard said, landing beside her. He watched all around as the Vanir of the company landed. "From the Wild Hunt, when King Orn divided the hunters by family. Orn is from the line of Ingmar?"

"And Kjorn's line would trace back to En," Brynja said, watching the prince land and give his orders to ready their camp. "Through Sverin. The bloodline of En has always ruled at the Dawn Spire, until now. Surely it's what the land and the gods know is best. Things have never been so out of balance before."

"We'll set it right," Shard said, and saw Ketil coming toward them. He forced himself not to flatten his ears. "Kjorn will set it right, I know he'll do well by this land. Fair winds, Ketil," he said as the gryfess approached.

"My lord." She mantled. "My daughters and I are prepared to hunt."

Shard deferred to Brynja, who knew the land. She inclined her head. "I'll gather some of mine. We hunted here often."

Ketil hesitated, but her gaze remained on Shard and she dipped her head. Even she wasn't so foolish as to wander in a land she didn't know.

"Keep alert," Shard said. "We're farther from the Ostral Shores now. There may be scouts from the Dawn Spire, and I think we'd all rather not have them see Kjorn just yet."

"Yes, my lord." Ketil inclined her head again.

As she left, Brynja leaned over to touch her beak to Shard's neck. "I miss the days when you hunted with me." Usually it was the duty of gryfesses to do the bulk of hunting for a pride, for they were more skilled and worked better in teams. To earn himself a place at the Dawn Spire that autumn, Shard had hunted with Brynja and the others.

He ducked his head, his heart quickening. "We'll have those days again. Right now, I need to—"

"I know. Go, plan with your wingbrother." She preened three feathers on his neck, then bounded away, calling for Dagny and two others. He glanced around and spotted Asvander a few leaps off, instructing his band to gather kindling. Toskil and the Vanir fell in with them, and Shard caught Asvander's gaze. The big Lakelander

Jess E. Owen

lifted his beak in acknowledgement, looking more confident and settled than he ever had before.

Kjorn trotted up, ears alert. "Ketil and Brynja seem to be getting on better?"

"Ketil won't insult her directly," Shard murmured, watching the huntresses gather from the assorted clans, decide a direction, and lift back into the air to hunt. "But she barely looks at Brynja, and I know she wishes I spent more time with Keta."

Kjorn hesitated, then asked, "Has Keta approached you herself?"

Shard dug a talon against the chalky earth. "No. I doubt if she's even interested, and I pity her."

"Or she's waiting for her mother to clear a path to you. Or, perhaps it's none of that and you're a self-absorbed jackdaw. Have you considered that?" Kjorn's voice was light, teasing.

Shard flattened his ears, looking over only to realize that Kjorn was enjoying the drama, and purposefully goading him. He growled, low. "I'm glad you're entertained."

"Do you think I faced no opposition to choosing Thyra?" Kjorn asked, studying his face. "A half Vanir?"

Surprised, Shard shook his head. He hadn't thought so. He hadn't thought anything about it but to be happy, for he loved them both.

The summer Kjorn and Thyra had mated, Shard had been so self-absorbed with learning he was a Vanir and learning from Stigr and trying to sort his place in the world, he hadn't known Kjorn had faced opposition at all. To all appearances, everyone had looked pleased with the match. Shard couldn't think of a thing about Thyra, his own nest-sister, to object over.

Then, he couldn't think of anything to object over about Brynja either. "But surely, because she was Caj's daughter—"

"No, Shard. There will always be someone who is unhappy with what you do, so you can only keep doing what is right."

Shard huffed a sigh. "I know it. Thank you for the counsel, Your Highness." He offered a dramatic mantle, and Kjorn cuffed his ears.

"Come now, let's get everyone settled."

The early evening light revealed scant kindling for their fires, so they lit only one. The huntresses returned before long with a single pronghorn, remarking that the herd seemed skittish, as if others had recently hunted there.

They set their usual watch, four gryfons posted around the perimeter, and the gryfesses divided the meat sparingly among the band. Shard walked among his Vanir as dusk washed the sky with indigo, and shadows pooled in the wells of the rolling hills. He spotted the Vanir sentry, standing on a low rise, outlined against the sky. When he realized who it was, he took a deep breath and climbed the rise to speak to her.

"Keta."

She turned, blinked at him, and mantled quickly. "My lord. All stands quiet."

"Thank you. You hunted, so you don't have to stand a watch, you know."

"I like it." She straightened and watched him respectfully, but not meekly. "I like knowing where everyone is, and seeing what's out there."

Shard inclined his head. She was a lovely gryfess. He felt strong affection for her, but in the manner of a younger sister or simply the bond of being Vanir—being part of the Conquering, reunited, and reforming their pride.

"I need to speak with you," he murmured.

"You are speaking with me, my lord."

Shard laughed, perking his ears. "Yes, true. I think you know what I mean."

She looked toward the sky, ruffling her wings, and stated, "My mother hopes you will cast off Brynja, and mate with me the next Daynight."

Shard hadn't planned to stoop so quickly on the topic, but since she had . . . "And you know Brynja and I love each other."

"Yes." Keta tilted her head to study him, then looked back across the landscape, eyes alert. "I won't lie, my lord. When we found you by the fire in the Outlands, and you declared yourself, and I knew we were going home at last—home, to a place I had only dreamed of—I admit for a little while I was smitten with you. The dashing prince who came to find us in our exile." She didn't look at him, but resolutely ahead, her nares blazing pink. "Yes. I'm sure I told my mother I was in love, and that probably got her on the scent."

Shard wanted to laugh, but held it in. He remembered how he'd felt when he'd arrived in the Outlands, after a long flight over the sea, and couldn't imagine that "dashing" was how he looked at all.

"And now?" he asked, amazed and appreciative of her honesty. But then, she had faced harder and more terrifying challenges than speaking honestly with a fellow gryfon.

"And now I love you as my prince, and I understand the difference." She turned fully to look at him, wise and wiry from her years of struggle. "And I would like to get to know my own home again, and my own heart, before I go on to choose a mate, whomever that might be."

Shard felt a swell of love and protectiveness that was completely unlike what he felt for Brynja or any other female he'd known. He wondered if this was the love a king felt for his pride. "I think that's wise," he said quietly. "I also waited longer than others in my year to mate."

Her eyes gleamed. "And it went well for you."

"It did." Shard perked his ears, watching her fierce eyes. "I am proud to know you, Keta."

"And I you, my lord."

Shard wanted to correct her, to tell her to use his name, but he managed to hold back. Stigr wouldn't approve. He had to remain a prince. "Thank you for speaking to me. I'll have Toskil relieve you in two marks."

"That will do," she agreed. Shard turned to go, feeling suddenly buoyant with that weight lifted, when she turned, opening a wing to get his attention. "My lord, one more thing?"

Curious, Shard stopped. "Yes?"

Keta ducked her head, submissively, and her tail twitched. "My nest-sister . . ."

"Ilse?"

"Yes. My mother found her starving in the Outlands, she raised us together. Though she was born in the Winderost, she also dreamed of the Silver Isles as I did. I know she is Aesir, but she fears you won't allow her to join us when we go home. She fears—"

"Tell her not to fear," Shard cut in firmly. "My wingbrother is Aesir. My nest-father is Aesir. My own father had a vision of our prides uniting in peace, and one of his last wishes was that I be raised among the mixed pride, even under the conquering Red Kings, so that I'd know them as my family."

Keta watched him with wide eyes, almost quivering with emotion.

Shard extended his wing to brush hers, meeting her gaze squarely. "Keta, all are welcome in my pride. Tell Ilse. And I will tell her too."

"Thank you," she whispered.

"Fair winds," Shard said, and left her to her quiet post.

Walking back to the main group of the camp, he took pleasure in seeing all the gryfons settled, talking amongst themselves, though some were grumpy over the scant food. When one Lakelander hollered that the huntresses had been lazy, Ketil suggested he go hunt for himself, and that was the end of that.

The groups—Vanir, Lakelanders, and the exiles of the Dawn Reach—melded decently. They'd been together at the Ostral Shores and for the most part overcome many of their differences, though Shard noted that they still claimed distinct, separate areas.

"Counting heads?"

Shard turned to see Asvander trotting up, and ducked his head. It felt lighter between them. They were comrades again, as they had been at the Dawn Spire before the issue of the arranged mating came up between them.

"If anyone's missing, I don't know who it could be."

"You were missing." Asvander gave his shoulder a friendly bump. "Kjorn hates losing sight of you, you know, afraid you'll slip away on another dragon quest. Have you eaten?"

At the question, Shard couldn't recall. The huntresses had returned and he'd helped pass around the food. His belly snarled, answering for him.

Asvander fluffed, and laughed. "Well that's settled. Too bad, there's absolutely nothing left." He gave a heavy sigh.

Shard shook his head sadly. "To think I've come all this way just to die of starvation."

Asvander laughed. "You know Brynja saved you a choice bit."

"At least someone cares." Shard searched his face for tension at the mention of Brynja, but there was none. They were settled, and Shard felt lighter still.

They turned and walked together toward the middle of camp, passing clumps of Lakelanders and Vanir. In the grasping glow of twilight he caught sight of Ilse with a group of the other young Vanir, and paused.

"I'll meet you at the fire," he told Asvander.

"I'll wait here." Asvander glanced at the sky, then around. "Kjorn said Vanir disappear in the dark and I want to see if it's true."

"He did not," Shard said, almost laughing. "Anyway you had plenty of chances to see us disappear at the lake."

Asvander watched him with suddenly less humor, searching, his falcon mask giving him sternness in the low light. "You do tend to slip away when no one's looking, Shard."

Shard chuckled, then hesitated, realizing it wasn't a joke that time. "What do you mean?"

Asvander looked across the camp. "From all you've told us, don't you realize? You said you challenged Sverin, then left your home. You came here, stirred up the Dawn Spire, and left—"

"You told me to leave," Shard said, surprised and wary. "All of you, you told me to run, and I had a vision to seek."

"I know." Asvander watched him, his expression turning hard. "But Shard, we couldn't find you earlier, and my first thought was that you'd left again."

"That's not my fault," Shard said, his ears slipping back. "I was speaking with one of my own. Must you know where I am every breath I take?"

"Yes. You're prince of an ally pride, and my friend. I must know where you are." Asvander tilted his head, then leaned in, head low in a posture to soothe Shard's defensiveness. "Shard, you're my friend and I respect you. But you do seem to have your own ends, and none of us know what you're going to do next. The way you tell it, you even left your dragon hatchling to fend for himself after riling up all the dragons in the Sunland. Do you realize you always leave right when the trouble begins?"

Shard began to answer, then stopped as heat flushed under his feathers and all along his spine. "I hadn't . . . thought of it that way, exactly."

"Think about it."

Shard stared at him, wondering how long he'd wanted to say that, wondering if he was right. Just when he'd felt things were settled . . . "I will. Excuse me."

He turned, not waiting for an answer, and walked to Ilse and the group of Vanir. They fell silent at his approach and some began to stand.

"Don't get up," he said quickly. "This will only take a moment. I just wanted to thank you again, all of you, for accompanying us and helping me to see Kjorn to his rightful place." Thinking of Keta, he met each of their gazes and added, "Know how glad I am to have

found you. Know that the very moment our work is done here, we
will fly home. All of us."

He didn't single out Ilse, didn't make a point of speaking about
the Aesir and the Vanir, but let his gaze linger on hers for a moment.
Her eyes shone, and she ducked her head with the others, murmuring
appreciation.

When Shard turned to go, Ketil rose from the group and trotted
to him. Eyeing Asvander, she asked quietly, "What was he saying to
you, my lord?"

Shard didn't look back at Asvander, but watched Ketil. "Maybe
something that needed to be said. Don't worry over it."

Ketil ruffled, eyes narrowing. "Well. Thank you for saying that just
now, for Ilse."

"Of course. And Ketil, your daughter and I have spoken."

Her gaze lit, then shadowed when she appeared to read his expression. "Oh?"

"Even if I were of a mind to change mates, she wants time. She
wants to go home. I think we all ought to focus on that."

She stiffened a little, then inclined her head. "Of course, my lord."

"And Ketil?" Shard glanced around at the camp, thought of what
Kjorn had said earlier, and looked back to her. Her ears perked but
she stood wary, defensive. "Thank you for coming with me. Thank
you for all you're doing for the Vanir. I'm very grateful you came to
my beacon."

Surprised, she lifted her head. "Of course."

"Fair winds."

"Fair winds, my lord."

As he walked away he felt she still stood there, watching him. He
wondered if she too thought he would disappear in the dark. *I did leave
the fire*, he thought, suddenly gloomy. *I gathered them all and left to hunt
down a missing gryfess . . . then stirred up the wyrms again.*

He met Asvander and they walked in silence to the single bonfire where Kjorn, Brynja, and Dagny sat talking. Stars mingled with

incoming clouds above, and Shard flopped down hard between Brynja and Kjorn.

"All well, Shard?" asked the golden gryfon.

"He needs to eat," Dagny said wisely.

"Don't worry," Brynja said. "We saved you some."

"I heard," Shard said gratefully. He felt Kjorn's gaze on him, searching, and knew he couldn't hide his mood from his wingbrother. He would ask Kjorn about Asvander's comment later, in private, if he had the chance.

The chance didn't come then. He ate the last of his meat, the camp settled as true dark claimed the Reach, and they all gave in to the exhaustion of a full day's flight.

Shard's gaze lingered on the red embers when the fire flickered low and Kjorn stretched out next to him, pressing his back against Shard's. The weight and pressure was comforting, but the moment Shard closed his eyes, he knew he should try to reach Rhydda.

Remembering Groa and her dream net, Shard slowed his breathing and pictured a spiral of sinew in a distant cave at the bottom of the world. He imagined flying along it, grasping at strands that became swirling stars, then eddies of wind. He touched the dreams of the gryfon camp with a sense of wonder and flew higher, then, feeling a touch of murky anger from somewhere, he stooped.

As he slid toward true dreams, he felt her. The hot, searing mind, devoid of words or reason and ravaged only with blood and fury and fear.

Fear.

Their bellies always felt hollow. Burning thirst cracked their tongues and hardened their hearts. The memory of green hills rolled in her mind, then confusion, a memory of soft piles of gold upon which they'd slept. Plump deer, fish, and birds on which they'd feasted.

Now, everything was lack, thirst, and fear.

Through her eyes Shard saw her brood, realized that he was dreaming, but she was awake, and in her mind, he was a daydream. He watched as they hunted in the night.

Rhydda. Did you hunt well? Did you feed your brood?

Darkness loomed like wings around his mind. Black boulders thrust up before him. She wasn't listening. Shard tried again, differently, instead imagining the warm scent of red flesh, the taste of pronghorn and what it must feel like to be a fat, sated wyrm.

Her thoughts turned to him, answering in an image. He saw blood spilling, splashing in dry dust, a sense of satisfaction so pure and whole he shivered.

That hoofbeast had a name, he thought softly to the she-wyrm. *Did you honor him? We honor all those we kill, even the simplest fish.*

Again, he saw black stones, this time smeared with blood. Her way, he thought, of shutting him out if she was angry, or if she couldn't understand.

Remembering how he'd crafted a dream with Groa, he opened his wings and made one for Rhydda, grabbing and weaving memories from the dream net. He showed himself crouched by a greatbeast, murmuring his name so he would take it with him to the Sunlit Land, murmuring thanks to a dying red deer, complimenting her fast run, thanking the brief, simple life of the fish he ate each day. He recalled the moment he'd spoken the name Ahote to a dying wolf prince who had attacked Shard's own family, so that even though they had fought, he would not die Nameless.

Blood and stone and mulling, muddy darkness. She didn't understand, or didn't want to.

Please, he implored. *You are more than this!*

He remembered the sunlight in her dream from before, and showed it to her. Sunlight on water. She lifted her head to see it, then sharp pain lanced across Shard's flank. He cried out, heard Rhydda roar, and realized it was her pain, a memory of pain, and then came a voice he did not know, but the timbre of it was familiar.

You are unworthy of the sun!
Back in your hole, beast.

Shard whirled, seeking the voices, and the dream he'd crafted for Rhydda crumbled into fire and blood—

—then Kjorn bumped him awake as the big gryfon rolled to his feet with a hiss of surprise. Shard held very still, stared at the pulsing embers, not sure if he'd ever actually fallen asleep. He tried to reconcile the sudden violence of his dream with the red embers, then realized there was quiet commotion around him.

"Who goes there?" barked Toskil, from the perimeter. Shard narrowed his eyes and looked up to meet Kjorn's gaze. Together they slipped around gryfons toward Toskil's post. Shard heard steps behind them and suspected Asvander and Brynja followed. Someone, Dagny, began to stoke the fire to give them light.

They found Toskil standing stiff at his sentry post, taking sharp breaths as he scented the air. Shard could just see him now that the fire burned up again from the center of camp.

"What is it?" Shard asked.

"Someone's moving about out there, but I can't see."

"Declare yourselves!" Kjorn boomed, making Shard jump. "We are friendly if you are. If you claim these lands, we're only passing through."

They tensed, standing in silence and trying to hear whatever movement Toskil had heard. The sound of a few gryfons standing, milling, moving to stand protectively behind Shard and Kjorn made it difficult to hear.

It was impossible to see anything outside the firelight.

Shard lifted his ears, and strode forward into the dark. Kjorn swiped for his tail and Shard trotted ahead. Toskil protested, but didn't grab for him.

"Show yourselves!" Asvander shouted. Kjorn cursed when Shard kept walking, but he and Asvander didn't leave the faint ring of light.

There, in the dark and the soft wind, Shard could see better, and hear. He shoved the troubling dream from his mind, and focused.

"If you are painted wolves, we're friends," he offered. "We have no meat left, but you may share our fire. Some of your number have allied with us—come and hear the tidings."

A hoarse laugh crackled. Shard swiveled to face the sound, staring through the dark.

"Painted dogs? Don't insult us."

"Us?" Kjorn demanded, and immediately more gryfons joined, ringing him and Shard protectively. Shard stretched up, looking over the heads of his protectors—Brynja, Ketil, Toskil, and other Vanir. The rest remained in the firelight.

At last the shadow moved, stalking forward, raising wings to reveal a gryfon form. "Us. The free prides of the Winderost."

"Free prides?" Asvander asked. "You mean poachers. Exiles."

"You would call us that."

Finally, Shard gleaned that the speaker was female, and definitely a gryfon, with raspy eagle overtones and the boom of a lion growl beneath. She raised her voice, as if make a point to those listening. "You, who think your claims on the land are stronger than others just because you can name more than one grandfather."

Asvander rumbled dangerously, and Shard heard Kjorn take a step.

"I am Kjorn, son-of-Sverin," the gold gryfon declared. "I have offered a number of your free pride followers a chance for honor and fellowship, to redeem their names and return to their home clans."

"I know who you are." Her voice lowered, dangerously soft. "I only wanted to see for myself, and show the others."

"And you are?" Kjorn asked, and Shard heard his patience waning.

"I haven't decided if you'll know me. Fair winds."

"Who are you?" Kjorn asked again, firmly, but silence answered.

Toskil shifted. No one else moved. Shard stepped toward the surrounding darkness and Brynja made a low, warning noise.

"Speak!" Kjorn demanded, ears raised, glaring.

Shard slipped around Brynja and through the protective ring of gryfons, completely out of the firelight and into the brisk, windy night. When others followed, he lashed his tail to order silence. He caught no scent of gryfon on the wind, heard only the faintest rustle of large bodies moving through the distant grass, running like lions on the ground, and already too far to pursue through the dark.

"They're gone," he reported, frustration and curiosity prickling his feathers. He scented Brynja before he saw her, and the stocky gryfess stepped up beside him and pressed her wing to his, a strong presence at his side. She had joined him in the dark, when the only others to leave the fire had been his own Vanir.

He brushed his tail against hers, and called to Kjorn over his shoulder. "I thought you said Rok leads the exiles. That he would bring them to your cause."

"I thought he did," Kjorn said quietly, from his spot within the ring of firelight.

"No one truly leads the exiles," Asvander said. "Obviously he's met some resistance. We'll post a double watch. Perhaps Rok has spread word of you, and it's only as she said, that she wished to see you for herself."

"But not face me," Kjorn growled.

Shard looked one last time out into the dark, then returned with Brynja and his Vanir to the fire. "Worry about the Vanhar first," Shard advised Kjorn quietly, for the gold prince still peered beyond the fire. "When Rok finds you again, you can worry about this."

Brynja spoke thoughtfully. "Who was she, I wonder?"

"A problem," Asvander said darkly, and ordered four more sentries around their perimeter before all tried to settle down to sleep. Shard felt too hot, with the fire blazing again, and more gryfons now sprawled around them protectively.

"It's all right, Shard," Kjorn murmured thickly, already falling asleep again by the sound of it. "I doubt they'll return."

"I know," Shard said, and didn't voice his real fear, of going back to sleep. The dream had come back to him, and he remembered feeling Rhydda's pain along his flank. As he neared sleep again it returned, flashing up his hind quarters, and he jerked awake, feeling as though he'd been slashed by claws or fire.

All slumbered around him. Kjorn hadn't even roused at his movement.

Holding his breath, afraid to look, Shard twisted and lifted a wing to study at his flank and leg. There was no trace of injury. No scar, no slash. It had truly, only been a dream. A memory. Rhydda's memory. He loosed a soft breath, laid his head down, and spent the remainder of the night trying to remember if the great she-wyrm had a scar as if from a whip of flame.

11
THAW

THE TROUBLE DIDN'T BEGIN RIGHT away, for no one knew Sverin was receiving red meat. Ragna, Halvden, and Eyvin had managed to bring the first kill back in relative secrecy, for most of the Aesir sheltered in their dens when it snowed.

On the third day, when Sverin ran out of venison to eat, Ragna returned to Star Isle with Eyvin. Without a third experienced hunter, they only pursued rabbits, but four of those would be enough to tide the War King over for some time.

Ragna felt the shift in the winds that meant spring was coming. Snow in the morning often melted into freezing rain by the afternoon, with blue skies at evening. It was her favorite time of year—chaotic, unpredictable and full of the rushing, rebounding energy of the awakening earth. She relished her time flying back and forth from the Star Isle.

"You seem pleased," Eyvin observed as they flew back to the Sun Isle, each with two rabbits clutched in their talons.

"Spring is coming. And with it, my Vanir, and my son." She looked over. "Your son Dagr, and your mate. It's very likely they will both return."

Eyvin's talons tightened on her rabbits and her ears slipped back. In her bright copper feathers, Ragna saw young Einarr's face, and she had to turn away as a sudden rush of sadness claimed her. The ocean rolled stormy and cold beneath them, but the clouds above dropped no rain.

"I would be glad to see Dagr again," Eyvin said at length.

"And Vidar?"

Eyvin didn't answer. Ragna didn't get a chance to question her further, for an angry shout echoed down the bronzy, dark rocks of the nesting cliffs.

"Ollar," Eyvin muttered. "What a waste of wings. If only he'd died in the wolf attack last summer."

Ragna looked at her, surprised. She'd never heard Eyvin speak ill of another Aesir. But then, Ollar, who stood on the edge of the cliff, hollering angry questions about the meat they carried, was one of the least-liked gryfons in the pride.

Caj, solid blue against the snow and muddy peat, trotted up to Ollar as Ragna and Eyvin banked to fly toward Sverin's den.

"Stand down, son-of-Lar," Caj boomed. "You will not question the queen."

"The queen," sneered Ollar, spinning to face Caj. "This is a mockery. She's weak. See, even though he's imprisoned and bound, she's too afraid not to do as the Red King asks!" He raised his voice, shouting at Ragna and Eyvin. "Here now, back to the Star Isle with you, and fetch enough meat for all."

"Shut your beak," Caj rumbled, "or I'll do it for you."

Ragna watched them from the corner of her eye, slowing her flight on purpose. Eyvin slowed with her.

"It's a mockery," Ollar raved again. "It's unjust. Why should a mad prisoner of war receive fresh, decent food, while the rest of us choke down cold, slimy poison from the sea?"

Eyvin tilted her head in toward Ragna. "I quite enjoy fish. I suspect Asfrid gives him rotten ones. It would serve him right."

"Will you take these to Sverin's den? I must see to this." Ragna offered the rabbits, flaring. Eyvin swooped about and took them deftly, winging off without a word.

Ragna glided down to land on the King's Rocks, where Ollar stood fuming, with Caj ready to leap on him. Green caught her eye and she saw Halvden, trotting up the cliff trail from his own den.

"What is your complaint, Ollar?" Ragna asked, as if everyone hadn't heard him from the rocks.

"You know it, white witch." Silver feathers had never looked so ugly, Ragna thought. Somehow his gleaming feathers, unnaturally metallic and bright, made him look spiteful, dangerous and wild, rather than handsome. "I demand red meat as well, or I'll starve myself."

"Good riddance," Ragna said, her skin heating with anger. It was not the first time the Aesir had called her a witch, accused her of bringing poor weather on them, blighting the pride, cursing all with her quiet presence. "Stand down. You embarrass yourself and undermine the peace we have gained here. No one else is complaining."

"Because they don't know." Ollar climbed the rocks, stalking her. Caj shadowed him, and his steady, rumbling growl warned the silver gryfon to go no farther. He ignored Caj. "I will tell everyone and we will force you to let us hunt decent food."

"Ollar. Stop this." Caj's feathers stood on end, his broken wing clamped to his side in a mud cast, his good wing arched high, tail lashing.

Perhaps Ollar, in his anger, forgot that Caj had beaten Halvden soundly even with a broken wing, and almost Sverin himself, for he whirled and hissed. "Or *what?* I can't believe your cursed mate has you so pressed under her talon you can't see what's happening. Go on and take that step, you limp-winged—"

Ragna surged forward, smashing into the Aesir who was nearly twice her size. If anger and violence was all he could comprehend, then she would act in a way he understood. Sheer surprise helped her land a few powerful swipes to his chest, and blood splattered his bright feathers and Ragna's.

"Stand down," she shouted as she slapped talons toward his face. He caught her swipe and she dropped, shoving forward to fling open her wings and push him back. "Or I will drive you myself into the sea!"

He roared, rearing back to his hind feet and tossing her away. Ragna rolled through the snow. Blue and green blurred past her, then coppery feathers like flame—Caj, Halvden, and Eyvin rushing in to defend her.

The shrieks and snarls drew onlookers from the cliffs, sea, and sky. Gryfons circled, calling to each other, trying to figure out what had happened.

Ragna lunged toward the fray and it was Halvden who whirled and gnashed his beak. "Stay back!"

"What's all this?" Thyra's ringing voice silenced all others. Caj and Eyvin subdued Ollar and pinned him to the ground as Thyra trundled forward. With a steady diet of good fresh food, her belly swelled and her eyes looked bright and clear.

"Son of Lar, how have you shamed yourself today?"

"This is none of your affair," Ollar snapped.

"You will answer your queen," Halvden said coldly.

"She's no queen of mine!" he said shrilly, and Caj ground his face into the snow with one foot.

"I see," Thyra said, and looked at Ragna. Her brown eyes registered surprise, and Ragna remembered Ollar's blood had splashed her feathers. Stigr had always warned Ragna of how grimly awful her pale feathers looked after fighting.

"He discovered we offered Sverin red meat," Ragna said, shuddering with nerves and with frustration as more gryfons gathered and began to mutter among themselves.

"And that is so Kjorn may see his father again," Thyra explained coolly to Ollar, who snarled inarticulately under Caj's foot. "Not out of pity for the War King."

"You are weak," grumbled Ollar. "All of you!"

"Will you respect my mate better, when he returns?" Thyra inquired, her voice steadily colder.

Ollar barked a laugh. "No. No I will not. Their whole line is cursed and broken, and look what following them has brought us. I have a weakling mate, and a weaker daughter who mated to a weakling who's now dead. The cursed kit will be born *weak*."

Thyra's eyes flashed and she stalked forward, a formidable sight despite her burgeoning belly. "You will not speak of Asfrid, Astri, or Einarr like that in my presence ever again."

"I'll do as I please."

Caj pressed down, Eyvin crushed against him with her weight, and Ragna watched him sputter and growl, then laugh hoarsely.

"I'll do as I please, because none of you have the courage to stop me!"

"If by stop, you mean kill, then you are right." Thyra's voice chilled Ragna to the bone. "None of us will kill you—"

"I might," growled Halvden, and Thyra snapped her beak, raising her head.

"None of us will kill you, because we are heartsick from war, and still we try to heal. But I won't tolerate this in my pride."

"Ha," rumbled Ollar. "What will you do, half-breed?"

"My daughter," Caj reminded him, his words nearly lost in a snarl.

"Ollar, son-of-Lar," Thyra said, opening her lavender wings, "your warmongering and discontent are not welcome in the new pride. You have until nightfall to leave the Silver Isles."

All fell quiet, stunned. Ragna looked slowly from Thyra to Ollar, then Caj, who gazed at his daughter with a mix of pride and shock. Ragna hadn't thought, after all the grief that exiling gryfons had brought to the pride, that Thyra would have it in her to do so. But it was that or kill him, or imprison him, and why should they spend their time feeding and caring for someone who bore them no love?

Even Ollar had gone silent for a moment. But not for long. "You can't—"

"I can, I am. Since you're unhappy with my rule, my mate, and the new pride, you're better off leaving us. I wish you fair winds wherever they take you."

Without another word, Thyra turned and strode away. Gryfons—Aesir, Vanir, and half-bloods alike—fell in behind her, asking questions, demanding to know about the red meat, and if she planned to exile anyone else. Ragna saw unfortunate lines of division forming again. Vanir walked together, and Aesir walked together, each eyeing each other suspiciously. Any trust they'd slowly built was gone, as each wondered if the other was getting special treatment, or special discrimination.

Ragna stood there, watching them depart. Caj stepped back and Eyvin let Ollar stand. "Say goodbye to your mate and daughter," the coppery gryfess said quietly. "Though I know you have no love for them. You owe them that."

At the edge of Ragna's vision she saw Astri and her mother, Asfrid, staring from the edge of the cliff.

"I owe them nothing," Ollar growled, backing away, his tail lashing. "They are weak excuses for gryfon kind. Poor huntresses, and embarrassing. You're all weak, and you will rue this cursed new pride and the pathetic princes you wait for."

With those words, he shoved past Ragna and leaped from the cliff. Caj strode up beside Ragna to watch him fly, making sure he navigated across the ocean, and not toward another island.

Halvden trotted up, hackle-feathers standing high. "Where does he think he'll go?"

For a moment only the wind answered, stirring the air. A light drizzle misted down. Caj shook himself, staring across the water, and said, "Home."

"Good riddance," Halvden hissed.

Caj eyed him sidelong, then met Ragna's gaze over Halvden's emerald back. It wasn't so long ago Halvden had displayed the same insufferable, dangerous arrogance. Ragna was pleased to see changes in him, subtle as they were.

"Thank you," she said to all of them, breaking the silence. The she added in particular, "Halvden, thank you for intervening."

He glanced at her, then turned his head away. "I should go back to Kenna now."

"Yes. Go. Caj, will you help Thyra and me to talk everyone down? They do deserve an explanation. We should have done it before, instead of skulking back and forth like thieves."

"Yes, my lady. Let me fetch Sigrun as well. Both sides have respect for her."

Feeling relief at the thought of her wingsister by her side, Ragna reminded herself not to try and do everything alone. "Of course, yes. Thank you. I'll just follow the mob and you can find us."

She stretched a wing to indicate the group of gryfons who still followed Thyra as the young queen walked along the cliff, calmly answering their questions.

Caj dipped his head, left her, and Eyvin followed him, leaving Ragna alone on the King's Rocks. For a moment she stood, looking back across the sea. She spied Ollar flying. Standing in the cold spring wind, she watched until he disappeared from sight, to make sure he didn't turn around.

12
SPRING RITE

A BLACK SERPENT'S EYE REGARDED HIM, scouring him for more dreams.

"Rhydda. Did you hunt well? Did you feed your brood?"

A dream formed for him of a night hunt, wyrms soaring across a ragged moonlit plain and coming upon a herd of pronghorn.

Shard, aware at once of his body by the cold ashes of their fire, Kjorn's warmth at his back, and of the sharpness of the dream, kept his breathing slow, trying not to wake.

"You are mighty hunters," he acknowledged. "Did you thank them for their lives?" He felt she had returned to her den, was sleeping, was listening to him more clearly because she was dreaming of him. He remembered the pain across his flank, the whip of flame. "What was that?"

Her hard, rumbling growl seemed to shake his body although they were lands apart. Stones jutted up before him. She didn't want to remember that pain.

"Why do you hunt us?" He showed her herself, winging after gryfons in the night, ravaging the Dawn Spire. With it he tried to impart the feeling of sorrow, but wasn't sure how to show her.

A tiny flame flicked in her. A tiny spark of understanding, or memory.

Then he saw a gleaming sheet of gold, inlaid with carved ruby. It was the sharpest, clearest thing in her mind, as if she'd seen it the day before.

It took Shard a dumbfounded moment to realize the ruby inlay formed the image of a gryfon. A tall, sleek, gryfon rampant, carved in ruby with eyes of gold. Recognition shot down Shard's spine.

It was not Sverin or Per, though . . .

"Dragon craft," he told Rhydda. *"That is dragon-made, and the gryfon is—"*

"Bright with dragon's blood," hissed a voice he didn't know. It was the same as the one who'd whipped her. *". . . hear me, beast!"*

Pain lanced across Shard's wings, then his face, and he lunged up snapping. He was himself, and Rhydda, and together they roared, rage consuming them at another slash of pain.

"Stop it!" he shrieked, spinning around to see his attacker—

"Shard. Shard!"

He came to his feet with a sharp cry, gasping hard in the quiet morning light. His chest burned. His neck and feet ached as if he'd battled a foe, and he glanced furtively at his talons, half expecting to see blood. But they were clean, gray, clenching at the dusty earth.

Kjorn stood before him, wings open as if he'd mantled over Shard protectively, the early sun sparkling on his golden feathers. Shard backed away from him, tail lashing as he scavenged his memory for the end of the dream. It slid away like wet sand and he snapped his beak in frustration.

"Mudding, windblown—why did you wake me?" he demanded, snarling at Kjorn. "She heard me! All winds, Kjorn, she was showing me! I almost ..." He trailed off at Kjorn's expression.

The gold prince stepped back, bemused, ears perked. "Shard," he murmured. "Calm down. I had to."

"Why?" Then Shard paused. All around him, the rest of their company was awake, some standing, some still laying down, or stopped in mid-stretch.

All stared at him with wide eyes and open beaks.

Kjorn lowered his head, regarding Shard warily. "You were screaming. I've never heard such a sound."

Shard gathered a breath, looking away from the staring group. "I'm fine. It was a dream."

"Shard—"

"It was a dream. I said the dreams couldn't hurt me." He looked around sharply at the rest. They broke their stares, looking away, then leaned in to each other to whisper. Every nerve along his spine prickled, and he took another ragged breath.

"Are you sure?" Kjorn asked sharply. "You don't know that. You didn't hear yourself. You sounded in true pain—"

Shard steadied his breath and met his wingbrother's gaze. "It was a dream, Kjorn."

Kjorn remained quiet, watching him with a hard look. Shard sought some sight of Brynja, and found her nearby, wings up, one foot half raised. She watched him with steady but calm concern. Unlike Kjorn, she seemed aware that his scream was from the nightmare. *Not a nightmare, a memory. Rhydda's memory.*

Shard glanced to the other Vanir, Ketil, her eyes wide as eggs. Another day of flying had seen them to the edge of the Dawn Reach, and this was the first time he'd managed to dream of Rhydda again.

He ducked his head, refusing to feel embarrassed, and addressed Kjorn. "You have to let me fight through the dreams for any hope of speaking to Rhydda."

Kjorn narrowed his eyes and ruffled his feathers, looking toward the dawn sky. "Very well. But you might have warned us what to expect."

Shard looked again at his talons, then shook his head. "I didn't know."

Asvander loped up to them. "The Lakelanders are ready to depart. All well, Shard? Bad dreams eh?"

"Yes," Shard said with feigned curtness. "I dreamed I had to serve you as a sentinel of the Dawn Spire. It was horrible."

Asvander's tail twitched, then he laughed, and even Kjorn managed a chuckle, though he watched Shard sideways. Brynja and Dagny approached.

"All stand ready," Dagny reported, glancing at Shard with concern.

"All well?" Brynja murmured, stepping up beside him.

"Yes." Shard touched his beak behind her ear, grounding himself in her scent. She fluffed her feathers and he promised, "I'll tell you on the way."

Kjorn nodded to Dagny. "Then let's fly. I'm anxious to reach the Vanheim Shore."

Soon they were airborne, and Shard's thoughts cleared in the bright wind, tinged with the faintest hint of rain. He spied the shadow of clouds on their horizon.

"Now tell me," Brynja said, pumping her wings and settling into a glide alongside him.

Shard tucked his talons into his chest feathers and recounted the dream. Off to his other side, he saw Kjorn's ear flick back, listening over the wind, but the gold gryfon let him speak to Brynja in relative private.

When Shard spoke of the ruby gryfon, Brynja sucked in a breath. "Kajar? The red gryfon," she said slowly. "It has to be Kajar, doesn't it? But you told us that the Sunland dragons had the feud with him, not the wyrms."

Shard tried to remember anything else from the dream, remember exactly what the hissing voice had said. The hissing voice, he became more and more sure, had to be a dragon of the Sunland. "The Sunland dragons I spoke to think that the wyrms were jealous of the gryfons, of the treasures and favor they showed the gryfons. Or at least," he added grimly, "that's what they told me."

Brynja tilted her head, eyeing a stretch of clouds that loomed closer. They flew lower than Shard would have liked, but it was that or go above the clouds, and they preferred to track the landscape. "Yes, I remember. You said that after Kajar went to the Sunland and they had the falling out with the dragons, the Sunlanders sequestered themselves."

"Which meant they didn't go to the home of the wyrms anymore, they didn't make them treasures, they didn't show them favor." Shard thought aloud, hoping he might speak an answer. There was something missing, some link, that would bring sense to the wyrm's hatred.

There had to be.

Hear me, beast.

"But one wyrm went to the Sunland," Brynja said quietly, and that was the part that burned his mind like a nettle, and would not be solved. Rhydda had gone to the Sunland, and she had almost told him what happened there.

"And that's all I know," Shard said quietly. "The chronicler tried to show me the truth, but we were interrupted. There's a secret they didn't tell me. There's something else. Something else about why the wyrms are angry. It couldn't be just gold and jealousy, could it? I could swear there was something she thought..." He trailed off, ruffling his feathers. "And Rhydda might have been about to remember for me, but Kjorn woke me up."

"You can't blame him," Brynja said. "You didn't hear yourself." When Shard didn't answer, embarrassed and angry, she said firmly, "We'll figure it out. These dreams, they're obviously getting clearer.

You're helping Rhydda to remember. Maybe you'll be able to speak to her, truly, to find common ground and peace."

They were all the things Shard hoped for, and had said aloud. But hearing another gryfon, his future mate, his friend, talking it over with him, Shard felt many times better. He was not alone. He didn't have to solve it alone.

"Thank you," he said, focusing on her stern and hopeful gaze.

"Just keep talking to me," Brynja said, the gray light bright on her face. "If the dreams get worse, or you feel in danger, you must tell me, tell Kjorn. You've been alone for a long time, but you aren't now."

That she echoed his thoughts made him laugh. She looked startled, then laughed as well, relieved. "Thank you," he said again, brushing her wingtip on his next down stroke.

They fell quiet then, and focused on flying as the weather began to turn windy and damp.

THE STORM UNLEASHED JUST as they spied the sweeping shore the Vanhar called home. Shard caught up with Kjorn to fly on point, and sentries rose through the gloom and battering sky to meet them.

"Fair winds, Kjorn!" A gryfess shouted through the driving rain. She winged up, looking them over, and Shard recognized her from the Battle of Torches.

"Hail, Nilsine!" Kjorn called. "Fine weather here!"

She laughed, and welcomed them to land, then ordered one of her sentries to take word back to their pride of the incoming force of gryfons.

Shard called to his Vanir for descent, gladly, for they couldn't fight the rain any longer. With Nilsine in the lead, they sprinted on the ground for shelter. This turned out to be a cliff that soared up majestically from the shore, riddled with dens and little grottos along the bottom. The wind lashed rain against the high ground and over the sea, effectively transforming the cliff into a sheltering roof. It was quiet and warmer under the overhang, with only drumming rain above, like a herd of Silver Isles horses parading on top of the cliff.

An uncountable number of Vanhar gathered on the beach, laughing, apparently in buoyant celebration.

Kjorn shook himself, dousing Shard with his drops, and Shard returned the favor, puffing up cold feathers away from his skin. A glance over his shoulder showed his Vanir looked more invigorated than worn.

"What's the occasion?" Kjorn asked Nilsine, just before a deafening crack of thunder. All fell silent, and heads turned expectantly toward the sea. Skyfire darted in silver claws over the white-capped waves. A cheer rose, laughter, and Shard chuckled, perking his ears.

"Spring rite," Nilsine said, looking over their group. "The first true thunderstorm of the season. Winter is leaving us. This year, Tor roars like a lion. A good omen."

Rather than look happy, Kjorn's expression darkened. "How long until the Halflight?"

"Two moons, no more." Her exuberance calmed. "Ah, yes. You think of your mate. Don't worry, my lord. We'll return you to her in short order."

Shard would've reassured him too, but he didn't feel so certain. Most of the Silver Isles gryfesses would whelp on or near the Halflight, the sun's turn toward spring. Thyra had demanded Kjorn be there for the birth of his kit, but Shard feared his task in the Winderost would take longer.

The gold prince tipped his head stiffly, politely. "Yes. But I've been remiss. Nilsine, you never received a proper introduction to my wingbrother. Rashard, son-of-Baldr, future king of the Silver Isles. Shard, please meet Nilsine, daughter-of-Nels, sentry of the Vanhar and lately a steadfast companion and friend."

To Shard's surprise, Nilsine mantled for him as she would a prince.

Of course, I am a prince . . .

Somewhere, he could imagine Stigr grumbling. He must stop looking surprised at acts of deference. At his back stood loyal Vanir. He would be a king. He dipped his head to her. "It's an honor. Kjorn told me all you did for him during his hunt for me in the Winderost, and I thank you for your part in the Battle of Torches."

"I was honored."

Shard nodded toward the rest of their companions. "I think you're acquainted with Brynja, daughter-of-Mar, of the Dawn Spire. But do you know Asvander, from the Ostral Shores?"

The gryfesses inclined their heads to each other. Asvander stepped forward with ears perked, but then Dagny moved in front of him, wings lifting as she eyed Nilsine.

Shard saw Kjorn mask a look of amusement. "And this is—"

"Dagny," Nilsine said, looking from Asvander to her. "I remember. Well met!"

"Well met," Dagny said, and flicked water from the end of her tail. To Shard's delight, Asvander leaned into Dagny just a little, perhaps reassuring her that he didn't plan to wing off with the sentry from the Vanheim Shore.

Ketil and her daughters came forward then, and thus continued a long and cheerful round of introductions as the rain clattered and thunder boomed.

Nilsine drew Kjorn and Shard aside. "I hope you will not feel offended," she began quietly. "Our elders won't meet with you during the spring rite, but they know you're here, they welcome you. And they look forward to speaking at sunrise, weather holding."

Kjorn eyed the rain and shivered. "Well enough. Thank you. I don't know that any of us want to stand around talking in this. While we're here, I ask another favor."

She regarded Kjorn with her strange ruby eyes. "I'll do anything I can to be of service."

Kjorn nodded to Shard, who straightened. "My wingbrother hopes to speak to your priestess."

Nilsine looked between them curiously. "Oh?"

"I was hoping she could tell me more about the vala," Shard said. "And ... their powers."

"I am certain she would be glad to speak with you." Nilsine inclined her head to both of them. "But for now, rest, eat. Let us revel in mighty Tor."

"Indeed," Kjorn murmured, and a timely roll of thunder punctuated their words.

SUPPER WAS FISH, AND more fish, a variety and amount which the Vanir and Lakelanders fell on with enthusiasm, while Kjorn looked rueful.

"You'll get used to it," Shard said.

"It isn't the taste. It's what it reminds me of." His ears slicked back, and his blue eyes shadowed, and Shard thought of what fish had meant to them, once. The act of hunting in the sea, forbidden by Sverin.

"It's over," Shard said quietly. They lounged now in a semi-private grotto carved into the cliff side, with a good view of the sea and the surrounding beach. Vanhar fledges and some of the Vanir ventured out into the evening to frolic in the rain, and this cheered Shard. "It's all over."

"But it lingers," Kjorn said, his talons sliding into the meat of the fish with vengeance. "Like an illness. Your exiles here, that was Per's doing, Sverin's doing. My bloodline, Shard. It doesn't go away. There will be a lot of work to be done here, and in the Silver Isles."

"And we're doing that work. You're doing all you can now. We will have peace, brother."

"Because of you, Shard," he said harshly, and Shard tensed. Kjorn sighed, tail dusting the sand. "Don't you understand? None of this is because of me, not even the allies I have here. You laid a path for my coming. And before that, you had a chance to kill my father. And you didn't. I can't say I would have done the same, in your place."

"Not before, maybe." Shard studied his friend, the long, strong lines of him, the exhaustion. "But now you would."

Kjorn flexed his talons in the sand and met Shard's gaze. "Yes. Now, I would do what I understand was a great act of honor and courage on your part." His eyes searched Shard's face, the whole history of their lives together, and their lives apart. "But only because of you."

"You were never your father," Shard said quietly. "I have faith you would have been more just."

"Maybe," Kjorn sighed. Then, with a stubborn and mischievous air added, "Because. Of. You."

Shard laughed, and Kjorn watched him. He saw, Shard thought, all they'd both become in the last year.

One year. This upheaval and change has taken course over one year.

One hundred years since Kajar had flown to the Sunland. Ten years since Per had conquered. And one year since Ragna sang the Song of the Summer King to the pride in the Silver Isles. So much could happen in a year. A lifetime could happen, Shard thought. Some lifetimes *did* happen.

Hikaru. With a talon of piercing fondness and regret Shard thought of the Sunland dragon, who would be fully-grown by summer, and old by the time the first autumn leaf dropped free. *I shouldn't have left him. I should have stayed. I should have demanded he come with me.*

"What is it?" Kjorn asked quietly.

"I was thinking of Hikaru."

Kjorn looked regretful too, for Shard had told him the whole of it—how a Sunland dragoness had left her egg to Shard's care, how he'd hatched it, raised Hikaru, taken him home to find help from the dragons in the arctic country at the bottom of the world. But he'd found only more secrets and fear, and Hikaru felt called to stay and help his kind. Shard couldn't begrudge him that.

When silence stretched on, Kjorn nudged him with a wing. "Should Brynja and I be jealous, or . . .?"

Shard blinked back to the present and laughed. "Eat your fish."

Kjorn separated flecks of meat from the bone with irritating pickiness. "You *did* take a wingbrother vow to this dragon."

Shard studied Kjorn's face, but saw no trace of true upset. Curiosity maybe, or a quiet awe. "He was my nest-son, and otherwise alone in the world. I had to."

"Hm." Kjorn picked halfheartedly at the fish, and the smell that rose succulent and delicious to Shard made Kjorn sniff reluctantly. "Well. Perhaps I'll take a wyrm for an extra wingbrother."

"If that'll make you feel better," Shard said gravely.

"It will, thank you."

The thought of Kjorn spreading wings with a wyrm seemed to strike them both at the same time, and was so preposterous that they both laughed. Then they bent their heads to discuss Kjorn's first meeting, the next morning, with the ruling council of the Vanhar.

As night deepened and the rain continued in long, lashing strokes over the ocean, noise and commotion dwindled. The Vanhar curled up under the shelter of the cliff and Shard and Kjorn's company joined them. Shard and Kjorn remained in their grotto, calling good night to those who passed them. Shard saw Brynja, but she only glanced their way, gave him a fond look and dipped her head, moving on to nest with Dagny.

"I wonder why she didn't join us for supper."

Kjorn glanced out at the rain. "I have an idea."

Shard watched him expectantly.

The golden prince stood, stretched languorously, and tossed his half-eaten fish out toward the beach. "You'll think it's self-indulgent."

"Most likely. Tell me anyway?"

Flopping again next to Shard, wings pressed together, Kjorn offered, "I think she's giving us as much time as possible, together before . . ." His tail twitched, and Shard made a quiet noise of understanding.

"Before we're parted."

"Yes." Kjorn sighed. "She gets you for the rest of your life together, each night and day, until you drive each other mad. You and I have only until my kit is old enough to be carried home."

Home, Shard thought, his chest constricting. *This is his home now.* "But surely, it isn't as if we won't ever see each other after that." He thought of Hikaru, he thought of how at last he had true friendship, honesty and respect within his realm of closest family and friends, and how fleeting their time together would be.

"Of course not," Kjorn murmured, resting his head over Shard's shoulders, as if they were fledges again settling in for an afternoon nap. "I hope that our kits will know each other. But it's a long flight, Shard, and perilous. I think we'll see each other, but not often. Not really. She's giving us time now, my brother, because after this, it won't ever be the same."

"No," Shard whispered. "I suppose it won't."

Suddenly grateful for Kjorn's uncomfortable weight against him, and his wing at an odd angle under the gold head, Shard shifted only slightly to avoid numbness. He would've said more but apparently the rain had exhausted Kjorn, and the gold prince was already asleep.

Kjorn returning to his birthright in the Winderost had seemed the best possible answer to Shard, but that didn't make it the happiest one.

Shard didn't move, and couldn't sleep then, as the rain fell on over the waves.

13
ELDERS OF THE VANHAR

"THIS GOLDEN SUNRISE BODES WELL for you, Kjorn, son-of-Sverin."

Kjorn stood once again before the half ring of twelve Vanhar elders, the high priestess at its center. But this time he was not alone. Shard sat to one side of the semi-circle and Brynja sat beside him, as did Asvander, Valdis, and Ketil, as chosen representatives of Kjorn's allies. Nilsine stood with them, which Kjorn saw the elders noting with sideways looks.

"It makes me hopeful," Kjorn said, looking at the sky. "We have moved into a hopeful time."

Rain-washed wind sent the long grass around them dancing, and Kjorn breathed deeply, smelling the fresh air and the salt waves. Behind them, the cliff dropped down to the glimmering sea, and the air smelled fresh and clean. All things seemed possible.

The high priestess circled slowly around Kjorn until she stood again before him. "When first you came here, you spoke only of finding your wingbrother. This you have done. We are all honored to meet the prince of the Silver Isles, whom the lions and painted packs call the Star-sent. We are glad to know that you two are wingbrothers, for this makes us hopeful that you will indeed rid the scourge of the wyrms from this land."

Kjorn bowed his head, glancing furtively to Shard, who twitched his wings encouragingly. "And we plan to do just that," Kjorn said. "We've come to ask your help."

"But that isn't all. My elders, the most aged, knowing, and wisest among the Vanhar, sat before you this winter past when you claimed to have no other aims in the Winderost but to find your wingbrother. They have questions for you now."

As the wind shifted around them like a playful kit, one of said elders stood, a graceful, hale-looking male whose feathers had paled with age.

"Son of Sverin. You claim to want to rid the land of our scourge, but that isn't all. Say with your own words what your final aim will be."

With another glance at Shard, Kjorn raised his head and opened his wings just a little, to catch the light. He'd often watched the effect his father's presence had on his pride, and if the Vanhar thought the sunrise boded well, let them see his golden wings.

"I've come to claim my birthright here as Per's heir, Kajar's heir. One who brought a blight on you, and one who fled it. I mean to rid this land of the wyrms, and take my birthright at the Dawn Spire."

"And you seek loyalty of the Vanhar," hissed an even older female, who looked too weary to stand, but her voice cut bright and clear ice. There was no weakness or frailty in the minds of the ruling council that Kjorn could see. "You seek submission, to bring the Winderost under one talon, answering to your whims."

"No." Surprised at her vehemence, Kjorn inclined his head, folding his wings again so as not to intimidate her. "No. I seek your alliance to drive out the wyrms. I seek your recognition, your friendship. Perhaps, one day, your fealty, but for now—"

"You lied," another male said bluntly.

From the corner of his vision Kjorn saw Shard begin to stand, looking indignant, and flicked his tail to stop him. It wouldn't do for his friends to rile, and Kjorn look too defensive. The words were true, if unfair.

"I didn't lie. At the time, my only hope was to find Shard and reconcile, which I've done, and now our aim together is to drive out the wyrms so this land can heal."

"And you can be lord over all."

Kjorn looked back to the female who'd spoken. "Not in the way Kajar's line was. But to take the Dawn Spire, to know alliance from all the gryfon clans, the wolf packs, lions, and the eagles, yes."

"Is this a promise as it was a promise that you had no other aims, before? Is your truth fluid, son of Sverin? Will you have a new truth, once the wyrms are gone? Will you bring warriors to the Vanheim Shore and demand that we bow to you and your heirs and come and go from the Dawn Spire on your whim?"

A claw of frustration curled in his chest and Kjorn narrowed his eyes. His friends shifted, looking from the council to him, and he forced himself to keep his wings folded, his tail still.

"No. That isn't my wish." He raised his voice, speaking to each of the dozen in turn. "I hope for gryfons to be united in brotherhood, to live at the Dawn Spire if they wish, or in their own homeland, and come together in times of need."

"Times of need," scoffed the pale, elder male. "In war, you mean."

"The lions have told us their vision," the priestess said quietly. "That you will stir the Sunwind. What do you say to this?"

A shiver nearly made him ruffle his feathers, but he grasped to his poise. He remembered the night. "I respect their vision. But I believe this Sunwind portends my battle with the wyrms, not gryfon against gryfon."

"It isn't for us to know," a wizened female remarked, glowering at him.

"No, it isn't." He turned to her, forcing himself to transform his needling frustrations with them into a sense of determination. He would not become Sverin, making speeches and promises meant to intimidate. It had worked on the Lakelanders and he'd meant every word, but the Vanhar were very different gryfons. "It isn't ours to know what the winds will bring us. But it is for us to choose how we fly them." He searched the faces of the council, and found only three who looked at all thoughtful and not stubborn. "If you choose not to join me in the coming battle, I respect that choice. I'm not threatening, I'm asking, offering. I am offering the chance to help, to be there to drive out the enemy, to give you back the nights you hold sacred—"

"And then?" broke in the male who'd called him a liar, standing. "After the dead are honored, you'll be here with wing and talon demanding that we bow! Mark my words, everyone—"

"That isn't—"

"He had no interest in this land until he came and saw opportunity." He turned his glower in Kjorn. "You are here to conquer, just like your cowardly forefathers!"

"No!" The shout broke from him, and he immediately took a step back, lowering his head.

A strange, buzzing quiet fell, and the Vanhar who'd managed to snap his temper sat back, looking smug.

At a loss, Kjorn sought Shard.

His wingbrother stood slowly, walked to his side. *He looks like a king,* Kjorn thought, a little dismayed that his wingbrother could be at once hapless and halting in accepting shows of fealty, and then a noble prince when required.

"I told Kjorn about the need for a king here." He spoke quietly. "A new king." The elders turned their gazes to him warily, and the high priestess perked her ears to his firm voice. "I left my homeland to find the truth of the Aesir coming there, and I found the Winderost, in turmoil. I know Kjorn better than you. I grew up with him, quarreled with him, made amends. For what it's worth to you, I know his sense of honor, and justice, and courage."

Shard looked at him with such faith and loyalty that Kjorn could only bow his head, breath catching. "Let me speak for him, though you don't know me. Let me promise that we are striving to find a way to make peace with the wyrms, but if that fails, it will be war. And let me speak as one who shares your desire for peace, for harmony, and tell you that if you choose to ally with any king of the Dawn Spire, it should be Kjorn."

In the silence, Kjorn heard voices down at the shore. Vanhar, going about their morning fishing, gossiping, happy in the fresh wind and the smell of the sea. He felt a fierce sense of wanting to protect it, them, all of them, though they weren't his. A few councilors muttered to each other, eyeing Shard.

"You do not know Shard, but you know me." Nilsine stepped forward to stand on Kjorn's other side. "This winter, the high priestess asked me to accompany Prince Kjorn on his quest to find his wing-brother, asked me to judge his character and his honor. I did this."

Kjorn watched her, grateful and not quite surprised. He had thought she'd had other aims when she joined him, but hadn't guessed it was to bring a report to the council.

That means that at least the priestess suspected I would eventually want my birthright . . .

The high priestess, orange eyes bright in the morning, dipped her head. "Tell them what you told me."

Nilsine's voice was flat, honest, unemotional. "I believe he is the true blood of En of the Second Age, daughter of the first Dawn Spire kings to rise above petty clan wars and our Nameless, brutal fight for survival." Her eyes, like red embers, scoured the elders. "I believe he comes in the name of peace, though that may mask itself in battle. We honor Tor above all, but it is bright Tyr who lends our talons strength in times of war, and it is Tyr who has sent Kjorn to us, Tyr who raises the Sunwind. The sun shone on Kjorn the first time he entered the Vanheim, and it shines on him still. I urge the council to consider these omens."

Kjorn stared at her, and saw Shard doing the same. Over her back, he caught Shard's gaze, and even he looked awed.

A female, younger than the rest but still older than Kjorn's father, made a show of clearing her throat. "Daughter of Nels, there are some here concerned than you are too fond of legends, and that you seek a hero from a song, not a king. I was your age in the time of Per, and it was no better then."

"Kjorn is not Per." Nilsine turned to her, but otherwise looked locked to the earth, like a stone. "And why should a king not be a hero from a song? All of my sentries will witness that Kjorn led us to battle against the great enemy, and others are already singing of it. Don't be blinded by your contempt for the old kings. This is a new day. We must fly to it with new, open eyes and hearts."

The elders exchanged looks, bent their heads, whispered. Kjorn flexed one shoulder idly, wondering how they managed to get anything done, ever, with so many making decisions and giving opinions.

Shard and Nilsine remained at his sides, lending their silent support, and Kjorn leaned on a hind paw to resist pressing to Shard for strength and patience.

When it seemed they might keep whispering and arguing until the middle mark, the high priestess raised her wings for their attention. "I have a proposition for the council." Her voice hushed them, but she watched Kjorn. "The council is concerned about your aims, about your desire for leadership. We have a ritual for any who wish to serve on our council. Since you hope to be a high king, I say that performing this ritual should satisfy their concerns."

The elders considered, began nodding, murmuring agreement. Hope glowed in Kjorn's heart. The priestess observed her council until they fell silent, then spoke to Kjorn.

"They are agreed. Will you do this?"

Kjorn perked his ears, invigorated by the promise of taking action. "Yes, I will. I would be honored to perform any task to satisfy the Vanhar as to my intentions."

"Good. Then I dismiss the council. The rest of your company is welcome to roam the shore as they wish, join us in meals and otherwise make themselves feel at home."

The council rose, stretching and speaking of breakfast, and Kjorn stood there, slightly confused. He glanced at Shard, who appeared at a loss, and Nilsine, whose red eyes gleamed.

"Did I ... did she not say there was a ritual?"

"Yes," said Nilsine.

"What is it? When?"

"You'll know," Nilsine said quietly, and Kjorn suspected her of being amused at his expense. "Or you won't. Either way, it will happen."

"Can you help me?"

"I already did. And will continue to, if I can."

Chagrined, Kjorn dipped his head to her. "Yes, you did. Thank you for speaking on my behalf."

Her gaze traveled out over the sea, and to the horizon. "I meant every word. Fair winds, I'm sure we'll see you later in the day. Prince Rashard, the priestess would like to speak with you." With that, she left, loping and opening her wings to fly and, Kjorn assumed, perform her duties as sentry.

"Kjorn." Shard's voice drew Kjorn back to him, and he looked worried, one ear flat, tail twitching. "I can stay with you until their ritual is complete."

"No," Kjorn said. "I have a feeling I should do it on my own. Whatever it is. Go on. It's important you find out if she can help you."

"Then I'll see you tonight." Shard eyed him one last time, then trotted away.

Feeling muddled, Kjorn watched the other councilors confer with each other, giving him sideways glances as they departed. He looked around for some clue. Asvander still waited there, watching him for direction. Kjorn shook his head slightly, lifting a wing to point toward the shore and indicate he and the others should go about their business.

"Son of Sverin."

Kjorn turned to look down at the old male who addressed him. It was the elder who'd called him a liar, and he watched Kjorn with a flat expression now. Kjorn controlled his tone. "Thank you for hearing me once again. I hope—"

The elder grated his beak in a sound of annoyance. "Come with me."

"Is this ritual to begin now?"

He didn't answer, but walked away along a narrow trail through the high grass and down to the shore. Kjorn glanced around once more and, seeing no one else, followed.

14
THE LAST VALA

"SO. THE SUMMER KING."

"Shard." He introduced himself again quietly to the priestess. The oldest of the Vanhar he had seen, she looked wiry and hard as a birch, and Shard wouldn't have challenged her to a race. Her eyes gleamed orange, an old, birdlike bloodline.

"Shard then, if you like."

They walked along the pebbled beach together, far off from the nesting area of the Vanhar. Shard hoped Kjorn was faring well with his test or riddle, and couldn't really blame the council for their wariness. He hadn't known Kajar, but he had known Per. Whether that gryfon had been more or less of a tyrant than Sverin, he could see why, among other reasons, the Vanhar had severed their ties long ago.

The waves washed over their talons and the cool slip of it sliding across Shard's hind toes sent invigorating shivers through him. The scent of fish and salt and grass, and the old gryfess beside him grounded him. A tingling warmth of anticipation flicked across his skin, making his wings twitch. Perhaps she would be able to help him.

She remained quiet, waiting for him ask his questions first.

"Nilsine told you that I dream?"

"Yes."

"I've had visions before," Shard said, and explained about seeing his dead father, about seeing the Winderost before he'd ever been there. He told her of hearing songs in the wind and Amaratsu the dragon who had called to him. Finally, as she listened in perfect silence, he told her of the spirit Groa, and of his dreams of Rhydda.

She stopped walking, so Shard did too. Gulls cried, echoed by kits cavorting farther down the beach. The priestess looked across the sea, and Shard thought she appeared wistful.

"So. She taught you dream weaving, and you're able to do it." Her attention turned to trail along the rolling knolls and waving sea grass, wet and lazy in the clean, gold light. "Just like a vala. Perhaps it is the trait of the Summer King."

"I think our kinds were one, once," Shard offered, hoping he hadn't offended her in some way by being a seer. "I think perhaps we Vanir came from this very shore."

"I know it to be true," she said, turning her gaze back to him. She studied him long, paying special attention to his wings, and then, he thought, his talons. He chanced a look at her feet as well. Her talons were longer than his, and hooked, and a trace of membrane like a seabird webbed each toe. The Vanhar seemed even more fit for life near the sea than he was.

"We let the ties die," the priestess said, still looking at Shard's feet thoughtfully, "because we'd never heard from the Vanir again. But if you are Shard, son-of-Baldr, and your father was descended from the first kings of the Silver Isles, the first gryfons to leave this shore, then you are a descendent of Jaarl, who could speak to any living thing, and did."

"Jaarl," Shard murmured. "Stigr told me of him. He said he spoke to whales."

Slowly the orange gaze found his eyes again, and Shard suppressed a shiver at her deep, searching expression. The warmth of dawn kept him steady. "Then surely of any of us, you, his descendant—trained by the last known vala, a dreamer, a seer—will be the one to speak to these wyrms."

"I don't know if I have the strength, the right words." Shard ruffled his wing-feathers, feeling restless, helpless. "Groa was a Vanhar. I was hoping you could tell me more of dream weaving."

The priestess shook her head once. "Groa, daughter-of-Urd, was the last vala of the Vanhar. Their lost art was precious, revered, and valued especially by the kings of the Dawn Spire." The priestess's gaze wandered back out to sea. "Perhaps it was the fear of the wyrms that drove it from us, or simply time. Perhaps all gifts fade with time. Many of their dreams and prophecies have yet to pass, and some even said that the coming of the Summer King would mean the end of prophecy as we know."

"I don't know if that would be a bad thing," Shard said, and she looked at him curiously. "Sometimes I didn't take action because of my dreams, for fear of doing the wrong thing. Sometimes I think I would've been better off never having a vision, and just making up my own mind."

Her short, dry laugh surprised him. "You sound like your wing-brother. We are to stir the winds with our own wings then?"

"Is that so bad?"

She studied him and resumed walking, but slowly as the shore grew rockier and harder on their feet. "Perhaps not. For an Age we listened to the Four Winds, but they could carry us only so far before we came to know of Tyr and Tor."

"The Four Winds . . . Someone, a Vanhar, sang a song after the Battle of Torches, about the Winds."

She turned and waded into the shallow water, as if to seek some strength from the sea, and Shard followed, shivering at the cold. "Yes. When we barely knew ourselves, still we knew the rain, the sun, and the wind. Of course the wind, which brought all things, good or ill, and each wind had its purpose."

"And you think Kjorn will raise the Sunwind, this wind of war?"

She glanced at him sidelong. "It was not I, but Ajia the Swiftest, who said that. I believe you're acquainted."

"We are." Shard ran his talons through the rocks beneath the waves, raising a cloud of sediment. "Do you think that either of you would be able to help me with these dreams? Help me get through to Rhydda?"

The priestess stood quietly for so long that Shard wasn't sure she would answer, or if she had one. The waves slid and pulled, slid and pulled.

"Visions that are given to me," she began slowly, "are just that. Given. I will hear a whisper, I will sense a current in the winds or have a flash under the moon from gentle Tor." She stepped around, standing in deeper water to face him. "Your gift is beyond me, but I will tell you what things I know. If you need strength to see farther, you may stand in the ocean, or under the fullest moon. For clarity, face headlong into a Starwind, or sleep on hallow ground, where the spirits may find you." She opened her wings. "These things I know, these things were passed from vala to priestess, before they all were gone from us."

"Thank you," Shard said, a light flick of desperation in his voice. "Is there any more you know?"

Her gaze hardened to a kind fierceness, like an older sister. "Tell me, you said you've had visions while awake?"

"Yes." Shard stopped fidgeting with rocks and straightened, raising his wings to soak up some sunlight. "But..."

"But?" She watched him sharply.

"But my strongest visions have always been ... always, near death." Shard had hesitated to say it, but once he did, the truth seemed obvious. "When I saw my father, when I saw others in the Sunlit Land, and when the white owl showed me the First Age and all were Nameless. Every time, I was about to die. I wonder..." He stopped, looking away from her fierce orange eyes.

"You wonder if perhaps you should place yourself in peril, to receive visions?"

Hearing her say it out loud, Shard felt embarrassed, but nodded once, not meeting her gaze.

"A reasonable idea," the priestess said, and he blinked at her in surprise. "But fraught with all sorts of complications. Not the least of which being that you surely don't wish to die, nor do your fine friends wish you to."

"No, that's true," Shard said. "But—"

"Your clear visions of those in the Sunlit Land came to you because you were nearer to it. But it is your life, your tie to the wind and the ground and water that will help you to reach Rhydda, who may be wild, but she is still a living creature, breathing our same winds, touching our same ground."

"The owl wasn't in the Sunlit—"

"Wasn't she?" the priestess asked gently. "Some messengers may travel between places."

"Munin," Shard murmured, struck to think that his friend the snow owl might be much more than she seemed. "He travels in dreams. And the owl told me once that it is the gift of her kind to know when another is going to die . . ."

"Just so. I believe you are best off trying to remain alive. Now, if you've had visions while waking, then I believe you might speak to this wyrm while awake, more in control, and more clearly than in your dreams." She kept her gaze on him now, a hawk stooped on its prey.

"Really?" Hope surged in Shard's chest and he took two steps forward, splashing her in his eagerness. She shook herself, but gave a soft laugh. He mantled, dipping his head in apology. "Can you help? We're hoping if I can make peace, then we won't need to fight them again. Can you show me?"

"I can guide you, but I am no vala."

"Yes, I'm ready."

She laughed, a warm rolling sound. "The wyrm slumbers during the day. Let us wait until the night, when you and I both feel strong, and she too is awake. If this helps you, I'll be glad, but beyond those things, you fly a wind I do not know."

Shard dipped down, inhaling the scent of the water at his feet, both to show respect and to hide his disappointment that they would not begin immediately. "Thank you. Tonight then. Thank you." She inclined her head. An odd thought struck him. "My lady, you've been so generous, and I see you trying to help Kjorn even though you're supposed to be neutral, I think. But you've only ever called yourself high priestess. I'd be honored to know your name."

Her topaz eyes crinkled with amusement, and the softer edge of her beak turned. "A thoughtful young lord. I hope you will be a thoughtful king. Son of Baldr, the highest priestess of the Vanhar must give up something for her strong ties to the wind and to the gods, and I, like the content birds, have given up my name. No, don't look so sad, it will be given back to me when I go to the Sunlit Land, and my voice, stronger than any other in my pride, will sing on. Like Groa, it may be there in the wind to guide others."

For a moment, Shard stood mute. *She gave up her own name for her powers to see, and even she claims they aren't powers such as I have, or the vala of old.* "Then I'm honored to call you high priestess, and to know you."

"And I you, Rashard of the Silver Isles. I will meet you again here, at the middlemark tonight."

Shard bowed, shivering with happy anticipation, and she left him, walking away through the water and barely leaving a ripple behind her.

15
KJORN'S RIDDLE

FROM AHEAD, THE ELDER RANDOMLY mused, "Which came first, the mountains, or the sea?"

Kjorn perked his ears. It was not a riddle—or perhaps it was—but a words from a song the wolves had taught Kjorn over the winter.

"The Song of First Light," Kjorn said, trotting to walk abreast with the elder, though it put him off the trail and into the high grass. He fell back again and walked behind, and the old Vanhar didn't speak again.

Which came first, the mountains, or the sea?

Kjorn tried to remember the rest of the song, and it came to him in the she-wolf's voice, Catori's voice. "Not even the eldest could tell, whether first came wave or tree."

One ear tuned to him. "Which came first, the silence, or the song?"

"Not even the rowan could say," Kjorn continued, "had it a voice, and lived so long."

The elder raised his voice.

> *"Only in stillness the wind*
> *Only from ice the flame.*
> *When all were Nameless, the wise will tell . . ."*

He trailed off and it took Kjorn a moment before he finished, "It was only by knowing the other, that they came to know themselves."

They walked on in silence, and Kjorn wondered if song lore was part of his test. He didn't ask, supposing the elder wouldn't answer anyway. They trailed down to the shore, and the soft roll of waves on sand reminded him sharply of home. Of the Silver Isles.

I am home, he reminded himself. No, the waves reminded him of Thyra, his beloved, waiting for him. It reminded him of his father, who might still be mad and Nameless and lost somewhere. His sense of anxiousness swelled, his driving purpose making him impatient. But he could not be impatient with these gryfons.

"Elder Elof!" a gryfon called.

Kjorn realized he hadn't asked the elder's name, but would remember it. Not even glancing to Kjorn, Elder Elof turned without comment to walk toward the voice—a gryfess fledge ten leaps away down the shoreline. She sat in a pile of knotted seaweed, and looked like a gray little storm cloud. Bemused, Kjorn followed.

"What troubles you?" Elof asked, sitting beside her. Kjorn watched them, standing somewhat awkwardly five paces away. The elder hadn't dismissed him, so he didn't leave, and stifled his sense of urgency.

"The net, I can't remember the knot sequence."

"Ah. A tricky one to be sure."

There was nothing to be done. He would have to wait. With a glance over his wing, Kjorn sat and watched them, intrigued.

He saw with no little surprise that the knotted mat of seaweed was actually a lacework net, such as a spider web. Looking away down the beach, he saw groups of Vanhar using other such nets along the shore and in the tide pools. He supposed they were used to catch and transport fish for Vanhar who were too old or too young to fish for themselves.

"There, you have it now?"

"Yes, Elder." She fluffed and looked happily at their work. "I can finish it now."

"Good." Elof stood. "Prince Kjorn of the Aesir will assist you. Fair winds."

He continued on down the shore, stopping to speak with every Vanhar he saw along the way.

Kjorn and the fledge stared at each other. At last he gathered his wits and inclined his head. "Fair winds. I'm Kjorn, son-of-Sverin."

The fledge perked her ears, and offered a kind of mantle while still sitting. "Ide, daughter-of-Tyg." She looked him up and down uncertainly. "Do you know how to tie a net?"

Kjorn drew a long breath, forcing himself not to look down the shoreline after Elder Elof. Perhaps his only riddle for that time had been to test if he knew the Song of Last Light. "I'm afraid I wasn't paying attention. Will you teach me?"

She brightened like sun coming from behind a cloud, and lifted the tangled seaweed. "Of course."

Kjorn sat beside her, and for the remainder of the morning, he learned how to tie a firm knot that wouldn't tangle, and to pattern in a series of diamonds, and how large to make the holes depending on what fish was desired. Vanhar stopped to stare at them. Kjorn tried to greet them all until Ide warned him against distraction, and chided him for inadvertently doubling a knot.

After that Kjorn bent his focus to the task, and when he raised his head again, was almost surprised to see the grand net he and Ide had created, and Nilsine standing before him.

"Decent work," she noted, and Kjorn felt a little spark of pride, even though the work took him from his purpose. "Come with me."

"Am I to face my test now? It's almost middlemark."

"One of my sentries has fallen ill," she answered blandly. "I thought it might interest you to take her place, and learn our night-ward border."

Kjorn stared at her. "Truly, Nilsine? Your council wishes me to perform their ritual or test to earn their trust. I cannot leave now."

"When the council wishes to test you, they will find you." She lifted her wings in invitation. "Are you so busy you cannot spare a mark of the sun for a patrol with a friend?"

Kjorn scanned the beach once for any of the elders. Seeing none, and all Vanhar happily engaged in fishing and flying, he looked to Nilsine. She would not lead him astray. He trusted her. "Of course not. Lead on."

Her ruby eyes shone with approval, and together they flew night-ward, while she spoke of their borders and their treaties with the lions, and other things she thought he should know.

Other things, everything but the ritual the elders had asked of him. For a mark of the sun he guarded the border with her and asked no more questions, for he knew they wouldn't be answered.

After that, one of the elders found them and asked if Kjorn would be interested in hearing the great sagas of the first Vanhar, and what they knew of ancestral dealings between the gryfon clans before the first king had risen from the red dust of the Winderost.

At a loss, Kjorn said he would be honored.

So it went the rest of the day, with odd errands and requests until sunset, and Kjorn still had not heard what task he was to perform, what ritual or riddle would win him the council's favor. He ate his supper in stormy silence, and not even Shard could rouse him from it. Then Shard left to nap in preparation for his meeting with the priestess later that evening, and Kjorn walked to the shoreline.

The broad nesting cliff of the Vanheim left the waves in violet shadow, but a slow sunset glittered gold farther out to sea.

A soft step in the sand made him turn. A Vanhar fledge stood before him, her tail ticking back and forth as if she stalked a mouse, her beak lifted to the evening wind as she sniffed uncertainly. Her wide eyes looked like pearls set in her face, milky and bright. She was blind.

"Son of Sverin?"

"I am."

When he spoke, her head tilted, ears flicking to focus on him. "I am the only acolyte of the high priestess. She wishes to meet with you tonight, at midnight, where the council gathers."

"Very well." Kjorn watched her, bemused.

The pearly eyes gazed at Kjorn, or something slightly beyond him. "Before you meet with her, think on these three things: what bears a gryfon when there is no wind, what treasure can be grasped only by claws open wide, and what is the measure of a king?"

Kjorn lifted a foot uncertainly, and had a feeling she would not repeat the questions if asked. "I will. Thank you. Midnight. Tell the priestess I'll be honored to meet with her."

She dipped in a brief mantle, and turned to stride up the beach. Kjorn watched her gait, and how she appeared to keep herself walking a straight line by listening to the roll of the waves on the sand.

He stood there until full darkness fell, then walked back to the fire. Asvander, Brynja, and Dagny sat there, swapping stories of their day. The Vanir sat away at a separate fire, chatting with the Vanhar and the Aesir of the Dawn Reach, and the Lakelanders kept to themselves.

Perhaps seeing his troubled expression, Asvander stood as if preparing for a fight. "Your Highness. What did that whelp say to you earlier? We saw you talking."

"That whelp is the only chosen acolyte of the high priestess of the Vanheim Shore." Nilsine's cool, smooth voice came from the shadows before she did.

"It's all right," Kjorn said to Asvander, then looked to Nilsine. "I think she gave me my test at last."

"Did she indeed?" Nilsine's ruby eyes were eerie and captivating in the firelight. All Kjorn could think of was how each of his allies in the Winderost embodied some element of his friends at home, and how dearly he missed Thyra.

To distract himself, he repeated the questions, since no one had said he couldn't ask for help.

"Water," Dagny said immediately. "For the claws open wide bit. If you squeeze your talons, it'll spill."

"Clever," Asvander said to her, and she fairly glowed.

"Or light," said Brynja, looking out toward the rumbling ocean and the stars. "If you closed your claws, you create a shadow."

"Ooh," Dagny said. "Even more clever, my sister. Yes, maybe it's light."

"Strength lifts a gryfon when there is no wind," said Asvander. "Or courage." Appearing to realize there could be multiple answers, he fell into unusually thoughtful quiet.

Kjorn listened to their ideas, meeting Nilsine's silent gaze across the fire. "Do you know the answers?"

"Perhaps. But I don't wish to be king, so my answers don't matter."

"What is the measure of a king?" Kjorn asked idly.

"His honor," Asvander said.

"His kingdom," said Dagny.

"His friends," said Brynja, and Kjorn looked at her, then Nilsine, curious if that was correct. She remained inscrutable, and merely perked her ears at him expectantly.

"Well," said Kjorn, "I have until midnight to figure it out."

"The second one is definitely light," Dagny said, and they dissolved into discussion again, while Kjorn wracked his memories for anything his father, Caj, and others had ever told him about being a king.

16
A WORD IN THE WIND

R AGNA PACED IN HER DEN, awake, wishing Sigrun was there so she wouldn't be so alone. At last, restless, she flew out under the moon, asking Tor's help. Milky white rippled across the molten black sea, and Ragna flew along the trail of moonlight for a time, her head clearing in the frosty night.

She thought of Baldr, bright Baldr, who lived on in Shard. Shard, who had been gone so long but who should be here, should claim his birthright. Shard, who should be her king.

But when Ragna closed her eyes, breathed the winter air and the sea and thought of the King's Rocks, she saw only huge, blood-red Sverin, his red meat, his collars and bands and eyes of gold.

Ten years he had oppressed them, forbidden their very life style, forbidden the night, the sea. Exiled any who broke his law.

And yet.

And yet, there had never been such disorder among the gryfons in that time.

He'd abused the wolves, the hoofed and thinking creatures of the Silver Isles, disrespected all living there.

And yet . . . the pride, as uncomfortable, tense, and divided as it had been at times, had been stable. It had been stable enough for Caj and Sigrun to fall in love, to bear a kit who grew into a huntress who would mate to Sverin's son. It had been stable enough for Ragna to keep her promise to Sverin, remain in the pride and watch over Shard. Stable enough, Ragna realized ruefully, to indeed become a single, if troubled, pride.

Before he'd gone mad, before his spiral into Nameless hatred that had been a mask for his fear, Sverin had ruled with a hard talon, but a steady one. He would have cowed a bully like Ollar in less than a heartbeat.

I'm losing my mind.

Ragna shut her eyes, sucking in a cold breath. After all she'd hoped for, that couldn't be the answer. It couldn't be the answer that he had, truly, done the best he could with what he'd had.

Is tyranny and oppression the only way to maintain stability? She thought of Baldr, who was not a tyrant, who had been loving, understanding, and strong as a rowan tree, always fair, never paranoid. But he had not ruled a mixed pride. She thought of Shard, who was all the things his father had been, but more so, for his heart was divided. Baldr had left him a difficult legacy.

Perhaps Sverin really was the best king he could have been, at the time. We are all only, ever, the best we can be.

"Bright Tor," she pleaded. "Let me see what is true. Let me know forgiveness. Shard," she breathed into the cold wind, "come home to me, my son, my king."

The night gave no answer, and she didn't know if her words would reach Shard. But now they were in the wind, her heart, her truth, and the wind could do what it would. Talons clenching, Ragna banked and soared back over the sea, speeding up with hard, fast wing strokes.

Looking down, Ragna spied a shadow roaming along the nesting cliffs. Her blood skipped, wondering who was out in the night.

"Who goes there?" she called. The shadow stopped, a head flew up, and Ragna saw wolf ears outlined against the snow. A song answered her, a long, low howl that became words.

"Which rises first, the night wind, or the stars?
Not even the owl could say,
whether first comes the song or the dark.
Which fades last, the birdsong or the day?"

The song trailed off and Ragna glided down, thumping in the snow, and finished the song. "Not even the sky could tell, Whether last stills the sun or the jay." She stopped, leaving it unfinished, for the verse's lines spoke of death. "Well met, Helaku's daughter. Thank you again for allowing us to hunt on the Star Isle. What brings you to my island? Why do you sing the Song of Last Light?"

"I have restless dreams," Catori murmured. "And my own mother is long to run with the Great Hunt, and she cannot answer my questions anymore."

Ragna felt her heart open with pity for the restless wolf. "And I can? Did you come seeking me?"

"Maybe I did. I ran all night, and my paws brought me here." Catori wrinkled her nose, showing Ragna the points of her teeth, but ducked her head submissively.

Ragna lifted her wings a bit helplessly. "I often listened to Baldr's dreams, though I don't know what help I was. What did you see?"

Catori lifted her nose to the night wind, and the black feathers twisted and danced against her neck. Ragna longed for Stigr, for his gruff, blunt answers. He would know what to do with a restless pride.

Exile them all, she imagined him saying, and thought of Shard, instead, and his love for Aesir and Vanir. She thought of Caj, who was fair, and Kjorn, who was honorable.

And Sverin . . .

"I heard a new song in the wind," Catori murmured. "A strange voice, at once young and old, a serpent in the sky."

Ragna shook her head a little, and wondered if Catori had learned some of her riddling speech from ravens.

"What song did you hear?"

"A song like no other in the islands." She stopped walking, her tail fluffed out and alert behind her, and looked out over the sea. Her ears perked as if she would see her mysterious dream serpent, or perhaps, like Ragna, she watched for Shard. Then she sang.

> *"The noble draw wind from the water*
> *The brave will call fire from stone*
> *The foolish seek gold in the mountain*
> *The last know that wood grows from bone."*

Ragna shivered as wind slipped cold claws under her feathers. "It sounds like one of our first songs."

"It does, and yet not."

"Wind rises from the water," Ragna mused. "Fools love gold, I understand. Wood grows from bone, yes. But I wonder how one calls fire from stone." Ragna laughed, letting another shiver take her. "I wouldn't mind knowing, on nights like this."

"Fire comes from Tor," Catori murmured. "Fire from the storm, and fire from the earth, from the heart of the earth, where it runs like blood. Perhaps it truly dwells in stone, and if you crack it open, it will bleed fire."

"You sound like a raven, dear one." Ragna touched Catori lightly with a wingtip, calling her back from the edge of her visions and rhymes. "Why does this dream trouble you so?"

She looked at Ragna, her eyes glowing in the moonlight. "Because it draws closer."

"Something coming this way?"

"Perhaps."

Ragna managed not to sigh, for she would be eternally grateful to Catori for helping Shard, for helping the pride, seeking harmony. But riddles grew tedious. "Come, my friend. Let's clear your head."

She dropped to a crouch, swinging her tail like a wolf inviting a friend to play. Catori laughed, crouched, then sprang away. They chased each other through the moonlight and across the plain to the birch wood, where Catori stopped. Ragna halted before running into her, but it was a near thing.

"Listen," the wolf whispered. Ragna perked her ears and closed her eyes since she couldn't see much anyway. The soft shuffling made its way through the wind that moaned against the tangled, naked tree branches. Catori glanced at Ragna in silence, ears forward, inviting her to hunt. Ragna nodded once, a small thrill squirming up in her. She had sworn, with others, not to hunt red meat on the island. But the wolves had their blessing from Tor, and a wolf invited her now.

By silent agreement they split, and Ragna knew that she was to flush the prey toward Catori, who was more likely to catch it in the trees. She suspected a snow shoe hare, and a light scent on the wind confirmed it. She caught movement and leaped, crashing forward on purpose. The hare sprang away. A muddy blur was Catori, flashing through the moon in the trees, then suddenly the hare was dodging back toward Ragna. Without thinking she hurled herself sideways, talons flinging out as if the hare were a leaping salmon, and caught it.

"Ah," she gasped, shocked that she'd been fast enough, then yanked the hare to her and dispatched it swiftly, by the throat.

Catori padded up, panting with hunt-excitement. "Well done, my lady. You are a huntress born."

"You should take it," Ragna said, looking at the blood on the snow.

Catori considered the hare, licking her muzzle, then ducked her head. With a mischievous air in her voice she said, "No. You may give it to the War King, with my regards."

Cold closed over Ragna's chest. "I will."

Catori tilted her head. "What troubles you? Helping your enemy? *Wood grows from bone.* We are all one. If we wolves can forgive Sverin, surely you can."

"It isn't that I can't forgive him. I've done that." Ragna tightened her grip on the dead hare. "It's that I fear I'm beginning to understand him."

Catori lifted her nose in a gesture of comprehension, then watched Ragna in silence, as if she understood how much more frightening that was. "Do you know how I met Shard?"

Ragna shook herself, certain Catori was leading up to something. "Only that it was during the hunt for the great boar. Sigrun thought as much, but he never told us anything else."

Catori walked in a circle around her, her voice low and sweet, like a song. "I met him first, before Stigr, though we had both been watching him for some time."

"Stigr would wait," Ragna murmured. "He was always more patient than I." Except for the one time it had counted, the one time when she should have barreled ahead, a War Queen, and driven out the conquering Aesir.

Catori stopped in front of her, her paws delicate in the snow. "Your son was afraid of understanding me once, too."

"He knew nothing true about wolves." Ragna looked to the moon for strength. "I know what the Aesir have done, I have seen it, lived it."

"And why?" Catori asked. "When we harried gryfon hunts, and fought, and harmed you, why?"

"Because . . ." Ragna ducked her head in assent. "Because you were under attack, first."

Catori lifted her nose to the wind, her gaze scanning the stars, and Ragna craved the peace and confidence the wolf appeared to feel. "So too, were the Aesir in pain. They fled their homeland, and it was Baldr who first perceived that, Baldr who asked that his heir be raised among them. But like my brother Ahote, the Aesir were not ready to accept peace, and attacked."

"Well I remember," Ragna murmured, and shut her eyes, as if it would block Baldr's death from her memory.

"Shard had a chance to kill Sverin," Catori said softly, and the wind flitted across the snow and through the clawing branches of the trees. "And he did not. If he does not fear understanding his former enemies, why should we do any less?"

"Thank you," Ragna said, turmoil still darting about her chest, but somehow she felt more accepting of it. "Thank you for the steady wisdom of the earth, dear one. I will think on it."

"Fair winds," Catori said. "Thank you for listening to my dream."

"Good hunting," Ragna said quietly, though she wasn't sure how much good either of them had done for the other.

With the hare in her beak, she trotted back to the nesting cliffs. Alert for other Vanir, or any other witness, Ragna slipped across the white snow, grateful for her plumage, and rather than fly, she climbed down the cliff face, feeling oddly like a thief, with the hare. One wing pressed to the stone wall, she trailed down to the massive cave mouth that led to Sverin's nest.

Vald barked from the entrance. "Who goes—oh. My lady?" He sounded uncertain, and Ragna remembered it was the middle of the night, she had a dead hare in her beak, and it was utterly foolish to be there. But she said nothing, letting the sight of the hare in the moonlight speak for her, and Vald and the other sentry stood aside.

She realized Sverin would be asleep, and felt even more foolish, not sure what she hoped to gain by being there, except that if she had to suffer restless nights, so did he. She began to turn around.

"I'm awake," he murmured from the nest. "What are you doing here?"

Ragna dropped the hare, ears perking. "How did you know who I was?"

"I know your step."

Taken aback, Ragna picked up the hare again, standing on her hind legs to toss the hare to him. She rested her talons on the edge of the nest, tail twitching. "There. With regards from Catori. The daughter of Helaku."

"I know who she is." He shifted. Ragna heard chains scraping, metal tumbling, and twigs snapping under deer hide. "Why does everyone think I had no idea what was going on in my own kingdom?"

"Not your kingdom," Ragna said harshly, defending herself against her own sense of empathy. "And you'll understand that I didn't think the names of wolves were important to you to remember."

"They became so."

"Well by any wind, here, more red meat." She tossed the hare up to the nest.

In the murky dark his feathers didn't show the way hers did, didn't pick up a trace of light, but when he moved, she saw the chains that bound his feet and his wings.

"I've only just finished the deer. Are you afraid I'll go mad from hunger in a day?" He was eating the rabbit. No false sense of pride there—he bolted it down and ducked his head. She didn't answer, and told herself he was right, and that was why she'd done it.

After a moment, he asked, "Why did you let me live?"

"I don't consider death a punishment," Ragna growled. "I want you to live, to face what you've done. I want you look into my son's eyes when he returns, and bow to him."

He seemed to have no answer for that, and somewhere in the cave, a small rodent scuffled about. The sound of the ocean came to them, and she wondered if it was soothing or troublesome to him. The sound of the waves had always rocked her to sleep. She wondered if it made him think of his mate, if there was a sound in his homeland that he preferred, that he'd missed hearing all these years. She remembered what Catori had said. He was not at first a conqueror, but an exile.

"Do you like the sound of the ocean?" she asked, unable to stop herself from breaking the silence.

"No."

"Because of Elena?"

"I never did. But Baldr died in the waves. Do they not trouble you?"

Ragna's heart quickened and she growled. "Baldr died at your father's talons. The waves have never troubled me and they never will."

He made a soft, derisive noise.

Ragna felt reluctant to leave, to go back to the whirlwind of her own head. Sverin said no more, didn't ask her a question, didn't move, didn't speak. The sentries remained silent at the entrance. Ragna stood there, and Sverin remained in his nest.

"I wonder." His soft words were so loud in the quiet it sounded like distant, echoing thunder. "If—"

Wings stirred the wind outside. Ragna's mind seemed to fly apart like a cloud of irritated starlings.

"What?" she asked him, burning with sudden curiosity. What was he thinking, while she stood in silence?

"Ragna!"

"Sigrun?"

Ragna turned and watched her wingsister swoop into the den, past the surprised sentries, suddenly embarrassed that Sigrun would even look for her here. "What is it?"

"A messenger!" Sigrun paused, eyeing the nest as Sverin's head appeared over the top. Then she huffed and looked solely at Ragna. "A sea bird! He said he that he's traveled all winter, over the starward corner of the world, and met Vanir there!" The healer spun in a circle, giddy as a fledge, and laughed. "He spoke with Maja herself, and even now, they're making their way home!"

"Halvden's mother?" Sverin mused. "Maja, who left a fish in my den before fleeing?"

"The very same," Sigrun said brusquely. "But you didn't know she also left the Isles last summer, seeking exiled Vanir."

Ragna remembered all of it. After wolves killed Halvden's father, Maja declared her freedom and self-exile by leaving a fish for Sverin and fleeing. Then she vowed to fly for Shard, to find any lost Vanir who'd flown starward. And now, at last, word that she was well and had found others. Sunlight flooded Ragna's heart. Vanir. Her Vanir, at last, flying home.

"This seabird," she began, "Is he still here? I'll hunt fish myself to fill his gullet."

Sigrun laughed and nudged Ragna toward the entrance. "Yes, come, we must meet him, and then tell everyone."

Ragna trotted with her to the entrance, then, as if tugged, found herself looking back at Sverin. In the faint moonlight, she saw his face, grim, silent.

"Fair winds," he murmured, averting his gaze.

"Fair winds—"

"Come!" Sigrun said, nipping her neck feathers lightly. Ragna shook herself, and without another look back they jumped from the ledge and flew down to the shore. There she spied the sea bird, bright under the moon, and a scatter of the other Vanir who'd apparently also grown restless in the moonlight and came down at Sigrun's shouting.

Ragna landed on the pebbly beach and trotted to the group. Not just any sea bird, but a great albatross from the farthest seas stood there, looking slightly uncomfortable at being surrounded by several gryfons, and standing on dry land.

"Hail, great wind rider!" Ragna said, bowing her head. "My wing-sister tells me you were kind enough to stop here on your journey, and bring us news."

"Windwalker," replied the great, white bird, watching Ragna with placid eyes.

Ragna opened her beak, thought a moment, and closed it.

"Not Wind Rider," he said, as if that clarified things.

Ragna tilted her head. "Pardon?"

"Great queen of gryfons," he said in a voice like an ocean breeze, "my name is Windwalker. You may call me by it."

"Forgive me. I ... thought that birds had no names."

"I was given one."

Surprised, Ragna actually took a step back from this strange bird. "By whom?"

He opened his long beak in what she thought was a gleeful expression, and extended his impossible wings. "By the Stormwing, by Shard, Rashard, the Summer King. Last autumn, after the starfire flew, I led him from a storm, and he named me over the sea."

Ragna sank to her belly on the sand, placing her eyes level with his, and tried to keep her voice from shaking. "Then, fair Windwalker, we'll be honored to give you a feast before you depart, if only you'll tell of the Vanir you met, and all you know of my son."

He folded his wings again, and began his tale.

17
DREAMS OF BLOOD AND STONE

WANDERING CLOUDS CREATED RACING MOON shadows along the shore, as if the light and dark were blown by an otherworldly wind. Shard trotted down the beach just before the middlemark, when bright Tor flew at her highest point. After supper the others had left him to nap, and now the chilly wind and silver sky brought him fully awake.

The priestess stood in the water already, her beak tilted toward the moon, a sliver of shining talon in the dark. Shard waded out to join her, sucking a breath against the icy waves. Tide was out, revealing long planes of stone that reached out into the water, strands of kelp, and bones.

"My lady," Shard greeted.

Tilting her head slightly to acknowledge him, the priestess closed her eyes. "Do you feel the strength of the waves?"

The water swelled up to his chest and he gasped as it slithered under his oiled feathers, then it tugged away, leaving him breathless. "Yes."

"Good. Let it keep you grounded here as you seek the dream. Do you feel the strength of Tor?"

Shard looked up at the moon, which commanded the rocking sea. Feeling tiny, he closed his eyes. "Yes."

"Good. She will guide you."

They stood in silence then as four waves washed up and retreated, and Shard grew accustomed to the cold. Down the shoreline, some Vanhar and others remained awake, but their voices faded into a pleasant background along with splashes and the turning of gravel under the waves.

"Tor," whispered the priestess, and Shard held a breath. "We seek your high sight. We seek your path along the stars. We, the Named, we your beloved, ask your strength."

A wave coursed up, splashing over Shard's wings. He clenched rocks and gravel, holding firm. The combination of majesty and fear sent a strange, exhilarating power through him.

"Rashard." The priestess intoned his name like a summon. "Rashard, see the star path, the dream net, as you have seen it before."

Rather than argue that he could only see it when asleep, Shard remained silent, and imagined it instead.

"Every detail," the priestess breathed, and for a distracted moment, Shard wondered if it was safe for such an ancient gryfess to be standing out in the freezing ocean.

"Breathe as if you sleep," she commanded. "I will not let you float away. See your dream net. Every detail. See how it is also the star dragon, the shell, the leaf. See how it is our own heart, unfolding forever into the world."

Shard's breath caught. No longer simply imagining, he saw the net as it appeared in his dreams, an endless spiral that wove and touched every living thing. Dreams sprinkled along it like stars—dreaming gryfons, distant lions, pronghorn, and birds.

He almost laughed, but instead he let the net carry him under the moon to the Outlands. Climbing and flying as if through a vast forest, just as in a dream, he traveled while his body remained there in the ocean.

"Be mindful," said a warm female voice, and he remembered the priestess. "She may not understand."

Shard dug his talons and hind claws deeper into the sand at the bottom, and let the waves rock him. Thinking of Groa, he let his mind slip into the water, down to the sand around his toes, the pull of sea. Down into himself. From there, he found the net again, and her.

Rhydda. She was awake. She sensed him, like a scent in the wind.

He thought of her name, and she lifted her head to it. They had finished their hunt. The scent of blood was sharp and fresh, and pride surged within her. A dream, a memory bloomed before Shard. She'd held back, watched the youngest wyrmlings run down a herd of pronghorn. The young ones had done well, had hunted alone. They brought her their kills.

"Rhydda." Shard didn't know if he whispered out loud or not, but he spoke to her, and she seemed to hear, if not understand. Where she was, clouds masked the moon, and darkness lay over her. "You're proud of them. Does that mean you love them? I know that feeling."

Sensing where he swirled and flew within the dreaming net, he crafted a vision for her of Hikaru's first hunts, of the first fish he'd brought in from the sea. With that he swept her in the emotion of pride. Her massive heart quickened, great gusts of air bellowed from her lungs, and for a moment he was with her, was her, was ancient, aching bones and bulging, weary muscles and fangs the size of a gryfon foreleg.

Yes, she knew pride.

She also knew injustice. Her young ones should not be hunting in this dusty land.

And she knew hatred. Heat suffused her mind, curiosity, anger.

"You once flew under the sun," Shard said softly, speaking carefully, painting his words with dream images. "You showed me. You flew over the sea."

Fire cracked across his head and he startled, jerking. Salt water lapped into his face, reminding him that his vision was not real. He was safe. The priestess would see to his safety.

"Show me," he growled. "Show me."

He thought of the gryfon cast in ruby and gold, but instead, saw a land of waving green grass hills and ash forests, and other trees he didn't know. They had huge, sprawling trunks and twisting branches and leaves like miniscule wyrm tails, like long slender spades. He saw caves, and a golden dawn. A wyrm emerged from the deep earth to see the sun—

Pain lashed across his eyes, a hissing, cracking voice.

Back in your hole, beast, until you bring gold. The sun is not for you. The sun is not for you.

Breathing hard, Shard forced himself not to shrink back, reminding himself he was safe, even as anger and injustice coursed through his heart.

"What's happening?" he asked Rhydda, and she showed him only that sunlight meant flares of pain.

"But you flew under the sun! You flew over the sea!"

"Caution," murmured the priestess, and the odd echo of her voice in the dream threw Shard from his focus.

Frustrated, he flung out across along the dream net and back into Rhydda's presence. She had stood, was pacing, wings flexing and flaring, and her brood milled and snarled and snapped around her, unhappy at her tension.

"Was that your home?" Shard asked. "What happened there? Was it the dragons?"

He showed her Hikaru again, the Sunland, the great mountains and the icy ocean. He showed her dragon halls of stone and ice, and the dragons themselves.

And she knew it. She remembered it. She had been there.

She held very still, and Shard watched her remember, the words overlapping from his last dream with her.

" . . .bright with dragon's blood," hissed a voice, and this time Shard saw the speaker, a half-grown dragon whose scales shifted like abalone shell. "You will know him and his cursed kin, because they are bright with dragon's blood."

"Kill him," rasped another, and Shard felt searing pain along his flank that he knew was Rhydda's pain, a memory of pain.

He tried to look at the injury but claws locked his head in place, forcing him to stare at the image of a gryfon cast in stone and metal.

"Kill him, beast, and you will be beautiful as we are."

"Kajar," Shard whispered. Rage and confusion boiled in his mind, but it was Rhydda's. "The dragons showed you Kajar?"

"Find him."

"They are murderers and thieves, and took what treasures we would have given you, and the blessing of our blood. Kill him and it will be yours."

"Kill him."

"Kill all of them."

In the middle of the scene, Shard remembered himself. He remembered he was supposed to be talking to her about peace, trying to understand her. In the dream he swiped and struggled, then reached for the ruby and gold gryfon, but the ruby feathers melted into the blood and the gold into fire. He jerked away, choking—

And he was hacking salt water, scrabbling for purchase on the sea bed. The priestess' talons locked on his scruff and she hauled him to the beach. Shard collapsed, gasping, and she shook herself before lying beside him to offer warmth.

Shuddering, taking another wheezing breath, Shard turned to stare up at the moon, then the priestess, who watched him calmly. "Did—did I fall asleep?"

"You were never asleep. You fell into the dream, though. I felt as you slipped from the net, and then you fell into the water."

"I see." Shard flexed his talons and hind claws in the wet rocks and sand. "But I did it." The realization filled him with satisfaction like a warm meal. "We did it. I did it, I spoke to her while we were both awake!"

"Truly, Tor favors you," she said, so softly Shard might have mistaken her tone for regret.

"I couldn't have done it without your guidance."

"You honor me." She looked away, to the moon. "Did you see anything that might help?"

"Maybe. I saw many things. I think the dragons did more wrong to the wyrms than they want to admit. I learned more, but I failed at speaking of peace. I don't know if Rhydda will understand." Feeling regret, Shard thought of how well the dream had started, with a feeling of mutual satisfaction in the hunt.

The priestess looked thoughtful, and she glanced down the beach, where a single fire flickered. "Speak also to Ajia, when you see the lions. She is a healer and prophetess, and may know older ways than I do."

"Thank you," Shard whispered, unable to bring any more strength to his voice.

"And also . . ." She hesitated, and the waves surged higher as the moon slipped below its middlemark and the tides shifted. "Also, be wary. Perhaps these wyrms are like us, and their Names are only lost in fear. But perhaps they are not anything we can understand. In my heart I think they are older, like the stone and the tree. Be wary what you show to her, what you say. She might not understand."

Or she might understand all too well, Shard thought, recalling Rhydda's surging sense of injustice at some wrong. "I'll be careful," he said. "I think that's all I can do for tonight. I think I angered her."

"Go to your friends," the priestess advised. "Go to the fire, enjoy the light of Tyr, clear your heart. We can try again as long as you are with us."

Shard stood and stretched the cold from his muscles. Drying his feathers at the fire and telling his friends about the dream sounded like the best thing he could think of.

"Thank you, my lady. Will you join me?"

"No." She stood, but didn't move when he stepped forward. "I will remain, and seek council from Tor."

Shard nodded once and left her. He found Asvander, Brynja, and Dagny sitting around a fire near the massive cliff, but he stopped just outside the ring of light. "Where's Kjorn?"

Dagny and Brynja exchanged a look, but it was Asvander who spoke. "We thought he was with you."

"Why would he be with me?" Shard peered down the line of waves, sparkling in the moon. "I've been with the high priestess for the last mark of the moon."

Asvander made a low growl and stood slowly.

"That's why," Dagny said by way of explanation.

"Shard," Brynja said, drawing his attention. Her gold eyes filled with wariness, which didn't help his mood. "Kjorn told us he was meeting the priestess at middlemark. So were you. We assumed..."

"He isn't with me," Shard said. "I haven't seen him since supper."

"You," Asvander barked, and at first Shard thought it was addressed to him, then heard a step in the sand behind. He turned to see Nilsine.

"Where is Kjorn?" Shard asked tightly, as politely as he could manage.

She lifted her ears. "Not with you?"

"No." Asvander strode forward, raising his wings. "Not with us. That fledge told him to meet the priestess a midnight, but Shard has been with her and didn't see him. What's going on?"

Nilsine looked up at Asvander placidly, unmoved by his show of aggression. "I have not seen him since we all sat at supper, here."

"You know," Asvander growled. "You know what these doddering councilors want from him. Is he in danger?"

Though worry and suspicion flicked in Shard's heart, he saw a spark of anger in Nilsine's eyes and felt reassured that she wasn't in on some plot.

"Rest assured if I thought he was in danger I would not be standing here talking with you."

"Let's find him," Shard said, stepping between him. "This has gone on long enough."

"Agreed." Asvander stepped back, though his hackle feathers ruffed up. "I'll arrange a search party. Dagny?"

"I'll help."

"Before you go," Shard cut in, "I don't suppose he told anyone *where* he was supposed to meet the priestess?"

"No, Shard," Brynja said. Her tail flicked back and forth in agitation. She looked at Nilsine. "If you know anything..."

"I do not. This is all highly unusual."

"And still not safe to be roaming at night," Asvander said.

"We know," Shard said, as his dream of Rhydda fell away in the face of this new problem. "Let's go. Brynja and I will look along the cliffs, with the Vanir."

"And I," Nilsine said.

"We'll search the beach," Dagny said. "It's all got to be a misunderstanding. The priestess is old, maybe she forgot."

Nilsine gave her a slow, burning look. "She would not forget."

"We'll ask her first," Shard said reassuringly. "Go, now. We'll meet back here when we find Kjorn or, when the fire burns low."

They split. Brynja and Nilsine followed him back down the shore to where Shard had left the priestess. If she had arranged a meeting with Kjorn, surely she could clear all this up easily.

But when they reached the spot where she had guided Shard, they found only an empty beach and the moonlit sea.

18

THE MIDNIGHT COUNCIL

WIND TURNED THE LONG GRASS on top of the sea cliffs into ripples of silver and white. Kjorn climbed up the cliff trail on foot, for even the Vanhar wouldn't fly at night with the threat of the wyrms.

He saw no gryfons, but he could smell them, as if they waited for him, out of sight in the grass. Growing weary of games and riddles, he stood in silence where he had stood that morning, and waited. The priestess had asked him there, so it was up to her to greet him.

The shush-shush of the grass seemed to echo the sound of the waves.

Feeling watched, tested, and un-amused, Kjorn was determined to show his patience. He sat, wings folded calmly, and watched the grass before lifting his gaze to the waning moon. His frustration ebbed with the decision to sit there all night if need be, and calmness took its place.

Then, someone spoke from the dark.

"What bears a gryfon when there is no wind?"

Kjorn flicked an ear, recognizing Elof's voice. The elder was off in the grass, somewhere, but Kjorn didn't need to see him to answer.

159

He remained sitting, and said clearly, "His wingbrother. As the vow says, *wind under me when the air is still.* When all else fails, our friends and family bear us up."

He'd had the evening to think on the questions, on his friend's ideas, and to come up with his own. Elof had tested him on his knowledge of the Song of First Light, so he thought perhaps some answers would be from songs.

"What can be held only in claws open wide?" The harsh voice of one of the female elders turned Kjorn's head, but like Elof, he didn't see her.

He thought of water, of light, but had realized another thing that, if grasped too tightly, would slip between one's talons. "Love," he said quietly.

A ghostly form approached through the grass. At first Kjorn thought it was the fledge from before, then realized it was the high priestess herself, silhouetted by the narrow moon.

"What is the measure of a king?"

Kjorn stood slowly, mantled, then closed his wings. "I've searched my heart and all my history, my lady, and I fear I can't answer. It could be his kingdom, his subjects, his honor. It could be his legacy. If you know the answer, I humbly ask for your wisdom, and I will do my best to fulfill it."

Her pale form looked like stone in the strange, faint glow of the night. "How has he fared today?"

It took Kjorn a moment to realize she was asking the elders, who rose from the grass in their semi-circle, which matched the crescent moon.

"He sang with me," Elof said. "He knows the old songs."

"He humbly wove nets with my grand-daughter," said another. "He does not believe himself above others."

"He flew duteously with the guard, serving as if it were his own pride."

"He heard our tales, and listened with true attention."

"He showed kindness."

"He showed generosity."

"He showed patience."

"He is honest in his answers."

The priestess turned her head as each spoke, and at last looked again at Kjorn. Little chills slipped down his back and he resisted the urge to open his wings, lest he appear nervous.

"And I say he shows wisdom, by asking for help with questions to which he does not know the answer."

Kjorn looked around the circle of ghostly elders, and bowed his head.

The priestess stepped toward him "You see, Kjorn, it was not whether your answers were right or wrong, but whether they were *honest.*"

She opened her wings, and when she said his name Kjorn looked at her again, mildly surprised. "You have been honest, and so we know these things about you. If you believe that it is our friends who lift us when all else fails, that shows me you can admit when you need help, which some kings may never do. If you believe love must not be clutched too tightly, that shows me your own sense of trust. If you believe you cannot know the measure of a king, it tells us you will be a humble and honest one, here to serve, not to conquer again."

Kjorn held a breath as understanding dawned that his test, his ritual, had actually gone on all day, and cumulated in the questions. Then he felt foolish for not realizing it, as obvious as the signs had been.

"Then have I satisfied you, as far as my intentions here?"

The priestess would have answered, if a booming shout hadn't scared the life out of Kjorn and every elder on the council.

"Your Highness!" Asvander lunged up the cliff, trailed by others Kjorn could barely make out in the dark.

"Stop!" Kjorn ordered. "We're—"

"What's the meaning of all this?" Asvander demanded, coming to Kjorn's side. He scented and then heard Brynja, Dagny, and Nilsine shortly behind, then caught Shard's familiar scent.

"Welcome," the priestess said, apparently unruffled by the intrusion. With a note of amusement in her voice she said, "You've come just in time for the council to declare the alliance of the Vanhar to Prince Kjorn, and pledge our warriors to the cause of defeating the enemy once and for all."

"Oh!" Dagny cried. "Breezy!"

Kjorn allowed himself a short laugh, and Shard came up on his other side.

"We were worried," he murmured, his wing pressing to Kjorn's.

"Clearly," said Kjorn, glancing to Asvander.

"I suggest we all go back to our rest now," the high priestess said. Asvander remained ruffled, but Kjorn knew it wouldn't take much to talk him down. The elders dispersed without further word, congratulations or encouragement.

Kjorn led his friends back down the trail toward the beach in thoughtful quiet.

Dagny's voice piped up. "So were we right about the riddles? Was it water, or light?"

THEY TOOK THEIR LEAVE of the Vanheim Shore with little fanfare two days later, now with a band of Vanhar warriors added to their number. Light rain gusted along the coast, driven by wind that smelled sweetly of spring.

Kjorn bid farewell to the council and the high priestess. He bowed to her, and she approached him. To Kjorn's surprise she dipped her head low as he bowed, and touched her brow to his, as he had seen her do with others, with warriors of the Vanhar.

"I wish you the blessing of each wind, Prince Kjorn," she said softly. "The light of Tyr in your heart, and the wisdom of bright Tor."

"Thank you," Kjorn said. "And I wish you ... fair winds."

They stepped away from each other, and Kjorn found his company gathered only a few leaps away. From the corner of his eye he saw Nilsine approach the priestess and receive a blessing, and it seemed to Kjorn that she remained the longest.

Asvander bellowed to his Lakelanders, Brynja gathered the Aesir of the Reach and Shard, the Vanir, counting heads. When Nilsine left the priestess and appeared satisfied with her head count, they set out.

Out of respect, they would walk into the lions' territory, as Kjorn had done before.

"You've met them before," Kjorn said to Shard as they strode through the tall grass, leaving the ocean behind. "They spoke of you."

"Yes, just once. They showed me the wyrms for the first time."

Kjorn flicked his tail, feeling disgruntled. "They didn't make you join them on a hunt before they would tell you anything?"

Shard laughed. "No, is that what they did to you?"

"Yes. I wonder why."

Shard ruffled his feathers, sprinkling Kjorn with drizzle. "I'm better looking, obviously. Or maybe better smelling."

Kjorn snapped playfully at his ears and Shard ducked, flicking talons out to smack Kjorn's shoulder. "Your Highness, be careful, you may start a war with my kingdom."

Kjorn sobered and his step slowed. Shard winced, perhaps seeing the joke was too close to recent events.

"Not funny," Shard agreed to Kjorn's silent sentiment. "Well enough. I would have summoned a dragon and beaten you, anyway."

"I'd like to see that." Kjorn laughed. "Then again, maybe not. Any luck with Rhydda?"

As the wind steadily brought the drizzle against them, Kjorn at last felt the chill.

"Maybe." Looking anxious, Shard straightened, setting a quicker pace that Kjorn followed. A respectful distance away, Nilsine, Asvander, and Brynja walked in the leads of their respective groups, and behind them, in rough formation, trailed the rest of their band, now swelled with the full ranks of the Vanhar warriors. Shard told Kjorn of his dream, how he'd sensed emotion from Rhydda. "And I think Ajia might be able to help even more."

"Well," Kjorn said, feeling more hopeful even as the sky darkened and they lost sight of the ocean. Drizzle turned to rain lashing down on them, making mud of the frost and ash. "This should be an interesting visit all around, then."

19

GUARDIANS OF THE FIRST PLAINS

To Kjorn's apparent surprise but not Shard's, a lion yearling met them at the border of the lands, where the uneven, grassy hills turned into a sweep of endless plain, dotted with gnarled trees, scrubby grass and boulders. The cub, who Shard would've equated with a fledging, greeted them somberly.

"Sons and daughters of Tyr. I am to lead you to Ajia, and the chief. They look forward to seeing you."

Kjorn slipped Shard a questioning, sideways look, and Shard gave his head the slightest shake. He hadn't met a chief either. Both of them thought Ajia led the lion pride, as the Vanhar priestess led hers.

"This way," said the young lion, turning about.

"What," Kjorn asked, "just like that? No riddles? No debates?"

"Kjorn . . ." Shard managed not to laugh.

"No moonlight hunts? I'm disappointed." He looked thoughtfully across the plain. "We're actually making progress."

Shard laughed quietly, following the grave, trotting lion cub as he parted a corridor through the tall grass. "And we weren't, before? Did you forget the Lakelanders and the Vanhar, and Brynja's supporters? And the rogues?"

"The rogues," Kjorn echoed. "But I wonder how Rok fares. We've heard nothing, except from those in the Reach who wanted nothing to do with me."

"I shouldn't have to tell an Aesir to remain in the present," Shard said, swatting Kjorn with his tail. "We have a plan, my brother. Let's stay on that wind. The Ostral Shores, the Vanhar, the lions, *then* the rogues. Then the eagles. Then—"

"The Dawn Spire," Kjorn said, though it sounded like a sigh, and he turned his head to look starward, though from where they walked, nothing could be seen of the great gryfon dwelling.

"The Dawn Spire," Shard said. "But now, the lions."

"Lions." Kjorn nodded once, casting Shard a grateful look. "What will I do when you're gone, Shard?"

He laughed quietly, though his chest tightened. "You'll have Thyra, of course. And she'll keep you on course much better than I can."

"Yes." The thought genuinely appeared to cheer him, as if he'd forgotten he had any support coming from the Silver Isles at all. "Yes, I will have Thyra, and maybe . . ." He trailed off. Around them, the drizzle lightened into a fog that smelled of wet earth. Sticky warmth infused the air and insects began a low, churring song.

"Maybe?" Shard prompted.

"Maybe," Kjorn murmured with a touch of bitterness, "my father. If he's come to his senses."

Shard dipped his head, but didn't answer. The last time Kjorn had seen his father, the Red King had fallen into Nameless madness and fled from him. Shard knew that place of grief, and it was not easy to emerge from it, especially bearing whatever burdens Sverin carried in his heart. Given the last ten years, Shard guessed his burdens were many.

They spoke no more, and followed the lion yearling as the wet grass thinned and squished under their feet, still dormant from winter. Shard perked his ears, trying to recall if he'd flown this far windward of the Dawn Spire, or if Ajia and her huntresses had met him closer. They must have, for the broad, pale landscape looked nothing like what he remembered.

"The border of the First Plains," Nilsine said from Shard's left.

Just as she said it, the yearling lion announced the same, and stopped, slinking around to face them. "Welcome, princes, Vanhar, friends. Where I lead you now is hallow ground, ancient and unchanged since the First Age, where my family dwells, where Tor first set paw to earth."

"You honor us." Kjorn inclined his head.

Shard marveled still at the change in his wingbrother. Kjorn, who had once scoffed to Shard—*was it only three seasons ago?*—that all the Silver Isles belonged to them, and he'd hoped to line his den with wolf pelts. Kjorn, who had courted war. Kjorn, who like his father and the other Aesir, had thought little of every other creature in the land and air.

Showing respect to all, now. Shard's heart bloomed, and eased. *He will make a good king, a good example for gryfons here.*

He thought of the story told to him by Groa, the truth of the Aesir's strange coloring. A dragon who'd loved Kjorn's great-grandfather had shown that love by blessing them—blessing, not cursing. But her gift had come with a warning. *With a dragon's blessing, everything you are will be more so.*

The sons and daughters of those gryfons had carried the blessing on, and their sons and daughters had, and they would, as far as Shard knew, for the rest of time. All of those Aesir descended from Kajar's band, Per, Sverin, Caj, Thyra.

Kjorn.

Kjorn was proud, noble, honorable and just. In general, he was kind. Shard thought if any of those things were enhanced by the dragon's blessing, it would only make him a better king. Sverin had failed, for he'd fallen toward the wrong qualities, Shard thought, with all the power of the dragon's blessing behind them.

The young lion, satisfied with their acknowledgement of the land, turned to lead them on.

A SCARLET, MISTY SUNSET blanketed the plains as they reached land that was familiar to Shard. The grass stood higher again, he smelled and heard a river, and within leaping distance stood stands of dark, grasping trees breaking the horizon.

Kjorn was looking around, nonplussed. "This isn't where we came before," he said to Nilsine.

"No." She stepped up beside them as Shard took in the welcome scent of water, stretched his aching forelegs, and noticed also the musky smell of lions that permeated the very soil. The lions themselves were either not there, or kept out of sight. "That was more nightward, more their hunting grounds I believe. This is their home."

"As she says." The yearling lion circled back to them. "Welcome. Now, you may prepare to meet our chief." He sat, ears lifting.

Kjorn and Shard looked at each other, and behind at Brynja, who merely blinked at Shard as if to remind him he had more experience with lions than she.

Even Nilsine looked bemused, and she lifted one wing. "If you please, what—"

"You're covered with dust and mud," the young cat said, his somber air cracking as he eyed them with unmasked disdain, his nose wrinkling to reveal the points of his fangs. "You reek of the sea. You may preen, or bathe in the river, or whatever gryfons do, but you must do *something* before you present to the chief."

Nilsine made an abortive noise to speak, but remained quiet.

"You want us to wash?" asked Dagny, and Shard thought she didn't know whether to be amused or insulted.

The young lion inclined his head.

Kjorn's eyes narrowed and it seemed it was only Shard, choking back a laugh, that kept him from being mortally offended. Shard had never heard of a Named creature offended by dirt. But then, he didn't know many large cats personally. Only Ajia, and he must have been clean enough for her then.

"You do look fairly awful," he said to Kjorn. Kjorn's ears slicked back.

Without another word, Shard led the way to the river. Behind them, the young lion relaxed, and began his own bath with his tongue.

And Shard did feel better, certainly refreshed, and maybe more princely, after a splash in the river and a thorough preening. The sun, setting leisurely, stroked the river with gold and red. *The days are getting longer.* Shard glanced around for Brynja, but she held off with Dagny some two leaps away, the wingsisters preening and laughing at their own private conversation. Shard huffed, then took a face full of water as Kjorn slapped water at him.

"Brighten up. You're the moodiest Vanir I've ever seen. Worse than Stigr these days."

"Tyr's beak," Shard said, mimicking his uncle. He shoved against the river bottom and smashed into Kjorn, giving the prince a good dunking to remind him who was the stronger swimmer. Kjorn came up sputtering and declared that bath time was over.

Though it was still sunset, a sliver of moon hooked in the orange sky as they dried and stretched away the aches from walking, and Shard shivered against the rising chill. He wondered, idly, if the lions would allow them a fire, and reached up to tap a talon against the little pouch that held his fire stones, to reassure himself they hadn't come off in the river.

The yearling lion appeared, appraising them, even going so far as to lean forward and sniff delicately at Kjorn's flank.

One golden ear ticked back, but Kjorn managed a neutral expression. "I trust we're more acceptable now?"

"Hm," said the yearling, circling away. "You'll do."

Some scents don't wash away, Shard thought, and managed not to say, realizing the lion might've hoped they would smell less like gryfons by the time they were done.

"This way."

Six gryfons fell into a line behind the yearling, Shard and Kjorn abreast, Nilsine, Dagny and Brynja, with Asvander warily taking up the rear. The rest remained near the river, in the company of two watchful, mostly silent lionesses and another yearling who had joined them during their bath.

Shard looked discreetly back at Asvander. The big Lakelander had been so silent the entire trip that Shard wasn't sure if he was uncomfortable in the First Plains, or still moody about Kjorn's test from the Vanhar. He would talk to Asvander, soon. After the lions. Certainly before battle, if there was a battle.

Away from the river, the lion scent saturated the air, and Shard perked his ears, looking around. He would be glad to see Ajia again, for she'd been helpful and kind, if mysterious. The chief he wasn't sure of, but obviously they were expected, so he hoped that was good. Beside him, he sensed Kjorn tensing.

"Your Highness," Shard said quietly, not in jest. "All will be well. We're obviously expected, we've both met their most important lioness, and made friends. I wouldn't worry. This isn't battle."

"Some friendships are like battles won," Kjorn answered cryptically.

It sounded so unlike something he would say that Shard wondered where he'd heard it, then their escort stopped. Before them, deep indents broke the long grass as if heavy bodies had slept there, and the ground swept up into a ragged bluff, reminding Shard of the landscape of the Dawn Reach. Scattered boulders piled to form small dens around the base of the bluff, and trees offered shade over those dens. Now, in the last of the sunset, it all cast long shadows toward Shard and Kjorn and their band, as if to reach out and grab them.

The sky and earth looked aflame. Shard felt a moment of awe and wondered, shoving down an absurd snicker, if lions had a flair for the dramatic.

"The Chief of the First Plains," the young lion boomed. "High leader over all the lion prides and favored son of Tor." He turned to gaze at the top of the bluff.

Shard and Kjorn looked up, ears lifting, as the first fully-grown male Winderost lion Shard had ever seen strode from behind the bluff to its top to gaze down at them. He heard Kjorn's breath catch, and thought his own did, too.

The chief's heavy frame reminded Shard of a gryfon of the Ostral Shores, bulky and low to the ground, though his size nearly rivaled Kjorn. A broad, barrel chest and shoulders tapered to sleek, muscled haunches and the narrow, tufted tail. His wildfire mane of gold and black framed a wide, angled face and yellow eyes. His heavy scent drifted to them, a tang of and meat and power, mixed, Shard thought, with the essence of multiple lionesses. Shard realized that while he stared, Kjorn had mantled low, and he quickly followed suit.

When he stood tall again he was gratified to see the great cat dip his head, though not deeply enough to be called a bow.

"Welcome to the First Plains." Shard had expected his voice to be mountain-deep like Helaku, the wolf king, but his timbre was almost mild, a tenor, a pure note that belied his size but fit him nonetheless, liquid and graceful. "We have waited for this meeting for a long time."

Kjorn stood, resettling his wings. "We're honored to stand in your home, and I hope for great things between us."

"Great things," the lion echoed, displayed his teeth in what Shard hoped was amusement. "Yes. Yes, indeed." He tossed his mane and called several names. Lionesses appeared out of the grass, out of the rock dens, and watched him attentively. "Find us a feast," he commanded, his gaze lingering on each of them with fondness and approval. "We know Tor, now in her claw time, will bless us with rich food for this meeting."

With not even a glance at the gryfons, the lionesses slipped away
into the twilight.

As the chief moved to step down from his place, Shard glanced to
the shaggy mane again, and saw multiple long, twisted locks with bits
of claw and talon woven in. A display of feathers of all colors and
sizes were knotted into the mane, and Shard recalled that Ajia wore
feathers too, but hadn't said why.

He examined the chief's, which started behind his ear with the
smallest, the yellow feather of a meadow lark, and trailed in a diagonal
curve down his neck, growing larger until they stopped in the center
of his chest. There Shard's gaze locked, and Kjorn's, for there hung
the unmistakable feather of a gryfon, a feather of the brightest red.

"We're honored," Kjorn said tightly, containing his surprise, Shard
thought. The red feather stood against the darkest part of the lion
chief's mane.

"Honored," Shard said, taking over when it was clear Kjorn would
speak no more. "I am Shard, son-of-Baldr, prince of the Silver Isles.
My wingbrother is Kjorn, son-of-Sverin, heir to Kajar and the lands
of the Dawn Spire."

The long tail swung back and forth and the lion displayed his
teeth. "I know."

"And will you honor us with your name?" Shard asked, while
Kjorn recovered from his surprise. He took a furtive glance around
for Ajia, and didn't see her.

"Yes, of course." He hopped lithely down from the slope and
advanced on them, a slow, rocking stride, leaving deep paw prints in
the grass and soft dirt. "I am Mbari the Brightest, the only son of
Badriya, Who is Pale."

"Badriya," Shard murmured, unable for a moment to remember
where he'd heard the name.

It was Kjorn who said, "You're Ajia's brother."

"Yes, though this has little consequence on our ruling now."
He stopped before them, just taller than Shard, but much larger of

frame. "She did speak well of both of you, and this will enlighten my decisions."

"That feather," Kjorn said, and Shard flattened his ears at the blunt remark. "Where did you get it?"

Usually I'm the one to speak impulsively.

Mbari looked at him with placid yellow eyes.

"That feather belonged to my father. How did you come by it? Why do you wear it? He never told me he had dealings with lions, what do you mean by wearing that to meet me? Is it a threat?"

"Kjorn," Shard murmured, surprised at the outburst, though saw that Chief Mbari's eyes only glittered with amusement, as if Kjorn were a small bug he planned to bat about in the grass. Or as if he were already batting him about.

"A threat? No. A promise, maybe. We met once over a kill, myself and the red gryfon fledge, though he didn't hear my words at the time. I bested him then, and his companion, though I only won the red feather, not the blue. I looked forward to meeting him again on better ground, and then, when he never came, to meeting you."

"You fought," Kjorn said slowly, "fought, and bested, my father? And Caj?"

"And a good match it was. But if we're to repeat all that is said this night," the lion purred, "it will be a long negotiation indeed."

Shard felt Kjorn's ribs swell with a great breath, hold, and release slowly. Clearly the feather was not meant to be an insult. Perhaps it was an honor, or a show of good intentions. "Kjorn," he began, but Kjorn canted his head. He appeared to be in possession of himself again.

"I look forward to meeting your family," Kjorn said with strict formality. "And discussing all that's important to both of us. And, if you're willing, to hear more of your meeting with my father."

Shard stepped forward. "And, as a show of things to come, and friendship, I'd like to offer you fire."

Mbari shook his mane in apparent pleasure as darkness thickened around them. "I've heard of this dragon fire. The birds make much of it. Yes, we accept." And to Kjorn he said, "Come, let us speak privately of our wishes, and of your father."

He turned to walk away, and Kjorn looked at Shard. "What do you think?" He hesitated, looking toward Mbari's disappearing form. The sun was gone, shadows crawled from the rocks and over the grass.

"Go on. I'll start the fires. And remember, these are friends. Whatever happened between him and Sverin—"

"If only he were here," Kjorn murmured, and Shard realized what was troubling him. He loosed a low, angry growl. "He should be here, beside me, but instead, he's ..." He didn't finish.

Shard touched his beak to a golden wing. "Kjorn, I know what it is to wish you had your father by your side. But you're here now, and he isn't. You've got to go forward with what you have now."

Kjorn eyed him, as if finally remembering Shard had never known his own father, then lifted his head. Whether Shard had truly gotten through, he couldn't tell, but at least his friend appeared genuinely calm now. "You're right. I know you are. You'll be well, with the others?"

"We're fine. Go on." Shard butted his head against Kjorn's shoulder, for Mbari was disappearing into the dark without looking back. "We'll see each other after."

Kjorn dipped his head and didn't run, but took long, dignified strides to catch the lion chief, and Shard turned to the task of fire.

"ANOTHER FEAST?" DAGNY LOOKED dismayed. They gathered dead branches from the trees and driftwood from the river bank, with the help of enthusiastic lion cubs. "This war is going to make me fatter than a grouse."

Brynja laughed.

Asvander murmured something in the negative and Shard, building another little pyramid of sticks, was distracted, looking around for a familiar lioness face. Ajia had not shown herself, and he tried not to be disappointed. She'd been so welcoming of him when he'd flown to find the lions, to learn more of the wyrms. Certainly she must know he was there, and he'd thought she would be interested in the fire, and all that had happened since they'd met.

"Shard," Brynja murmured, slipping up next to him. "Are you well?"

Am I well? Shard twisted a cluster of dry grass in his talons, thinking how short a time ago he would've given anything for Brynja to walk up and stand so close and speak to him so softly.

Am I well? He thought how short a time ago it had been that he'd learned to make fire, that he hadn't known when or if he would see Kjorn again, that he'd thought he could solve every problem of the world by talking. How long ago since he'd kept a newly-hatched dragon warm in his wings, then the same dragon had carried him safely from the grasp of death. How long ago since he'd left his home . . .

"Shard." Brynja nipped him, bringing him back to himself.

How long ago since she asked her question? He thought wryly. "Too distracted for words. I hoped to speak to Ajia, but I haven't seen her."

"You think she can help you more than the priestess did?"

"I think she can help me in a different way." Shard lifted his wings restlessly, soaking up the strength and determination in Brynja's expression. "I hope she can help me figure out what to say, or show, to Rhydda."

After a thoughtful moment, Brynja said, "I don't understand this dreaming that you do. But I know it is real, and I have faith in your strong heart. Don't you? You're the one who inspired us to band together, to listen, to see beyond our own borders and troubles. What do you fear?"

Shard twisted grass, looking down at his talons. "Before, in the Silver Isles, I spoke to the wolves, to boar, to creatures no one thought could speak. Here, I spoke to the lions, the eagles, the painted wolves. I spoke to the blackfish, even though they didn't listen. I even spoke to the dragons. I haven't been afraid like this before, afraid to speak—"

"Afraid to be wrong?"

"Afraid to be wrong," he agreed, breaking a twig in two. "Brynja, what if I really can't speak to them? I've failed every time."

"You haven't failed at all. Rhydda has shown you things."

"But she doesn't answer. She shows me pain, anger, hatred. What if she doesn't understand me? What if they really are Nameless, Voiceless, like fish in the sea, and I'm wasting my time?"

"Then we will fight," she said firmly. "As we did before. We will fight, and drive them from this land. This doesn't all rest on your wings."

"Yes," he said, feeling hollow. "We will fight. And many will die."

"They'll die anyway," she said, tossing her head. "Of old age, or disease, or flying in a storm. We are warriors, Shard, proud to fight, proud to die to defend our home."

"I only hope we don't have to fight. Again."

She nuzzled under his beak. "So do I, Shard. So do all of us."

Shard drew a breath, letting her scent calm him. "I can sense that Rhydda *feels*, but I can't get through to her."

Brynja watched him through the dark, and he heard her talons shifting in the grass. After a long moment, she spoke. "Maybe you haven't tried to rise too far, Shard." She leaned in, pressing her shoulder to him, giving her strength. "Maybe, to do what you hope to do, you must still rise higher."

The words struck to his bone.

Brynja nipped him lightly and stepped away, raising her head. "Now light your fires, my prince. Let them see the blessing of Tyr!"

Shard nodded and withdrew his fire stones. Yearling lions clustered in a tense ring around them, cubs, younger lionesses, all watching with gleaming eyes. Sparks fell to the tinder bundle as Shard struck the stones together, then caught and flickered and smoked. Shard coaxed them with little drafts from his wingtips, and a rolling gasp and murmur of appreciation swept the lion pride as true flame crawled over the tinder.

Delighted, the lions frolicked around the fire. The gryfon band gathered from the river and slowly the two groups merged. Shard observed that the Vanhar had an easier time speaking to the lions, but many of the Lakelanders didn't understand them at all. This made for a few misunderstandings, but Asvander remained close to his group, keeping tempers in check. Shard grew restless, and remained at the outskirts of the firelight.

Around him, the courteous, cautious voices of lions and gryfons made a low, pleasing murmur in the night. Kjorn hadn't yet returned from his meeting with Mbari, but the yearling who'd led them there assured them Kjorn was safe, that they were only talking. Asvander and Dagny were indignant, and agreed they would seek Kjorn out if he didn't return by midnight.

Shard's belly was too tight to eat anything, though not because of Kjorn. He trusted the lions. No, he needed more help.

Before, he'd sought out Ajia on her own ground. Perhaps, even now, she still expected him to do the same. With a quiet word to Brynja, he left the circle of firelight completely and walked out into the night.

20
BREATH OF TOR

S HARD CREPT THROUGH THE DARK. A breeze that mingled the humid scent of spring with the chill of winter brushed his flanks and face.

He walked, almost gingerly, knowing the lions probably had eyes on him though he couldn't see them. He walked until the sound of voices faded and there was only wind, the river, and his own footsteps. Insects chirruped and pulsed in their song. As his eyes adjusted to the dark and the familiar sea of stars above, Shard stopped, craning his neck to look. His gaze followed the clustered band of silver that stretched from one horizon to the other, the dragon stars. Midragur.

He didn't think he heard anything, but a sense drew his gaze back to earth, and a small hope kindled in his chest.

"Ajia, the Swiftest," he greeted, mantling though he didn't yet discern her through the grass and blackness.

Then grass shifted and he turned his head, seeing her outlined against the sparkling reflection of stars in the river. "Star-sent, you return to us, with your Prince of War."

"He isn't. He hopes for peace."

"Hope is not a goal." She was facing him, her tail toward the river. "Peace is. Even now, the Sunwind rises. All of his preparations are not toward peace, but war. "

Shard hadn't thought of it quite that way, but he inclined his head. "Yet, I chase the wyrm in my dreams, and Kjorn promises if I can find a peaceful solution, he'll honor it."

When Shard stood tall again, the lioness had stepped closer, and he caught her scent. The familiar tang of it reminded him of the first time he'd seen the wyrms, and he shivered.

Her eyes glinted like stars in the gloom. "I have watched you, and him, and I see that you hold each other's hearts. So I will trust what you say. But keep a steady eye, for he comes from a history of war, and sometimes we can only walk the paths we know."

"We're making a different path now," Shard said, defensive but proud. "He and I together, and the others. Trust me in that."

"Still Tor shines on you, Star-sent. I hope your wings will part this growing storm. I hope the breath of Tor will disperse the wind of war."

A memory came to him, odd in that place, of a forest turning sweet with autumn. He remembered the caribou king, Aodh, telling him a new rhyme he'd heard in the wind, a song that, coupled with the starfire, had spurred Shard to travel to the Winderost, then on to find the dragoness Amaratsu and Hikaru.

It is for gryfons to see, Aodh had said, a lifetime ago. *To hunt, chase and catch.* It was for the hoofed to listen, he'd said, to listen to the wind and earth.

I hear the Silver Wind itself.

He'd said it was for gryfons to see and hunt, and to see, one must look. But Shard had looked, and he hadn't seen. He couldn't see what Rhydda wouldn't show him. He should have learned the whole truth while he was in the Sunland. He shouldn't have let the dragons imprison him, shouldn't have fled. He should have learned the truth, and now he had lost his chance.

Stigr had wondered what wind Shard was following. Kjorn was raising the Sunwind, the wind of war. The Vanhar had sung a song after the Battle of Torches. *A new wind, a bright wind, a silver wind is blowing.*

From across the sea, a memory answered him.

The Silver Wind is the truth.

"The Silver Wind," Shard breathed. "The breath of Tor. Is that what you speak of? The Silver Wind, the truth?"

"The first, the highest," the lioness said, echoing the words Stigr had uttered to Shard what felt like a life time ago.

"I try to find the truth, to speak it, to use it. I try to reach the wyrm, Rhydda, but …"

"You still try to speak with the wyrms, but they don't hear?"

"She hears, but then I lose myself in the vision, and I wake as if from a nightmare. If I could stay focused, and remember myself …"

Her head tilted, and he caught the outline of the feathers she wore about her neck. "Tell me your tale, young prince. Walk with me, tell me what befell you during the end of winter, and what you have tried with the wyrm so far."

She turned and Shard trotted to her side, grateful to have found her, and found her welcoming. He didn't question why she hadn't come to him. It was probably right that he had sought her.

Together they walked upstream, with stars peering overhead and the river muffling his story. He told her everything from the time they'd met to him fleeing the Dawn Spire, taking Hikaru to the Sunland, and returning.

"A dragon," Ajia mused. "A true dragon, and even he couldn't speak to the wyrms? Something has eaten their hearts, or they have no hearts at all, as we feared. This does not bode well."

"No," Shard agreed. "It doesn't bode well, but I know they have hearts. Rhydda feels, she feels for her brood, she fears the sun, but I don't think they always lived in the dark. I dreamed with her, and I know she once flew in the sunlight. I don't know what changed."

Pain flickered in his mind, sunlight and pain, linked. To Rhydda, sunlight was pain.

But she once flew under the sun . . .

They came to a slow bend in the river and Ajia paused, turning to look at the water, ears perked. Shard remained quiet, certain she was seeking a vision in the starlight on the water.

"With the priestess of the Vanhar, you dreamed." Ajia batted a paw into the water, as if to test the temperature. Shard found the gesture strangely endearing, and wondered if she'd seen a fish, or if it was simply a thoughtful sort of fidget.

"Yes. I saw her clearly, while I was awake."

The lioness drew back from the water and faced him fully, her braid of feathers outlined by the crescent moon, her face in shadow. "Dream with me now. This is a hallow place, this river, old and steady and abundant. I believe it will give you strength, and I will help you to remember your purpose, and not be fooled by the dream."

"I'll try," Shard said.

"Try?" Ajia asked. "Do you try to fly, or do you simply open your wings and soar? Do this with me. We will face the wyrm together."

She stretched out on her belly and extended her paws toward him. Shard lay down in front of her, with the high grass on one side, the river on the other, sand under their bellies and starlight on their backs. He closed his eyes. He sought the net.

Ajia shifted forward and her large padded paws touched his talons.

Faster than before, perhaps because he'd already done it, or perhaps because he was much closer to Rhydda now, Shard found the wyrm's presence. He slipped close to her with an image of rolling green hills, as she'd shown him before, the place he believed to be her home.

"Rhydda." He tried to keep his voice light, soothing, as if speaking to a kit. "Don't you wish to go home? Why all this anger, this mindless hate?"

"Hate stems from fear," Ajia said, her voice thrumming and low. "As courage stems from love. What does she fear?"

"What do you fear?" To get the idea across to Rhydda, Shard painted a dream of himself, facing his first sea dive. He let the sense of fear wash over him. He showed her Lapu, the boar, and felt fear again, and sent her a feeling, a question. "What do you fear?" he whispered again.

Sunlight gleamed in her mind.

"Why?" Shard asked her.

Pain.

Her great wings flared and he felt caught, swept into the dream.

Warm paws flexed against his forelegs. Claws dug at his skin, not piercing, but reminding him where he was. "Smell the river," murmured the lioness. "Feel the earth. You are safe here. Remember your purpose."

The ocean and the priestess had given him strength to practice his dream weaving, but here, the lioness, with four paws firmly on the ground, kept him from forgetting himself. From his safe place in the grass with Ajia, he watched Rhydda's memories unfold again, and was not distracted by her pain.

The voices of dragons overlapped with hissing and crackling fire.

"Kill him, beast, and you will be beautiful as we are."

"Find him."

"They are murderers and thieves—

"—took treasures meant for you . . ." a talon slid down her jaw, then pierced, a sharp pain like a hot coal.

". . . and the blessing of our blood. Kill him."

They showed her a gryfon crafted in ruby and gold.

"Kajar," Shard told her. "His name was Kajar, but he's dead. He's been dead for almost a hundred years." He didn't know how to show her at first, so he showed the sun and moon, rising, setting. He showed her green summers and white winters passing.

"Kill him."

Somewhere outside himself he heard a deep hum, and knew Ajia was keeping him rooted to the First Plains.

"Kill all of them."

Shard strove to tell Rhydda that all her enemies were dead. He showed wyrmlings hatching, as he imagined them to, gryfons being whelped, growing, dying, two generations of gryfons. He showed her Kajar and imagined a mate for him, their son Per, and his mate and their son, Sverin, a red gryfon like his grandfather.

A great red gryfon, with flashing eyes like gold.

Her thought of the ruby gryfon blended against Shard's memory of Sverin. A vision of Sverin decked with dragon gold, scarlet in the sun, standing at the edge of the largest of six isles in the starward-most corner of the world.

A dry, wicked rumbling snarl coursed through Shard's blood, and he and Rhydda turned their faces from the desert to behold the moonlit sea.

Shard gasped, jerking from the vision. His heart scrabbled at his chest. He stared directly into Ajia's eyes, silver in the starlight.

"I have to find Kjorn," he breathed, standing. "I fear I've just . . . I must go. Forgive me. Thank you. Thank you for your help. I don't think I'll lose myself again."

She stood, like liquid moonlight. "I'm glad to have helped you, and I wish you fair winds."

Her voice held a note of finality. Shard hesitated. "You won't come and see the fire?"

"I have no need. I will stay in the dark, and keep vigil with Tor in her claw time."

"You told me you would stand with me if we faced the wyrms."

She watched him without blinking, and he wondered if she'd seen what he had, in the dream. "And, if we face the wyrms, I will. I wish you good hunting, Star-sent."

The sharp moon edged her in pale light, and the river leaped and laughed. Her voice sounded like an intonation, warm, thrumming from her chest, from her heart. For a moment, Shard imagined she sounded like Tor herself. "And I wish you *peace*, Prince of the Silver Isles."

21
THE SUNWIND RISES

I T WAS NEARLY MIDDLEMARK WHEN Kjorn returned with Mbari to the fire and feasting. Brynja told him Shard had gone to seek Ajia, so Kjorn didn't worry.

"So long as he comes back," muttered Asvander, casting frequent glances beyond the fire.

"He'll come back," Kjorn said. "You're fretting like a nesting grouse."

"He has run off before," said Dagny, defending Asvander.

"He'll come back," said Brynja, so Kjorn didn't have to. Still, now Kjorn felt uneasy, and found himself checking over his shoulder more often than not, peering into the dark for his friend.

Meanwhile, Mbari told the tale that he'd told to Kjorn, of meeting Sverin and Caj. The lion chief held his pride rapt as he paced and cavorted before the dancing fire, shadows leaping and crowding around him.

"...and so we three, new initiates in our own rights, meet over the carcass of a pronghorn. The red gryfon, red like the morning sun and Sverin by name, the son of a king, stands before me so." He ramped

184

to his hind legs, crouching back, and the shadows behind him almost looked like great wings.

All the gryfons sat utterly entranced. Behind Mbari, the lionesses hummed a low, pulsing rhythm. Kjorn glanced to Asvander and saw the Lakelander still looking grim, his gaze flicking to the dark.

"And the blue gryfon, blue as the summer sea, Caj by name and from a line of warrior lords, circles round me so." Mbari dropped to all fours and prowled, drawing back his lips to reveal long teeth. He perked his ears alertly and narrowed his eyes. For as much as a feline could emulate a gryfon, Kjorn thought he captured Caj's humorless demeanor well enough.

"This is the good part," Kjorn murmured to Asvander, hoping to distract him from being suspicious of Shard's intentions. His wing-brother would return. Kjorn knew that. Asvander perked his ears obediently.

"Leaps the red gryfon, Sverin!" Mbari leaped, smacking a paw near the fire to send a splash of smoke and embers skyward.

"Oooh," purred Dagny appreciatively. The cubs and yearlings yowled and cringed in delight. Kjorn winced, grateful the ground was still damp from rain.

"And I know it is a ruse, and turn rather to meet the blue, Caj." He spun, fighting an invisible, leaping foe, long claws slashing wide.

Mbari prolonged the tale, re-enacting the fight where he always appeared to think just a moment ahead of Sverin and Caj, and eventually drove them off out of sheer frustration.

During the re-enactment of this portion, a shadow slipped through the gryfons and Dagny shifted near Kjorn to make room for Shard as he returned.

"Did you find her?" Kjorn asked under his breath.

Shard nodded, once, not sitting. "I need to speak with you."

"Soon," Kjorn promised, his gaze on Mbari's performance. "I don't want to insult him."

Shard fell silent, standing and watching. Kjorn felt his tail twitching, and was unnerved by his restlessness.

Mbari whirled to a stop at last, all four paws on the ground, and raised his head, pacing. The lionesses' chant dwindled, softly underscoring the end of the tale.

" . . . and never once did they hear or seem to understand my words, my challenge, then my best compliment on a fight well fought. But I did find the red feather, and kept it as a promise to meet again, as a symbol of my victory and, I hoped, honor." He stopped before the fire, panting lightly in the heat, and sat, his tail tucking around his haunches.

"Tell them of the feathers?" Kjorn asked, for the gryfons still wondered among themselves whether the feathers were a sign of honor, or battles won.

Mbari shook his mane. "We wear feathers thus, to adorn ourselves from those whose qualities we admire. The lark's sweet voice, the swallow's speed, and beauty of the falcon. The gryfon's mighty strength." He extended a paw toward Kjorn, and inclined his head in gratitude. Shard sat, at last, perhaps sensing this was going to go on longer than he'd expected. Kjorn nudged him reassuringly.

The steady humming of lionesses ceased, and the silence pulsed loud. The fire popped.

"Now," Mbari intoned, "bright Tor brings to us the Star-sent, and the son of Sverin, who will be kings. We will help the golden son of Sverin win back his kingdom and drive away the screaming wyrms. We will win back our sacred nights. We will find new honor and brotherhood with gryfon-kind!"

The lions stood and blared their agreement. The gryfons stood, raised their wings, and roared approval. Surprised by the sudden declarations, Kjorn stood, and Asvander stood at his other side, roaring from deep in his chest. This, Kjorn knew, was the kind of ally the Lakelander had hoped for, more so than the passive Vanhar.

Shard stood more slowly, as a show of faith, but raised no shout of his own. Asvander bumped Kjorn firmly, and he raised his head, offering a hearty agreement. The firelight painted bright, warlike eagerness over the faces of gryfons and lions.

"We will fight!" Mbari roared, standing tall, his tail lashing.

"*We will fight!*" agreed the lions of his band.

"We will breathe the Sunwind, and we will follow the prince to war!"

"To war!"

"With great eagles and gryfons above us, and the painted packs beside us, we will fight!"

"We will fight!"

Kjorn could do nothing—he'd waited too long to speak, and now the fervor drove itself, like the fire. He felt Shard's reproachful look burning into his feathers.

Mbari raised his face to the sky. "At last we will drive out the enemy, at last, as one, we go to war!"

"*To war!*"

Kjorn opened his wings, and all the gryfons around him let out a roar boomed like thunder over the First Plains.

"*TO WAR!*"

"WHAT IN ALL WINDS was that?" Shard demanded. He trotted with Kjorn away from the fire, for the lion's theatrics and the war chants grew more intense than the Vanir prince looked ready to handle.

"Don't worry," Kjorn said, stopping once they'd reached the taller grass and the dark. "It's bluster. It's good, Shard. We're only cementing our alliance—"

"It's the Sunwind! The wind of war!" Shard flared his wings, looking as if he might burst from the ground out of sheer frustration. "You said if I could find a peaceful solution—"

"Better they shout it all out now," Kjorn said, keeping his voice calm, "than arrive eager for battle at the Narrows when all will be meeting. It will be tense enough as it is."

Shard looked wary, but backed a step away and folded his wings. "I trust you, Kjorn. I trust that you'll keep your word."

Struck, Kjorn growled. "Of course I will. I don't want the battle any more than you do. Now brother, please, tell me what was so urgent."

In the glow of the fire that reached him, he saw fear steal over Shard's face. "I saw Rhydda again. She showed me things—Kjorn, I believe the dragons taught her, trained her to fear the sun. I believe—"

"Trained her to fear the sun?" Kjorn imagined the massive wyrm and could not think of anything that could cause her fear. Then he recalled Shard's descriptions of the dragons—how huge, how intelligent they were.

"Yes. Is it so hard to believe?" Shard's ears perked, and he searched Kjorn's face earnestly. "Per and your father taught me to fear the night, to believe that the very moon might burn my wings off."

"Oh." Understanding, and ashamed once again by his legacy, Kjorn motioned with a wing for him to go on.

"I believe they can fly just fine during the day, but they've been afraid to. She showed me, also, that the dragons showed her a red gryfon and told her to hunt him. Kjorn, I've shown her Sverin. I fear—"

"Your Highness." Asvander's voice came from the dark, then Kjorn made out his silhouette against the fire glow. "Forgive the interruption. The chief wishes to see you."

"Thank you, in a moment." Kjorn tried not to flick his tail in irritation. "Shard, please finish."

Shard continued, eyeing Asvander sideways, and the Lakelander didn't bother to leave. "I fear she might have misunderstood me. I fear she will try to find the Silver Isles."

Utter cold washed Kjorn's skin. He remembered the terrible wyrms, their Voiceless hate, their deadly claws and sharp spade tails. He thought of Thyra.

"My lord," Asvander began hesitantly. Kjorn looked at him, his mind alight with fear for his family. "My friends," he amended, looking at Shard and then Kjorn again. "Surely you don't believe this dream is so real that you could have shown her Sverin and she understood? And that she could even find your islands? Could this not be just a simple dream, a worry?"

Though Kjorn wanted to believe Asvander might be right, Shard's feathers ruffed up and he moved a step forward, more aggressive than Kjorn was used to seeing him. "My visions are real, Asvander. These are very real I promise you. Kjorn, it was real."

"I believe you," he said, quietly, forcing the words out because they were true. Soft wind off the river brought the rich scent of water and mud. All Kjorn could think of was the Nightrun River in the Silver Isles, his Aesir, his father, Nameless and lost, and his mate, and the terrible nightmare that might even now be flying their way.

"My lord," Asvander said. "Surely not."

Kjorn laid back his ears. "Don't overstep yourself, my friend. It couldn't hurt to send scouts along to the Voldsom Narrows, to alert the eagles and to begin a search of the Outlands. If the wyrms are gone, then at least we've skipped a war here." He tried to lighten his voice and sounded only dreadful even to his own ears.

"I'll go," said Shard immediately. "Let me go, since I can at least speak to Rhydda."

"After a fashion," Asvander said, eyes narrowing. "It's foolhardy for us to send a prince."

"Then go with him," Kjorn said, not wanting to lose Shard at his side, but at the same time knowing it was the most logical course. It would be foolish not to send the only gryfon who might be able to get through to the monsters, even if it was a prince. Even if it was his own wingbrother. "Take the Lakelanders, the Vanhar, and go with him. I will find Rok and treat with the rogues, then meet up with you before the dark moon."

"We can leave tonight," Shard said, ears lifting.

"No," Kjorn said sharply. "If the wyrms are still here, they will hunt you for flying at night."

"If they're still here," Shard echoed.

Kjorn watched him a moment, still feeling torn. "We'll split up in the morning. Asvander, make your preparations tonight."

"I will, sire. The lion chief still wishes to speak with you."

"I'll be along."

Asvander took that as the intended dismissal and left them.

"Thank you," Shard said quietly.

Kjorn, distracted by his fears, shook himself and looked at his friend's earnest face in the dark. "For what, Shard?"

He stepped forward, almost timid, as if they were back in the Silver Isles, and Kjorn a prince, and Shard . . . what he had always been.

"For believing me."

"I don't know that I quite believe all of it," Kjorn said, watching his face in the dark. "But I trust you, and isn't that good enough?"

"It is. Kjorn, I'll do my best to end this."

"I know. Come, let's tell our company the new plan."

The rest of the night passed in conversation with the lion chief about the best strategy for land-bound animals in a fight with winged beasts, followed by brief, troubled sleep for Kjorn.

In the damp chill of early morning, they divided their number.

Brynja would go with Shard, but most of her Aesir would remain with Kjorn while he sought out the rogues and their leader, Rok, who was a friend of Kjorn's. He had arranged to meet them at the new moon, with all those Rok could gather. The Vanhar and the Lakelanders would fly with Shard to meet the eagles and begin scouting the Outlands.

All stretched, spoke quietly, bid their new lion allies farewell until they met again. Kjorn made his goodbyes to Mbari and turned to see Shard loping up to him through the grass.

"Fair winds, brother," Kjorn said. "All ready?"

"All ready." Shard bumped his head firmly against Kjorn's shoulder. "Don't look so glum. Whatever happens, we face it together."

Kjorn nodded, once, but the forced cheer in Shard's voice didn't encourage him much. "Thank you, Shard. We'll see you soon."

Shard turned to go, and Kjorn raised his wings and crouched, calling the order to fly. But just as their first down strokes beat the grass, a lioness bounded through the gathered pride, breathless as if she'd run for a day.

"My chief! Great chief. A messenger came in the dark hours. I met her, and my huntresses hold her at our starward border."

Kjorn landed, Shard beside him. The others touched down in rustling disorder.

Mbari, lounging in the grass at the base the bluff where they'd first met him, flicked his ears forward. "What messenger? What do they say?"

"A gryfess." Her whiskers wrinkled. "She says she comes from the Dawn Spire. She says she bears a message for the son of Sverin."

22

FROM THE NIGHTWARD SEA

RAGNA SLICED TALONS THROUGH THE foaming chop, barely missing the shining back of a herring. The wind gusted so hard she could've shouted a curse and no one would have heard. Instead, she flapped and tucked, flapped and tucked, swooping through the currents of wind over the water. Around her, ten huntresses and two fledges also battled the wind and sea, having more luck than she did.

Shouting drew her ear, then, "My lady—Ragna! Wave!"

Ragna snapped a look over her wing when she should have been flapping, and the rogue swell rolled and leaped like a living thing, caught her wing and chest, and plunged her under water.

Roiling bubbles, drifting ice and startled fish met her blurry, spinning gaze.

Calm! Calm!

Bone-chilling cold grasped her haunches, her face, sliced under her warm, oiled feathers. *Think, think, think, keep moving, don't lock up. What would Stigr say?*

She held a breath, letting the wave suck her down and in, then as the tension broke she kicked hard for the surface, fighting numbing leg muscles. The thought of having to fly out brought a shriek of dismay to the edge of her throat, but she managed an encouraging shout instead. Gryfesses clustered overhead, shouting in panic. One spotted her, pointed, and winged closer.

"I'm all right! No, stay at a safe height, I'll…" before another large wave hit, and using the heat of embarrassment to warm her muscles, she pushed through the water with hard kicks and paddled to build momentum.

Like a gull, like a gull, they're watching you, daughter-of-Ragr. Be a queen, a Vanir.

She felt the moment, slapped her wings to the water and thrust herself up, not thinking, just working, shoving, flapping. An awkward, stumbling, lunging takeoff brought gasps of delight from the mix of Vanir, Aesir, and half-bloods above her.

Pride flushed her muscles and she loosed a derisive churr at the water. The others laughed.

Even as she worked to fly higher, she was grateful to see dark clouds on the horizon. "A storm comes," she said, forcing her voice to be light, even as quivering weakness stole between her muscles and bones. "Let's be in. We'll fish again at dusk, weather holding."

"Yes, my lady," they chorused, and she turned to the nesting cliffs to hide what she knew was a pinched, relieved expression. That had been far too difficult. She must not fall again.

I've been too idle. I am in my prime, not some elder, brittle twig. Stigr would laugh his feathers off at a fly-out like that, and they praise me.

Solid wing strokes warmed her trembling muscles and she thought she should go to Sigrun's den. Mostly to set an example—a crash always warranted a visit to the healer, for injuries one might not feel until later. But rather than Sigrun's den, Ragna's distracted course led her to the wide entrance of Sverin's prison. An older Aesir male and Vald stood watch, moved aside to allow her to land, and greeted her.

Sverin prowled about his nest, she saw, muttering darkly. Ragna caught Vald's eye questioningly.

"For the last half sun mark," the orange Aesir murmured. "He's been—"

A clatter of metal on stone finished the explanation, and as Ragna strode forward into the cave, she saw that the red gryfon was dragging all the gold from his nest to pile in a corner.

Ragna stood well back. "Sverin."

It was not an orderly process, but savage tearing and tossing, soft curses. Incongruently, he wore two of his most favored bracers on his forelegs, ones twining with gold filigree and shifting brown and gold catseye gems.

"Sverin."

His head jerked up and he swiveled, ears flattening. To her surprise, when he saw it was she, his ears relaxed and his expression cleared, but his tail twitched in restrained agitation. "My lady."

"Are you quite well?" She eyed the treasures warily. She had not at all enjoyed the sight of him muttering to himself, though it had seemed in frustration, not the rumblings of a mad creature. She hoped.

"Indeed." He glanced behind him at the raw pile of dragon gold, then looked back to her, challenging.

Ragna found herself pleased to see that his nest looked normal again, padded only with deer hide, soft fir branches and the jutting base of stick and stone. "Do you find it too difficult to sleep on now?"

"It was always too difficult to sleep on. Did you have a purpose here, my lady, or may I return to my business?"

"Don't let me keep you." Ragna's mind scoured itself for a reason, any reason to be there.

But he didn't wait for her reason. He inclined his head, reared up to the nest again, grasped clusters of small rings she had seen the Aesir wear on their front toes, and flung them into the pile. When Ragna didn't speak, his ears flattened, and he asked, "How fares the pride?"

She knew the unspoken question. Were they still fighting over meat? She considered lying. "Fortunately, Thyra has not had to exile anyone else. But tension remains."

He made a low noise and Ragna watched the crimson hackle feathers prickle. "Yes. It would. When you ban a gryfon from eating his preferred food."

"I know the feeling well."

He paused, but didn't look at her. "I have faith you and Thyra keep everyone well in wing."

"Thyra and I, Caj. Halvden." At the name he paused again, feathers sleeking back down. "He's growing up at last. If we can forgive him his trespass, so should you."

"He lied to me. He turned me against my own son."

"You turned yourself," Ragna growled.

He shoved from the nest to stand on all fours again, talons slapping the stone floor. Feeling odd to be defending Halvden, Ragna lifted her wings in challenge and heard Vald shift in the entryway. Sverin's gaze lifted beyond her to the sentries. He stepped back, inclined his head, and met her eyes with a smoldering look.

"Is this a mockery, my lady? Why do you come here? At first I hated you for this light, weak sentence, for I knew I deserved more. I know what I would have done in your place."

"I'm not you—"

"But now I see what the true sentence is. You, flying in and out each day to ask me one question or two, to watch me circle the walls, so you can revel in my imprisonment."

"That isn't the sentence." Ragna stood, rooted, drawing her strength from the stone at her feet. With the golden treasures shoved to a dark corner, the den regained some of its natural scent. The metallic odor that had infused the nest gave way to Sverin's own, and with it rolled the memory of the last ten years. "And that isn't why I come."

Isn't it punishment? Ragna realized slowly. *Is that why I come? To show him what it felt like to be trapped and helpless while he did as he pleased?*

But now she wondered how often he had actually done what he pleased, or how much he did to distract others from his own guilty secrets.

"It isn't why I come," she said again firmly, for he stared at her with a look she hadn't seen since his madness still held him. But it was an expression of clear, clean anger, not masked by layers of lies.

"Then why? If you wish to drive me Nameless again with anger, these pointless visits are a good start."

Ragna glared at him, felt her ears slipping back defensively. "I came to check on your welfare."

"Don't worry, your sentries have me well in wing."

Ragna shifted her feet, her own temper growing, anger at him, at herself, unable to recognize or admit why she had come.

A sudden, hard brightness came to his eyes. "You pity me."

Coarse laughter drew itself from her throat and her neck-feathers stood on end. "Believe me I don't."

One red ear twitched back in uncertainty. Seeing his honest confusion and frustration, Ragna understood herself at last, by his frank, flat expression.

"I come here . . . I come to see you in your right mind. To wonder what might have been if you had grieved openly, admitted fault, and been a proper king."

"Ah." Both ears slanted and he turned from her, wings flexing against the golden chains. "You come to *regret*. A typical Vanir. Living in the past. You offered me a weak punishment and now you wander in and out, fretting, regretting, waiting." He sat, lifting a foreleg to remove his gauntlet. Ragna watched with some satisfaction as he appeared to struggle with the twin clasps. They had clearly been designed for gryfon talons, but in his agitation, he couldn't manage. "Always waiting, the white Widow Queen."

"I can make your punishment harsher if you'd like." Stung by his remark, she drew herself up and paced to his pile of gold, making a show of picking through it disdainfully. To think how her heart had caught at the sight of them when they first arrived in their magnificent regalia, talons overflowing with treasures. Though not Sverin, at first. At first, the only gold he had carried was Kjorn. "I spare you for your son's sake. For mine, so he may face you again. And because you were a king."

"A tyrant, you mean?" He managed one clasp, and the sound of his beak grinding with frustration was too much for her. Ragna walked around to face him. Without hesitation, for that would look frightened and weak, she sat before him, and touched a talon to the clasp, offering.

Like a stag, Sverin froze, his gaze inquiring. She only tapped her talon once on the gold, so he inclined his head with royal courtesy.

"Yes. A tyrant." She spoke and he watched as, with smaller, clever talons made for fishing, she unclasped the gauntlets, thinking he must have had help before. It seemed that the dragon treasures were easy to lock, but not so easy to release. "But a king nonetheless, and I meant to treat you with courtesy at least."

More courtesy than you showed us, she added silently.

He didn't answer, holding so still she heard the breath through his beak, the beat of his red heart under red feathers. She set one gauntlet aside and worked on the other, ears flat, avoiding his look as she continued.

"If you prefer, I will cut your rations, tuck you away in a cold, forgotten cave too small for you, and allow no one to speak to you again. If you prefer, I can make you truly suffer."

She set aside the second gauntlet and stepped back from him, feeling Tor's thunder rise in her heart. He could bait her. She did not have to rise to it. "I will do all those things, and we'll see how long you remember your name. You forget us, who had to live through your madness. I won't try to drive you to that place again. Soon you'll be Kjorn's to deal with, and I will be rid of you."

"Will you indeed?" Sitting on his haunches, he flexed his forelegs. "I wonder if we'll ever truly be rid of each other."

Ragna narrowed her eyes, uncertain how he meant it. As he sat forward, then stood, Ragna shifted farther away, saying only, "We will. Our sons will return soon."

"Ah yes," he murmured, silhouetted in the mouth of the cave. His heavy frame was impressive, regal, and terrifying. If only, Ragna thought, he had used all his power to protect, to be strong, to rule well, rather than terrorize.

Regret. Typical Vanir.

"Our sons," he mused. "We became who we are for our sons. Now they're gone, and who are we? And then they will return, and who will we be?"

Ragna didn't know how to answer that, for she wasn't sure what he was asking. She walked toward the entrance. As usual, there were too many questions she couldn't answer, and too many answers would lead to regret anyway. Low evening light cast a sheen on the water far below, and Ragna shivered.

"I saw you fall, and fly out again, out there."

She turned, tail twitching. The mention of it seemed to remind her body and it threw itself into dramatic, aching awareness of the growing bruise where she'd hit the water. "Yes." She offered no more, for he would surely be thinking of Elena, who had fallen. Elena, whom Ragna hadn't been able to save. Elena, who had drowned.

He ducked his head, loosed a rough, dry chuckle. "I confess that for a moment, my heart stopped. But you flew out."

"A typical Vanir," she said, ears flattening.

Sverin's head lifted, cocked, searching to see if she was joking. Ragna couldn't decide, and kept her expression flat. When he said nothing else, she turned, flexing her wings.

He stopped her again, she heard his talons touch the floor as he stepped forward. "It was impressive. Very impressive. I . . . I am glad to see the Vanir fishing again. My lady."

"Yes." Anger burrowed deep in her chest. So many years he had oppressed their ways, and now he spoke of being glad. "I am too."

She shifted to go.

"Ragna. Please."

She shut her eyes, thunder and skyfire lashing in her heart. She opened her wings, whirled on him with a snapping beak, unable to contain herself any longer. "*What?*"

He stood tall, regal, tail low. "You must forgive me. You must know that I understand now the evil that I—"

"I did forgive you."

"Assure me again," he said quietly. "I saw you flying. I saw all of you, fishing, I saw you flying over the sea, as is your right. I know you fly at night. I know it brings you joy. You don't understand what we faced in the night, in my homeland, and why I was afraid. You must forgive me for taking that from you. For taking that from Rashard."

Her breath swept from her. She pressed her hind paws hard to the rock to keep from flying at him with beak and talon for saying her son's name. "I do, I did. But it remains a wound. You understand the feeling."

Gold eyes searched her face in the last gray light. "I do."

Silence clotted the den, and she sensed the guards standing rigid, ears perked firmly forward, trying desperately not to eavesdrop.

"Fair winds, son of Per." She turned, unable to look at his face any more.

"Ragna. If you truly come to see me in my right mind, to check on my welfare . . . thank you."

She couldn't answer that. She thought it might be the last time she came to the den, for in there, she seemed to forget everything outside of it. Her splintered pride, her missing son, the long remains of winter. In there, she only marveled at the change in him, and filled to brim with regret and anger. In there, she was only picking at her wounds.

Typical Vanir. She couldn't answer, but she turned to look at him again. Though the cave was dim and growing chilly with evening, a light touched his gold eyes, seeming to change his face to something younger. Hope.

"Sverin—"

Outside, a gryfess's high scream tore the air.

Sverin's eyes widened, his ears slicked back, and he made an abortive movement toward the entryway.

"You stay here," Ragna growled, coming to herself again, and flung herself out of the cave, ordering Vald to keep Sverin there. It was no longer his pride to protect. In that, he had failed.

She flew up, scouring the cliffs and surrounding land with her gaze. The brief storm had passed by them and the sky was clear. In the twilight, gryfons had gathered in the snow on top of the cliffs to eat. Ragna expected to see blood, fighting, some shocking new thing to fall across their way and block a path to peace.

But she only saw Astri, stumbling through gathering gryfons and the snow, star white and shouting Einarr's name.

Confused, Ragna turned, flapping hard. "What in every wind is ..."

She heard more shouting, old Vanir shouting, half-bloods. She spied Sigrun and Caj, and dove, stumbling a landing beside them. Sigrun, with an expression of pure triumph, lifted her beak to point to the sky. At last, feeling slow, Ragna looked up where they were looking—high and toward the sky to the nightward horizon.

And there, she saw what they saw.

In a long, wide, wedge formation, like geese, flew creatures too large to be geese.

"Tyr's wings," Caj breathed. "It's ..."

"Einarr!" Astri screamed again. And indeed, the last day's light bounced off coppery feathers of the leading male, but Ragna knew at once it wasn't him. He was stockier, this gryfon, his wings longer, at least two years older than Einarr had been. Anticipation quivered in her chest.

"No, dear one," she heard Astri's mother say. "It's not him . . ." Growing commotion drowned her out. Gryfons flocked up from their nests, from the sea, from the river. They ran and gathered there by the King's Rocks, staring. Gasps fell out, some shouted names, some launched into the air.

As the arriving gryfons grew closer, Ragna counted at least forty. Since the albatross's word, she had waited every day for Maja and the Vanir she'd recovered to appear on the starward horizon.

But this was not Maja and her band.

"It's Dagr," Sigrun whispered. "Ragna, he's returned! He found Vidar, and those others, they're . . ."

"All Vanir," Ragna said softly, stunned. The albatross had told her of Maja, not Dagr. Sverin had exiled Dagr last summer for waiting too long to take up the challenge of initiation. When Dagr learned Shard was true price of the Vanir, he had flown nightward to find his father and others on the same day Maja had, flown in Shard's name to find the Vanir. And though they'd had no word at all of how he fared, here he was, and Ragna had to gather her wits, to reconcile her surprise and her joy.

"So it begins," Caj said quietly.

Ragna snapped back to attention. She realized she had a duty to set the tone of this arrival, and fast. She couldn't stand there like a tree. She bounded forward and jumped into the sky, winging a long circle around the pride and the arriving Vanir. Some were Ragna's age, some Shard's age, a few older. Most of them landed hard and collapsed with relief onto the packed snow.

"My pride! My Vanir, my family, welcome home!"

At the sight of her, pale and strong against the deepening evening, the pride fell to quiet whispers, and tension stretched its wings over them. The returning Vanir appeared surprised to see Aesir in the mix, even though Ragna was clearly no longer under Sverin's power.

Surely Dagr and Vidar would have prepared them for the mixed pride, would have told them that some were true mates, some had mixed families like their own.

Dagr flew to meet Ragna. "All hail the queen! Ragna the White! See, I bring you the indomitable Vanir who flew beyond the nightward horizon!"

He laughed, and she laughed, wanting at the same time to weep. Other gryfons called her name, familiar voices she'd thought lost forever. Faces she'd dreamed dwelled in the Sunlit Land turned to see her and laughed and called their loyalty.

It was chaotic, it was too soon, it was not as she'd imagined it would be. Yet, the sight of her bedraggled pride sank in at last, and she let joy steal over her.

"You're sooner than expected," Ragna said, flapping in a quick circle around Dagr. "And bold! What made you fly here, when you didn't know how we fared?"

"From a safe distance, my father scouted and saw Vanir flying over the sea, fishing." His eyes glinted as he hovered, straining against the cold air. "It was a welcome sight. This, more than anything, told us the Red King was no longer in power, told us it would be safe to come home."

Ragna laughed as she realized that would be an obvious sign. She remembered who she was supposed to be. The queen of the Vanir, mother of the true prince, not the widowed, lost gryfess who wandered in and out of her enemy's prison to check on the state of his mind. "No, he is no longer in power. And you're a very welcome sight."

In a colorful bunch to one side, the old Aesir watched, wary. Caj and Thyra went to them. Ragna trusted them to handle that half. As for the rest...

She had not been prepared for them to arrive so soon. She hadn't thought it would be so abrupt, so unexpected, but surely would be after the Halflight, or early summer, or not until Shard's return. There was much to do.

"But where is our prince?" Dagr asked, stealing the thought from her as they swooped around each other to stay aloft. He was all brightness and strength, though he'd grown thin. "The Vanir fly free, which means we've come too late for the overthrow?" He eyed the Aesir below, whom Ragna had clearly not exiled nor imprisoned. "Where is the son of Baldr?"

"He's . . . oh, but there's too much, and you've flown far. Land with me," Ragna said. "Land, all of you! Rest, eat, we'll tell all the islands, and I'll catch you up on what has passed."

In his eager face she saw Einarr, and like a bolt the thought nearly dropped her.

I'll tell you your brother was slain. Her throat clenched.

She caught sight of Vidar, and he called a greeting. Vidar was Dagr and Einarr's father, and one of Ragna's old friends. Sverin had exiled him for the crime of flying at night. Weight dragged at her wings.

Dagr landed with Ragna. Vidar touched ground some leaps off, looking around for Eyvin, his mate. Ragna spied her, standing away with the other Aesir, but she did not immediately go to him. Vidar paused to bow before Ragna, and before she could wonder at Eyvin's hesitance, Astri approached through the muttering throng of gryfons.

The little white gryfess trundled to Dagr, ears perked, face burning in the twilight. "You're . . ." Her expression broke, crestfallen.

She couldn't really have thought it was Einarr, could she? We left him to rest on Black Rock.

"Dagr," he said cautiously, watching her with gentle curiosity. "Son-of-Vidar. I knew you as a fledge, but I regret I've forgotten your—"

"Astri," she managed, staring at the gryfon who looked so like her mate should have, in perhaps three years. "I'm . . . I was . . . Einarr's . . ."

Ragna watched, sapped of strength to intervene. By any wind, she decided, it was right for Astri to tell Einarr's family. Ragna looked sideways at Vidar, who was watching Astri, then, slowly realizing, he raised his head to search the gathering for his younger son.

So invigorated by the arrival home, it seemed Dagr didn't notice Astri's sorrow at first. "Einarr's mate! Ah, yes, Shard said he'd won a fine huntress, and I see he was right." He dipped his head to her. "And has already started a family of his own I see. I should rush to catch up, if any gryfess will have an *exile*." He laughed, and no gryfon around seemed able to move. "But come now." He opened a wing to embrace the dainty white gryfess, as if they'd been close all their lives. "Where is Einarr? I've brought our father home, whom he hasn't seen in . . ."

At last, he paused. At last, halted by the look on Astri's face, Ragna's face, and the silence that fell over the pride at Einarr's name, he fell quiet. His ears tilted back in uncertainty, and he appeared to realize there was one face not there to greet him.

"Where is my brother?"

The wind moaned across the rocks and the ice that jutted from the sea. The buoyancy dissolved from the gathering. Distantly, Ragna heard a raven call, and watched as the simple question rent open the fragile wounds in her pride.

Astri drew herself together, lifted her beak in a show of pride, and managed four words. "Einarr flies with Tyr."

Wind stung at Ragna's face and she closed her eyes.

"No," Vidar breathed at last, "my son?"

Ragna could not look at him.

Dagr managed only a sharp growl of negation, and Astri loosed a soft, choked sound before she collapsed under the wing of her new brother.

23
THE INVITATION

THEY SOARED ON A HIGH, warm wind.

"I guarantee this is a trap," Asvander said again, calling over the wind for Kjorn's ears. Shard glanced over at Kjorn, who merely shook his head. Shard, Kjorn, and Brynja flew at the head of a diamond with Asvander, Dagny, Nilsine, and Ketil ranged behind.

Asvander had argued the moment Kjorn wanted to go. First, Kjorn had wanted to go alone, merely to hear the message. Shard insisted he accompany, then Asvander, Brynja, and Dagny also volunteered to go. And since Shard was going, Ketil demanded a Vanir be present for his interests. Shard tried to remember the time he'd been able to do things without an entourage, and decided he missed it. Still, the presence of his friends, future mate, and a member of his own pride always at his side had begun to feel normal.

For a moment, he remembered the summer before everything was swept up into madness, and he, Thyra, and Kjorn had frolicked before their initiation hunt.

Only a year ago. A year. Less than a year. How many times have we all been reborn in these seasons?

Meanwhile, Kjorn didn't answer Asvander. He didn't have to, Shard knew, and they flew in silence. Whatever message, whether truly from the Dawn Spire or elsewhere, they had specifically named and asked for Kjorn. It was not in him to ignore it. The exhausted lioness had told them that the gryfess waited with other lioness hunters at the border. That alone surprised Shard, that a gryfon would respect the boundary of the First Plains.

They had little time to discuss the matter further, if anyone had a mind to, for they were nearly at their destination, according to the lioness's description.

"There!" Shard stretched a talon to point, and Kjorn followed his direction. Three lionesses lounged in the grass around a gryfess, who sat stiffly, searching the sky. Her gaze found them. Her ears perked, and she stood.

Just as Shard recognized her, Brynja cried out.

"Sigga!" She tightened her wings, paused, glanced at Kjorn. "My lord. She is—was—one of my huntresses. I'll introduce you." And without leave, Brynja tucked and dove. Dagny followed Brynja's lead and they landed first, trotting forward to meet their estranged comrade. Ketil winged up closer to Shard, wary of the whole thing, and Nilsine seemed to share her caution.

Kjorn looked at Shard, who clenched his own talons. "I knew her," Shard confirmed. "We hunted together. We weren't exactly friends, but if anything it means the message is truly from the Dawn Spire."

From him, Kjorn looked to Asvander. "She is honorable," Asvander said. "Dawn Spire to the core. I don't believe she would desert or bear a false message."

"Well enough," Kjorn murmured, and at his signal, they glided down to land.

Brynja bounded up to Shard, her face alight.

Shard felt better just looking at her. "Did she have news of your family?"

"Yes." She stretched her wings happily. "They're well. Orn didn't imprison either of my parents, for they weren't really involved with you or any of it." A chilly, bracing wind made dignity and quiet conversation nearly impossible, for their feathers ruffed all the wrong ways and the whipping grass made them raise their voices.

"You weren't really involved either," Shard muttered. He had been the one to draw the wyrms down on the Dawn Spire, but Orn, the current ruler, had considered his friends traitors for associating with him.

She nipped his ear lightly and, opening her wings for attention, led the males back to the huntress. "Sigga, let me present prince Kjorn, son-of-Sverin. Kjorn, Sigga, daughter-of-Syg, huntress and lately, messenger."

Sigga mantled respectfully, though she eyed Shard with a dark look. When she straightened, her gaze was only for Kjorn. "Well met, my lord. I am sent to invite you to the Dawn Spire."

"Invite? Or command?"

Shard watched Kjorn carefully, saw his ears tilt back, his stance stiffen. They had not planned on revealing his presence to the Dawn Spire until all their allies were certain, and assembled. But Shard didn't know how long they really could have expected to move large numbers of gryfons, painted wolves, eagles, and lions around without someone noticing. Still, he wondered how they knew of Kjorn himself.

Sigga laughed, too brightly. Shard supposed Kjorn could be intimidating. "My lord, I am one gryfess. I certainly can't command you anywhere. You are invited, an honored guest, to speak of . . . current tidings."

"And if I don't go at your invitation?"

"Then I am to tell you that we hold a gryfon who claims to be one of your captains, working under your command to gather others in preparation for a war."

Kjorn's expression grew icy. "What gryfon?"

"Rok, son-of-Rokar."

Kjorn cursed. Shard glanced around as if he might see confirmation of the claim—but then, it couldn't be a lie. There would be no reason for the Dawn Spire to know the exiled gryfon now served Kjorn, except if they had captured him. Kjorn touched a talon to the chain he wore, a chain that represented promises between himself and Rok. "Yes, he is one of mine. But my war is against the wyrms, not the Dawn Spire."

Sigga's expression grew serious, she ducked her head a little. "We know. That is why I was sent. I was told to tell you this—come, present yourself to the king, be known, be seen, and stop skirting the borders like a rogue thief in the night." She raised her head, meeting his gaze fully, and seemed to take a bracing breath. "Come and see the Dawn Spire."

Kjorn glanced to Shard. Shard tilted his head slightly in negation, and tightened his talons against the grass. Something didn't feel right, but he had no answer for Kjorn.

Asvander did. Feathers ruffled, wings lifted in agitation, he snapped his beak. "If Orn thinks he can lure the prince in with some—"

"I'm only the messenger," Sigga said tightly, not looking at Asvander. Her gaze remained fixed wholly on Kjorn. "Take what you will from my message, but please give me an answer to return, or accompany me yourself. Prince Kjorn." She appraised him, extending an inviting wing starward. "Won't you come and see the Dawn Spire? Won't you come and see your home?"

Shard saw, immediately, that Kjorn could not refuse. A light had come into his face at continued talk of the Dawn Spire, a fierce longing, a hunger that Shard feared would steal reason from his head. "I will go," he said quietly, and in his face they saw there would be no arguing.

So, rather than argue, they planned.

Shard, Brynja, and Asvander would return to their larger group, and lead them on to the Voldsom Narrows, with warrior lions following on foot behind. There they would meet the eagles, the Lakelanders who would be traveling with Stigr and the rest of the Vanir, and the Serpent River pack of painted wolves. There, they would wait for word, or for Kjorn himself for the final onslaught against the wyrms.

Nilsine would go with Kjorn, for protection and to represent the Vanhar. Dagny would go with him, for she knew the Dawn Spire, had family there, and could protect him and speak for the gryfons Orn had exiled.

"Won't you take more?" Asvander asked. "We'll send along more Lakelanders and the Aesir of the Reach to protect you."

"No," Kjorn said. "I don't want to look like I plan to attack. An escort will do."

Asvander exchanged a dark look with Shard.

Ketil listened to the plan, and spoke up quietly, surprising Shard. "As much as I wish to stay by your side, my prince, I will go with Kjorn if you permit it, to represent the Vanir."

Shard tilted his head, studying her stiff posture, and worried that she might hold too much of a grudge against all the Aesir in general to make a good representative. But then, so had Stigr. With her eyes she challenged him, lifted her beak, and opened her wings a little in deference.

"Thank you," he said at length. "I accept. I know you'll speak well for us."

"Thank you, my lord. Please tell Keta and Ilse." She mantled. Shard fluffed and resettled his wings, and looked at Kjorn, gauging him.

Kjorn nodded to the rest, and drew him aside to speak privately. "I haven't forgotten your worry. Send your scouts to the Outlands and see what the wyrms are up to." His gaze trained starward, toward the Dawn Spire. "I want to be prepared as soon as we arrive." As if sensing Shard's unhappy expression, Kjorn finally turned about to meet his gaze. "Shard, if you can reach Rhydda before we go to battle, and change her mind, all the better. If she's gone," he drew a deep breath, "we shall make all haste to the Silver Isles."

"I feel strongly you shouldn't go," Shard said quietly. "Even more strongly that I should be with you."

"I do too." Kjorn loosed a wry chuckle. "I don't have a warm feeling about this. But I have keen huntresses at my side. We'll remain aloft as long as possible. Shard, you have to investigate whether the wyrms have gone or not. I must attend to Rok and make sure they've treated him well. He's been loyal and I can't return that favor by ignoring his capture."

Shard had almost forgotten about Rok. "Curse your sense of honor," he said, nipping the air in frustration.

"You would do the same for one of your own."

Shard tried to think of another argument, but by the fierce light in Kjorn's face, he knew it would be windless, get him nowhere, win him nothing, and now he was just wasting time.

He remembered what Asvander had said. "I suppose I won't do you any good at the Dawn Spire anyway. Orn hates me."

"That too," Kjorn said.

Inspired, Shard slipped the pouch with the dragon firestones from around his neck. "Here, at least. Take these." He stretched his foreleg, offering. "Give them back their fires. Return to the Dawn Spire in glory, bearing Tyr's flame."

"Ooh," Dagny said, and they both realized the others had been eavesdropping anyway. "Breezy. Good idea, Shard." At Kjorn's look of confusion, she added, "The wyrms destroyed our fires when they attacked. Pyres fell or were allowed to die."

Asvander stepped up beside her. "We don't have firestones like the dragons—we came upon it by luck after skyfire struck dry wood a long time ago. Now you can bring it back. A fine idea, Shard."

"A fine idea indeed," Kjorn said, accepting the pouch and slipping it by the leather thong around his neck, where it rested with the golden chain. He drew close, resting a wing over Shard's back to say farewell. "Never fly alone," he said, voice low. "Promise me, Shard, that you will not face her alone again."

"I won't," Shard said. When Kjorn didn't move, he echoed Kjorn's words. "I promise I will not fly alone, Kjorn. Never again. For you, for Stigr, my mother, and my pride. I promise. And *you* stay alert."

"Of course. Fair winds," Kjorn said tightly, drawing away. "We'll meet you and the rest at the Voldsom within five days. If we don't—"

"Five days," Shard said. He stretched out his wing, and Kjorn extended his to cover it.

Kjorn looked at the others who were leaving with Shard. "Fair winds. Thank you."

The gold prince's ears lay half slanted, his tail twitching intermittently. Catching Shard's gaze, he dipped his head, then looked starward. "Let's not delay any longer."

"We fly," Shard said.

With a firm nod, Kjorn turned away, jumped into a lope, and took to the air with the gryfesses forming an honor guard behind him. Shard stood, watching Kjorn's bright form against the sky, and his throat caught.

"Shard." Asvander bumped him firmly. "It's the right thing. Orn wants no part of you, and maybe it's better this way. Kjorn can reunite with his mother's sister. The queen," he reminded Shard. "He can make his first approach to the Dawn Spire alone. We'll be there for him at the Voldsom. It's only five days."

"Yes," Shard added dryly. "What could possibly go wrong?"

Thinking of at least a dozen possibilities in the span of a heartbeat, they all looked skyward again. But, rather than make him feel worse, Shard found the thoughts made him break into nervous, hearty laughter. Asvander followed suit.

Brynja spread her wings. "Let's fly. We have a lot of ground to cover, not to mention explaining to rest of the allies why Kjorn has left without so much as a fair-winds-to-you."

"Let's fly," Shard agreed. The chilly wind grew damp as they soared, and rain speckled the dry ground as they reached the lions' den again.

There, they told Mbari of Kjorn's invitation to the Dawn Spire, and they bid farewell to the lion pride, promising to meet them at the Voldsom in five days.

By the time they explained everything to rest of the gryfons and convinced Nilsine's Vanhar not to go after her, and Keta and Ilse not to go after Ketil, low gray clouds rushed across the plains as far as a gryfon could see. Rain lashed down as they took wing, and the ozone scent of skyfire suffused the air, along with rain and the petrichor from the earth.

"I hope this isn't an omen," Asvander shouted at Shard over the rain.

Shard thought if it were any omen, it was a good one. Rain was spring. Rain was change, and life, and skyfire. "Maybe it's a blessing," he offered. "Fire, and then rain. Perhaps it's a blessing from Tor!"

Some of the other Lakelanders had words for that, but thunder cracked and drowned them out.

"We need a warrior blessing," Asvander said grimly.

"Or a huntress," Brynja said, eyeing the sky.

To Shard's surprise, Keta stroked hard against the rain to catch up with them. "Prince Rashard and Brynja are right! My mother taught us a rhyme." She raised her voice high, cutting through the rain, her gaze on Asvander now. "Tor is the mother, but also the huntress!"

Ilse's voice raised with Keta. "Tor is the thunder, Tor is the thunder..."

"Tyr is the wrath and the rain!"

Keta spun, flapping, looking surprised as a Vanhar gryfon swooped in below them, echoing and adding to the rhyme. "We know this one too. Surely the Vanir of the Silver Isles are one blood with us."

Shard laughed, and called out as rain battered and slid down his face. "Tor is the thunder..." He would have answered Asvander's grim look, but a low, thrilling hum wove through the storm. The Vanhar, and the Vanir, chanting.

"Tor is the thunder, Tor is the thunder!
Tyr is the wrath and the rain.
Tor is the thunder, Tor is the thunder!
Tyr is the wrath and the rain!"

Thunder boomed and broke across the sky and the flying gryfons shrieked, then laughed and soared high, weaving in dodgy imprecision that neither Asvander nor Brynja bothered to correct.

"I'm coming, Rhydda," Shard whispered into the storm, his words in time with the chanting and the thunder. "I'm coming to face you again, and you will hear me."

Thunder rolled out in growls like a gryfon mother warning a beast away. Rain fell, and they flew hard, rebelliously high, toward the Voldsom Narrows and the Outlands where the wyrms dwelled.

24
ORN'S MESSAGE

KJORN FLEW AT THE HEAD of his small wedge of companions, every now and then eyeing the dark storm that had rushed in windward of them. Shard would be flying in that storm.

"Shard," he muttered, "watch your back."

"What, my lord?"

Brought out of his thoughts by Nilsine's frank, clear voice, Kjorn shook his head, shifting his wings to soothe his irritated flight. "I was thinking aloud."

He felt the stares of the gryfesses on his back, and kept his eyes resolutely forward. Behind him, Nilsine resumed her conversation with Ketil, about the similarities of their prides. The other half of the wedge, Dagny and Sigga, caught up on tidings from the Dawn Spire. Kjorn flicked an ear to that, to the news that Dagny's family was well, and Brynja's family was well, though watched. Orn spared no one if they were suspected to have helped Shard, or incited the attack on the Dawn Spire.

"Be prepared," Sigga said to Dagny, and he thought, a little to him. "It will not be as you remember. Many of the outer towers are toppled. The great red bridge on the dawnward border—"

"No," Dagny whimpered. "Not my bridge?"

"Smashed," Sigga confirmed. "The smaller three to the starward outskirts remain." She watched Dagny, then averted her gaze. Kjorn's feathers prickled with further unease.

"Brynja and I would always meet under that bridge," Dagny said quietly, her wing strokes leaden. "In the evenings, to catch up on the news after I lit the fires."

Sigga made a clipped noise of sympathy, and when Kjorn peered back at them, she was looking at him. When he met her eyes, her ears slicked back and she looked away, dawnward, folding her talons in what looked like apprehension.

Outer towers, toppled. A stone bridge smashed.

A shudder rippled over Kjorn's skin to think of the wyrms, powerful enough to smash rock. A warm, climbing thrill followed the shudder. They had routed the monsters once, and they could do it again if needed.

Then he thought of Shard's dream, and at the idea of the wyrms marauding in the Silver Isles, his skin went cold as snow.

"I have fought and won against the wyrms once," he said, forcing himself to remain in the present. "If honor and courage remains, then nothing is broken. The Dawn Spire is more than towers and stone."

Sigga sniffed, one ear ticking forward, then back, and he knew her thought.

How would I know such a thing?

"Wait until you see it," Dagny said, her voice brightening, though edged, and Kjorn understood why she and Brynja were wingsisters. Her determination to be cheerful was impossible to break, and always a comfort.

Meanwhile, Nilsine and Ketil had fallen quiet. "Beware, my lord," Nilsine said, "of any expectations."

The heavy scent of rain gusted intermittently, but the storm crawled along the border of the First Plains and didn't drift starward. For a moment, Kjorn suffered the mad fantasy that the rain was following Shard, and he wasn't sure if that was good or bad. Good, he thought after a moment. It would wash away the ash from Midragur, and Shard liked the rain.

He registered Nilsine's comment. "How do you mean?"

"It would be wise not to have expectations about what it will be like when you return," Ketil chimed in, her voice warm and warning.

Kjorn eyed the Vanir thoughtfully. "I suppose you've been thinking about that a lot lately. Returning home, I mean."

He didn't mean it to sound cruel, or like anything but an observation, but she looked struck, and turned her face from him. "Ketil," he said swiftly, "forgive me. I'm on my own wind, thinking of Shard, and my aunt at the Dawn Spire. I didn't mean any offense."

With a quick glance at him, she rolled her shoulders in a shrug and said quietly, "I only meant it might not be as you remember."

Kjorn nodded once, turning forward to behold the distant outline of the Dawn Spire. "Fortunately for me, I remember nothing at all."

KJORN HAD PLENTY OF time to ponder his past and his legacy as they soared closer to the Dawn Spire, but still he was not prepared for the sight of the aerie. As late afternoon touched the face of the Winderost in pale light, Kjorn stared at the place of his birth, and at the ruin that had surely come with the attack by the wyrms.

Towers of stone jutted from the earth and stood tall, but some were only half as high as the others, with newly crumbled red stone around their bases. Kjorn counted at least four of those, smashed. Arches of stone rose and thrust toward each other fruitlessly, spanning only half the distance between each other. Broken bridges lay in marbling shades of ochre, umber, and red, red stone.

He'd thought he would remember it, but the only thing vaguely familiar was the drifting scent in the air. Nilsine flapped up closer to Kjorn as he lifted his head, grasping for something, anything familiar. He curled his talons, staring hard.

"My lord," Nilsine said, her voice touched with warning.

Kjorn realized voices called to them, ordered them to land. He flicked his ears, noting that sentries stood on the high towers and some even on the piles of rubble. He remembered nothing about any of it. He didn't remember the ancient formations of stone, vast and dazzling in their color and formation, nor the lay of the landscape beyond it. He didn't remember the way the sentries were posted, nor the stream that ran out of the aerie and broke into the lands beyond.

It felt nothing like arriving home. His idea of home was still the Silver Isles, and he shook his head, hard.

This is my home. Was my home. And it will be again.

Four more sentries left their posts. Warning tapped at Kjorn's heart. Four well-built Aesir of the Dawn Spire flew hard at them, folding their wings, calling orders and questions, and Kjorn turned to them to answer.

Too late, he realized that more gryfons stooped at them from above. And they were not slowing down to ask questions.

"Kjorn!" Ketil swooped forward, wings fanning in a hunting flare. Kjorn had time only to suck in a breath before the gryfess struck him hard, knocking him out of the way of the warrior who dove at him, and under the four sentries.

As Kjorn caught a breath, he whirled, stroking the air to gain his equilibrium and understand that they were not being stopped, or welcomed, but attacked.

Four more sentries converged from behind.

"Contain him!" barked a male.

"Mar?" Dagny cried. "What are you doing?"

The male, ruddy in color, flashed her a look of regret before calling down two of his warriors on her. Kjorn scoured his mind for memory of the name. It gnawed with familiarity.

"Sigga!" Dagny shouted, "how could you trick us? We hunted together!"

"That's why the king suspected me of treason as well." The gray huntress circled the fight, her voice raw. "He threatened my family if I did not bring Kjorn this far."

Above Kjorn, Nilsine swooped to distract and avoid their attackers, but wouldn't engage in battle, and Ketil slashed and fought against the largest of the sentries. Dagny shouted their names, imploring them to stop, even as they drove her to the ground. As Kjorn chose a target and pushed up higher, weight slammed into his back and talons gripped his wings at the joint.

He shrieked, hind legs thrashing as he fought to spin and see his opponent, slashing talons at the next gryfon to flare in his face. The male Dagny had called Mar grasped for Kjorn's forelegs, and all their wings beat in chaotic disarray, smacking each other, swiping faces. Kjorn had to duck his head to avoid stiff flight feathers slicing his eyes.

They sank. The gryfon riding his back dug talons into Kjorn's wing joints to force him to fold and turn, driving their whole knot of feathers and beaks to the ground. Kjorn hit first and gryfons piled on to pin him down.

Shouts broke the dusty air, and Kjorn sucked in a beak full of ashy, red dirt. *Stupid, stupid, stupid . . .*

"Mar, look—"

"After her!" barked Mar, and Kjorn squirmed to lift his face from the ground and see who of his number had escaped. Before he could discern anything in the dust and chaos, talons swiped near his eyes and he jerked his face away.

Mar, Mar, why do I know the name?

Four gryfons pinned him, one straddling his back, another sprawled across his hind legs, one nearly sitting on his wing. At least he wasn't trying to break the wing, Kjorn noted with festering rage. Nearby he heard Dagny, her voice raw and sounding as if she wept. Then it was muffled as if someone held her beak shut.

"I will come peacefully," said Nilsine's smooth, calm voice. "Lay talons on me and I will snap them off."

So Ketil had escaped. Indignation and hope flurried in Kjorn's heart. Their last conversation, what had he said? She might have been insulted. He'd apologized, but he didn't know if she would flee him and take this turn of events to Shard, or return to the Ostral Shores, to her Vanir, and simply wait out the rest of this farce to go home. Or perhaps she would be captured. He didn't know. He knew only that he'd failed the gryfesses who'd accompanied him, and now the gryfon called Mar was staring down at him.

"I came peacefully," Kjorn growled against the red ground. Dust blew into his face and he coughed, which caused the warrior sitting on him to press talons harder against his neck, grinding his head against the ground. "At the invitation—"

"There was no invitation," rumbled Mar, stepping close so his shadow fell over Kjorn. "You have no friends here."

"My mother's sister, the queen—"

"The queen has no idea you're here, or even alive. We're to keep it that way." He took a short breath and lifted a foreleg, revealing a rock clutched in his talons. It was big enough, hard enough, to break Kjorn's skull.

"Why a rock?" Kjorn rumbled against the ground, stalling, desperate. The big gryfons pressed him against the ground. He couldn't move.

"They don't want royal blood on their talons," Nilsine said drily from nearby. "What a mighty group of warriors."

Mar snapped his beak at her. A muffled squeal rose from somewhere, Dagny. Crouching back, Mar raised the rock high.

Nilsine loosed a blood-chilling shriek and Mar dropped his rock in surprise, then whipped about to stare at her. Kjorn bucked against his captors, and they answered by grinding him flatter against the ground. Through talons pressed hard to his head, he saw two big warriors fall on Nilsine, pin her wings, and grasp her beak shut as they did Dagny.

"You know this is right," Mar growled at Nilsine, then at Dagny, who jerked her face from him. "If he shows his face it will be chaos, and he comes from a line of cowards. "

Dagny's eyes blazed. Kjorn stared, straining his talons against the ground, trying to shove off his captors. They hadn't clamped his beak shut. He still had his voice, but he didn't know what to say. He would have one chance, one plea, one promise to give these gryfons to save his own life.

He scrabbled against the dirt as Mar retrieved his rock and stood over Kjorn. The late light shone at his back, painting him in bloody silhouette.

"Forgive me," he whispered, "bright Tyr."

"Do it quickly, Mar," growled the biggest gryfon pinning Kjorn. "Or I will."

Brynja, exploded a bright voice in Kjorn's memory, and he sucked a hard breath. *I am Brynja, daughter-of-Mar.*

He jerked his head to meet Mar's eyes as the rock swept down. "Brynja follows me—"

Surprise flickered in the warrior's face, then pain cracked Kjorn's head. Then, nothing.

25

A GATHERING OF ROGUES

BRYNJA CHOSE THE SPOT TO land, as darkness swamped under the clouds and the rain lightened to foggy drizzle. The long flight brought them to the border of the Voldsom Narrows, a network of canyons and crags where the gryfesses of the Dawn Spire had once hunted.

In fact, the great eagles of the Winderost claimed the lands as their own hunting grounds, and only recently, with Shard's prompting, had Brynja or anyone else bothered trying to listen to them. Now they were staunch allies against the wyrms, who stalked and lived in the Outlands, on the border of eagle territory.

As Shard took a head count, making sure none had been lost in the storm, Brynja trotted up to him, ears alert. "I'll take some and fly ahead to alert the Brightwing Aerie that we're here."

"It's getting dark," Shard remarked, looking across the nearest crevasse, where mist drifted from far below, presumably a stream at the bottom.

Brynja chuckled. "My Vanir prince, afraid of the dark? It was you who taught me to find the light."

Shard stretched his wings, keeping them warm in the cool, damp air. "I meant to say I would go."

"Shard," she said quietly, "you need to remain. Half of the gryfons in this band fly only for you, and Stigr will have my tail if anything happens to you."

"Then you should stay too," Shard said, stubbornness rooting in his chest. "You will be my queen."

"We'll go."

Brynja and Shard turned to see a trio of gryfons—Keta, Ilse, and Toskil, approaching with heads low in respect. Keta spoke for the group. "We'll scout ahead, meet with the eagles in your name, and begin the search for the wyrms."

Breath lodged in Shard's throat. Arguments rose in him, caught in his chest, and smothered there, as Stigr's request echoed on and on. *Let them serve you.*

He wanted to shout no, that it was too dangerous for all of them, but then Asvander was approaching, ears forward.

"I'll assemble Lakelanders and any of the Vanhar who wish to scout," he said. "But not tonight. Everyone," he looked at those who were gathering, "after that flight, we need rest. Do you agree Shard? It's best not to fly at night yet. The eagles are expecting most to be gathering soon anyway so we shouldn't surprise them too much."

Shard agreed quietly, and Asvander and Keta walked among the volunteers, telling Shard what they would do while he stood there, wanting only to go himself, to spare them, to make sure it was safe.

Isn't that what princes do? Lead?

"Let them," Brynja whispered. She'd drawn so close, the whisper was only another echo in his head. "Let them serve you."

Before he could answer, a battle scream ripped the air, and Shard's relaxed band sprang into a chaos of flaring wings and ramping gryfons and shrieked challenges.

They had not posted a watch upon landing, nor scouted around, nor thought at all about danger for they weren't yet in the Outlands. They'd heard no wyrm shrieking, but suddenly battle was on them.

A voice boomed above it all. Asvander, shouting, *"Form up!"*

Shard whirled, pressing his wing to Brynja's, part of a line that flowed into an outward-facing ring. The shriek came from above, and so their heads turned. Gryfons. Shard spied them against the dull gloom of the clouds. Gryfons, not wyrms. Still his heart scattered.

"Who goes there?" he called, nudging his wings open against Brynja, on his left, and Toskil, on his right. He stepped forward, though not far from the ring.

No answer. The wave of gryfons in the air—he counted only ten—dove, and Shard watched as the Vanhar leaped to meet them, wings beating the air. But this left their ring broken, and even as the Lakelanders moved to close it, Shard heard the rush of wings that meant the first ten attackers were a distraction, and the true assault now came from behind.

"Behind!" he yelled, but was too late, and others had already realized the mistake. Thirty gryfons dove in silence from above, and Asvander roared in challenge, breaking the ring to lead his wave of Lakelanders forward.

"Exiles," Brynja said to Shard, ears forward, "rogues. If they were here to meet Rok—"

"And he's at the Dawn Spire," Shard said grimly, "they'll think they've been betrayed." Shard backed out of Brynja and Toskil's space to give himself room, and shoved hard from the ground, wings flapping hard. Gryfons smashed into each other all around, battling with fierce and angry shrieks.

"Stop!"

They fought without strategy now, having used up what appeared to be the only trick they knew in the pre-emptive, pinscher ambush. Shard tried to shout again, then a shriek warned him of impending attack. A stocky, long gryfess the color of ash and bone flew at him, talons splayed. Shard's gaze darted around, and he held his air, flapping hard, preparing to dive at the last moment.

She closed fast. One wing beat more and she would be upon him.

Then a gray and russet blur barreled into her from the side. Asvander, bowling her over and through the air.

Shard caught a breath and stroked higher, nearly losing sight of the skirmish in the whirling, low-lying clouds. He scoured the battle, saw his own Vanir fighting gamely from the ground beside half of the Lakelanders, saw the Vanhar forming into more precise wedges for defense and attack, and saw that the exiles had no form at all and would soon be driven to ground and subdued if they did not surrender.

Shard tried to discern a leader among them, and heard Asvander shouting. He and another Lakelander held the big female who had attacked Shard, and she was shouting at her band to stand down.

With a painful lack of care or discipline, they kept fighting with seeming glee. Shard peered around and chose a target, a smaller male who looked to be an exiled Vanhar. Just as he angled his wings in preparation to dive, two gryfons stroked in to harry Shard's target to the ground. Almost before the fight began, it was won.

Then he heard Brynja. "Shard!"

The Vanir echoed her, calling for him, for their prince. *As if I was a lost kit,* Shard thought, disgruntled and shamed that he had missed the brief skirmish, though he'd only flown above to get focus and try to spot a leader. But it had all happened without him. For half a wing stroke, he was tempted to fly on, to venture into the Outlands, to hunt Rhydda down and end Kjorn's war before it began.

The thought of the look on Stigr's face, or what it would do to Brynja, or what his Vanir would think of him if he left again lowered him below the clouds.

"I'm here," he called, circling once, gliding in to land near Brynja. "I'm fine."

"Of course you are," she said, feathers fluffing as she swiveled to eye him placidly. "I just didn't know where you *were*."

Shard huffed, grateful she trusted his fighting ability, ashamed again that, perhaps, she had thought he might've run. He turned to take in the rogues. "Now, who have we here?"

All around, gryfons of his mixed band held the rogues in check, snapping beaks and threatening with wing and talon if they tried to fly.

The fight mostly appeared drained from the exiles, as if they'd only had one good effort in them. Shard and Brynja walked to Asvander and one of his Lakelanders, who held the big, pale gryfess between them, wings overlapping her to keep her from flying, each gripping a foreleg. If she hadn't been hunched she would have stood tall and bulky, her head and breast pale as bone, her broad wings darker gray.

"An exile from the Ostral Shores," Asvander informed Shard, who could have guessed by her color and bearing. Asvander seemed glad and frustrated at the same time.

"We came for Rok," she said, snapping her beak. "But like the thieving coward he is, he did not come, and is probably laughing somewhere at that muddy shore he calls home. To think he promised that a prince would actually be interested in restoring us."

Not wanting to waste arguments, Shard raised his wings. Perhaps his small stature, his foreignness, or the fact that others demurred to him made her fall silent and perk her ears. "Rok was captured and is held at the Dawn Spire. Even now, Prince Kjorn has gone to see to his freedom, and gain the alliance of the Aesir there."

Her head tilted, regarding him. "Why should I believe you?"

"You don't have to," Shard said, growing edgy as true darkness fell. The rain had stopped, otherwise he would have suggested they fly on, into the Voldsom, for the shelter of the canyons. "But you see here I have warriors of the Ostral Shore, Vanhar of the Vanheim, my own Vanir whom you won't have known, and Aesir once of the Dawn Spire. If that isn't proof enough—"

"He promised to meet us," she snarled. That tone rang familiar to Shard, and he perked his ears, listening. "And here we've sat, in the rain and wind, with eagles circling like buzzards, watching us."

"Wait," Shard said slowly. "I know you. You came upon us in the Dawn Reach not a fortnight ago! You wanted to see Kjorn for yourself but then you disappeared. So, Rok convinced you to join us after all?"

"Yes, then he ran away, and this glorious prince is nowhere to be found. Only you." She looked less than impressed. "Who are you?" She shifted, glaring at Asvander, who pressed his down in warning against her back.

"I know him!" hollered a rogue gryfess from down the line. "The painted wolves call him—"

"I am the Star-sent," Shard said, raising his voice, feeling it couldn't hurt to stir some wind, to try to impress upon them the importance of their presence there. "I am Rashard, son-of-Baldr, prince of the Silver Isles in the Starland Sea. I am wingbrother to Prince Kjorn. I am called the Stormwing, called, by some, the Summer King. I'm here to help the Winderost, to help Kjorn." He glared at her. "To help you, if you'll hear us out. Rok and Kjorn will keep their promises to you. Rok helped us to fight against the wyrms. Where were you for that?"

She fluffed, shrinking back a little in Asvander's grasp.

Shard stepped forward, narrowing his eyes. "In five days time you will see here the greatest meeting of creatures that perhaps the Winderost has ever known. The lions of the First Plains, the eagles of the Voldsom, the painted packs, the gryfons of the Ostral Shore and the Dawn Reach and the Vanheim, and, we hope, the Dawn Spire. Now, you know who I am. You can stay with us or you can flee, but I won't tolerate skulking ambushes and attacks based on false information."

Her beak had fallen open, her lashing tail now draped listless in the mud.

Even Asvander stared at Shard as if he did not know him. Beside him, Brynja seemed to ignite with pride, and extended a wing to touch Shard's side.

"Well," the female rogue mumbled, every feather standing on edge as she jerked her gaze from him, "why didn't you just say so?"

"Welcome to our company," Shard said shortly. Darkness closed swiftly under the cloud cover. "I think it's past time for the rest of our introductions."

SHARD WOULD HAVE ENJOYED a fire, with the damp ground and the chill, and hoped his fire stones were serving Kjorn well. Their camp remained in gloomy darkness.

Rather than follow the big female, whose name was Hel and whom Shard had assumed was leading while Rok was absent, the rogues wandered or kept to themselves. A few fell timidly or boldly into the groups to which they felt they belonged—the Lakelanders or the Vanhar. One old male got to talking of exile with Keta and Ilse, and made himself comfortable with the Vanir. Hel fell in with the Lakelanders, and as Shard circled their encampment, seeing to it that all were present and comfortable, he overheard her telling Asvander part of her story.

"…because I'm not a fighter by nature. My father kicked me from the nest when I wanted his affection, rather than spar with my sisters."

To Shard's surprise, Asvander ruffled his feathers in apparent agreement. "I had a disagreement with my father over my returning to the Dawn Spire."

Shard paused, listening openly, as it was dark and they likely wouldn't see him anyway. Disagreement was a mellow word. As Shard had understood it, his father had all but disowned him until they'd settled things back at the Ostral Shores.

"Yes," Hel said. "At least you had honorable intentions. I'm just a peaceful coward."

Asvander's laugh apparently woke several gryfons, who hissed and muttered at them to hush. "That's not what I saw today."

"I was angry."

"Then be angry at the wyrms," Asvander said quietly.

"When the wyrms fly, I don't know that I won't flee." Her low, grumbled words resonated over the gathering.

For a moment, Asvander was silent, and Shard had to hold his tongue or give away his eavesdropping.

"None of us know that, Hel," Asvander finally said. "But here is the thing that has worked the best for all of us—think hard on what you love, and why you fight, and the wyrms won't be able to frighten your name from you."

A rough laugh. "Does my estranged family count?"

Feathers rustled, and Shard thought maybe Asvander nudged her with his wing. "Of course."

Shard slipped on, heard more quiet conversations along the same lines, some snoring.

Familiar, comforting scents drifted to him with the evening chill, along with the mineral scent of mud and the earlier rain.

He walked from the camp, his eyes adjusting to the dim starlight that twinkled through the breaking clouds, and stopped at the edge of the first crag in the earth at the bounds of canyon land.

The shallow canyon cracked just beyond his feet and zagged away to join the larger network. Twitching his ears to and fro, he heard water running below. No wind blew, and a few tendrils of mist drifted up from the streams, caught in starlight, and made it look as if the earth were breathing smoke.

He heard a step behind him, and knew it was Brynja. She walked up beside him, pressing her wing to his, but kept her silence as he stared over the Voldsom.

"Listen," he whispered. Brynja glanced at him, then turned her face and her ears, searching the still air, beyond the muffled noise of their band, for any sound.

"It's peaceful," she said quietly, leaning into him.

"Yes." Shard's tail lashed, and he clenched restlessly at the dirt. "You don't find that strange?"

As it dawned on her, she looked at him once more, then out over the canyons, staring, searching, her ears straining one way, then the other. "The wyrms?"

"They're awfully quiet." As he said it, he realized they hadn't heard any wyrms at all over the last days, even so close to the Outlands. Before, they had nearly always broken the night with their screams.

Beside him, Brynja shuddered. "Why?"

"I don't know," Shard said, voice low.

"Is it *possible* that you've gotten to Rhydda?"

"I suppose," Shard said. "But I fear what got through." He explained about the dream of the dragons, Kajar, and his thoughts of Sverin and the Silver Isles.

Brynja lifted a wing and draped it over his back. "Shard, even if that's so, she doesn't know the way. If she flies toward your home, she might well get lost over the sea before she ever finds the Silver Isles."

"I hope for that, then," Shard said quietly. "Or that on some chance, she simply goes to wherever her home is."

For a moment more they stared out together across the misty labyrinth, and Shard knew with climbing dread that he would have been less disquieted by the familiar shrieking of the hunting wyrms than he was, now, by their strange and utter silence.

26
SVERIN'S PENANCE

"I AM GRET, DAUGHTER-OF-GUNNR. GUNNR, MY father, who was killed in the Conquering."

The Vanir gryfess stood before Sverin, and Ragna saw that she quivered, though with fear or rage was unclear. The day dawned crisp, cloudless, and bright, and the scent in the air hinted at wet earth rather than winter. Across the expanse of the Sun Isle, the tips of brown grass showed through melting snow.

Sverin stood on the King's Rocks, wings bound, as still as the dark rocks themselves. A clustered line of Vanir waited to climb the rocks, tell their tale, and demand his penance. It had not been Ragna's idea, but perhaps it should have been.

Two guards flanked the fallen king, and Ragna watched his face steadily, waiting, wary that one too many stories of pain may crack his mind, which she still considered fragile.

Gret's pale, brown tail whipped back and forth. She sucked a breath and snapped her beak once. "My father was killed. Then after battle was done, one of your Aesir killed my mate." Her gaze lashed the gathering, pleased to not see him there. He was one of the gryfons

230

who had fallen in the battle with the wolves last summer. "He killed my mate, and my yearling kit. Then he expected me to mate with him. What do you say to this, *Sverin?* When I refused him, when I fought him, your father banished me." She raised her head, and though her voice trembled, she seemed to find strength in the dawn, in Sverin's silence. "He sent me to exile for refusing to mate with a murderer, with a coward. What do you say to this, *my lord?*"

Ragna's skin prickled and she shifted her feet. Before, they had simply accepted the way of the Aesir, the way of conquering, like barbaric, Nameless animals, letting them take over by brute strength. Now they had to face that. She watched Sverin carefully, fully expecting him to blame his father, to blame the dead Aesir, to remind her they were gone now, and she was home.

"I should have intervened," murmured the red gryfon instead. Ragna watched his face.

Gret's feathers ruffed slowly, her talons flexed on the melting snow. "You should have," she breathed, voice tight. "Yes, you should have. My mate and my kit are dead."

"Forgive me," Sverin said, his voice careful, low, and pinched, though his severe, golden eyes never left her face. "For all that you endured. I hope you ... find peace."

Gret loosed a sound of disbelief. "You have no right. You have no right."

"Forgive me," Sverin said again, louder, for all to hear, and lowered his head.

Ragna's muscles trembled. It was the tenth such tale, the tenth heartbroken confession and demand for penance and closure. The tenth time Sverin asked forgiveness, and was refused.

No, she thought, wanting to collapse with weariness. *No, it's I who should be asking forgiveness, I who should have spoken, who should have intervened. I should have been stronger. But I was too silent, too afraid for Shard.*

The regretful, waiting Widow Queen.

Briefly, Ragna shut her eyes. Astri had demanded this. Astri, demanding it of Thyra. Let Sverin see and hear and suffer his crimes again in his right mind. All had agreed, all but Ragna, and Caj, who stood on the rocks as well, watching his wingbrother's face, his own a dark, cobalt mask. Seeming to feel her look, he glanced over, and appeared surprised by whatever he saw in her face. Ragna tightened her expression.

"Gret, you may step down," she said.

"All winds take you," she hissed to Sverin. "The queen is too merciful. I hope your wings remain bound 'til they rot. I hope *your* son dies at the claws of his enemies, as mine—"

"Gret," Ragna said again, swiftly, for quick fury swept over Sverin's face before disappearing again, like the shadow of a cloud over plains. "Step down. I will hear the rest of your grievance later, if you wish."

Gret looked to her, eyes narrowed, then mantled and stepped down. Two more replaced her—a brother and sister who were only fledges when the Aesir killed their parents in the Conquering. They'd fled, raised themselves in the White Mountains, but, fearing discovery, left the islands and flew farther nightward.

"Nothing can repair that," Sverin said, so quiet Ragna thought he meant it only for them. They looked surprised, the female angry, the male confused, as it almost sounded as if he were trying to counsel them. "I hope you'll find happiness now, with your pride."

"We'll find happiness," the female, Istra, growled, "if you suffer as we have."

"Perhaps I will, yet." The words held no trace of mockery, but drew another growl.

"Istra, Istren, step down," Ragna said quietly. Her strength for this exercise waned. She trembled as if she'd sprinted leagues up hill, and she wondered if they'd really been doing it for a full mark of the sun. She might break before Sverin did.

Another widow came up, and spoke of how bravely her mate had fought, and how bravely he had died. Then a male who, like Stigr, had left of his own accord rather than be ruled by the Aesir. After him came another orphaned kit, now grown into full hatred, for it was Sverin himself who had banished her mother and herself when she was still fledging. Her mother had died in exile.

Ragna watched them, watched Sverin, her heart pattering along as if she were in a fight, not standing still on the snow-covered rocks under a strengthening sun.

At last a lone male advanced through the cluster, and the sight of him made Ragna's heart seize. Silence settled as he climbed the rocks and stood before Sverin. His wings were rich brown, eyes gray, the feathers about his face prematurely pale. Ten years ago, a lifetime ago, he had been a friend. Now, to Ragna's eyes, he looked like a ghost.

"I am Vidar." His voice checked as his gaze traveled, mute, discerning, over Sverin's broad, bound wings, his broken posture, his silent face.

Each crime was equal in weight, stinging in pain and numbing with horror. But time had done its work on many of them, like water over stone, smoothing, softening pain into new shapes of strength, regret or resolve. Not this one. This wound remained sharp, fresh, and aching.

"Vidar," he tried again, coarsely, "son of ..."

Sverin sank to the ground, dropping his head until his beak grazed the snow. His wings flexed as if he would mantle. "Son-of-Eirikur. Forgive me. There is no excuse, no recompense to give, no crime I regret more than Einarr's death."

His voice rasped, cracked over the name. His eyes darted to his own talons, as if he still saw blood there. Ragna's muscles cramped as she forced herself not to intervene. Caj stepped forward and she cast him a warning look. Eyes narrowing, he stood down. She wondered what he saw in her face, if she looked cold. She wondered if he thought she was cruel, and if she even cared what he thought.

"He did everything for you," Vidar said, his voice as warm and rich as Einarr's had been, a singer's voice carrying clearly over those gathered. "He dreamed of being a warrior."

Sverin's ears slicked back against his skull and his black talons crunched the snow, but he didn't look at Vidar's face again. "He was a warrior. Braver than all, braver than I ever was."

Vidar stared at him, and Ragna could see he had no words.

"He stood against me," Sverin said, loudly, against the snow, then raised his head, pushed himself to his feet, as slowly as if he weighed much more. He looked around, tail lashing. "He stood against me at the height of my madness, when I would have exiled Thyra herself." His voice strained and his gaze flicked around until he found Caj, the sight of whom seemed to steady him. "He stood against me when others would not." He drew a breath, and looked directly at Ragna.

Ice lanced down her spine.

Sverin looked away from her, back to Vidar. "He died as he lived, a warrior, with a true and courageous heart. There is nothing I can do to change the past, but I beg that someday I will have your forgiveness."

Vidar's wings opened slowly, his beak. He stood like a witless, vengeful hawk, ready to fly. The guards near Sverin tensed, and Caj looked ready to leap. Ragna did nothing, staring, her whole body locked to the snow and stone.

"Someday?" Vidar whispered at last, looked around him, and folded his wings. "No. I will not add hatred to the burden on my heart. I cannot bear the weight of it." His eyes never left Sverin's face, and though Ragna didn't see pity, neither did she see hate. "Son of Per, for my part, I forgive you."

Sverin released a soft, strangled sound, and bowed his head. Ragna felt a dizzying rush of relief and gratitude for Vidar's decision.

Surprise and some unhappy mutters swept the Vanir who had already stood before Sverin, including Dagr, who sheltered Astri under his wing, as if they hadn't separated since the day he'd returned. Eyvin stood apart from them, her eyes narrowed.

Vidar cast Ragna a quick, piercing look and an abbreviated mantle, then strode down from the rocks. When another moved to step up, Ragna forced herself forward, opening her wings to draw attention.

"That's enough. Enough for today. He will hear all your grievances, I promise, as will I." Their pain was as much her fault as any. She saw as they confessed that Sverin was right. She had been idle. She had been cowardly, had waited too long. "But it's enough for today," she murmured. "To your fishing, and your nests. I promise, we will hear more tomorrow."

Caj stepped forward, dipping his head close to her. "Thank you, my lady. That was a kindness."

She swiveled, watching him and feeling blank and cold as the snow. "I did it for myself, Caj." The guards flanked Sverin and they walked down from the rocks, to the trail that led to his den. "I don't know how much more I can bear, or if it is wise to pick our wounds this way."

He nodded once, and Ragna resisted the urge to lean on him, understanding exactly some of the things Sigrun admired. Even with a broken wing, he emanated strength like a mountain. It was not his physical presence Sigrun had fallen in love with.

"It hurts us all. If you don't believe me, look around. But we're rotting with hate and pain. It's got to be dealt with, and I hate to say it but we can't wait for Shard and Kjorn to return. Sigrun would say you must lance a rotting wound and release the poison before you can heal."

A laugh scraped out of her. "Yes, she would say that. You listen well." To hear him say Shard's name picked at the ache in her heart. She wondered how much the old Aesir missed his nest-son, how much he cared for him.

He tilted his head, watching her, she thought, with a measure of concern. "I try."

Ragna looked away. "Go to him. Please."

"Yes, my lady."

He bowed his head and left her. Ragna looked around and spotted Vidar, walking along the cliff's edge, head low. Her own heart warned her not to go to him, not yet. Or maybe it was fear. Fear that his pain would turn itself to anger with her.

Either way she stood there, staring around as the pride dispersed. She could only hope she looked regal and watchful, but feared she might only look like the rest of them—exhausted, agonized, and lost.

When Shard returned, she wondered if he would be the balm she hoped for, or if it would open the wound again. When Maja, Halvden's mother, returned with more Vanir, she wondered if they'd relive this again.

And again. And again, to the end of our days.

The overthrow of the Aesir, Ragna thought bitterly, was nothing as she'd dreamed it would be. The naïve fantasy of a fresh widow felt distant, unfamiliar and hopelessly foolish in the face of ten years gone by. That summer past, Sigrun had urged her to act. She should have then, that very moment, not by singing a song, but by naming her son plainly and challenging Sverin.

She should have acted when Helaku the wolf king was alive, when he might have stood with the Vanir instead of attacking the entire pride in his righteous fury.

She should have acted years ago, when Sverin exiled Vidar for merely flying at night.

She should have acted after the Conquering, should have taken the Vanir into exile and let the Aesir have the nesting cliffs—given up their home, but kept their lives and freedom.

The moment Per slew Baldr, she should have acted.

But instead she hid, she bided, she kept Sverin's secrets, and her own, and she waited.

The waiting, regretting Widow Queen.

Perhaps it's best that Sverin went mad, she thought, now watching Vidar, *for I would have kept waiting for Shard. And if he'd never returned, I might be waiting still.*

A breeze that smelled more of rain than of snow touched around her beak and eyes, and she searched for clouds over the sea. A large part of her still searched for Shard, but she could no longer wait for him to rule the pride.

Feeling resolute and determined, she decided to have a feast that very night. Despite their pain, they had much to celebrate, and she would declare a feast. A feast with food for all. Fish, delicacies. And she would ask the wolves for permission to hunt meat for the Aesir, red meat—deer, birds, and hare.

Surely Catori would be glad to help Ragna achieve some bonding and harmony within her pride. She would provide for her pride—*all* of them, a celebration of their healing wounds, of their returned families, and those still to come.

Refreshed by the idea, she opened her wings and sprang from the ground to find Sigrun, and plan. As she wheeled about, the sight of a large flotsam in the water caught her eye. Feeling grim, she winged out to see what washed in from the ocean.

At first, she thought it was a massive sea bird, an albatross, but size and the color told her the truth.

A gryfon, a silver gryfon, floated on the water.

"Hail!" Ragna called, distaste sharpening her words. "Ollar! Are you injured?"

There was no answer. Ragna dove hard and hit the waves, swimming toward the floating gryfon.

The scent hit her first. Bloated flesh and death. She gagged, horror and confusion flooding her veins with fire. He was not injured.

He was dead.

"Sigrun!" she shouted. "Help!"

She grasped a splayed silver wing and him hauled toward the shore, letting the waves roll her forward. She told herself it wasn't far. By the time she was halfway, Sigrun had found her, and Vidar with her. They dove into the water beside Ragna, and together they swam the lifeless body back to the beach.

Twilight brought a frosty chill as with tight, cold muscles they dragged Ollar's body away from the water.

"Why bother?" Vidar grunted, helping Ragna lay the body out on the gravel shore. Ragna wondered if Asfrid or someone else had told him of Ollar's exile, or if he was simply angry with the Aesir in general.

"Our honor is defined by how we treat others," Sigrun said quietly, sounding very much like Caj. She turned Ollar's body to determine what killed him.

"Sea wolves?" Ragna asked haltingly.

Sigrun jerked her head sideways, sharp negation. "No. We would know without question."

They all examined the body, the silver feathers, hindquarters, throat, head, and found no injury. An icy cold seeped into Ragna's heart.

"He fell," Vidar said darkly. Ragna watched him quietly. "Or dove. He couldn't fly out, and drowned." He met Ragna's gaze. "It was a long flight for us. I know there were times I thought I wouldn't make it. Perhaps he was simply exhausted, and we all know an Aesir might not be able to fly out."

"Perhaps," Ragna said quietly, but felt troubled. The Aesir had all made the flight over the sea once before. "Let us at least bear him to Pebble's Throw."

"A warrior's death rites?" Sigrun asked, ears flicking back. "Burn him as we did Per? Does he deserve it?"

"As you said yourself," Ragna murmured. "Let us treat him honorably, whether he deserves it or not. It isn't for him, but us. Vidar, will you fetch Dagr and Halvden, and tell Caj what's happened? We'll need help with the body."

"I will, my lady." He took off, and Ragna hung her head.

"I was going to plan a feast," she said to Sigrun, feeling suddenly weary. "A feast, to celebrate the Vanir, and ask the wolves for their blessing to hunt red meat."

"I think it's a fine idea," Sigrun said, sounding distracted. Ragna watched her friend, still prodding the body, checking under Ollar's tail, then walking back up to examine his nostrils. "Oh, ah ha," she said, touching a talon to Ollar's beak. "Look, Ragna."

"What is it?" Ragna peered. Stubbornly, Sigrun merely pointed. Finally, just inside the nostril, where it couldn't wash away in the sea, Ragna saw a speck of dried blood. "Blood? Yes?"

"His heart," Sigrun said, prodding the big gryfon's ribs. "I've seen this in rabbits. I don't think he drowned."

Ice slithered down Ragna's spine as she met Sigrun's eyes. "Then?"

The healer narrowed her eyes. "If I was guessing, then by Tor's wings, I would swear he died of ... fear."

"Fear?" Ragna asked. "A gryfon, die of fear? Of what?"

Sigrun shook her head, and slowly they both turned their gazes toward the dark horizon.

27

SILENCE IN THE NARROWS

ORNING SAW LOW CLOUDS GUSTING across the Voldsom Narrows, and Shard and Brynja led their party forward to greet the eagles before they began searching for wyrms. The Vanir, Lakelanders, and rogues flew in a rough formation toward the eagle aerie.

No drizzle fell, but wetness clung to the air, but fresh with spring. They had four days until Kjorn arrived, rallied their forces, and attacked.

Then, the flight home. The immensity of Shard's tasks spread before him like a field of lava.

Wind rippled across his back.

Rise higher.

Shard snapped from his reverie, staring around for the voice he thought he'd heard.

Brynja, flying beside him over one of the canyons, tilted her head inquiringly. Shard curled his talons together. "Did you say some—"

"Ho, gryfons!" called a bright voice. "Ho, Shard of the Silver Isles!"

"Hildr!" Relieved to see a familiar face and hear the she-eagle's voice sounding friendly, Shard dipped in to greet her and the three eagles that flew with her. "Hildr, daughter-of-Brunr."

"Shard," she said again, eyeing him. They had not seen each other since the Battle of Torches when she'd called her eagles in to help Kjorn route the wyrms. "Brynja, of the Dawn Spire, well met. You seem underfed."

They both laughed. "You seem fed well enough," Brynja observed.

"Yes." The smaller eagle circled them, and her companions hovered with effort, beating the air to remain in a rough formation. They were about a third the size of a gryfon, but Shard had seen them hunting and fighting, and didn't underestimate their strength. "Hunting has been good in the Voldsom along the river. Have you noticed the quiet?"

Shard exchanged a look with Brynja. "We have. We mean to scout for the wyrms, to get their whereabouts to tell Kjorn for the final battle."

"We have been scouting since the rains began," Hildr said, nearly crowing. She swooped above them, gazing across their company of gryfons. "Come, bring your raggedy band to the river, and I will tell you what we know."

As dawn lightened the gray clouds, warming and turning the moist air sticky, Shard and Brynja led their mixed group down into the canyon. A series of wolf dens scattered along the river, and above those Shard saw hollows and cliff-side nests, reminding him, with a sharp pang, of the Nesting Cliffs of his home. His heart quickened. *Soon.*

Hildr caught them up on events in Voldsom since the battle. For a time they heard the wyrms hunting in the Outlands, but unusually, they had not broken the line of the jagged mountains on the night-ward side of the canyons, nor flown near the canyons themselves. They'd spooked them, the she-eagle claimed, put the bright fear of

Tyr's fire into their hearts. Now, it was silent. They heard no wyrms, saw no wyrms, smelled no fresh scents.

Rather than feel glad, Shard fretted, wondering where the wyrms were, and what they were up to. He tried not to imagine them arriving at the Silver Isles, falling upon his unsuspecting family—but Brynja was right. They wouldn't know the way across the sea.

Shard told himself the wyrms were in hiding after the Battle of Torches, and that it would not be a waste of time to look.

Upon hearing Hildr's news, Asvander, Hel, and Brynja sorted their gryfons in scouting bands. Keta led the Vanir, with Toskil and Ilse helping.

Afternoon fell with breaking clouds. Shard paced by the river, planning to scout with the Vanir.

"And Shard." Asvander lumbered up to him. "You stay here."

Shard fluffed, lifting his wings, tail flaring and lashing in an unconscious effort to make himself look even half as large as the Lakelander. "I will not. I know the Outlands just as well as any other. Better, in fact—"

"Your Vanir know the Outlands, and they have volunteered to lead the scouting parties. The rogues, my warriors, and Brynja's allies will go. You will stay here, *Prince* Rashard." His expression softened from stubborn to concern. "For Stigr and Kjorn's sake, at least. If you insist, I'll stay behind as well."

Shard felt rooted. He looked beyond Asvander to his clustered followers, the Vanir who'd come to serve him. The Vanir who served Kjorn's purposes, now, because they knew it was as Shard wished it. They had volunteered to fly back into the dead land of their exile to find the enemy. And he would sit here, tucked away like a nestling, while they all risked themselves.

He felt short of breath.

"Shard, my friend. My brother by battle." Asvander loomed back into Shard's line of sight. When Shard looked at him, ears flat in consternation, Asvander laughed and snapped his beak in mock aggression. "Someone must be here for the great gathering. Brynja is staying too, and she fought me harder than you are now."

Shard eyed him. Oddly, it did make him feel better. "Why? I'm one of the fastest fliers—"

"Were," Asvander said with grim pleasure. "Your Toskil might give you a run, and Keta. Let them serve you. You're a leader now. You've done and seen things none of us will in this life, and you've all but returned a proper king to the Dawn Spire for us. Let us help you. Let us serve."

It sounded so much like Stigr that Shard shut his beak. Brynja approached, and with a glance at their faces, seemed to guess what they were talking about.

"Someone has to be here," she murmured to Shard. "Shard, we need to be here for the gathering. The lions will likely arrive within two days, and who knows how quickly the rest of the Lakelanders and the painted wolves will come? Think of Stigr. If he arrives only to find out that you've disappeared into the Outlands, none of us will survive until the battle."

Shard managed a laugh. "I yield."

"Good." Brynja ruffled her feathers, stretching her broad, ruddy wings. "Then I'll tell you the groups, and who will be flying where."

As they sat, Hildr flew to them and offered her fastest scouts to accompany each group. As Shard watched them all finally take to the air and depart, he wondered with an out-of-place sense of misgiving how Kjorn fared at the Dawn Spire.

VAGUELY, HE REMEMBERED THAT outside, night had fallen. Tucked next to Brynja, he had fallen asleep to the murmur of other gryfons. Now he sought the dream realm, seeking the net that wove through the stars. He sought Rhydda.

A raven's dark laughter followed him. Though the sound surprised him, Shard ignored it. Munin had shown him false things before, images and events out of context that put fear into his heart. He didn't need anymore fear.

Spiraling in a dream flight, he grasped the net and flung it out wide, seeking wyrm dreams of blood and stone.

Images, laughter, raven wings flapped and scattered around him. He slipped across the dreams of the sleeping gryfons around him, many of which featured Kjorn and glorious battle, and fire.

Rhydda!

A long, clattering raven call mocked him across the stars. *You've scared her away, mighty prince,* Munin rasped, now winging in beside Shard.

Shard tried to shove the raven back.

You've reminded her of finer things and greener places. The raven flapped his wings, conjuring up images of molten earthfire surrounded by icy sea, pine woods, and a distant range of mountains.

"Did she fly home? Was that my last dream? Tell me!"

O' Summer King, I warn you, spring has come sooner than you know, and your pride will fly or fall without you—

With a flick of his wings, Shard dove down, leaving the raven behind in mottled, unformed images. Soaring in the odd half-light of the dream, Shard scoured as far as he could stretch, following the long spiral of scattered light.

A dragon's voice whispered, *You should have flown. You should have flown when you knew the time was right.*

"Amaratsu?" Shard cried, whirling.

A raven wing struck him and knocked him into a blazing fire. Shard was consumed in laughter and hot flames, and Munin's voice rang on and on. *You should have flown, you should have flown, you should have flown when your heart called you home!*

Munin had him now, caught in long spindly claws, and tossed him down on a familiar cliff of the Star Isle. There he found Catori, and called her name in relief. But the red she-wolf stood at the edge of the cliff and stared out over the sea, ears perked, and did not see or hear him.

Oh what darkness, her warm voice howled into the wind, *oh what darkness have we lived to see?*

He shouted her name, thrusting his wings open. When she flicked an ear his way, he managed to shove forward. His talons sank into the ground and he slogged toward his friend, her winter fur whipping in a wind he couldn't feel. *"Catori!"*

At last she turned, but as she did her red fur warped into stone-hard, leathery flesh, wings ripped up from her back and flared open, and Rhydda's gaping jaws met him with a hollow roar.

"OH, SHARD!"

"I'm all right," Shard whispered, freshly awake, not moving. Brynja huddled over him. Darkness cloaked the night outside the den in which they sheltered. The murmuring music of the river grounded him. His heart didn't race as it did after most nightmares. His blood felt cool, calm. He didn't trust Munin's visions. They had always led him false.

"Did you see her?" Brynja hung over him, protective, stroking her talons down his back.

"I don't know." Shard shifted and stood, touching his beak to her neck in thanks for the comfort, and walked to the edge of the den. "It felt more like a nightmare than a vision. A raven dream." Wind blew steadily against the canyons, and Shard perked his ears.

Brynja stood beside him. "I haven't slept. I haven't heard anything. Any wyrms, I mean. But maybe the scouts will turn up something when they depart tomorrow."

"Maybe so," Shard said, grasping at the edges of the dream even as it slid from him.

You should have flown, the raven's voice cackled. He saw Catori, her face aflame with horror.

You should have flown home.

He shuddered. He could not leave Kjorn. He promised not to fly alone. Even if it wasn't a raven dream, there was nothing he could do yet.

Outside the den, a lookout called a warning. Shard and Brynja trotted out, ears alert. He found himself absurdly hoping the warning was about wyrms, but the voices were familiar.

" . . . Rashard? Where is the prince? I have ill tidings!"

"Ketil?" Shard's heart clenched. If Ketil had found them at night, and was alone, that did not bode well.

Stars formed a glistening corridor over their heads and shed enough light to see Ketil gliding down to meet them. Two of Shard's Vanir had stood watch on the canyon rim, and they all flew down to land by the river. Waking gryfons peered out of the abandoned wolf dens, and eagle heads poked from nests, silhouetted against the stars. Ketil mantled before Shard, her feathers in disarray, winded and worn.

"My lord. It was a ruse. Kjorn, Nilsine, and Dagny have been captured, and I fear the warriors who met us meant to kill him. Forgive me for fleeing, but I knew it would be better to escape and tell you than to fight, lose, and leave you wondering."

"You did the right thing," Brynja said.

Ketil shot her a quick, surprised look, then dipped her head in gratitude. "I fear I was too slow. I got turned around when I flew to lose my pursuers and lost an entire day. We could reach them faster if—"

"I know the way," Brynja said quickly. "It will take us only half the night to return there. You did well, you came as swiftly as you could."

They continued speaking, but Shard stood in a daze as anger rushed him.

Captured. Meant to kill him. A ruse.
You should have flown.
I have to go.

Raven wings blended in and around his thoughts, and suddenly he realized he'd been speaking out loud. "I have to go." Gryfons clustered around him, telling him what to do, telling him he couldn't go, himself, alone, to the Dawn Spire.

Shard flung his wings open and ramped to his hind legs, his feathers catching starlight. "No, I *will* go. This is my doing, bringing Kjorn to this land. *I* will go. I have unfinished business with Orn and the Dawn Spire."

Brynja and the others stood silent.

Before Shard could speak again, Asvander rumbled, "Not alone."

Shard fell again to all fours, looked at Brynja, then at Ketil. "I will—"

"Not alone, Shard," Brynja said sharply. "Kjorn went practically alone. Don't you see what you're asking of us?"

"Forgive me, my lord," Ketil said, "but don't be a fool. Don't waste the loyal hearts and talons that you have here."

Three heartbeats passed in quiet, and in it, Shard imagined what Stigr would say, what Kjorn would say. Then, he remembered he had promised he would never fly alone again. The wind left his chest, and he ducked his head. Gryfons crept from their dens, listening, catching up in muttered whispers on what was happening.

"It will be dangerous," Shard said. "Orn hates me, blames me for the destruction and deaths from the wyrm attack, and perhaps rightly so. The wyrms haven't shown themselves but it's possible they would hunt a large band of gryfons flying at night. We—"

"All haste, Shard," Brynja said quietly.

Shard shook himself, raised his head. "Who will go with me?"

A chorus of voices shouted in the night.

28

KJORN'S HOMECOMING

A HORNED ACHE IN HIS SKULL brought Kjorn around, but when he opened his eyes he saw only darkness. For a moment he feared blindness from the blow to the head, then, feeling foolish, knew it was deep night. He twitched, checking his limbs, scraping his thoughts and awareness back together.

They'd been tricked. Attacked.

Captured.

But not killed. Surely, Kjorn thought, if Mar and his warriors hadn't killed him, they wouldn't have killed Dagny and Nilsine.

Ahead of him, he smelled fresh night air, but heard paws and talons pacing on the rock. Sentries, guarding him. Kjorn pushed up to sit. His head bumped hard rock and he hissed, squirming back down. Testing his wings, he found he could only extend them a third of the way open before they struck rock. A tiny cave then, a cell. Festering indignation roiled under his skin, which encouraged the pounding in his head.

"Sire?"

Kjorn shook his head. The voice rang familiar, muffled, and seemed to be coming from somewhere above.

"Fraenir?" he ventured. Kjorn hadn't seen the young rogue since he'd gone with Rok to help gather the free exiles scattered across the Winderost. This explained why.

"Yes, it's me. Oh, but we're glad you're awake."

"We?" Kjorn asked, ears swiveling to place the voice. Definitely above, speaking in another cell.

"Tyr's foot," said a new voice, male, also familiar. When Kjorn shifted, a rock dug into his wing. "I thought they'd killed you the way they stuffed you in that cell. Like a grouse, for later."

"Rok?" Kjorn leaned forward but didn't try to crawl out, wary of the pacing sentries. "Where are we?"

"As far as I can figure, we're where they take prisoners to forget about them." His voice came more from the side, an adjacent cell.

"Rok . . ."

Rok had pledged his lot to Kjorn, and fought gamely in the Battle of Torches, so he'd almost forgotten the rogue's ironic and stubborn nature.

"We're at the windward-most edge of the aerie," Fraenir supplied more helpfully. "There are guards everywhere, I know, I tried to fly out once. You can't. There's a small canyon, and a wall with cells dug, like a honeycomb—"

"Pipe down," barked a third voice, from outside.

Just as Kjorn contemplated what would happen if he simply crawled out the front entrance of his cell, he heard a pair of sentries stride by again, saw their movement against the rest of the dark. They stopped in front of Kjorn's cell.

"He's alive," one remarked to the other, his tone dropping with a troubled note.

"I am," Kjorn said. "I demand to see the king."

Silence. They didn't bark at him as they had Rok and Fraenir, and Kjorn took that as good news.

"Or the queen," Kjorn hissed, shifting. "My mother's sister."

"I've tried to tell them all that," Rok drawled. "But maybe they'll listen to royalty." He didn't sound optimistic.

"Be quiet, poacher."

"Deserter's son," chimed the other guard.

"My father was more loyal to Per than you are to your own mother—"

"Enough," Kjorn warned, then looked back to the sentries. "What will Queen Esla do when she learns I'm here? This is a poor way to treat even a rival prince—cowardly, and dishonorable, and Orn will hear it from me. I have forces gathered he cannot conceive of, and when they begin to miss me—"

"Silence."

Kjorn perked his ears as a new speaker joined them. He knew that voice. "Mar."

"You remain alive at the king's mercy," said the older sentry, approaching through the dark. "We're instructed to end you, if we deem it necessary." His tone shifted as he clearly turned to address the other sentries. "Go on now, to your patrol."

They obeyed and Kjorn peered hard, seeing Mar's form shift closer in the starlight. When it fell quieter, Kjorn knew the other sentries had completely gone. Mar stretched out on his belly in front of the cell so he faced Kjorn at eye level, though they could barely see each other in the night.

"We were commanded to kill you before you reached the Dawn Spire."

"So I surmised," Kjorn said quietly. He hoped Rok remained silent, hoped he understood how vital this moment was.

"You can't kill him," Fraenir said, quiet, and it was Rok who snapped his beak to shush him.

Mar and Kjorn stared at each other in silence.

"She's well," Kjorn said, answering the sentry's unspoken question. "Brynja is well." He decided not to mention Brynja casting off her betrothal to Asvander in favor of Shard.

"And Valdis? I heard nothing after I helped her escape with Stigr."

It took Kjorn a moment, then he realized that Valdis was Mar's sister. He knew Valdis was Brynja's aunt, but hadn't made the connection. So, Mar had helped prisoners escape once before. "She's also alive and well. They help me to gather forces to fight the wyrms."

"I've told him all this," Rok growled from above. "Proud fool."

"You never told me my daughter lives," snarled Mar.

"I didn't know you had a daughter, did I? You might've asked me the tidings instead of—"

"Rok." Little talons tapped along the inside of Kjorn's skull where Mar's rock had struck. He flexed his talons against the ground, sensing a delicate opportunity. This gryfon had raised Brynja. Surely his ideals couldn't be far from hers.

"Mar," he said quietly, firmly. "Honorable warrior of the Dawn Spire. You pulled your strike to spare me. You know I am the grandson of Per who was king here, and Orn was set to rule in our absence. He has kept the pride well in wing, but I've returned, and it's clear to me his time is done. You know why I came, aside from seeing to my fellows here."

"I'm flattered, sire," Rok said wryly before Mar could respond. Rather than grate, his sarcasm seemed to make the situation seem less dire. Kjorn wondered if Mar tolerated the chatter because he knew Rok's family was once of the Dawn Spire, exiled for being too loyal to the line of Per. "But you've got to admit you botched this rescue. Have you got my chain? I miss it."

Kjorn sighed, and he heard Mar make a soft, grim noise of amusement.

"So now," rumbled the sentry, regarding Kjorn frankly and with almost a parental air, "what shall we do?"

Even Rok kept quiet at the question, and Kjorn could practically hear Fraenir quivering with anticipation through the rock.

The answer came to Kjorn as surely as if Tyr himself whispered in his ear. "I think," he said quietly, "we should rather ask ourselves— what do we hope our sons and daughters tell their sons and daughters about us when singers tell our tale?"

For a moment Mar regarded him levelly. Then he shifted and stood. "I have served the king of the Dawn Spire all my life, and only faltered recently, when I felt his judgment was flawed."

"It's still flawed now, I can tell you."

"Rok," Kjorn said, exasperated.

"It is," growled the rogue. "He exiled my father for being too loyal to Per. Mark my words, he'll do the same once he learns you helped Stigr and others escape, Mar. Maybe he cared about family and loyalty once, but now he's only clinging to the high tier like a kit on a bone, and can't see that fellow gryfons aren't the threat in the Winderost."

Mar didn't answer, but he also didn't stop Rok from speaking. Following a quiet instinct, Kjorn edged forward in the cell. Mar did not stop him, didn't raise an alarm. Kjorn crawled out, watching him, holding a breath. When Mar regarded him in silence, Kjorn stood. He was taller than the middle-aged sentry, but Mar was strong, a gryfon in his prime. His silhouette reminded Kjorn very much of Brynja, and, when he thought about it, Valdis.

When Mar spoke, his gaze wandered past Kjorn, keeping an eye out for fellow guards. "I would like to see my daughter again."

"We can see to that," Kjorn said. "I know your conflict, Mar. You're an honorable gryfon. I've been in your place. I know you don't wish to betray your oaths, but I ask you to do what you believe is right."

Mar's tail lashed, and he loosed a hard breath, looking around at the cells, then at Kjorn. "If you become king here, will you have oath-breakers in your pride?"

"Did Orn also not make oaths to protect his pride, his family? How has he kept those, by putting fear into the hearts of those most loyal?" Kjorn hated Orn's treatment of all of them, by the whole messy affair. It all could have happened much more cleanly. "I will have honorable, brave gryfons in my pride, who tell me when I am wrong." Feeling bold and sure of himself, Kjorn stepped forward, opening a wing. "And I tell you that, since Orn has pushed this fight, I believe many will be making new oaths by the next sunrise."

Mar stared at him, then, to Kjorn's pleasure, the guard mantled low. "I will be among them. Come with me."

Fraenir whimpered. "Hey—"

"You too," said Mar. "And Rok. But we must be silent."

THEY WALKED ALONG A trickling stream, Mar with head held high. Kjorn forced himself not to stalk. Mar said sneaking would only draw attention.

This way, in the dark, the other sentries would hardly take notice if they saw six patrolling gryfons calmly walking out of the prisoners' area. They walked in threes—Mar leading Nilsine and Dagny whom they'd also freed, and Kjorn leading Rok and Fraenir an inconspicuous distance behind. Dagny had barely been able to conceal her delight, and begged Mar's forgiveness for ever doubting him.

Now they simply walked out of the small canyon that held all the cells, and followed the brook upstream, into the night toward the windward-most border of the aerie.

One mighty tower drew his eye at the border, precariously tall and carved in odd curves and scoops, carved by the winds since the First Age, until it ended in a platform that was just wide enough for a gryfon to stand on—and one did, a single sentry.

"The Wind Spire," Mar said softly to Kjorn. "A place of honor for the sentries of the highest regard to stand their watch." Lowering his voice, Mar added, "Your father stood there, once, when he was prince."

A jolt quickened Kjorn's heart, and he looked at the spire again, knowing its history, knowing his father's talons had touched it, knowing it had meant something to Sverin, to Per, and to Kajar. To himself.

"How fares he?" Mar asked, hesitant. "Your father?"

Kjorn only shook his head, tail twitching. "I don't know."

They stopped at the outskirts, where two great towers marked the end of the aerie, the rock formations fell away, and the land swept out again into empty desert. They stood in the shadow of the two stone towers, and just beyond them was the Wind Spire, and the sentry.

"Wait here," Mar said quietly. Before Kjorn could protest, Mar flew directly to the top of the spire, up to speak with the gryfon there.

Kjorn turned, looking behind them at the vast towers and pillars of the aerie, outlined now like great, frozen beasts under the stars. It had been foolish to come under Orn's terms. He wondered how much more foolish it would be to run away in the night.

Nilsine and Dagny drifted ahead to keep watch, leaving him to his thoughts, alert and waiting for Mar.

Rok strode up beside him, beak open. Before the rogue could ask, Kjorn slipped the golden chain from around his neck and returned it, wordlessly. His talons brushed the leather thong, on which hung Shard's fire stones.

Even Rok seemed to know this was not the moment for a wry comment, and glanced back to the aerie as he slid the chain around his neck. "Good of Mar to help out," he said, as if he couldn't stand the silence. "I thought he was a good sort. Not that I doubted you, of course. You would've figured it out."

"Thank you," Kjorn said dryly.

Nilsine approached, her steps deftly silent on the hard earth. "What is he doing up there? We should get moving, sire."

"Assuring our escape," Kjorn said, and the word tasted bitter on his tongue.

"Ever in a hurry," Rok murmured. "You haven't even said hello."

Nilsine's feathers puffed. Kjorn eyed them sideways, knowing their unhappy history of Rok poaching on Vanhar lands, and Nilsine catching him at it. He began to wonder how often Rok let himself be caught on purpose, just for chances to run Nilsine's feathers the wrong way.

"If it weren't for you," Nilsine said coldly, "we wouldn't be here."

"That's not really true," Dagny said as she returned to Kjorn's side.

"Be quiet, everyone. Please." Kjorn's head pulsed. "We wait for Mar. He's making sure the sentry won't sound alarm."

He wanted to curl up and sleep for a day. Even as he gazed across the desert night and thought of the relief he would feel at fleeing, his whole heart strained against it. He found himself oddly grateful that Fraenir stepped up next to him, for his size and bearing were very much like Shard—and he remained silent.

At last Mar returned, gliding back down to land in front of Kjorn. "She'll cooperate and turn a blind eye while you run. Stay aground for as long as you can," he instructed. "I'll stand the watch here to see you off. No one will follow if I can help it."

"Thank you, Mar," Dagny said. "We'll tell Brynja everything."

"I hope to see her soon," Mar said, eyeing Kjorn.

"My lord," Nilsine said, "let's be off."

Kjorn gazed at each of their faces. It was Fraenir's face, fierce and dedicated, that made his decision.

"I'm not leaving." In the blazing starlight, Kjorn could see the surprise that ticked one ear back and widened Mar's eyes. "This is my home. I'm here now, and I won't run away like a . . ." he'd planned to say thief, but with a glance at Rok, he said, "like a rabbit, in the night."

"You mean to go to Orn," Mar said flatly.

"No." Kjorn glanced around, noting the straggled shapes of kindling scattered across the ground. He brushed his talons over the pouch and the firestones. "I mean for Orn to come to me."

29

FIRES REKINDLED

COASTING LOW, SHARD SWEPT ACROSS the Winderost night, guiding his fellows by the stars. The wyrms usually hunted at night, and the moment he lifted into the air, his heart shot to a dizzying speed. He fought to keep his breaths even. The cool, damp air soothed his nerves, and the fact that Ketil had just flown this very stretch of ground.

She hadn't mentioned any trouble.

I shouldn't have let Kjorn go with only two for a guard. I knew he was walking into a snake nest with Orn . . .

Flying so low his wings nearly brushed the ground, Shard checked the stars and aligned himself along the great Bear. He'd learned that autumn to follow the line from the Bear's shoulder and hind foot, and that would lead him to the Dawn Spire. It might have been faster to fly high, but he couldn't convince himself or most of his company that the wyrms wouldn't find them.

The flight felt as if it took an age, gliding hard through the night, fighting the coolness of the ground, constantly checking above and around for signs of the wyrms. After two full marks, Shard realized he'd pulled too far ahead of his company, and heard Brynja hissing for him to slow down. Other than that, it was silent.

Oddly silent, for the number of gryfons who flew behind him.

In the end, it had been easier to sort out who would stay. Most of Shard's Vanir, the rogues, and the Vanhar remained behind, for the Vanhar wouldn't fight against other gryfons. They promised to scout the Outlands. Half of Shard's Vanir, many of the Aesir with Brynja, and roughly half of the Lakelanders flew in a long, wide formation behind.

Whatever Orn had in store, Shard was certain he wouldn't expect so many gryfons, and they would be ready. Ready, if Kjorn was injured or . . . worse.

The horror of the thought chilled Shard's muscles. The notion that he might have led Kjorn to his own execution and been far, far away when it happened sent cold and fury through him, and sharp, gnawing panic.

Then, an impossible glimmer snapped him from his growing dread.

An orange star winked and twitched some leagues ahead of him. Shard shook his head. Had he never seen fire, he would have mistaken it for a spirit, a spark, a reflection of starlight on water.

But he knew it to be fire. Since there had been no skyfire this far starward that he knew of, Shard guessed that Kjorn had made it, for Kjorn had the dragon firestones.

"*Kjorn!*" Surging forward, Shard rose higher and beat the air, plunging fast in great scoops and dives. Of course he was too distant to be heard yet, but the relief that burst open had to be voiced. He shouted his friend's name again, and the gryfons behind him strained to keep pace.

"Caution!" Asvander called, and Shard agreed.

They spiraled higher as they approached.

"Only one fire," Brynja observed, maintaining a circle just under Shard. "What shall we do, Shard?"

Shard hadn't expected fire, which surely meant Kjorn was alive.

Or Orn stole the dragon stones and figure how to spark a flame . . .

"If I may," Asvander said, beating the air near Shard.

"Yes, please."

"Let most of us land and approach on foot, where sentries are less likely to be watching for us. They'll expect us from the air. And they won't be able to see as well beyond the firelight. We can see what's happening and how best to approach, and leave our main force in the dark."

"Yes," said Shard, relieved he'd brought his friends after all. "Approach the fire, see what's happening. I'm going to stay aloft."

"I'll stay with Shard," Brynja said.

"Let's do it," said Shard, and Asvander peeled off, communicating their plan more quietly to the larger company, who followed him to the ground.

For the next moments as Shard and Brynja flew, it was silent. They couldn't see the rest of their fellows once those gryfons landed, and Shard was grateful.

"It looks awful," Brynja said quietly.

"I'm sorry," Shard said, looking toward the Dawn Spire.

"It wasn't you."

In the glow of a single bonfire, he made out the broken spires and bridges, and shuddered at the memory of lashing wyrm tails and powerful bodies smashing rock.

They glided closer, as silent as their wings would allow, and flew high above the Wind Spire and the fire that burned on the ground.

If there were sentries posted, they paid no mind to Shard and Brynja, if they saw them all.

As they drew nearer, Shard spied Kjorn, gold awash in orange flame, throwing great logs of juniper onto the bonfire at the border of the aerie. Recalling the stores of wood the gryfons of the Dawn Spire had once collected for their nightly fires, Shard wasn't surprised he was able to create such a blaze. Other gryfons worked with him—Shard made out Nilsine, the exile Rok, and Brynja's father.

"Oh, Father," Brynja breathed, her voice a mix of relief and pride.

Shard didn't see Dagny, and his heart quickened again.

He appeared to have arrived at the beginning of whatever was happening. Shouts rose, night sentries staring from their posts, but too amazed to move as Kjorn built his bonfire.

Brynja and Shard circled above the firelight, high above the Wind Spire, but were able to hear what happened next.

"Gryfons of the Dawn Spire, behold!" Kjorn's voice boomed in the dark, as if the fire itself had a voice. "Wake!"

"We fear the night no more!" roared Mar, leaping up to shower bark and kindling onto the roaring blaze and sending up a spiraling wave of sparks and spitting flames.

Movement in the air caught Shard's eye and his heart stuttered to his throat as he whipped around.

"Ssst, Shard! Brynja!"

In the growing, golden light he glimpsed Dagny, circling over them.

"Oh, Dagny!" Brynja exclaimed, flying up to meet her wingsister. "You're all right!"

"I knew I saw something," Dagny said, and didn't seem worried about the volume of her voice. Shard could see why, with the bonfire and Kjorn, big and golden and yelling, holding everyone's attention. "I thought you were just a very small wyrm," she chittered in amusement.

He saw that she held an unlit brand, of the kind the fire-keepers of the Dawn Spire used to light the nightly fires.

"What's happening?" Shard asked.

"The king has returned," Dagny said, at once with a grave and impish air. "I think he would've been subtle and polite, had Orn not knocked him in the head and imprisoned him. Now he's going to make a show of it."

"Oh." Shard looked down at the bonfire, casting Kjorn in molten gold, and listened to the cries of amazement ring out from all quarters of the aerie, and thought his wingbrother had succeeded. Fledges romped forward to behold the blaze, grown gryfons climbed or glided down from their nests, but the sentries remained at their posts. Shard could imagine their dilemma—attack the gryfons who returned fire to their home, or not?

Clearly they waited on Orn, who had yet to arrive.

"I'm going to him," Shard said, readying his wings to dive.

"No! Shard, wait, please." Dagny stretched her talons out to him. "You're a little late, but he won't mind."

"Late? Who won't mind?" Shard stared at her.

Dagny laughed. "Oh, Kjorn knew Ketil escaped. He knew once you heard he was captured, you would be on your way. He asked that when you show up, you help me."

Brynja laughed beside him, and Shard felt flustered to know his wingbrother knew him so well. She swooped a happy circle around Shard. "Help him with what?"

"Fetch a brand," Dagny crowed, holding out her talons to show that she held the dragon fire stones. "We're going to make the sun rise."

RATHER THAN MEET THE fire and strangeness with hostility, gryfons of the Dawn Spire poured from their nests, some dragging nestlings. A great throng ringed the bonfire, and Shard glanced back once during his task to see Kjorn outlined by the blaze, standing still and solid as a figure carved of gold.

The sentries, by that time, abandoned their posts. Dagny, Shard, and Brynja flew unimpeded to the great towers that still stood and still held remnants of kindling from the fires that had once burned every night, until the wyrm attack put them out.

While Kjorn waited for the aerie to gather to his silent beacon, Shard and the others rebuilt the pyres, but waited to light them until Dagny gave the word. Since Kjorn was being dramatic, she'd said, it was all in the timing.

"Here," Brynja said, gliding down to toss a load of branches on the top. "That should do it."

Shard dragged one last crackling juniper log and stuffed it into place. They stood on the pyre together for a moment, and Shard butted his head against Brynja's wing. "Thank you. For coming with me."

She ruffled her feathers, nipping his ears in reproach. "I told you once, Rashard, I'm not letting you fly from me again. But I'm glad you went after your wingbrother." She swiveled, and in the distant firelight, he could see her eyes gleam. "You wouldn't be the gryfon I fell in love with if you hadn't."

From the edge of the aerie, Kjorn's voice boomed like a rock-fall. "Orn, son-of-Throsver!"

Shard tensed, crouching and ready to fly. Brynja laid her wing over his back. "No. This is his to do."

Dagny swooped down to land with them. "Here," she whispered to Shard, though they were well out of earshot of the bonfire and Kjorn's audience if they spoke at normal volume. She handed him back the pouch with the fire stones. "I was going to do it, but it's better if it's you."

Shard slipped the leather thong over his neck and murmured his thanks, and felt better for having them. Not only were they the key to his fire, but in a way, they were his only remnant of Hikaru, even though a spirit had given them to him.

"We should get word to Asvander," Shard said, remembering the Lakelander waited just beyond the firelight.

"I think he'll figure out what's going on," Brynja said dryly.

Dagny nodded. "Once we light the fires, he'll know we're here."

They huddled then, in silence, watching below. Dagny waited for a signal.

Kjorn paced a circuit around his bonfire, and the whole aerie of the Dawn Spire stared as if he had walked out of the very flame.

Off to one side, Shard spied the exile, Rok, wearing his gold chain, his stance proud as a warrior now. His gaze was trained warily on Kjorn and the gryfons who surrounded him. Eyes gleamed in the fire, beaks opened, talons scuffed the dirt, but none made a sound except brief whispers, excited fledges and the smallest kits, who didn't know better.

Kjorn halted, tail whipping, and opened his wings. The firelight bounced gold off his feathers and Shard heard gryfons actually gasp and whisper his name before he spoke.

"I am Kjorn, son-of-Sverin, and I have come home. Where is your current king? Will the regent of the Dawn Spire not come and greet me?"

"I'm here."

Shard crouched, tail tip flicking, and pricked his ears as the throng parted for their current king. Brynja lowered herself next to Shard, with a glance at Dagny, but the other gryfess shook her head once. It was not time to light the pyres yet.

Shard had to admire Orn. The gryfon looked as Shard remembered him, bulky, tall, his feathers a modest, tawny hue with the faintest hint of sage green in the firelight. He was drawn more haggard by the long winter and the deaths during the Battle of the Dawn Spire. In facing the grandson of the king who'd left these Aesir in his care, the blazing flame and all it meant, Shard thought he looked admirably calm.

"Such theatrics, grandson of Per." Orn's gaze traveled up the pillar of flame, and a rush of whispers went in the wake of his words.

Theatrics indeed, Shard thought. *He brought your fire back to you.*

Expressions turned dark. Muttering rippled through the gathering, but Shard couldn't hear if they were against Orn, or in agreement.

Orn's cool look returned to Kjorn, and he didn't look as if he planned to acknowledge the miracle of the fire at all, but changed the subject. "Grandson of the coward who left us to the scourge of—"

"Speak of cowardice," Dagny muttered, and Brynja and Shard both hushed her.

"Yes," Kjorn snarled, cutting Orn off. "Let us speak of cowardice. Let us speak of how I was attacked, and dragged back to the place of my birth like a pronghorn carcass—"

"Enough." Orn drew himself tall. "Back to your nests, all of you." He whirled, wings open. "All of you, now! Walk on your own, or be *escorted!*"

"I say let them stay," Kjorn declared. "Let them stay, and hear us speak."

Slowly Orn turned back, every hackle feather on end, the odd shadows from the waving fire flaring and shifting over his features. "Very well."

"And let us meet in a more suitable place."

"Now," Dagny jabbed Shard with a talon. "That's my cue. Now, Shard, light the fire."

Quickly Shard withdrew the firestones, talons fumbling so he nearly dropped and lost them in the dark. He drew a breath, slowed down, and struck sparks while turning an ear to the kings.

Orn hesitated, then answered. "Yes. A fine idea. To the Dawn Spire itself. All of you."

Shard struck the stones together again. Sparks jumped, caught, and little flames licked up and trickled through the pyre. Quickly, Dagny brought forth brands she had built from their old stores of pitch and rough matter, lit them, and handed one each to Shard and Brynja.

"Brynja, light the crescent. I'll handle the rest. Shard—"

"I can't. I have to go to Kjorn, now."

The great mass of gryfons below had turned, following Orn as he led the way, with Kjorn shortly behind him. They were silent, walking toward the namesake of the aerie, the massive, twisting, crescent tower of stone.

Dagny hesitated, but must have seen something in Shard's face that told her not to argue. She took the flickering brand from him.

"I'll see you after, then!" With that, she hopped off the tower and glided toward the inner aerie.

Shard looked to Brynja. "I'll see you after."

"Be careful. Please." She looked him up and down, then flew toward the next pyre, the flaming torch grasped carefully in her talons. Shard had taught her to fly with fire, and it took some willpower not to stand and watch her proudly. As she paused near each, lighting the masses of stick and brush, flames licked up high. Then the next, and the next.

So in that way, as Kjorn, the mass of gryfons who followed in a daze, and Orn, walked, fires leaped up in their wake. Gasps of delight filled the night, along with exclamations of surprise and wonder.

Shard flew first to the outskirts to quickly gather Asvander and his band and catch them up, though they'd surely seen for themselves from where they'd waited. Then they winged fast to meet Kjorn and the mass of gryfons at the Dawn Spire itself, as fire sprang to life around them and the whole aerie glowed like sunrise.

30

PRINCE OF THE DAWN SPIRE

K JORN AND THE HOST OF gryfons approached the twisting spire of stone that was the namesake of the whole aerie. He kept his breath steady, his steps slow and deliberate, and admired the spire to distract himself from the throng and from Orn, who walked ahead.

Thick and curving like a crescent at the bottom, it jutted up from the ground like a gigantic fin, tapered and twisted near the top. Ledges ringed the inner curve and created sitting places, the tiers that the gryfons used to define their rank.

They filled it to the brim now, for Orn had been unable to keep out all of the gryfons who wished to see the confrontation, and the sentries became all but useless at controlling the pride. Some wedged at the ground-level entrance to the floor of the spire to watch, others flew up to take their places on the tiers.

One young gryfess, clutching a nestling, reached out to stroke Kjorn's tail feathers in awe as he passed, holding out her kit as if Kjorn might bless him. He paused, touched his beak to the fluffy head, and murmured his thanks. Other gryfons pressed at him, some in awe, some muttering darkly about his cursed feathers, until

265

to Kjorn's surprise, Asvander thunked down from above and drove back the onlookers. Mar was not far behind him, shoving through the crowd.

"What are you doing here?" Kjorn almost laughed in relief.

"I'll give you one guess," Asvander said.

"Shard—"

"I'm here!" His wingbrother appeared, like a shadow, swooping down out of the dark and nearly squashing the nearest sentry, who scrambled back with a hiss. But, Kjorn noticed, did nothing to stop him.

Kjorn did laugh, then. "I knew you would come."

Fierce green eyes scoured him. "Are you all right? Ketil said they attacked you."

"Well enough. A bump on the head." Kjorn glanced at Mar, and didn't elaborate.

The big sentry looked at Shard. "Brynja?"

Shard tilted his head to nod toward the fires. "She's helping Dagny. She'll be along. There's a good number of us, if anything happens."

"Thank you," Kjorn said with true gratitude, then observed as Mar simply stared at Shard a moment, and the gray gryfon ducked his head.

"Now if you don't mind," Kjorn said, nodding toward the mass of rustling, talking gryfons.

Shard lifted his ears. In the corner of his vision Kjorn saw other gryfons landing—his allies, Vanir and Lakelanders, ringing the inner crescent with the other onlookers. "Go, brother, we're here for you."

Kjorn nodded once and strode past them. He couldn't halt his momentum now and give the pride a chance to doubt his resolve. He walked directly to the center of the floor.

More gryfons flew in, old and young, stacking the tiers with shocked feathered faces and wide, staring eyes.

Kjorn paced a circle around the floor of the crescent, opening his broad wings in the swaying light of torches set into the rock walls at every level. Dagny had gone ahead, as promised, and lit the brands for Kjorn. He could see the effect it had on the pride as they gazed in amazement, first at the fires, then Kjorn himself.

He stopped again in the center of the packed dirt floor. "Hail, gryfons of the Dawn Spire! Hail, Aesir! Know that I am Kjorn, son-of-Sverin, who is the son of Per. Know that I am the rightful prince and future king of the Dawn Spire and the Reach, lord of the Ostral Shores, and brother to the pride of the Vanheim Shore."

At last silence fell, a rustling, buzzing, tense stillness.

One glance over Kjorn's wing showed him that some of the allies who'd followed Shard there saw faces they recognized, saw friends, sisters, brothers, relatives. A season ago, all of the gryfons had nested together.

Shard caught Kjorn's gaze as he circled around, gave his head the slightest nod.

Kjorn steadied himself. Pulsing, hot anger at how Orn had kidnapped him drove his long strides as he paced another circle. This was not how he had planned or hoped for it to happen. Orn had begun this with his cowardice. All pretense of camaraderie had fled Kjorn's heart. The Dawn Spire belonged to him, and these gryfons needed a new king.

He tilted his wings so the firelight could shine through his long flight-feathers and flash when he shifted. In that moment Kjorn understood that his father had always purposefully presented with his back to the sun, had known what effect the sunlight had on his feathers. Regret clawed his heart to think of Sverin, and he forced his father from his mind.

He gazed up at the rows of standing places, and wondered what tiers all the cursed Aesir of the Silver Isles had held.

Not cursed, he reminded himself. *Shard said we were blessed with dragon's blood, that everything we are will be more so.*

Warm, prickling pride flushed his skin.

He looked up, wanting to imagine his father at the top, only to see that Orn himself stood at the highest tier. And beside Orn . . . Kjorn had to remind himself that the gryfess above him was not his mother. His mother was dead.

"My mother's sister," Kjorn called to the queen, a severe, but lovely, tawny gryfess with eyes that matched his own. "Lady Esla, I bid you very fair winds. You know me."

If she felt anything at all, she held it absolutely frozen behind blue eyes. "I know you, son-of-Sverin."

Kjorn craved more, but understood why she couldn't yet give it. The acknowledgment was enough for that moment.

"Son of cowards," boomed Orn. "Son of the cursed, who left their curse to us."

"I had better plans for our meeting," growled Kjorn, and the acoustics of the curved stone carried his voice to every tier. "You have forced this by my kidnapping and attempted murder." Dark gasps and murmurs swept the crowd. "But know this—you may still have honors and comfort for you and your family for the rest of your lives, if you bow to me this night." He met the astonished eyes of the old regent, stepping forward. "You have my gratitude for stewarding the pride for so long, but the time has come for you to step down."

"I will not bow to you." Orn's low rumble rolled down the rock crescent. "You will bring your curse back to blight us—"

"I won't argue with you, Orn," he declared. "Though I must believe that Per left not because he was fleeing, but in attempt to draw the wyrms away. Either way, it was not me. I know the truth now. I've come to set it right. I've come to drive out the enemy."

He raised his wings higher, and let warm firelight touch his face. "I have now at my command the strength of the Ostral Shores, the Vanhar, the exiles from all lands beyond, and the estranged Aesir from the Dawn Reach. You should know that they wish me to assume my place on that tier where you stand, and they will fight to see it so."

"You're lying," Orn snarled, his hard gaze turning squarely on Shard. "You have exiles, oath-breakers and traitors at your back, and they'll do you no good in battle. Your coward father did not even join you—"

"So too do the lions of the First Plains, the united packs of painted wolves, and the eagles of the Voldsom Narrows wish me to assume my place as king."

Kjorn drew a long breath, and glanced over his shoulder at Shard. His wingbrother tilted his head in encouragement before his gaze flicked to the restless mass of gryfons all around them, then back to Kjorn with a pointed look. Kjorn agreed. This couldn't go on much longer, especially not with Orn pointing out Shard's presence there.

"I challenge you," Kjorn said flatly, not planning to waste more time or energy arguing, nor to let Orn insult him or his forefathers any more.

As soon as he'd landed, Kjorn had begun sizing Orn up. Older, yes, but wide in shape and larger, he reminded Kjorn of Hallr, Halvden's father from the Silver Isles. They shared a common ancestor, Ingmar, of heavy, mountain stock. A gryfon just past his prime, he still looked able and ready to fight. Kjorn had faith he could defeat him, but knew it wouldn't be the best way.

"What," Orn scoffed, "single combat? I know stories of the duels of kings. A barbaric practice of the Second Age. You defeat me and win all these gryfons' hearts and minds, is that it?"

"No." Kjorn folded his wings, lifting his head high. "I challenge you to follow us to the Voldsom Narrows, and on to the Outlands. I challenge you to follow me into battle against our mutual foe, and to let these gryfons fight. Fight alongside me, and after, if you still feel you are king of the Dawn Spire, we will settle then."

The crescent was still.

All the eyes that had stared at him now stared at Orn, waiting on his answer. At last Orn's eyes gleamed with understanding. Kjorn didn't just want to win the Dawn Spire, he wanted to win hearts. He wanted peace, he wanted the gryfons to desire his leadership, not to blame him for turning families against each other.

"You will kill us all," Orn breathed. "You know not what you face."

"I do know," Kjorn cut in quietly. His voice carried up the echoing stone. "I have faced and routed the wyrms once—"

"Lies," Orn hissed again, but Kjorn saw his surety slipping, his fearful walls cracking before the restless pride of gryfons around him.

"It is the truth," Kjorn said firmly, and behind him, his allies shouted their agreement. Kjorn continued. "We have fought the wyrms, and we have won. We can do it again, this time once and for all."

"You're mad," Orn growled. The sharp desperation of fear and doubt tightened the old gryfon's eyes, sleeked the feathers of his head and neck. When he realized the crowd of gryfons was now intent on Kjorn's every word, his desperation seemed to grow.

Kjorn's gaze slipped to Lady Esla, and the gryfess was watching Orn with a neutral expression, though her ears had ticked back a slight degree in disapproval.

"It's my understanding," Kjorn continued, "that those raised at the Dawn Spire are raised as warriors, proud to fight, and ready to die. Or has that changed since Per left?"

Orn gazed at him, and Kjorn saw not anger or hatred, but sudden, impossible weariness. "But die for what?"

"What more honorable way to die than in defense of our very home ground?" Restless murmurs agreed with him. "The Dawn Spire itself stands. You have families and warriors here, still, ready to serve. How have you honored those who died during the wyrm's attack on our home? Will you honor them by further hiding in dens like rabbits, fearing the night, as I was raised to?"

Kjorn cast his gaze around the crescent, meeting as many eyes as he could before returning his gaze to Orn. "Or will you honor them by finishing the fight, once and for all? Stop cowering, and lead gryfons to their rightful place alongside all the Named creatures, as lords of the Winderost!"

For what seemed a year, Orn stared at him.

A male voice near the top tiers broke the frozen quiet. "I, for one, will fight." Searching, Kjorn found Mar. Gryfons swiveled and craned their necks to see him. Mar looked at Orn. "With or without your blessing, sire."

"I will fight," rumbled Asvander, coming forward beside Kjorn. "Will the sentries of the Dawn Spire join me?"

A cautious rumble of affirmation answered him from all corners of the crescent.

"I will fight!"

"I would die for the Dawn Spire!"

Calls and battle cries echoed down the ring. The silent chamber exploded into shouting and roars.

"Let our kits see us fight for our home!"

"This is a true king!" yelled a grizzled male. "I will fight even if it be my last."

When the wave faded, a single, flint-sharp voice rang out. "I, too, will fight."

Orn looked in shock to his mate. "Esla, this is madness. Think of our son."

The queen perked her ears, watching in challenge. "I am, my lord."

At that, Orn looked beaten. A rush of giddiness nearly quenched the anger in Kjorn's heart. A steady, beating murmur rose in the gryfons surrounding them.

The words were *we will fight*, and wings opened to beat the air.

Talons slapped the stone.

Like a thundering heartbeat in the Winderost night, the will of the Dawn Spire made itself known.

Kjorn walked the circuit of the floor, once, roaring his approval, letting gryfons touch his bright feathers for whatever meaning it had for them, and shouting his call to action.

Feeling fierce, he ended at Shard, turning to look at his friend in triumph. "Shard!"

"Congratulations, brother." But Shard didn't look triumphant or pleased.

Kjorn's thundering heart skipped to see that, standing half in shadow, half in fire, the son of Baldr watched him with uncertainty. The quiet, gray gryfon watched him, his green eyes holding something older than his years, something that shot doubt down Kjorn's spine. He found he could not look away.

"I need to speak to you about the wyrms." Shard's gaze didn't leave his face. They might've been the only two gryfons standing there. Kjorn began to speak, and Shard lifted his head higher. "Now."

31

CURSE OF THE AESIR

SALTY WAVES BUBBLED AND TRICKLED around Ragna's talons as she combed the beach below the nesting cliffs. She tossed a mollusk onto a pile she was collecting, and eyed a gull that waddled too close.

"Ahh, a little food?" His elegant beak opened wide. Dusty, speckled feathers marked him as a juvenile, and she realized she hadn't heard a gull speak in years. They were getting bolder, or she was no longer afraid to hear them. As promising as it was, their words didn't add much meaning to her life.

"Great lady! Great queen! Have you food? A little token? Ah?"

"Away with you." Ragna swiped at him and he trundled back, opening his wings. As a fledge, she had learned the hard way not to feed gulls out of kindness. Offer one a morsel, and soon the rest would mob her.

Spring was sluggish in coming, but all the ice was off the sea and the ground, which made foraging and fishing less treacherous. Ragna spent most of her afternoons away from the others now, telling herself she enjoyed the solitude, puzzling over Ollar's strange death and the promise of Maja yet to return.

Enough Vanir had returned that they taught each other fishing, brought in decent catches, and she didn't have to brave the icy water again. Let younger huntresses do that. Cold still stung the winds, and when it precipitated, it became more icy rain than snow.

The mussels were for Thyra, who in the late stage of her pregnancy couldn't seem to get enough of them. Ragna cared for her, because helping Sigrun took her mind off other things, and she felt that showing Thyra respect won her some peace from the Aesir.

"Kind lady!" other gulls called, floating above her. "Lovely lady, kind queen, a little food? Ahh? Food for poor and loyal beggars? Ah!"

Ragna growled. She remembered how Stigr used to lure in hordes of gulls with herring scraps, then dive into their midst just to watch them explode into winged clouds of white. Hard longing for her brother and her son must have made her look wretched, for even the gulls decided not to trouble her further. The youngest beggar took off, crying for its mother.

"Pale fools. Not two thoughts to bash together and make an idea." A sharper voice, edged with more intelligence, addressed Ragna from above.

Mantling over her precious pile of delicacies, Ragna peered up to see a skua on the boulder nearest her.

"Now *I*," croaked the dusky seabird , "I would give you news, great lady, in exchange for a bite. News, from over the sea."

Ragna huddled over her hard-collected treasures. Skua were notorious bandits, unscrupulous thieves. As a fledge, she'd been attacked by a pair, and lost the very first fish she'd ever caught. "What news?"

"First, food."

Ragna grabbed a mollusk and made to toss it to him.

"Crack it!" demanded the pirate bird. "Crack it, or I'll forget everything I know from hunger."

"Pest," Ragna growled, and smacked the shell against the boulder. She tossed it up to the skua, who caught it in his beak, then picked out the meat. Ragna waited.

"Many creatures," he said, one webbed foot nudging the discarded shell off the boulder. "Flying this way over the sea."

Her blood surged and she stood, wings open. Maja, at last! Or maybe even Shard. She hardly dared to hope. "From what direction?" Instinctively, Ragna looked windward. "How far away, by your reckoning?"

"Not far. But I can't quite remember." He opened his long wings and bobbed his head, opening his beak. Ragna grumbled and cracked him another morsel, tossing it high. He caught it, ate it, eyed her, and laughed, shoving from the rock to glide out over the choppy water.

"Wretch!" Ragna shouted. His laughter rolled into long calls, and frigid water washed over her toes, as if Tor scolded her for dealing with thieves, anyway.

"Can I be of help, my lady?"

Ragna whirled, ready to snap and pluck the next Nameless bird to interrupt her solitude. But rather, there stood Vidar, his presence oddly like a balm.

Like her, he was ever-wrapped in his mourning, his losses clouding him like fog over clearer water. Though it had only been three years, the sight of him still surprised her. The sight of every face that had gone missing during the Conquering and in the years after surprised, delighted, then saddened her. The way he had forgiven Sverin made her proud of him, sad for him, and glad to know him.

He was a well-built Vanir, slender, but every rift of his body lined with muscle from fishing and flying. His feathers were like Sigrun's, brown but intricately patterned as the pale sand of a river bed. The sight of him brought Ragna comfort, for it reminded her of happier days, her kithood, her old friendships. She longed for Baldr, for Stigr.

At least, she thought, fighting bitterness, *I still have my wingsister.* Though Sigrun would be run ragged until the females whelped, and her heart ran ragged by Caj tending to Sverin.

And now Vidar, back from exile, father to a slain son, watched her with the implacable calm of a still lake, reflecting her own musings back at her. She remembered, with painful nostalgia, that he had once thought to court Sigrun, but Stigr would brook no competition even for a gryfess he hadn't openly claimed, and had driven him off with a single spar.

"Yes," she managed tightly to his offer of help, realizing she stood there silently. "If you would help me carry these to Sigrun's den, I would be grateful."

"Shall we gather more, to replace what you gave the bird?"

"Yes," she said again, with relief. Clouds crawled along the dawn-ward horizon, and she wanted to enjoy the weather while she could. She hadn't wanted to go back to the cliffs just yet, not face anyone else. The gulls had left and so she felt less wary of leaving her bounty. Keeping some attention trained on the pile, she walked with Vidar farther down the beach.

"How fares Dagr? He seems to have fallen in well enough with the others." By others, she meant the males his own age, the half-bloods, and the other Aesir.

"Well enough. He barely leaves Astri's side, and I believe she finds true comfort there."

Ragna felt a little relief. They walked on in quiet for a few moments before Vidar spoke again.

"I saw Eyvin this morning."

She had noticed that Vidar and Eyvin were no longer nesting in the same den. Ragna hadn't intended to ask him anything about her, but since he started it, she lifted her ears. "Oh, yes?"

Vidar looked impossibly weary, his voice dull and deep. "She isn't the gryfess I remember. After the Conquering, Ragna, I... She seemed so strong, so sure." He paused to dig at a promising pockmark in the sand. "We did love each other. I wanted a family. She was honorable. Like Caj, I suppose. I thought she would accept me back."

"She is honorable. But even the best of us have our breaking points. Sverin sent you away, and killed—"

"Yes." With a huff, he shoved his talons into the sand, and came up with a clam. "Ha." Crouched, he turned and tossed the clam to the rest of Ragna's forage. Then he remained there, staring at the line where the ocean met the sky.

"Vidar," Ragna murmured. "Are you all right?" The moment she asked, she felt like a fool. Of course he wasn't.

"I miss him," he said tightly, looking down at the sand on his talons. "I miss my son, and my mate, and the life we were trying to make. Curse it! Bright Tor's wings, I never should have flown that night. I don't know what I was thinking!"

As if a wing slapped her, Ragna realized, suddenly, how self-absorbed she had been. She'd been avoiding Vidar, but he didn't blame her, or Eyvin, or possibly even Sverin for any of it. He blamed himself for being exiled.

"Oh, my friend," she whispered. "Vidar . . . It was Per's ridiculous laws. It was never your—"

"I left my sons," he snarled, turning his eyes to her, his features ragged, beak agape and eyes wide as if in physical pain. "All because I just wanted to stretch my wings in the starlight. I knew better. Ridiculous laws or not, I knew them, and I made a choice."

Watching him, Ragna saw as if in bright crystal what Sverin saw when he looked at her. Regret. Anguish. Useless remorse over things that could no longer be changed.

The regretting, waiting Widow Queen.

Perhaps, in this, the Aesir had the right of it.

"Let us mourn," she said, haltingly extending a wing to cover him. He thrust up his wings to shrug her off. "My friend," she continued. "Let us mourn, and then move on. There's much to be glad for. You have a son, still. You have a new daughter, who will bear Einarr's kit. And Eyvin—"

"That is all true," he said gruffly, not looking at her. "But not Eyvin. I've begged her forgiveness. She won't give it. She thinks I exiled myself on purpose. I cannot be with her now. I hope . . . I hope she returns with the Aesir to their land."

Never in all her days had Ragna heard of a mated pair of gryfons parting ways except by death. Such a bond was unbreakable in Tor's eyes. Sigrun had once said she thought love was like a broken wing, to be set and re-set after such tests and trials, and grow stronger at the broken points.

Ragna wasn't sure she could agree. How many times could a wing be broken and re-shaped until it lost its power, and never could fly true? If Vidar and Eyvin had changed too much, perhaps they couldn't love each other anymore.

Ragna wondered, then, if the opposite were true of enemies.

A stiff breeze gusted off the sea, and the skua's words came back to her.

She embraced her new thoughts with relief. "I believe it may almost be time for those decisions. The thief told me he saw creatures flying over the sea, a great number of them. It could be Maja, or even Shard."

Vidar looked at her, ears flicking back. "Creatures, though? He didn't say gryfons?"

The question Ragna had dismissed before rose again with his simple observation. "I . . . thought he'd said it that way just to vex me."

"That sounds more like something a raven would do." He studied Ragna thoughtfully, then looked out over the ocean, squinting against the gray glare on the waves, his voice dipping with foreboding. "Whatever he meant, I'm sure he meant it truthfully."

Feeling suddenly chilled by the rising wind, Ragna looked out toward the water as well.

How far, by your reckoning?

Not far.

Not far for a small seabird was not far at all, for a gryfon.

"My lady," Vidar murmured, and pointed his talons windward. A creeping cold gnawed up Ragna's muscles as she followed his indication, and along the horizon, she spied a dark line. She would have called it clouds, but it undulated with the movement of living things. It might have been a mass of gryfons, but she knew in her heart it was not.

She knew the flight of gryfons, even an unorganized group, but she knew not this movement, this slower, writhing mass of bodies flying hard toward her islands.

"What in all blazes," Vidar breathed, pressing protectively closer to her. It was tempting to stand there, to stare, to wonder, as one might halt in the path of an avalanche to behold its might even at the risk of burial.

Queen, her heart reminded her in a whisper. *Act.*

"Come," she said, steeling her voice. "We must tell everyone. We must go. Now. Find Thyra, and Sigrun, and bring them to Sverin's den."

She didn't know the name of the nightmare flying their way, but she had a feeling that an Aesir would.

"Yes, my lady," Vidar said, and took off. Ragna followed. A few gryfons stood on the cliffs, looking out over the sea. She heard remarks of wonder and fear as they, too, spied the dark mass.

Flaring hard, Ragna dropped onto the rock landing outside Sverin's den. The guards at the mouth of the cave, Andor and Halvden, startled aside.

"My lady—"

"Fetch Caj," she said. "Bring him here, and any elder Aesir you see along the way." When they blinked at her, she gaped her beak and flapped her wings once, raising her talons. "Do I mumble?"

They sputtered and jumped from the cliff. The wind of their beating wings swept across Ragna's face and back and she shouted into the den.

"Sverin! What blight is in my skies? Sverin! Come out now, and see what I see!"

So bright was the day, and so dim the cave, she barely saw him until he emerged from the back of the nest, where he'd clearly been sleeping. He slept too much. It wasn't healthy for a grown gryfon to sleep so much, but then, she thought, what else was he to do?

After his atonement, as Thyra called it, when he'd finally heard the last of those who wished to lodge complaints against him, he barely stirred from his nest but to eat. Ragna didn't pester him after that, and got her reports on his sanity from Caj.

"My lady?"

She'd never seen him look un-regal, except in his madness, but now his feathers pressed flat to one side of his neck and a small twig stuck out from the long feathers of his chest. Ragna managed not to slap it aside so he would look more like a warrior, more ready to deal with whatever was heading their way.

He shook himself, rustled, sleeked again and gazed at her, puzzled and wary. They had barely spoken since the end of the atonements.

"Come here, and look. What do you see?" She resisted the urge to shove him, not that it would have done any good. He looked as though he weighed much more than he did, for how slowly he picked himself across the stone floor. But he stepped outside with her, and narrowed his eyes against the light.

"You haven't come in days." His voice barely registered, low and rumbling.

"Look, look, there." Ragna jerked her beak. Standing a wing-length away from him, she watched his neutral face, then looked out to the horizon, peering at the strange, squirming shadow.

"Clouds," he rumbled. "The shadow of a storm."

"It isn't," she hissed. "Look at it. What is it?"

His crimson hackle feathers, those that faded like sunset fire in scarlet on his back and wings, slowly ruffled. "Clouds."

"Son of Per."

His black talons clenched so hard at the rock she thought they would break. "It isn't possible, they don't fly in the day."

"Is this your scourge?" Ragna backed away from him, seeing a change stealing over his face, seeing horror seal back his ears and turn the blacks of his eyes to pin pricks. "Did you bring this to my home? What is it, Sverin, speak!"

His name was slipping from him, Ragna saw. He didn't hear her as he backed away, back toward the darkness of the cave. "They only fly at night, this can't be—"

"This is your curse?" she hissed. "You brought your curse to my islands, and you will not flee it now! Stand and be a king! Be the king you never were." She leaped, and without slicing with her talons, slapped him across the head.

In shock he fell back from her, and stared, half crouched. In a fight, she was no match for him, for any Aesir, but he looked cowed, amazed she would touch him.

"Sverin," she growled. "Son of Per. Father of Kjorn. Once-king. You will not flee this fight again. Tell me what flies our way."

He stared at her, and she knew he saw her, heard her, that he still knew his name. But the breath came from him in hard gasps, his wings twitched under golden chains and he seemed to have lost his voice.

"For Kjorn," she said, and watched light come into his face again. "For Kjorn, Sverin. For your pride. Tell me what flies our way."

His beak tapped together. He stepped toward her, looking grateful, his gaze fixed upon her face—as if to look away, or to look outside again at the encroaching monsters—would drive him back over the edge. "I can't," he breathed.

Then he didn't have to. In that moment, Andor and Halvden returned, and at their heels flew two elders of the Aesir, Vidar, Dagr, and Sigrun. Shuffling on the rocks outside told Ragna that Caj and Thyra climbed down the cliff trail.

Sigrun found Ragna, pressed her wing against Ragna's. "Dragons," uttered the healer. "My sister, my queen. The curse of the Aesir will fall on us."

"We must flee," said Caj, and to hear those words from him, above all gryfons, sent quivers of terror down Ragna's back.

"Surely not," she said. "We can fight—"

"Do you want to know what Ollar died of?" Caj snapped.

Ragna and Sigrun looked at him, and Thyra, whose lovely lavender face was drawn and pale around the eyes, her feathers sleek as a threatened serpent.

But it was Sverin who answered. "Fear," he hissed. "He died of fear. We will all—"

"Silence," barked one of the elders. "It was your cowardice that brought—"

"Must we really run?" Thyra asked her father. "We have Vanir now, more warriors, surely—"

"We cannot fight them!" Sverin said, his gaze wholly trained on Ragna. "Tell them this is foolish, tell them . . ."

"Stay with us," Ragna said to him over the sudden chaos in the den, the two elders arguing, Halvden and Andor stepping from their posts to listen, Caj and Thyra arguing. "Sverin." Ragna couldn't look away from his face.

"My brother." Caj's calm voice and raised wing silenced the din.

With relief Sverin looked at him, away from Ragna, and for a moment it was as if the sun went behind a cloud, so intense had his attention been on her. Ragna drew away to listen to Sigrun, to hear what the other Aesir had to say, since Sverin had failed her.

"Tell me exactly what they are," she said to Caj.

The big Aesir, his wing draped over Sverin's back, spoke quietly, his voice flat. "Great beasts, my lady. Reptile, winged, as long as ten gryfons beak to tail and taller than a cedar."

"I will send scouts, to speak—"

"They don't speak," hissed one of the elders. Sverin had fallen silent, huddled under Caj's wing like a fledge. "They destroy. They consume your name. They—"

Caj interrupted, still matter-of-fact. "They're Nameless, Voiceless. They don't understand. They won't hear even if you go yourself, my lady."

"Like a mouse spying a serpent," said the female elder, "you'll lose your name. You'll die of terror, just like Ollar."

Caj nodded once, and the fact that he didn't argue or claim that was exaggeration steeled Ragna's resolve. "They hunt gryfons. But they've only ever flown at night. We thought they couldn't, in daylight."

"Well they're flying in the day now," Ragna said, doing her best not to snap and snarl. Perhaps it wasn't the fault of the Aesir the wyrms had come. Or perhaps it was, and they'd been lucky these ten long years. But obviously they'd caught wind of their cursed prey over the sea, and now came to finish whatever was on their long and hateful agenda.

Ragna tried very hard not to blame them, and mostly failed.

"What will they do?" Thyra asked, with eyes only for her father.

"They'll attack," Caj said, his voice pitched so low it sounded like falling stone. "They'll slaughter without sense, reason, or honor. And we don't have the strength to fight them. In this, you must trust me."

"Then we must leave the cliffs," Thyra said briskly, looking out to the horizon.

The mass defined itself now. Ragna counted over a dozen individual creatures. She couldn't quite make out their forms, just the individual motes in the dark cloud.

From the dawnward sky, clouds piled on themselves, turning iron with a storm. Thyra looked back to them, her gaze lighting on each face when no one answered her. "We must get all of the young, the old, and the pregnant females to safety."

"Where?" The hopeless rasp came from Sverin.

All eyes slid to him. His red feathers ruffed up, talons clenched the ground, and ears lay flat to his skull. "Where do you think we can go?"

"Underground," Sigrun said quietly, eyeing Sverin, and Ragna could tell she didn't add, *like when we fled from you.*

Caj nudged Sverin, voice firm. "To the caves, my brother. To the wolf caves, underground. They won't find us there. You'll—*we'll* be safe."

"Then let us go now," Thyra said. "They're moving fast, so we must go now, calmly, and orderly. I will gather the pregnant females with me. Mother?" It was a request to follow.

She walked to the entrance and paused, looking at Halvden and taking his measure.

With a sideways look at Sverin, Thyra gave her orders to Halvden. "Gather all able-bodied, gather all males of fighting age, and all females not heavy with kit, all fit to fly. Gather all who called themselves the King's Guard this winter past, and prove yourselves. You are my guard now, and you will hold back this scourge until the pride is safe—until your mate, and your unborn kit, and the rest of the pride are safe. My father believes you could be a great warrior. Now is your chance to prove it. Do you understand?"

Halvden gazed at her, and Ragna saw a trace of determination lace itself across the emerald face. He mantled, low. "I do, my lady."

With a glance at Sverin, whose crouching and cowering did nothing to inspire, he rumbled Andor's name and both sentries left the cave. Dagr left with them.

Ragna heard them shouting names into the wind as they sprang into the air. Thyra left the cave with Sigrun and the two elder Aesir, and Sigrun gave Ragna a fierce, encouraging look on her way.

"Sverin," said Caj. He, Sverin, and Ragna were the only gryfons left in the king's den. "Sverin, come, help me guard the rear. This is our chance for redemption, my brother, our chance to face—"

"They never fly in the day," Sverin rasped.

Caj drew back from him, folding his wing. "Sverin."

"I won't," he growled, whipping back. "Have you forgotten how horrid. . . ."

Caj stepped toward him and Sverin jerked back with a hiss.

"Go, Caj," Ragna snapped. "We're wasting time. I will speak to him."

"I can't leave him, not again—"

"To your daughter," Ragna said. "Caj, go to your daughter, to the pride. *They* need you. Sverin is able but unwilling. Others need your help. You know this danger, and they do not. Go to them."

Visibly torn, Caj stared at her, then Sverin, who hunched near his nest, his gaze now fixed on the line of darkness. Distantly, thunder cracked. Then someone called for Caj, he gave Ragna a pleading look, and he left.

Ragna eyed the growing cloud of wyrms, and tried to imagine herself as ice, clear and strong. They would be on the nesting cliffs fast, and Halvden would certainly have the chance to prove himself.

They all would.

32
THE WINDS OF WAR

S HARD WATCHED KJORN PACE BEFORE him as a cloudy sunrise glowed around the Dawn Spire. They'd been given a great nest high in the cliffs, lined with soft pelts and chips of juniper bark at the back for a fresh scent.

Around the fires, hearts grew alight with war.

The night before, Shard had managed to tell Kjorn of the silence in the Voldsom and the Outlands, then they hadn't gotten to discuss it further, as gryfons dragged him away, demanding stories of the Aesir who had left ten years ago.

Shard had been mobbed by friends from the Dawn Spire. All night, it felt, gryfons had assailed Shard with their disbelief that he lived, with questions, with relief, or sometimes with anger.

While Kjorn walked among the pride, Shard gave up and had tried to stay out of the way. Brynja helped him find a quiet corner to observe, then had left to spend time with her family. In the smoke and firelight, in the shouting and singing and boasting, the night had seemed an endless, chaotic dream.

Later he'd met Mar again, and Brynja's mother, both of whom seemed unsurprised at Brynja's announcement that she and Shard had chosen each other. The more difficult conversation, about Brynja leaving the Winderost for the Silver Isles, would come another time.

No sooner had he finally found Kjorn again, when Queen Esla herself bid Kjorn come and meet her kit, his cousin. Shard hadn't seen him again until the prince crawled into their quarters and collapsed in a heap at his side.

So he hadn't gotten to speak to Kjorn, truly, until the morning. *After* he'd gotten his blood hot surrounded by battle-ready gryfons who'd been chafing to fight their enemy for years.

At last Kjorn stopped in front of Shard, and he saw by the cant of the golden head he'd made a decision. "I think . . . we should still be prepared for a fight. The wyrms could be in hiding."

Shard dug a talon against the dirt floor. He smelled rain. "I'm telling you, they aren't there. I know it in my heart. Have we heard roars? I and others flew across the land last night, and not a wyrm in sight. Before, they always came down on any who flew at night, if they could find us. And my dream, Kjorn. Rhydda was flying over the ocean. She remembered a red gryfon, and she saw Sverin in my mind."

Kjorn ducked his head, looking outside. His feathers puffed slowly against the chill, or with frustration. Without lifting his head higher, he looked at Shard, fierce as a mantling hawk. "We have to meet at the Voldsom, at least. We have to honor the plan we told the Lakelanders, the lions, the Vanhar. Shard, half of the reason the gryfons of the Dawn Spire are following me is because they finally get to fight their enemy."

"I think it would be wasted time." Shard tried to keep his voice neutral. "Don't you think they would still follow you, if you offered them peace instead of war?"

Kjorn paced, tail lashing. "I do see your point, Shard. I do. Please understand that we have to try. We have to go, we have to look. I've told everyone there will be a war."

"You told everyone you would rid the Winderost of the wyrms, and maybe you already have. Maybe they fled after the Battle of

Torches." Below them, voices stirred the morning air. Warriors emerging from their nests to meet at the Wind Spire. Shard hesitated before adding, "Do you remember what Ajia and the Vanhar told you, that you confessed to me?"

Looking lost, Kjorn stared at him. "Which part?"

"I came to find the truth about why your grandfather flew to the Silver Isles." Shard stood, managing to hold his tail still, to hide his growing frustration and dismay. "Then, I thought that you would make a better king here, because you are honorable and true, and it's your birthright. But now—"

"I'm raising the Sunwind."

"Yes," Shard said quietly, and Kjorn gusted a sigh. "The wind of war." He stepped forward. Kjorn eyed him warily. "You told me you would be open to peace, but all I see is that you're preparing war, preparing everyone else for war, letting gryfons like Asvander tell you it's what everyone wants—"

"I have to honor the plan," Kjorn said, lifting his wings.

"Kjorn, if the wyrms are flying to the Silver Isles, we have no time to lose. Think of Thyra—"

"I am," Kjorn said, his voice harsh. Shard regretted pushing him, but his muscles felt tight with unease and foreboding. "I cannot leave things uncertain here before I return with her. Shard . . ." He met Shard's gaze, then looked away. "Just, promise me you will stay by my side."

Shard gazed at him, struck. Then he realized Kjorn thought that if he disagreed with him, Shard would fly, would leave on his own, return to the Silver Isles.

And the worst was, he'd considered it. "Of course I will, Kjorn. You do understand my urgency though?" Shard asked tightly.

"Yes. I do. I promise, my brother." Such relief glowed in his face, Shard felt horrible for ever considering leaving on his own. "Whatever happens here will happen swiftly. I will see to it."

"Just remember the dragon blessing," Shard said quietly. Kjorn tilted his head, and Shard recited, "*Whatever you are will be more so.*"

Kjorn lowered his head briefly, touched Shard with his wingtip reassuringly, then pivoted and leaped from the den. Shard stared after him, at the hole of empty, cloudy sky and the view of the canyon beyond the den. Weariness needled at his eyes.

He walked to the edge of the den, looked out over the Dawn Spire and the ruined towers from his previous mistake.

The dragons of the Sunland had a unique way of training their warriors, relying on principles of the elements. They learned the way of earth, to be steady and defend. After that, they learn the art of airy evasion, then of fire, to attack. And they learned of water, to flow, to use their opponent's strength and energy against them, no matter what direction it came at them.

Today, Shard thought grimly, *I will be like water.*

Spying Kjorn gliding through the canyon, he leaped and sped to catch up, in silence. They flew toward the nightward edge of the aerie, and without further words, they landed at the appointed spot to wait for the rest of Kjorn's army.

As warriors, huntresses, young, and old, gathered to follow them, Shard watched for familiar faces. He saw those he'd hunted with that autumn past, saw those who'd fought when the wyrms attacked the Dawn Spire.

The queen came, and many gathered near her, rather than Kjorn, as if unsure whose war they were fighting.

There was one gryfon Shard didn't see. As the Dawn Spire mounted its army in the morning light, Shard searched for Orn.

Brynja found Shard as the last of the volunteers flocked to Kjorn. "What troubles you?" Her voice was husky, her body roiling with the tension before a fight. Shard leaned into her, seeking enthusiasm.

"I don't see Orn."

Brynja tilted her head, searching, then lifted her beak to point to the Wind Spire. Shard looked up, and there spied the aging monarch, watching his pride pour out of the Dawn Spire to Kjorn's side. He watched, Shard thought, with regret, with anger, his wings open slightly as if he could mantle and shield them all.

As if he sensed Shard looking, Orn met Shard's eyes across the distance.

Compelled by a gnawing mix of strange pity and frustration, Shard dipped his head in respect. Orn stood frozen a moment, then inclined his head. The old king watched as Kjorn called the final summons, watched as the gold prince sprang from the ground, and Shard sensed he was watching still as his pride of ten years left their home to follow Kjorn to battle.

THE SUN WAS HIGH on their backs as they came in sight of the Voldsom Narrows.

Shard tried not to look behind them again. Foreboding closed a storm over his heart every time he beheld the host that Kjorn led toward the maze of canyons.

Over three hundred gryfons strong, all the able-bodied Dawn Spire Aesir, with some just barely out of fledge-hood and eager to make their initiation by battle against the wyrms. A contingent of ten healers joined them, with apprentices beside. Kjorn appointed Asvander First in Command, and he led a long, multi-tiered wedge of sentinels. Huntresses, in their own ranks, flew above.

"Kjorn," Shard murmured, then had to raise his voice over the wind. Many flew in silence, but many talked, and Shard fancied they sounded like a windstorm through pine trees, and that he could hear the thunder of three hundred hearts.

"Yes?" Kjorn looked fully at him, as if to prove he was still listening and paying attention.

"Some of them are too young."

"Of course they are." Kjorn glanced behind them. "They'll stay at the back, assisting the healers. But this is a moment that will be legend, Shard. I couldn't refuse them a chance to witness."

"Couldn't you?"

"Shard, it's already decided. They'll be as safe as they can be. They saw their home attacked by the wyrms. Let them fight."

Shard ground his beak and shifted his talons in his chest feathers, his gaze darting back to the young, chattering fledges that flew at the bottom of the ranks below them. The youngest appeared to be just short of four years. Shard thought of his friend, Einarr, who had been barely seven at the time of his initiation, and had still been considered young.

"Do you remember the boar?" Shard asked quietly.

War, battle, glory—the more Shard saw, the less he liked it. He remembered a time when he'd wanted glory, desired nothing but to show his bravery and courage, to fight for his pride, to prove his worth. Then he had seen his first true test, and felt his first true fear. Perhaps he was not a warrior. Perhaps at the end of his days he would not be worthy to fly with Tyr in the Sunlit Land, but he wearied of fighting.

A whisper warmed his heart. *You were worthy without ever seeing battle. You were worthy the moment you listened to your own heart.*

Kjorn was arguing. "... a chance to face the enemy, and their fear, head on. They've already seen it, when the wyrms attacked the Dawn Spire. Let them *choose* to face their fate. I said they would remain in the back. This is difficult enough, Shard, please, I need your support."

Shard fought against more arguments. But he didn't want to be seen further questioning Kjorn in front of everyone. "You have it, Kjorn."

Gratitude flickered in Kjorn's face. "Thank you. I promise the fledges will stay with the healers."

That soothed Shard's nerves, until they drew nearer to the Voldsom.

The broken canyons remained the same, but Shard heard Kjorn draw a sharp breath, his eyes widening, and when Shard followed his gaze, he saw the greatest host of creatures he'd ever witnessed in his life. For a moment he slowed, flying to a near standstill so that his wings almost stalled against the brisk wind.

At the dawnward rim of the canyon, the lions had gathered. Shard spied Mbari, and three other healthy, big, male lions prowling amongst rank upon rank of lionesses and mane-less youths.

A good stretch starward gathered a legion of painted wolves, many of their heads lifted to behold the host of gryfons flying in. They had banded in smaller family groups of ten or twenty, and ranged all along the rim. Some trailed down into the canyon, but many stopped to watch.

And the eagles. Eagles carpeted the walls and ledges of the canyons, soared through the air to meet Kjorn's army, or circled lower above the river, watching the gryfons below.

The Lakelanders and the gryfons of the Dawn Reach had arrived, and appeared to have claimed the dawnward bank of the Serpent River at the bottom of the main canyon. With them, Shard saw the rest of his Vanir, thought he caught sight of Stigr's black feathers.

On the opposite bank, the scouts who'd flown with Shard, the warriors of the Vanhar, Brynja's huntresses, and the exiles who followed Rok, all clustered and talked and laughed, and exclaimed to see Kjorn flying at the head of the Dawn Spire gryfons.

It was unimaginable.

The noise, the eerie sight of so many former enemies gathering together, and the suffocating waves of anticipation thrumming from the canyon nearly sent Shard reeling.

"Well." Kjorn's talons slowly clenched tight as he, too, took in the sight. "It begins."

33
THE VOICELESS HORDE

RAGNA APPROACHED SVERIN. HE EYED her. She watched him slipping between himself and a Nameless, terrified creature.

"What frightens you so?" she murmured, though her own heart
had quickened despite herself. She could *feel* the line of the enemy on
the horizon, as if a hurricane of hatred and fear gusted toward them.
The storm wind didn't help, smelling of rain and chill, and skyfire
flashing on the horizon. Normally thunderstorms thrilled her, but not
that day.

"You'll see," he growled.

"No, you will tell me. Tell me in your Tyr-given voice. Tell me,
Sverin, son-of-Per, what it is you fear."

His eyes of molten gold found her, glinting like the metal in his
nest. "I've seen them kill. I . . ." he shook himself. "Don't you see? All
my life they've hunted gryfons. I was never safe. I couldn't leave my
nest after dark. Their horrible shrieking filled my dreams. As a kit, I
had a nightmare that I'd hatched from a wyrm egg and they killed me
on sight. My fledge-mates who stayed out too late hunting near the
wyrms' borders were killed." Ragna shuddered, and Sverin's hackle

feathers raised. "They stink of death. Their fangs are the length of your leg. They don't hear, they don't speak. Like empty shadows, they don't know fear or love—"

"But you do," Ragna said firmly. Outside, Halvden and Thyra and Caj called orders. Gryfons whipped past Sverin's den on the wing, pregnant gryfesses climbed the cliff. "Tyr burns in your heart. Think of Elena, think of Kjorn. You know love, and courage—"

"No. I have never known courage. I was born hearing their screams, I was born afraid."

"You can atone now," Ragna urged, though her patience teetered on a cliff's edge. Cold wind swept into the cave, and clouds blotted over the sun, dimming the air around them like evening. "You can fight, now."

Staring at her, feathers sleeking down, he whispered, "I cannot. You'll see, and when you do, perhaps you'll think better of me."

Before Ragna could speak, animal screaming shredded the air in the distance.

A pure fear slithered through her. She clung to the ground, feathers lifting, and managed not to spring away and flee.

"You see," he whispered. "You see? They will take everything from you. Your love, your courage, your honor. Your very name—"

"I am Ragna." She ground the name from her beak, wrenching her gaze from his pathetic, huddled form. She strode to the mouth of the den and flared her white wings against the storm. "I am Ragna, daughter-of-Ragr, queen of the Vanir."

Without a glance back at Sverin, she leaped, and the wind nearly bashed her against the cliffs. She slipped into it, fell two breaths, found a sliver of lift and pushed herself higher, high into the air where Halvden was leading his warriors. Below, Caj, Thyra, Sigrun, Dagr, and Vidar herded the pregnant females up the cliff. Ragna saw them stumbling, stopping to stare out over the sea, crying out in fear.

"Sons and daughters of Tyr and Tor!" Ragna cried, "strengthen your hearts! We have not come through sorrow and war to become

Nameless, not now that we are close to being whole. We are one pride! We are strong! Hold to each other!"

Whether her voice helped, or the sight of her, pale against the blackening sky, gave them courage, she didn't know, but they appeared to collect themselves and move. Caj shouted encouragement. Thyra remained close to them, never pulling too far ahead, nudging them along.

Ragna turned, circling, wheeling hard against the wind to keep an eye on the approaching monsters. Their scent brushed her, decaying meat and oiled, reptilian flesh. A primal, ancient terror woke itself in her and seized at her muscles. Surely, the first fear ever felt by the first Nameless creature couldn't be worse than this. She shook her head, hard. She would not end up like Sverin, puddled in fear in the dark.

"Warriors to me!" Halvden's voice, scraping against the wind, brought her round. If *he* could hold on to himself, so could she.

As her insides quivered, she beat her wings. "I am Ragna," she breathed. "Queen of the Vanir."

The monsters, a league out across the sea, clarified against a backdrop of driving ice and rain. Ragna stared, and with sharp eagle eyes saw them in horrendous detail.

The largest led them, a hulking creature of impossible length and girth, with a hairless hide the color of dry mud. Two bat-like wings, leathery and veined, pumped against the storm wind. A long tail ended in a sharp spade, and the long, muscled neck ended in a wedge-shaped head crested with horns. Staring, Ragna knew in her gut the monster was female.

The rest of the flock swooped, squirmed, and flew in a swarm behind. For half a breath, Ragna thought of landing, cowering, calling the others down, presenting peace instead of a fight. But she had already made that mistake when they welcomed the Aesir, long ago. She remembered Caj's warning that the wyrms would not understand even if she did offer peace.

Looking at them now, she understood that he was right, that these creatures wouldn't have known the difference between peace, war, or cowardice at all.

Her mind reeled at the sight of their talons, their whipping, deadly tails. She hovered, staring. They were too close. She saw them, and knew she beheld her death. They would fall upon the pride and kill them all.

"Lady Ragna!" boomed a male voice. "Steady, my queen!"

Ragna shook her head hard, and saw Dagr. "Dagr—"

"Go to safety, I beg you." The coppery gryfon swooped around her, gave her one last look, and flew to Halvden to help rally the warriors who already joined him. Ragna wheeled, hearing Halvden shouting orders, sounding older, sounding confident.

"Form up! We will distract them away!"

With a flare of hope, Ragna saw the gryfons obeying him. All the gryfons—Vanir, Aesir, half-bloods, worked as one, forming into clustered ranks, prepared to meet their enemy.

Ragna glanced down at the fleeing pride, dots of color and wings, racing across the snowy plain to the river. Caj and Thyra's voices rose above the wind, guiding them. It was dangerous for the females to move too quickly, stress themselves and risk their unborn kits. But they had no choice.

A second monstrous scream split the air, echoed by terrified gryfon cries below. Ragna whipped around to see the oncoming monsters. She couldn't flee now. Despite Dagr's wishes, Ragna knew she had to fight. She was a huntress, she was able-bodied. She had to fight.

She had to do *something*.

Halvden was shouting orders. "Hold here, hold at the cliffs!"

Dagr added, "Distract them from the forest!"

Ragna swooped forward to join two half-bloods, Andor and Tollack, beating the air as they watched the dragons swarm.

"Maybe they'll flee," croaked the younger Tollack, a half-blood of mottle gray coloring with a falcon mask.

"If they smell *you* they will," said Andor, weakly.

Ragna laughed for both of them, hoarsely, to show them it was all right to laugh. "Steady," she said firmly to Tollack, who didn't even look amused.

The gryfons hovered in a stacked formation, forming a wall of wings and talons in the air over the nesting cliffs, a first and last line of defense against the horde.

The big she-beast flared her wings, and loosed a discordant, shattering howl that raised Ragna's feathers and nearly sent her reeling out of the sky to cower on the ground.

"Steady," said Tollack next to her. Then, "Andor. Andor!"

The other half-blood had actually begun to sink, with a mewl like a kit. Tollack smacked his head with a wing and he rose again, beating the air by Ragna.

The horde surged toward them, at least a dozen huge bodies hurtling out of the storming sky toward the gryfon ranks.

A few gryfons faltered, as if to break the line.

"Wait!" Halvden yelled. Ragna hovered, wings beating the air. The scent of oncoming rain and rotting meat clung to the wind.

Ragna could nearly hear all the desperate gasps and growls from down the lines.

Screaming monsters drove toward them, deadly tails whipping behind, claws the size of Ragna's hind legs extended, giant mouths agape to show fangs encrusted with blood.

A few gryfons dropped from the ranks with terrified cries, diving toward the woods. Ragna swore.

"Hold . . ." Halvden snarled to those remaining.

The monsters closed, fifty leaps, twenty, ten. Ragna's belly turned to water.

Halvden shot down like a green stone in front of the wall of warriors, shouting, "Scatter! Now! NOW!"

As the monsters closed, the hovering wall of gryfons burst apart in fifty directions.

With Andor and Tollack, Ragna peeled away, shrieking to loose some of her terror and to form a distraction. The monsters smashed into the ranks of flying gryfons, horned heads snapping this way and that, tails lashing, claws swiping randomly at Ragna's warriors.

A smaller, dull green beast focused on Ragna, loosing a guttural scream that almost shattered her heart with fear. She spun in the air as Stigr had once taught her, and drove under him. Behind her, Andor and Tollack cheered at her aerobatics, then split, forcing the beast to choose between them. It lurched after Tollack, tail slashing the air behind.

"Don't be heroes," Halvden was yelling, "just keep them flying, keep them away from the pride!" Surprise and pride bubbled in Ragna's chest that Halvden was leading so well. He had come very far. Then, with sudden shrillness the green gryfon shouted, "King's Guard to me! To the woods, the woods!"

Ragna, veering hard, saw that the big dragoness was not fooled by their chaotic display, but flying over the whole scene toward the fleeing pride.

"Warriors to Halvden!" she barked. "Dagr, Andor! Tollack—"

She whipped around, and her heart clutched to see Andor spiraling toward the ground, one wing flailing uselessly. Tollack was diving, diving for him. Ragna swooped down to aid them, when another beast closed on her, screaming and gnashing its fanged jaws. Her ears nearly burst at the noise.

Fear swamped her like a wave, as it had in her youth when a great sailfish had dragged her deep under the ocean. She couldn't move but to hover, beating the air and staring at the approaching, winged death.

A body slammed into her.

Eyvin, nearly mad with terror. "Fly, Ragna! Curse it!"

"Eyv—"

"Fly!"

The monster collided with Eyvin, and Ragna swooped down out of their tangled, battling path. She hated herself for it, but she had to stay alive. She had to be queen. She remembered Halvden, and the monster flying toward her fleeing pride. Andor, falling toward the ground.

Distracted, she realized there was still one color she didn't see with those fleeing, nor in the sky with Halvden. No flash of scarlet met her gaze in the storm wind, on the ground or in the sky.

A sense of fury mingled with helplessness in her heart. The invading creatures would slaughter her pride, kill or harry the pregnant females to death if Halvden couldn't stop them, and Sverin, the War King, would die cowering in his den. Even though it was his legacy, there was no part of Ragna that truly wished to see that.

Sverin's grandfather took dragon gold, and brought this curse on us.

Dragon gold.

Thunder clapped, as if Tor herself roared in rage.

An idea butted past Ragna's terror. She shoved her wings hard, soaring back to the nesting cliffs as unholy roars shattered the air, as the monsters battled her pride.

Halvden's battle roar thundered in the sky, and in the corner of Ragna's vision, as she navigated the storm, she saw warriors closing ranks with him to fly at the marauding queen, attacking in a series of wedges, like geese.

Then she saw no more, for she had to pay attention to her own flight or end up dashed on the rocks as the wind rose fast. She flew low, under the main fighting, down to the cliffs.

Angling hard, she swung herself back into Sverin's den, the wind beating at her rump and nearly bowling her over. Ignoring Sverin, who crouched in the deepest corner with his head bent into his chest feathers, Ragna leaped at the nest that dripped with dragon gold.

His head came up slowly, his voice raw. "What are you doing?"

"I see you can still speak," Ragna snarled. "We are in battle." She curled her talons around chains, bejeweled bracers, and shining rings, and hauled them from the nest. Hobbling between her hind paws and her talons, full of gold, she heaved herself to the front of the den.

"Ho, great dragons!" she shouted. "Hail, cursed enemy! Is this what you want?"

Behind her, Sverin gasped a protest. Ragna ignored him, kept hold of what she could reasonably carry, and jumped from the den. Sinking steadily with the weight of the gold, Ragna yelled challenge into the storm.

"Here!" Her voice cracked into an eagle chirrup. She bellowed again, deep from her chest. "Is this what you've come for?" Skyfire crackled as she brandished a chain, illuminating the gold.

Monster heads whipped her way as the treasures flashed. Grunting with the weight, Ragna managed enough lift to crash atop the nesting cliff.

All but the largest shrieked in seeming glee and swung toward her. Dagr's cry cracked the air, dismayed at seeing her call the monsters to her.

Ragna screamed at the nightmare horde. "Take it! Take all of it!"

As the leading male dragon, a grey beast the length of ten gryfons, dove at her, Ragna flung five sparkling, golden chains over the cliffs.

Jaws snapped three leaps from her, then the monster turned, and dove. Its brethren focused on Ragna as she cast the gold away. Above, in the chaos, her warriors caught on. Multiple gryfons dove toward the nests of the Aesir. The half-bloods and the Aesir themselves were large enough to bear the gold away from the nesting cliffs, and Ragna saw some flying along the cliffs, some risking themselves farther out to sea.

This had the desired effect, and drew the dragons away from the rest of the fleeing pride. She noticed that as they pursued and tried to snatch at the gold, they always veered shy of diving into the water.

The rain hit as Ragna snatched another treasure from Sverin's den. Blood pounded her ears as the icy rain slithered off her oiled wings.

The nesting cliffs glittered with discarded treasure. The beasts fought each other now, and chased any gryfon bearing bright things that caught their eye. The largest female loosed an angry, bone-rattling roar as the monsters left her battle and began squabbling among themselves for gold.

Not wanting to risk them catching sight of the fleeing gryfons again, Ragna soared out over the water. Three of the smaller beasts pursued her over the icy, frothing waves. Ragna blinked hard against the driving rain and pretended it was only gryfons behind her, gryfons, nothing more.

The treasure she carried was a collar, so heavy it dragged her flight, and she knew after two moments flying with it she wouldn't be able to draw the wyrms out and still have strength to carry it back while out-maneuvering her pursuers.

She would have to drop it.

She gave the treasure one last look. It was wrought with intricate designs and crested with shifting catseye gems. One of Sverin's favorites. He had worn it often. Ragna flung herself around so the marauding dragons could see her clearly, and with pleasure, dropped it into the sea.

Two immediately tucked into dives, shrieking and snapping at each other, trying to catch the collar before it hit the water. One pulled up, unwilling to dive into the waves, and the second fell hard and fast, catching the collar in a single claw. Then a wave surged and knocked the wyrm into the water. Ragna didn't see if it flew out.

The third was smart enough to figure out Ragna was to blame, and drove toward her. Ragna slipped under him and zipped above the waves, panting, staring hard through the rain toward the nesting cliffs.

In the distance she saw a line of gryfons against the naked birch woods that flanked the river. They disappeared from her sight in the tree line, and she knew they were safe. It looked as if most of the pregnant, elder, and young had made the river, made it to the entrance of the underground caves.

If I can just make it back to the cliffs myself . . .

"My lady!" Dagr shouted, flying out from the cliffs to meet her. Over his shoulder he called to others, "I found her!"

Multiple gryfons followed Dagr and converged on the dragon that pursued her, driving it back. Dagr, still clutching a golden bracer, whipped once around the beast's head. He flung the bracer at the monster's head and flew away, and the monster followed, striking randomly at gryfons who chased him.

Ragna followed them, flying high.

"Dagr!" she shouted. "Dagr! Halvden, retreat! Our pride is safe!" She tilted back, almost upright, ramping midair and flashing her wings. "Retreat!"

With the weakest of them to safety, Ragna hoped to spare as many others as possible.

The warriors appeared to hear, breaking off from the monsters. She saw them leave in strategic clumps, some staying to harry the marauding beasts in to confusion, others peeling away and flying to the woods.

Ragna soared over the cliffs, then dove down. As the monsters gathered their wits, she saw it was almost safer to fly low. To her relief she spied Halvden, shouting her order to retreat, calling gryfons to him. Ragna flew hard toward the woods.

A baleful roar struck the air. She'd lost track of the fighting, of the marauding queen, and could not look behind her. Terror drove her, flattened her ears, whipped her forward without looking back.

She should have looked back.

A gust of rotten wind bowled her beak over tail to crash, splayed in the slush and mud. Another guttural roar shook the earth and rattled her beak and her bones.

"RAGNA!" someone shouted, a gryfess—in the chaos, she didn't know who. Ragna gulped a breath. Scraping herself up, she whipped her head about in time to see the she-monster slam to the ground and duck her long neck, blaring a challenge at Ragna.

It was not Halvden or Caj who leaped past Ragna to come to her defense, but Sigrun, her own wingsister returning from the woods. Sigrun, followed by Gret, by Tollack, by Vanir and half-bloods and then a cloud of angry, shrieking gryfon voices, led by Halvden from above. A chaos of dragons descended with them, and tails and horns flashed like skyfire and hail.

Ragna watched, numb, as wyrms and gryfons whirled around each other. She saw gryfons fall to the ground and remain there.

"Fly!" Sigrun shouted, wheeling around the great, horned head of the dragon queen. "Ragna! Remember yourself. Fly!"

A gray beast snapped at Sigrun and she peeled off, leading it away from the river. Others followed. Ragna swallowed a stone in her throat, moving one locked hind leg.

Move. Move. MOVE!

The she-monster lunged forward and Ragna leaped back. A flash of emerald swept in front of her and she pitched sideways as Halvden skidded to the snow, roaring and lashing his talons. Ragna saw the dragon's tail whip up and screamed a warning, too late, but wily Halvden, trained under Caj, had already leaped up to evade.

He was still too slow.

The deadly spade rounded, caught his foreleg, and Ragna saw a spray of blood and heard Halvden's curdling shriek of pain. She stood locked in the snow, wasting his bravery, wasting his effort to protect her, a queen he didn't even love.

An angry, shrieking roar broke through her shock and sorrow.

The dragoness reared up to her hind legs and Ragna scrabbled back in the sludge as the monster turned to behold Sverin.

Sverin, standing twenty leaps away, clutching shining bracers and collars, blood red against the rain and mud and snow.

"Is this what you've come for?" he snarled at the rearing dragon. His wings were still bound. Ragna's blood seemed to lodge in her veins. "Well take it! Take all your cursed chains of gold!"

He flung the treasures at the dragon, and others whipped about to see, but she lashed her tail, warning them back.

"Sverin!" Ragna shouted. "The pride is safe, flee—"

The dragon lunged, her great claws swiping the air, but Sverin ducked under her massive paw, rolled, and came up on his hind legs.

Then, with a roar that bounded across the cliffs, he shoved open his wings.

Ragna stared as golden links snapped, flew apart, and glittered to the ground. He bellowed a challenge and the dragon queen answered with a roar like an avalanche, stamping the ground, tail whipping high. Her wings flared, darkening their sky. Sverin crouched back, ears flat, and sank toward the ground, his eyes losing their light.

"Sverin!" Caj's voice cracked through the rain. "Sverin, run!"

The red gryfon's gaze darted past them, to the fleeing warriors. Most of them had made it to the woods. Some remained, to help gryfons like Ragna who stood, mute, staring at the horror of the dragons. Without their queen guiding them on, most of the smaller beasts broke off from fighting to gather the gold still scattered along the cliff.

"Sverin!" Ragna yelled, coming to her own senses, coming out of her shock. "Sverin, the pride is safe, fly with us!"

He backed away from the dragon, wings opened, his beak and eyes wide. Ragna feared he'd lost himself. His gaze darted from the gold he'd thrown to the dragon, who stalked him, ignoring the treasure. Then his gaze flicked to the last of the gryfons, fleeing into the woods.

"Brother!" Caj shouted, leaping forward through the mud and slush.

"It's not the gold," Sverin rasped. "She doesn't want the gold."

He looked at Caj, then met Ragna's eyes, spun, and shoved hard from the ground. With a nasty bellow, the dragoness followed, lunging hard into the rain.

Sverin's scarlet wings beat hard against the storm—Ragna realized he hadn't been eating fish, that his wings wouldn't be as impervious to water as a Vanir's. The monster had eyes only for Sverin, it seemed—and when Ragna realized that, she realized Sverin had not fled, but purposefully flew, to draw the great she-beast away.

And it appeared to Ragna's eyes that she was slowing down. The wyrms were slowing. Whether injured or exhausted, she didn't know.

"Sverin!" Caj cried, lunging up beside Ragna. "Ragna, please..."

With a curse, Ragna looked once more at the bodies of her fallen, counting at least Andor, Gret, and many of the Aesir. She didn't see Halvden. Warriors tried to drag bodies toward the forest. Others hobbled, bloody and wounded, or fell beside their fallen comrades, with horrible cries that sent Ragna reeling back to memories of the Conquering.

Except this time they had been united—Aesir, Vanir, and all their new, mixed generation, fighting together in horrible, heart-wrenching unity against an impossible foe.

"Help them," she gasped to Caj. "Do not leave anyone for these monsters to find, alive or dead."

"We won't, my lady." His gaze strayed to the smaller dragons, wrestling and fighting over gold. They would surely find the rest in the cliffs, and take over Ragna's home.

"Go," Caj urged, his gaze searching the sky for his wingbrother. "Thank you."

Without looking back again, Ragna focused her gaze on Sverin's distant red wings, and shoved from the battleground into the storm.

34
GREATMEET

THE SCOUTS SHARD AND BRYNJA had arranged before Shard left for the Dawn Spire had not returned. Eagles reported the gryfons had flown farther into the Outlands to search for signs of the Wyrms.

Kjorn sent out his own. So did the Lakelanders. So did the Vanhar, and the painted wolves, and the eagles, each believing their eyes and ears to be superior.

The lions did not deign to send scouts, but made sure Kjorn was aware they *would* send scouts, if he thought it necessary. As it was, they seemed content to share in the afternoon meal and made a point of saying that certainly the eagles and gryfons had the situation covered, though lions would have been faster, if it were not so difficult to cross the canyons of the Voldsom.

The painted wolves met that statement with derision and howling laughter, then made a point of taking excursions up and down their labyrinths of trails through the canyon and calling to the lions from the opposite rim.

Shard lost track of Kjorn after they had to part ways—Shard to meet with his Vanir, and Kjorn to treat with the leaders of each group. He hadn't even had a chance to speak with Stigr, who, along with Asvander and Valdis, attempted to keep the Lakelanders of the Ostral Shores and the gryfons of the Dawn Spire from arguing.

Shard observed all this with growing tension, until he felt his wings might cramp and fall off.

The Vanir gathered to Shard, waiting on his word, seeking him out for orders—in general, he thought, keeping him in their line of sight. He busied himself and them by making sure everyone had a den, or at least an overhang under which to duck if the weather turned again. With the painted wolves returned, the empty dens Brynja and her huntresses had used for a while that winter were reclaimed, so they moved farther downriver into the canyon.

After the battle, they would depart for the Silver Isles.

Shard checked in with each member of his pride. Shadows kept the canyon cool down near the river, and many of the Vanir worked at the river, fishing to help feed the multitude of animals. Nilsine's Vanhar joined them, not inclined to arguing or empty boasting. This put them in good graces with the eagles, to whom fish was a great delicacy.

Shard found old Frar lounging by the bank, calling advice to the younger, fishing gryfons.

"Not bad, not bad, but if you angle so your shadow throws upstream they won't see you coming!"

"Frar," Shard said respectfully. The old gryfon looked up in surprise and shifted as if to stand. "No, rest. How was the journey?"

"Fair, my lord." He looked grimly toward the canyon walls, and they heard shouting among the Lakelanders. "That's a talon-happy bunch, I'll tell you. I think they like nothing more than being insulted so they can fight."

"I'm inclined to believe you. But don't worry." Shard touched his beak to the old gryfon's wing. "We'll be going home soon."

"Good, very good, my lord. You'll find your Vanir strong and ready."

"Thank you," Shard said. He watched the gryfons fishing for a moment, and considered joining them, then decided he was better off watching and keeping an eye on things.

Tension swelled between the canyon walls. Small, brief fights broke out along the river at least once a sun mark as the long, long day stretched on. Old enemies meeting again, rivals, friends who didn't trust each other as they once did. Some blamed others for the wyrm attack on the Dawn Spire, and the different creatures barely maintained peace with each other.

The painted packs called challenges and boasts to the gryfons of the Dawn Spire. Not everyone clearly understood each other, Shard saw. Not everyone was truly listening. Some only heard gryfons snarling, or wolves barking, lions growling.

Shard remained close to the Vanir, feeling stubbornly that it was not his place to keep anyone from fighting. Kjorn had chosen this. For now, Shard would protect his own.

The great roar of talk and commotion that had filled the canyon to the brim during the day faded off as night closed in. It seemed scouts had ventured so far into the Outlands that none would return that night.

Each group posted their own sentries along the wall of the canyon, the river, and a few on the far rim to cast their gazes toward the Outlands. No one flew once darkness fell.

Stars pierced the night. Brynja and Shard lit a great bonfire near the Vanir camp by the river, and Shard was grateful for her quiet company.

"You're not happy," she said as he drew out his fire stones.

"No, I'm not happy." He sat near the bundle of grasses and twigs. Some enterprising Vanir had been smart enough to set some grass out in the sun, giving it time to dry from the rain the previous day, and now Shard used it to light the first fire. "I believe the wyrms are gone, and Kjorn still insisted on bringing everyone here."

The sparks flared, raining from the stones in his talons and lighting a grim expression on Brynja's face. Then it was dark again. Shard struck the stones again, again, until an ember caught and glowed. In that whisper of light he felt Brynja watching him. He waved his wing gently at the ember, fanning it to a trickle of flame, and stuffed the little tinder nest under their kindling.

"I can speak to him."

Shard wanted to shake his head, to growl, to ask her why she thought she might have a better chance than himself, but he didn't. "If you think it will help."

"Shard. What aren't you telling me?"

He tucked the fire stones away in their pouch and glanced to her, backing away from the kindling as his blaze grew, spilling heat and light. "You know what I think. The wyrms have gone. They could very well be searching for the Silver Isles right now. There's no reason to have summoned everyone here, and now we can barely keep them from fighting with each other."

She inclined her head, and he couldn't help but admire the gold of the fire on her face, the splash of red flecks along the paler feathers near her beak. Her eyes, stern, made him check his skepticism. "What would you have done, in his place?"

"With my wingbrother arguing against me? I . . ." Shard trailed off. He and Kjorn had advanced a long way since they'd both left the Silver Isles. They saw each other more clearly. They saw themselves more clearly. "I would have . . ." Shard sighed, digging a talon against the dirt. "I would have wanted to check for myself."

"There's trust," Brynja said quietly, "and there's leadership. Kingship. If Kjorn hadn't doubted that the wyrms were gone, someone else would have. He's doing it to stay everyone's doubts, not just his own."

"But I would have checked for myself, *then* brought my army."

"Fair enough." Her tail twitched back and forth as she watched him. "Would you like me to speak with him? We share distant bloodlines, we are both Aesir of the Dawn Spire."

"Thank you, Brynja, but we're already here. We must fly out this wind where it takes us, and hope it doesn't end with all these armies fighting each other."

"Well aren't we the hopeful bunch." Stigr approached Shard from the river, Valdis at his side. She almost never left his side, like ballast, as if her presence somehow balanced his missing wing. Maybe it did. "Meanwhile, the rest of the camps are getting jealous of this blaze. The Lakelanders and the lions have kindling gathered for their own bonfires, if you have time."

"Give me the stones, Shard." Brynja stepped forward, ducking her head. "I will light a few more fires while you two catch up."

Shard hesitated, then took the leather thong from his neck and slipped it over hers. As she raised her head, she brushed her feathered ear along his and nibbled lightly with her beak in a way that washed a shiver down his back.

"Be of a bright heart, my lord." She drew back to watch him sternly. "It's one of your traits that I fell in love with."

"Yes, my lady," Shard said quietly.

"Valdis," Brynja said with more air, "will you join me? I've missed you. We can find my father and catch up."

Valdis eyed Stigr. "I suppose I can trust you not to get into trouble for a few moments?"

"I'll give it a try." They grazed beaks in a fond gesture and the huntresses left, leaving Shard alone with his uncle at last. "Let's have a walk by the river, and you tell me what's got your ears flat."

They reached a place where the river widened and the choice was turn around, swim, or fly. They turned, now standing well in darkness beyond the fire. More fires winked to life in the moments Shard and Stigr stood in silence. Three in the canyon, two above for the lions and for the gryfons of the Dawn Spire who didn't wish to nest so closely to the wolves and eagles.

"We heard no wyrms either," Stigr said at length, staring at the river. The muttering and rumor that the wyrms were no longer in the Outlands had clearly spread—or perhaps began on its own. "On the journey from the Ostral Shores."

Shard's gaze slid to his uncle's shoulder and the thick scar where his wing used to be. The last time he'd made a mistake, his uncle had paid a horrific price. Now everyone cried out for battle, for justice, for war, and Shard felt squeamish and uncertain. He didn't know what was right anymore.

"I don't know what to do, Uncle." Shard sat as close to Stigr as he could without nudging his uncle into the water. "If the wyrms are gone, I know Kjorn will deal with the consequences here. We will, together. Then I must take the Vanir home. And then? If the wyrms are nowhere to be found? I spoke to Rhydda. I'm learning her past. Do I pursue her until we understand each other?"

"That's a lot of questions about things that haven't happened yet," Stigr said quietly. "Why don't you focus on the wind that's under your wings now."

"The wind of war," Shard said sourly, dipping his talons idly into the slow waters of the river. Farther downstream he knew it broke into dangerous rapids, but this area flowed full and slow, and soothed him.

"You're a good warrior," Stigr said. "What do you fear?"

"It isn't fear so much as . . . I know that the Winderost has been terrorized by the wyrms, and that they seem to kill out of hatred and without mercy. I know I should wish to fight. But I don't. I don't want to fight the wyrms. I don't want to fight anyone. But I know Tyr looks highly on brave warriors, and I fear I'm becoming a coward."

He held his breath after this admission, and waited, shamed, fully expecting his uncle to call him on his cowardice. He watched the older

Vanir's face, edged in starlight, the scar of his missing eye a testament
to his own courage and warrior heart.

"Well." He sighed, and Shard flinched a little. "Who really knows
what Tyr looks highly on. We all seem to die, lose wings, eyes, love,
and friends without much regard for who is a better gryfon and not.
There is a difference between being a coward, and not wanting to
fight." Stigr's tail swept the sand, back and forth. "Shard, I will always
look highly on you for following your heart, for trying so hard to do
what you think is right, and by that I mean, what you think will be best
for everyone."

Shard sat very still, ears tuned to his uncle's every breath. It wasn't
the answer he had expected, but perhaps it should have been. "The
Summer King is supposed to bring peace."

"That's not exactly what the song says, actually," Stigr said. He
went on, looking down and digging a talon into the sand of the riv-
erbank in a fidget similar to Shard's. "Shard, we can't always know
what's best for everyone. These warriors of the Ostral Shores, for
instance, they'll never feel worthy and whole if they don't see battle.
That is in their hearts."

He looked down the river toward the distant bonfire. "The Vanhar,
on another wind, seek peace and wisdom. We Vanir like our harmony
too, but we will fight if needed. I believe bright Tor blesses those who
seek understanding and peace, but for a worthy cause, I'll go to battle
with Tyr's light in my heart." Stigr tilted his head to eye Shard with his
good eye. "Knowing all that, who's to say what's best for me?"

"Valdis?" Shard joked weakly, and Stigr's rough laugh was a balm.

Once again, Shard's throat locked to know that he would be leaving
Stigr in the Winderost, the closest gryfon to his own father that he'd
ever known. Briefly, with regret and guilt and a touch of anger, he
thought of Caj. But he could not fly that wind now.

"Rashard. Son of my wingbrother." Stigr stood, walking around
to stand between Shard and the river. "Do you understand what I'm
telling you?"

"No, Shard admitted, almost laughing, until Stigr gusted a growling sigh.

"I'm telling you that you aren't a coward. And you haven't failed. You've done all we could have ever asked, and more. The Summer King listens to all, speaks to all, his wing beats part the storm. He is borne aloft by the Silver Wind, by the truth, by understanding, as you are."

The black gryfon raised his head, eyeing the twinkling stars, and the fires on the rim. "This will be Kjorn's kingdom now, and he'll win it, and rule it, as he sees fit. You can do your best to avert him from evil air if you see it, you can stand by him if you wish it, but in the end, you can only serve your own heart. I follow and help you because you are my prince, and, I believe, my Summer King, and because that's all my heart has ever told me to do."

Shard closed his eyes, grasping the sand and gravel in his talons as if it would keep him from flying apart. "Thank you," he whispered.

"Come now." Stigr perked his ears toward the fires. "I think I hear another argument breaking out. What do you suppose it's about this time? Wingspan, or the advantage of beaks over fangs?"

Shard managed a laugh, and walked close to his uncle, and for a few moments he felt like himself again. For a few moments the stars seemed clear, his path felt right, and beyond it all he knew he would be going home soon.

Between himself, Stigr, Kjorn, Asvander, Nilsine, and the other leaders of eagles and wolves, they managed to avoid any more arguments that evening.

Then dawn brought no word from the scouts.

Nerves and tempers flared as cool, damp wind gusted through the canyons and along the river. Impatience and suspicion showed itself in duels that became brawls which turned deadly, and most over misunderstandings. A young lion was nearly slain in a duel with a gryfon of the Dawn Reach.

Kjorn stepped in then, ordering all gryfons unable to control themselves to keep to their own camps. He posted level-headed sentries around, those trusted to soothe tempers and stop fights before they began.

Ajia set the young lion right—their healer, their priestess, and Mbari forbade any lions from mingling with gryfons again, for the time being.

Shard and Kjorn passed the rest of time with the leaders by planning strategies for facing the wyrms with the best strengths of their gathered warriors, but that ended in arguments too.

The Vanhar attempted to sing some of their old songs, and were silenced by loud and boorish complaints from the Lakelanders. Shard watched the goodwill and battle-frenzy stretch taut, tighten, and begin to fray.

A second night brought a gloomy, strained silence over the Voldsom.

A second dawn brought back Shard's Vanir scouts, and they had no word of the wyrms. That afternoon, the eagles returned. The Lakelander scouts and those of the Dawn Spire returned with the same reports.

The wyrms were nowhere to be found, and no fresh tracks, scat, or kills. Shard wanted to feel vindicated, but he only felt worried. He thought of the Silver Isles. Once or twice when he was near Kjorn, he noticed the prince's smooth, cool expression faltering, and seeking Shard out with growing apprehension.

The last of the scouts, the painted wolves, returned at dusk. They came at a lope, breathlessly, with the same news as the rest. They brought this word to their leader, Ilesh, who sent a messenger to the bonfire of the Ostral Shore gryfons, where Kjorn had chosen to spend his evening.

Shard sat with him, Brynja next to Shard, with Stigr and Valdis to one side. The leaders of the Lakelanders had claimed spots nearest the fire, and they stared at Kjorn after the painted wolf gave her report.

"I will tell my leader you know all that we know," she murmured, "and we will wait for your word." She slipped away into the shadows again.

In the silence, fire popped and hissed along nodules of sap, sending a sweet, sharp aroma. Shard stared at Kjorn's face, which appeared to have hardened into true gold, for all Shard could read his expression.

"Don't," he breathed, for Shard's ears alone.

"I wasn't going to say anything," Shard began.

Lofgar, the big, scarred, rough Lakelander that Shard recalled from the last meeting at the Ostral Shores, made a rough, derisive noise. Kjorn's gaze flicked to him, but he did not move as the big Lakelander stood. The firelight threw a massive shadow on the canyon wall behind his massive frame.

"Well, my friends." His powerful, burred voice reverberated with unfortunate clarity up and down the canyon walls, and his beady eyes fixed on Kjorn. "*Someone* has made fools of us all."

35
KJORN'S CHALLENGE

"THAT ISN'T TRUE." KJORN REMAINED seated, but Shard stood, eyeing the Lakelanders warily.

"You knew the wyrms were gone!" Lofgar shouted.

Shard eyed Kjorn, wondering, after his challenge with the Vanhar, if he would answer that honestly. Kjorn glanced to Shard, and then back to Lofgar.

"When I summoned you, and all the rest of these warriors here, I didn't know if the wyrms were still here. I had suspicions, but you must believe that I thought they remained."

Around them, Shard sensed Stigr and Valdis moving forward to flank Kjorn. Brynja stepped around behind. Asvander and Dagny parted from their company across the fire and walked casually to stand behind Shard, as if the heat was too much for them.

Lofgar gnashed his broken beak. "I knew this was a terrible idea from the start, allying ourselves to the Dawn Spire after it was their ilk who brought the enemy on us, then refused to fight them. Then, he promised a grand war, and now the enemy has fled."

"Funny." The steely voice was Valdis, and Shard looked to her warily. So did Lofgar. "I thought the Ostral Shores broke ties with the Dawn Spire when Orn refused to fight the wyrms. Kjorn wants to fight the wyrms and now you're angry with him?"

"Because he lied," Lofgar hissed. "I see no wyrms here."

"I didn't lie," Kjorn said, his voice low. Shard pressed close to him.

"And other reasons," declared a female Lakelander, from behind Lofgar. "You seem to weigh the opinion of savage painted dogs and grass cats equal with ours. We don't like it."

"Your reasoning seems muddled," Valdis said, dangerous and silky, "like your mind. Let those wiser and with a better memory plan your battles for you."

Shard thought Lofgar would leap. His feathers puffed out and his tail whipped back and forth, actually slapping the gryfons behind him until they stepped back. "Say that again, arrogant, Dawn Spire vulture—"

Valdis stood, hackle feathers lifting. "Your reasoning seems—"

"Enough," Kjorn said.

Nilsine, followed by Ketil, and the she-eagle Hildr, glided down and landed several paces away from the fire, approaching quietly, as if they'd heard the commotion. In the light, Nilsine's strange red eyes glowed like gems.

"Nilsine," Shard greeted, using her as a distraction to stay the tension. "We were just discussing what to do, now the scouts have confirmed the wyrms are gone."

Nilsine looked between all of them, clearly noting the tension. "I see."

"Oh good," Lofgar grumbled. "The fishmongers are here to smell up our camp."

Nilsine's ruby eyes flicked to him. "Better a fishmonger than a warmonger. Live by war, and you will die by war."

"Better to die by war than old, limp, and flea-bitten in my nest."

"Lofgar," Asvander admonished, eyes narrowing. "You insult our allies."

"Don't address me, son-of-Asrik. You can't even keep hold of a mate for more than a fortnight." He whirled back to Nilsine. "Why are you even here? Pacifist, cloud-chasing—"

"Watch your words," Kjorn said, his voice low and grating. "The Vanhar are friends to me."

"My lord," Nilsine began, but Lofgar cut her off.

"I thought *we* were friends to you as well, *my lord.*" Mocking Nilsine's respectful address, Lofgar furthered the insult by mantling low, dipping his head to them both. "She insulted me, too. But I see, like your father, you're brave when there's no real enemy, and your words are the only thing impressive about you."

Shard growled and moved forward, but Stigr, who had been sitting in silence, beat him to it. Apparently unable to stand further insult to his new chosen monarch, he leaped and swiped his talons through the embers at the edge of the fire, splattering Lofgar's bowed head with burning coals and sparks. The big gryfon scuttled back with a choked gurgle of surprise, batting at his face, though Shard could see that nothing was truly burning.

"Wretch! Wingless, one-eyed—"

"Show respect to the prince!" Stigr demanded. "You gaumless, thin-feathered jaybird. I've a mind to show you what I can do with one eye and one wing and if you don't shut your broken beak. You saw Prince Kjorn fight at the Battle of Torches, you saw Nilsine, Valdis, and all here prove their mettle against our common enemy. Why stand here now and throw insults? This pointless nattering is why your cursed land is broken."

"Enough of this," Kjorn said, holding himself tall, though he flicked a look of gratitude to Stigr. Shard stood next to him, quiet, wishing he could will strength into his wingbrother. "We will hold a council at dawn, with representatives of *all* of my allies present, at the top of the canyon above these dens. If anyone has concerns before then, you know where I've made my nest."

Without even a look at Shard, Kjorn turned from the firelight and walked into the dark, with so heavy a step and grim an expression, not even Shard dared to follow.

A RING OF CREATURES gathered in the sun's first light. Shard had slept little, so weary he couldn't even pursue Rhydda in his dreams to see where she might be.

He looked now with unease at the faces before him, a great circle near the canyon rim. Shard had started a fire in the center so everyone would know where they gathered, to offer warmth and perhaps some sense of fellowship. To his left stood Kjorn, who Shard was certain hadn't slept at all. The golden prince's blue eyes were dull with weariness and his tail hung low.

Beside Kjorn, and ringing left, stood his aunt Esla, tawny and blue-eyed, Nilsine, Asvander, the rogues Rok and Hel, and three leaders of the Lakelanders—Lofgar, Asrik, and a female whose name Shard hadn't learned.

To Shard's right sat Stigr, Valdis, Brynja, Ketil, and the she-eagles Hildr and Grunna, who spoke for the Brightwing aerie, the strongest and largest of the eagle clans. Next to them stood two painted wolves, Ilesh and his mate, their rangy, spotted coats exotic in the morning light, their dark faces shadowed and enigmatic.

Mbari the lion chief lounged with Ajia, and from the corner of Shard's eye their crests of feathers made him think of gryfons. The lioness caught him looking, and held his gaze before lifting her eyes briefly. Shard looked up, heart thudding as if he might see wyrms there. But vultures circled, curious at this gathering of enemies, hopeful, perhaps. Beyond them, silver clouds feathered a pearly sky, not yet blue with morning.

May we rise higher, Shard thought, closing his eyes, though the voice in his mind sounded more like Ajia than his own.

Kjorn's deep voice gathered his attention. "Welcome, friends, allies, warriors." Low murmurs answered him. All watched, ears lifting, heads tilting to regard him. Lofgar was looking away toward the canyon.

Subtly, Shard touched his wing to Kjorn's. If he felt it, the big gryfon didn't respond, but continued. "As all of you know, our scouts have found no trace of the wyrms in the Outlands. It is my . . . it is our belief they have left these lands."

"Truly," Hildr the she-eagle exclaimed, opening her broad wings to look larger amongst all the large creatures, "we put the fear of bright Tyr into their hearts at the Battle of Torches. We should have known that when they fled, it was forever!"

Kjorn dipped his head to her. Shard noted disgruntled looks on some of the Aesir faces—the Lakelanders, Queen Esla herself. He realized they still couldn't understand half of what Hildr said. He had grown so used to listening deeply to understand creatures other than gryfons, he'd forgotten not everyone listened so. Nervous, he glanced around for signs of understanding, even as Kjorn spoke.

"Yes," Kjorn agreed. With a look around, he seemed to note what Shard had, and repeated what she'd said. "It seems we did, and they have fled. And now—"

"Now, we're better off without a battle," said Hel, and Shard remembered that she had called herself a coward. "If any of you can't see that, you're bigger fools than I thought. Though we could have told you the wyrms were gone."

"Then why didn't you?" asked Lofgar, glaring.

"They wanted to see us all fly out here for nothing so they could laugh," muttered the female beside him. Hel crouched back, narrowing her eyes.

"I *would* expect an exile to come running at the promise of a meal," snipped Valdis from beside Stigr. The black gryfon eyed her reproachfully, for he had been an exile from his own pride, and not out of opportunism. She flattened her ears and looked away as she appeared to realize her sharp tongue would not aide Kjorn's cause.

"I am disappointed," rumbled Mbari, though the lion chief didn't stand. His tufted tail dusted the ground, and he watched Kjorn with hooded eyes. "Very disappointed indeed that this battle did not come. We would have sung of it for many generations."

"But," added Ajia, eyeing Mbari sternly, "we do not believe you deceived us, Prince Kjorn. As healer and singer of my pride, I am glad not to see battle. I will say it, and proudly. In my dreams you raised the Sunwind, but now a new wind is blowing. I hope it will lift your wings higher, beyond war."

Kjorn inclined his head to her, and was about to speak, but Lofgar barked, "What are they saying? Tell them to stop grumbling like savages and speak properly. Tell those eagles to quit chittering."

"Tell him," Hildr rasped, a warning look in her eyes, "he may not understand us, but we understand him."

Mbari stood, and his full height and girth was nearly a match for Lofgar. "Yes, tell him we understand his disrespect all too well."

"Gibberish." Lofgar watched the big lion stand, looking smug. "Maybe it's the soft muzzle that does it ..."

Mbari bared his long, shining fangs. "Tell him he will not find my muzzle soft, if he does not shut what remains of his beak."

"Lofgar," Kjorn warned.

"Why is he here?" growled Ilesh, suddenly, the painted chief's round ears laying back. "He has no wish for harmony in these lands, only fighting. Many times we tried to speak to the gryfons of the lake, but they do not hear. I will not speak to those who cannot hear."

"What's he saying?" grumbled Lofgar.

"I'm beginning to agree with you," Stigr muttered to the painted wolf, who made a low noise.

Lofgar raised his wings. "Listen, you—"

Nilsine made a sound of disdain to cut him off, tail ticking back and forth. "If *you* would listen properly . . ."

Lofgar's attention whipped to the smaller Vanhar, and he broke the ring, stepping forward in threat. "Don't preach at me, fishmonger. Your kind are so soft-hearted and cold it's a wonder you don't melt in a hot summer win—"

To Shard's surprise, it was Rok who lunged first, smashing into the wider Lakelander with a vicious snarl. Asvander's father Asrik, and the female beside him leaped to Lofgar's aide. Mbari darted in with a delighted snarl, claws flashing, even as Shard and Kjorn rushed forward, shouting for all to calm down.

Shard whirled about, opening his wings when he heard others following. He stopped Stigr, Valdis, Hildr, Grunna, and Asvander all from diving into the fray. "No!" When the painted wolves trotted forward, Shard snapped his beak. "Ilesh, stay here!"

Behind Shard, he heard snarling, lashing wings and snapping beaks, and Kjorn's voice, demanding that all of them stand down.

When the gryfons and other creatures before Shard halted, he whirled and grabbed the cool end of a burning branch, leaped over the fire and joined Kjorn, slashing the fire in warning at the tangled knot of gryfons and lions fighting.

Cries of alarm and flailing wings and paws ended with Rok and Mbari scrambling back, Ajia slipping to Shard's side, and Kjorn lunging in to shove Lofgar back and out of the circle of leaders. Asrik and the female Lakelander shrank back from Kjorn's fury.

With a snarl, Lofgar swiped at Kjorn, and the gold gryfon bellowed a roar and broke into an eagle screech, leaping so fast and unexpectedly even Shard stared. He knocked Lofgar to the ground and, using his momentum, shoved the Lakelander through the dirt to the edge of the canyon and pinned him there, locking talons over his throat.

"You will leave this meeting. I need honorable warriors who know when to fight, and when not, who don't insult and pick quarrels with my allies. You are *dismissed.*"

Lofgar grunted, wings splayed, and eyed the canyon below him. If Kjorn shoved him, he would have little time to correct and would likely end up dashed on the rocks below. "You can't—"

"I am."

The wispy clouds above had burned off, and light came over them, shining on Kjorn's bright feathers, lighting the faces of all who stared. Kjorn raised his head and Shard watched, setting his brand back in the fire.

Swiveling, but still holding the Lakelander down, Kjorn declared to the gathering, "Know this! We came here for a war, but that war has already been won. I thought, truly, that the wyrms remained, that we had a battle still to fight. I tried to trick none of you, I came in good faith as you did. Now we fall back into old enmity, old disputes."

Clenching his talons against a protest from Lofgar, he continued, tail lashing, wings lifting. "I see a gathering of creatures bold and willing, ready to fight and to die for *our* land, our families. But are we willing to do anything else? Are we willing *not* to fight? I thought my challenge here was the great enemy, the wyrms. But I see it is not. I see clearly now that my challenge . . . our challenge on this day, my friends, is not war."

His gaze raked the staring eyes and found Shard, locking hard on him. Shard lifted his head in encouragement.

Kjorn, his voice strong, his eyes lit with the understanding of what Shard had tried to tell him all along, said, "It is peace."

36
THE SILVER DRAGON

THE DENSE PINE FOREST OF Star Island should have surrounded Ragna like an old friend, but it had grown alien by time and distance. The scent of resin and green needles reminded her of younger days, adventures with Sigrun, Baldr, and Stigr, and filled her heart with longing.

But she couldn't afford to long for younger days just then. She stalked through the forest, every feather on end, hissing Sverin's name. She had pursued him and the dragon through the rain all the way to Star Isle, watched the horrible creature flying, then slowing down, bellowing rage.

Then, for apparently no reason at all, the monster had retreated. The last Ragna saw of her, she was roaring for her horde and flying nightward in a weary, lurching way.

Reptiles, she thought grimly, entering a clearing still patched with snow where the shadows of the trees kept the ground cold. Perhaps, like true lizards, the beasts would have been slowed by the freezing rain and the icy Silver Isles night. With any luck at all, they would be too sluggish to move for awhile, recovering from the cold and whatever long flight they had made over the sea.

Ragna knew she should have checked in, told the pride she was alive, found out who all had been lost, but a more pressing duty urged her to hunt through the forest.

"Sverin!" Ragna hissed, perking her ears. The clearing stood silent. Not even the birds sang as the sun rose and glittered trails across the snow. All the islands seemed shocked by the arrival of the marauding dragons.

Ragna thought grimly of Sigrun and how she would be worrying, but her worst fear was that Sverin had been scared Nameless again, that he would once again plague the islands with his thoughtless killing and terror.

Although, compared to the monsters, Ragna supposed Sverin was about as dangerous as a snow bunting.

She risked raising her voice, not sure where the wyrms were sheltered, when they would stir, or how well they could hear. "Son of Per!"

Surely he would've remained on the island. He was hesitant enough to fly before, and now that they knew the monsters flew in the day time, she doubted he would open his wings at all.

The crunch of talons in snow sent Ragna whipping around, heart soaring to her throat, wings flinging open. Not realizing how terrified she'd been that the wyrms might appear any moment, it was strange to feel calm and relief flood her at the sight of Sverin, slinking toward her from the cool morning shadows.

"What are you doing here?" he rasped.

Ragna eyed his wings, unbound and half-furled over his back like a shield to ward off attack from above. She had never seen him on the Star Isle, and he looked strange and more out-of-place than ever in the dense pine trees.

"Looking for you. Or was my calling your name confusing?"

"Where are they?" he growled. Ragna, eyeing the sky, slipped out of the clearing to join him in the trees. Her heart still trotted in her chest like panicked deer.

"I don't know. If they're smart, they would've flown to Pebble's Throw for the warmth." The idea occurred to her as she said it, and scant relief slowed her blood. Yes, they would've followed any currents of heat toward the lava flows ...

Ragna blinked, looking at Sverin's open wings, and with sharp amazement remembered him snapping the chains. "You," she breathed, glaring at him. "You could have done that any time. Those chains never held you."

For a moment he didn't speak, and she feared for his mind. At last, the great scarlet wings folded, with neat precision, and he raised his head to a formal angle. "I told you," he said quietly, "I wish to see my son again."

Ragna simply looked at him, feeling foolish, feeling patronized. "You did it for show."

"I did it for you, yes," he said. "For you, and for Thyra. To show them I acknowledge you both as queens."

"We don't need ..." She stopped. They did need his acknowledgement, she and Thyra and even Kjorn, or the old Aesir would not follow them, despite all Sverin had done. Now, by allowing himself to be imprisoned, he had still done what was needed to give the pride what small scrap of stability he could.

For whatever it's worth, now, she thought bitterly.

"Thank you," she said, knowing her voice sounded too cool, and not caring.

"You came for me?" His voice was quiet again, his eyes on the jagged slivers of sky between the trees.

"Of course I did." Ragna lifted her head, sniffing warily, ears flicking, and heard nothing. It was more eerie than calming. "What would we do if you were flying about Nameless *and* these creatures were terrorizing the islands?"

He looked down, his gold eyes spearing her like a talon on a fish. "I don't think I will fall Nameless again."

Ragna wasn't so sure, but she wasn't going to argue with him. "Let's go. We must return to the pride, we must go underground."

Crimson ears ticked back uncertainly. "Underground?"

"Yes. Where we hid before, when . . ." *When you killed Einarr and threatened the rest of us with exile or death.* She met his eyes, said it all in her silence, and he looked away. Ragna realized she didn't quite know where there was an entrance to the underground labyrinth on the Star Isle, but she didn't want Sverin to see her uncertainty.

Turning, she boldly walked into the open field and strode across, not looking back. After a couple of heartbeats, she heard Sverin follow.

They re-entered the chilly cover of trees on the other side of the meadow, and Ragna kept her eyes sharp for holes in the ground, and scents of gryfons or wolves. Not a bird or a small creature moved in the brush. It was as if the islands were deserted, afraid to release a breath or a sound.

The flick of a shadow in the corner of her eye made Ragna pause mid-step, talons raised. She squinted, sniffing slowly.

"Do you understand, now?" Sverin asked quietly.

Ragna loosed a harsh breath, flicking her ears forward, away from him. The faint smell of wolf drifted to her, but in the cold she couldn't tell how fresh it was.

"I understand why you wanted to take your son away, but not everything after. Not the Conquering. I will never understand that."

He fell silent again. If he had hoped for more understanding or reassurance from her, she had none to give.

Then, he spoke her very worst fear. "If Rashard flew to the Winderost, you must know that he probably met these monsters."

"I know," Ragna said tightly. An icicle of fear twisted through her chest.

"You must be prepared. Both of us must be prepared." His voice was like iron—cold, hard, yet with a heady strength. "If our sons—"

"Shard lives." A voice drifted from the trees, a female voice Ragna knew, but it was not a gryfon.

Sverin's hackle feathers prickled, and he and Ragna turned to behold a pack of wolves approaching through the trees. Relief swelled over Ragna at the interruption. They had kept Sverin from speaking a horrible possibility—instead, Catori said what Ragna most needed to hear.

Ahanu, the young wolf king, led them, but beside him walked Catori, and it was she who had spoken. Behind her walked Tocho. The rest of the adult pack halted, then milled, behind them.

Ahanu stopped, lock-legged, when he saw Sverin.

The sight of the red War King in his forest laid back the young wolf's ears, raised his lip to a snarl to show yellow fangs. The wind stirred the feathers braided into his shaggy coat, and they flicked together, gray and gold. Signs of friendship and trust.

Sverin's gaze drifted to the blue feather Tocho wore, then settled on the gold feather at Ahanu's neck. No one spoke.

Catori caught Ragna's gaze, dipped her head. "We heard the terrible battle. We saw the creatures. We checked the tunnels and found your pride there. Caj told us that you led the largest of them away, and I promised Sigrun I would hunt for you. Tocho told Caj he would hunt for you, son of Per," she said softly. "And he chose to remain with Thyra."

A grating growl rolled from Ahanu's chest. Catori nosed his cheek. "Brother. We left our war and our hatred on Black Rock this winter."

"*He* was not with us on Black Rock."

Sverin stepped forward, toward the wolf king, whose forests he had poached for ten years, whose brothers and sisters he'd sent gryfons to kill, and whose father had died by Sverin's own talons.

The pack shifted behind Ahanu and Catori, and Ragna held her breath.

Sverin opened his flight-feathers, and Ragna tensed, but the War King splayed his blood-red wings low, and mantled before the king of Star Island.

As he had with every Vanir who stood before him and listed his sins, he lifted his eyes to Ahanu's and said, low but clear, "Forgive me."

Ahanu tossed his head as if struggling to release himself from the yoke of his anger, from the growl locked in his throat. His sister pressed to him with a low, comforting sound. As a mother, Ragna almost longed to go to him and wrap him in her wings. But it would not do. Instead, she gazed at Sverin, unbelieving.

"We have a common threat, now," Ahanu said at last, shaking himself hard. "We will stand with the gryfons of the Sun Isle, for we also have a common hope, for peace, I think. I see Tyr's light in you now, Per's son, if not Tor's. I see you have changed. I see all that, and still my heart hurts for all that has passed."

"Know that mine does too, Helaku's son."

Shock slid down Ragna's backbone to realize that he understood the wolves, and she wondered when he had started truly listening. She wondered if it was when Kjorn had left, or during his imprisonment, or perhaps when Vidar had forgiven him. He caught her stare, and tilted one ear in acknowledgement of her surprise, but gave no explanation. Perhaps even he didn't have one.

Ahanu saw that he understood as well, and to hear his father's name seemed to pull a shadow from him. Ragna saw him remember that his father had also been lost to anger and hatred, nearly Nameless by the end. His amber eyes pierced, then lightened. He looked from Ragna to Sverin and slowly lowered his tail. With his pack surrounding him, the wolf king managed a stiff dip of his head. "Then let us have an understanding at last."

Sverin didn't rise, and Ragna met Catori's eyes in amazement. The she-wolf's reddish coat was bright in the dark woods, her amber eyes shining. She had been a friend to Shard, a guide, a fellow seer. "Catori. You said my son lives."

"Oh yes. And I have even more joyous, and curious news to add. Will you come with us?" She glanced to Sverin. "Both of you."

Sverin looked wary. Burning with curiosity and hope, Ragna trotted forward, not bothering to urge the red gryfon one way or the other. If he wanted to remain in the woods, alone, then he was welcome to. After a glance at Ahanu, who tilted his head in polite encouragement, Sverin followed at a step behind Ragna.

Ahanu, Catori, and Tocho led the way, picking up to a ground-devouring lope. Ragna and Sverin followed, trotting, leaping over fallen trees and rocks, and the rest of the pack streamed behind them. They ran in silence.

One glance beside her at Sverin showed a determined expression, narrowed gaze, and curiosity to match Ragna's own. To her surprise, she saw no hint of anger or irritation that he was forced to run on the ground like a wolf—then, she thought—neither of them wanted to risk flying with the monsters at large.

They remained under the cover of cedar and pine and grasping, dark rowan still naked from winter. The wet scent of thawing ground filled Ragna with the wild hopes of spring. It felt good to run, to stretch her anxious muscles and feel the earth under her.

Then they came to a place Ragna had seen only once, in her youth.

The great rowan tree that the wolves called home stood as the crown over a jutting mass of rock that broke up through the forest floor. Roots entwined with rock and earth, forming hollows and holes where the wolves denned, and the branches creaked in a growing wind.

Oddly, a thick coat of snow piled on top of the jutting rock base, all about the rowan roots, shining silver and cut with shadow in the morning light. Ragna would've thought even the bare branches, spiraling like a thousand talons into the sky, would've been enough to keep snow from the ground beneath.

But she was distracted from that strange sight by realizing that she smelled not only wolf scent all around the den, but gryfon. The strong, heady, downy-feline scent of familiar gryfons filled her senses.

"Who is here?" Ragna whispered. As she asked it, Catori came up beside her, and she saw gryfon faces peek out of the wolf dens, a dozen or more, young and old. They were almost all familiar to her. They were all Vanir.

A gryfess stepped forward from the rest, and Ragna recognized Maja, Halvden's mother, who had flown starward in Shard's name to find the rest of the lost Vanir.

Before Ragna could close her beak or ask a question, the Vanir gryfess mantled low, and spoke haltingly.

"Forgive us our cowardice, my queen. We arrived in the night. We heard the roars of the monsters even across the ocean as we flew nearer. We didn't dare go to the nesting cliffs. Most are weary, ill." As she stood tall again, her gaze switched to Sverin. Thankfully, he remained quiet, and lowered his head. Maja looked back to Ragna with a guarded expression of triumph.

"We didn't know the state of things, and we didn't know what battle you fought. Our guide suggested that we not join the fight yet, that we had no chance against the foe, that you would want us to remain safe. So we landed on Star Isle, and the wolves welcomed us, sheltered us, and told us all that has passed."

Ragna stared at Maja, around at the other Vanir she had gathered from the highest quarter of the world, then registered the one thing in her story that sounded odd. "Your . . . guide?"

Maja hesitated. "Yes. We met him over the sea, and he told us of the monsters, called wyrms, and of true dragons, and an ancient, unforgiveable act that has caused all of this."

Sverin's ears perked, and slowly he raised his head. He was staring at the rowan roots above the rock dens.

"Wyrms?" Ragna asked. "You mean, the monsters? Then what are dragons?"

Maja's whole face lit as if the sun had broken through the dense, dark branches. After an encouraging whuff from Catori, the gryfess tilted her head to look behind her, at the pile of snow. Sverin also stared at the pile of snow.

Then Ragna realized it was not snow.

It moved.

Her eye caught on the edges of the palest silver scales and she realized the pile of snow was tightly stacked layers of serpentine coils. She saw that the slashes of shadow were black wings like swan wings, and her beak opened slowly as an elegant, wedge-shaped head rose from the shimmering silver, and regarded her with luminous eyes the color of the sun. A soft nose like a deer sniffed the cold air, and two whiskers drooped elegantly from the long snout.

"Fear not," he said, the voice a strange mix of foreign, windy whispering and the incongruent burr of a gryfon accent.

Then, his gaze fell on Sverin and he loosed an inelegant squeal of surprise and delight, breaking his spell on Ragna.

To Sverin's credit, he did not look afraid, but watched the creature in pure amazement.

"Oh, this is good," said the serpent. "This is good, that you've come. You're even redder than I thought, I must say. It's very surprising. You look like Kagu in his spring scales—"

"Pardon me," Ragna said. Catori pressed reassuringly against her wing and nosed her feathers. The gigantic eyes found her again, the coils loosened from the rowan, and he flowed toward her. It was only Catori's warm presence at her side that stopped her from stumbling away. "Pardon, but what, and who are you?"

"Oh!" he purred, climbing down from the rowan mound and settling back into a crouch, like a mountain cat. "You are Ragna, I know you are. He has your very eyes, and I think he must be built a bit more like you than his father, for from this angle, you almost—"

Catori whined in amusement, giving the creature a pointed look. He drew back, drew up, and up, tucking silver claws neatly against his chest.

"Forgive me. I'm so weary from the flight and so excited, so pleased to see you." He glanced to Catori, Ahanu, then Maja and Ragna again. "I have much to tell you."

"My king," the wolf Tocho murmured from behind Ragna. "While our noble friend catches them up, I will tell the other gryfons Ragna and Sverin are well?"

"Yes," Ahanu said, not taking his eyes from Sverin. Watching Sverin, Ragna thought wryly. Of all the remarkable things in that grove, Sverin was what the wolf king would watch.

"Thank you," murmured Catori, and the gold wolf sped off into the trees. Ragna noted none of the wolves or Vanir seemed amazed by the silver serpent, realizing they had all spent the night together, and she couldn't fathom where he'd come from or what he was about.

Sverin spoke, repeating Ragna's question. "Yes, clearly you have much to tell us. But who are you?"

The serpent opened his slender black wings and inclined his head. "Son of Per, and Ragna the White, have no fear. I am a friend to gryfons. I'm here to help you. I am a dragon of the Sunland, apprentice to the Chronicler. I've come here to help, and to tell you a sad history that will make some things clearer."

He looked at Ragna with a soft gleam in his eyes. "But more than anything, you should know that I am Shard's wingbrother, Amaratsu's son, Hikaru."

37
THE MEASURE OF A KING

T HE COUNCIL STRETCHED THROUGH THE day, and the fledges whom
Shard had called too young for battle took on the duty of finding
kindling and wood for the fires.

Kjorn was grateful they found a way to keep busy, grateful they
hadn't had to see a battle.

The fledges, with the yearling lions, juvenile eagles, and some
young pack members from the painted wolves, declared an unsteady
truce and dissolved into exploration of the canyons, short hunts for
small game, and gathering wood.

Kjorn set adults to keep an eye on them and make sure no fights
broke out, but once the battle fervor dissolved from the gathering, the
youngest of their number banded together in fellowship. Kjorn called it
a good sign, an opportunity. That their youngest could display tolerance
and peace, he proclaimed, should show that they could do no less.

He hoped everyone took the hint. The rest of the long, agonizing
day, he spent in negotiations.

He almost would've preferred a battle.

Clouds gusted across the Voldsom but didn't rain, and the wind
died as the sun shone again in the afternoon. The gryfons and eagles

traced maps in the sand of the landscape as they knew it from above, with corrections from various clans, and they laid out new borders. Old borders. Ancient borders, from the time of the first gryfon kings of the Winderost before the Aesir claimed more than was their right.

The arguing and the insults threatened to split Kjorn's skull.

Still, every time he looked up, Shard was there. Shard, whose mild expression was like a cooling balm. Sometimes, he would furtively imitate Asrik's sour expression, or a murmur a joke for Kjorn's ears alone, and Kjorn had to fight laughter.

"You're doing well," Shard murmured at the first evening mark.

They ceased negotiations for the night, now that Ilesh and the wolves were happy with the hunting grounds surrendered by the Aesir and the Lakelanders. Brynja, Nilsine, and others had gone to hunt, for stretched tempers would surely snap back to violence if there was no food. "Kjorn, you looked like a king today."

The words helped, and Kjorn knew he meant them. But it didn't cool his worry over the tensions, or his fear that the wyrms would find the Silver Isles before he could go home to his mate. His sense of urgency swelled.

"Thank you. Shard, it sounds foolish to admit, but I realize I wanted..." Glancing to the side, he saw the lions and the painted wolf leader in conversation, saw that the gryfons of the Ostral Shores and the Vanheim were at last speaking civilly, now that Lofgar had been dismissed and another had taken his place in the council.

No one was eavesdropping and he and Shard. He strained, tried, wanted to tell his true heart to his wingbrother, but it sounded both foolish and vain. He said it anyway. "I wanted them to see me as a warrior. A hero."

Shard chirruped in amusement and Kjorn glared at him. Ruffling his feathers, Shard said, "They know you from the Battle of Torches. And look at what you've done here. Can't you be a greater hero for leading no one to their death?"

Kjorn looked away at the fading light in the sky, and laid back his ears. "I can't explain it to you. You have a peaceful nature."

"At the end of all this," Shard said quietly, "you'll have the peace you promised everyone, and be a wise ruler. Everyone is listening now, Kjorn. Even Asrik can understand the lions. The Aesir of the Dawn Spire have an agreement with the eagles, the respect of the painted packs, and respect *for* them. Isn't that what you wanted?"

"Of course." He thought of all he'd learned in the Silver Isles, his new friendship with the wolves, his new respect for all Named and thinking creatures. Shame coiled to know that a small part of him *had*, in his deep heart, wanted a war.

A part of him still wanted it. A part of him still wanted to face the wyrms in combat, to slay one, as Shard had done, to let them see his fury and take vengeance on them for terrorizing his land and his father and taking him from his birthright. Part of him had truly wanted a war that would gloriously win him his kingdom, so that he could be a true hero, remembered as the king who drove the wyrms from the Winderost.

It was difficult to make ballads about treaties and councils.

"You'll be remembered." As if reading his mind, Shard walked up alongside to press his wing to Kjorn's. "You'll be remembered, and your kits and the new lion cubs of the First Plains and the eaglets who hatch this spring will know it was you who gave the heart and courage of the Aesir back to them, it was you who united the Winderost—not in war, but in peace."

Kjorn looked over at Shard, at his short, slim, unassuming, life-long friend. An ember flared and clawed his heart and he didn't know if he felt love and gratitude, or regret. "Was it truly me, Shard?"

Green eyes met his calmly, and Kjorn saw again a strange, eerie new depth to his friend's gaze. He wondered what Shard had seen. He wondered at the land of the dragons at the bottom of the world, at the visions of the Vanir, at the dreams where Shard claimed to fly in the mind of the wyrm queen, Rhydda. He wondered many things he was certain he'd never enjoy answers for.

"It was you," Shard said, in Shard's own voice—not some strange seer, not some mystical Vanir, but himself again, scrawny and wry and admiring. "Of course it was. You could have ignored everything, battled Orn and claimed the Dawn Spire and set gryfon against gryfon, but you didn't."

Kjorn huffed a long breath. "If you say so."

"I do."

"Well," Kjorn said, turning away again and twitching his tail. "If I have the blessing of the Summer King..."

Shard laughed and bumped him. "Now finish up your treaties so we can fly home."

Kjorn's heart darkened, and he thought of Thyra. He prayed to bright Tyr that the wyrms were lost over the sea, or had simply flown to their own muddy homeland. He was about to speak when a voice from above drew their attention.

"Hail, my lord!" A young gryfon circled, and Kjorn recognized Fraenir. The former rogue had fallen in happily with Asvander and the rest of the Guard of the Dawn Spire. "Your presence is requested at the dawnward border of camp." He sounded almost as if he might laugh.

"Why?"

Dipping low, wings beating, Fraenir met his gaze. "Orn has come."

Kjorn and Shard exchanged a look, and as sunset cast purple across the sky, they bounded forward, leaping into the air.

A RING OF SENTRIES stood around Orn, and Esla, who had come to greet him as well. In all the haste and planning, Kjorn had still barely spoken to his mother's sister, nor met his own cousin who was still a nestling. He knew, somehow, that much of it would have to wait until after he'd gone and returned from the Silver Isles again.

Standing with his mate by his side, Orn looked rested, regal, alert. His stern gaze fell on Kjorn as he landed, and then Shard with some skepticism.

"I hear your great enemy has fled."

"Our great enemy." Kjorn folded his wings and walked forward, twitching his tail to let Shard know he would handle Orn alone. "Yes. The Battle of Torches drove them out after all." He decided to leave out the part about Shard speaking to Rhydda, and Shard didn't correct him. "A mere show of bravery was all it took. They are Nameless, Voiceless cowards, and I doubt if they'll ever return."

"Perhaps." The older gryfon appraised him, and Kjorn was half disappointed to see that he was calm, but pleased to see he was not amused that Kjorn's great war would not happen. Around them, sentries stood tense, including Asvander, Rok, and Fraenir, ready to leap and defend Kjorn at the first sign of aggression. It wouldn't do.

"You can go back to the perimeter," Kjorn said, addressing Asvander mostly. "I think lord Orn and I have an understanding."

Asvander grated his beak together in protest, then called an order to disperse.

"That was big of you," Orn said, and now it was only he, Esla, Shard, and Kjorn. The tawny gryfess watched Kjorn quietly, her severe, pale blue eyes alert, her manner tense. He knew she was an ally, but also that she had no desire for Orn to die. Yet the issue of the Dawn Spire remained.

"No it wasn't." Kjorn gave him a measuring look. "Do you think I fear you?"

For a long moment, Orn watched him. Then, to Kjorn's surprise and the rest, he laughed, a harsh, hard laugh. "No. No, son of Sverin. I can't see that you fear much of anything. I wanted to believe you a warmonger, a conqueror, brave when it suited you, cowardly like your father when the winds shifted. But I see you are a different gryfon. How, I couldn't say." His gaze did drift to Shard, then, who inclined his head.

Esla spoke to Orn, her voice like silky wind. "My lord, you see what has happened here in the meantime."

"Yes. Indeed." Orn looked around, his short ears twitching. "When I heard the wyrms didn't show, I expected to be wading in the blood of these lifelong enemies. I expected bodies, and grudges, and

I'll admit I'd hoped to revel in your failure and take my pride home. Well."

He stopped, watching as, in the distance, a yearling lion, an Aesir fledge, and a lanky painted wolf pup raced up over the rim of the canyon. Each bore a stick for the nightly fires, in a friendly contest as if they'd known each other all their short lives.

"Well," he said again.

"Well, indeed," purred Esla. "My lord."

Kjorn felt Shard's eyes on him, and wondered desperately what his wingbrother was thinking. He'd thought of challenging Orn, of slaying him in single combat and claiming the king's tier of the Dawn Spire. But here stood an aging, reasonable gryfon, father of a nestling who was also Kjorn's own cousin, and with a mate who was blood to Kjorn.

"What am I to do here?" Orn asked quietly.

Kjorn couldn't answer, for he asked the same question of himself. A part of him wondered if he deserved the Dawn Spire at all, if he had not won it in battle.

The raspy laughter of eagles and gryfons, growling boasts from Mbari, telling stories around the orange fire, and the rapt exclamations of young gryfons told Kjorn a different story than war, and his heart warmed a little. Once not so long ago, Shard had not been afraid to tell Kjorn he wanted his birthright back, and surely he had earned it. Kjorn stepped forward, raising his wings.

"I want the Dawn Spire, Orn. You see what we've done here. I want to stand where my forefathers stood. You've watched over the land these ten years, and for that I thank you. But my sun rises now, and I want the kingdom." Haltingly, he bowed his head. "But I want it only with your blessing, regent of the Dawn Spire, for I know that is the only way for true peace, and my own heart."

Esla loosed a pleased sound, and Shard touched his wingtip to Kjorn's flank in approval. Stars pricked the sky, Kjorn kept his head low, and at last Orn tucked his beak down, though his ears perked attentively.

"Truly, you are different than your forebears." He lifted his head, ears alert, eyes bright. Kjorn saw that he was not any kind of grasping, aggressive warlord, but only a gryfon who had been chosen to rule, who wanted the best for the pride. They both understood that the best meant the less fighting, the better.

"Your blessing?" Kjorn asked again, quietly.

"You have my blessing," Orn declared. "My support, my fealty, Kjorn, son-of-Sverin." He raised his voice a little. "I think everyone here can see there is only one king of the Dawn Spire."

Kjorn didn't realize they'd gathered an audience until they heard the hush that followed Orn's statement, and Kjorn glanced to the side to see all manner of creatures watching them. They'd slowly gathered to witness, and the first to raise his voice, to Kjorn's surprise and his eternal gratitude, was Stigr.

"Hail Kjorn, king of the Dawn Spire!"

Shard joined him, Valdis, Asvander, and his aunt, all the voices Kjorn knew. The lions roared their approval, the eagles swooping through the dark, cheered him, and when he looked again at Orn, the older gryfon mantled, straightened, and raised his voice with the rest.

When the fervor died and all began to disperse, Shard slipped to Kjorn, and draped his wing over Kjorn's back. "Well done, your Highness. With Orn on your side, the Dawn Spire will be secure while you return with me to fetch the others."

"Yes," Kjorn said quietly, understanding the hint. "It will." He stepped away and met Shard's eyes. "If your Vanir are well..."

Shard studied his face, and Kjorn felt the sense of urgency kindle between them. "Yes," he murmured.

Kjorn watched as his wingbrother's gaze wandered the gathered creatures, settling briefly on Stigr who was laughing with Valdis and Asvander. Then his eyes found Kjorn again, and he raised his head. "I'll spread the word not to stay up too late celebrating. We can depart at dawn."

38
LEAVETAKING

A STIFF, COOL WIND GUSTED ACROSS the Voldsom, but from where Shard stood on the rim, he spied good weather dawnward. They would leave today, fly across the Winderost to the Dawn Reach and depart from that shore, where Shard had first arrived. It was, as far as anyone knew, the most direct route back to the Silver Isles.

Nerves and relief mingled in his muscles to at last be embarking on the journey home. Behind him, the Vanir woke, stretched, and the canyons filled with their buzzing anticipation.

The final evening of negotiations had seen old alliances renewed, new alliances forged, and Kjorn firmly recognized as king of the Dawn Spire.

It was the greatest meeting ever known by the Winderost since the Second Age, and so Kjorn declared it the Greatmeet, a rite of peace, and had asked that every clan of creatures send leaders to meet once again each year, every year, in the spring, to keep strong the bonds they had tied there. All agreed.

Shard had thought he would feel more pride, more awe, but all he felt was relief that it was done, and anxiousness to get home.

Shard had bid goodbye to the eagles, the painted wolves, and the lioness Ajia. He'd bid goodbye to all in the Winderost who were at the Greatmeet and who knew him, who considered him a friend.

All but one.

"Good day for flying," Stigr remarked, walking up to Shard's right side.

Hard talons seemed to grasp Shard's throat. He nodded once.

"I'll be all right, you know," Stigr went on, blunt, as wry and dry as the first night Shard had met him on Star Island. It felt as if his uncle's voice and presence permeated the wind all around, reverberated in the dust and in Shard's every feather. "I'll be all right, here. I see now what you see in Kjorn. He'll be a good king. And I have Valdis—"

Shard turned and buried his face against Stigr's neck, grinding his beak against fledge-like whimper. "*I'll* miss you, Uncle. You did everything for me, and I—"

Stigr tucked his head over Shard's and drew a ragged sigh. He preened one feather briefly, in a paternal way. "You'll be all right too, Shard. You will."

He stepped back, appraising Shard with a critical eye. Shard realized how desperately he would miss everything about his uncle, how he'd imagined their life in peace back in the Silver Isles.

"Thank you for everything you did for me," Shard said, ducking his head in deference.

Stigr laughed wryly, looking over his wing at the mix of Aesir and Vanir behind him, the strange harmony. "No, Shard. Thank you."

"Stigr . . ." Shard bit back more words and shut his eyes, trying to will some strength into his voice.

Stigr smacked him over the head with a wing. Shard jumped, laughed, and shook himself. "I'm complimenting you," he grumbled. "I want to remember you bright, happy, princely. Give it a try."

Shard laughed again and sleeked his feathers with more dignity, raising his head. Behind, the others waited, quietly preening, stretching, readying.

"I'll still miss you."

"I hope so," Stigr said wryly. "But not too much. I think we'll see each other again. I want to meet your kits. Maybe you can even drag that sister of mine here some day."

Shard nodded once. There was much to do before any of that might happen. But he said only, "I will."

Wind brought the scent of sage, a good dawn wind that would help them rise high and cover a lot of ground. They heard Kjorn, bidding farewell to those who would keep order while he was away, and gathering those who meant to escort him to the Silver Isles.

He heard Brynja and Ketil, counting heads among the Vanir. But no one approached Stigr and him. No one would interrupt or rush them.

Stigr stepped in close to Shard again. "I want you to listen to me one last time, Shard. And listen well." Shard tilted his head, ears perking obediently. "You've got to let them serve you. The Vanir. You've got to let yourself be their prince. You were born to a great line, you've done great deeds already, and you've got work yet to do. At first they saw Baldr in you. Now, they see Rashard, the Summer King, and love you in your own right. Let them. I've said it once. I say it again now, while I have your ear."

"I know." Shard's ears flicked back self-consciously.

"I don't think you do." He perked his ears sternly, watching Shard with piercing fondness. "Let them help, obey, and protect you. Above all else, when this is done, *you* must remain, you must be there to rule your pride."

"I know, Uncle." He pressed his talons into the hard earth, breathing the scents of the Winderost.

"You keep saying that, but listen to me, nephew. Valdis told me when they came upon you in the Outlands, you'd practically challenged that big she-wyrm to single combat after finding Toskil's mother dead. That won't do. It's well enough that you're their hero now, but now you must stay alive. Stay alive for them, for your mother and the pride, and the work to be done at home."

Stigr's true meaning sank in slowly, like water to his skin. Anything could happen on the journey. Even now, the wyrms might be ravaging Shard's own homeland. "I'll have Kjorn at my side, too."

Stigr glanced over his shoulder. "I know Kjorn thinks he would die for you, I'll give him that. But in the moment he'd have to decide between saving you and surviving, he would decide to live. For his pride, for the rest of his family, even if it meant losing you. You must be willing to do the same." Shard began to argue, but Stigr moved his head sharply in negation. "That's what it means to be a king. He knows that. You need to know it too."

"I would die for any of them," Shard said, eyes narrowing.

"I know, Shard. So do they. But they don't need you to die, they need you to *live*. A living king is better than a dead one. Remember that."

"Stigr—"

"A living king," he said again, very quietly.

Shard drew a slow breath. His mind flickered to an old vision, a dream of a red gryfon and a gray gryfon battling over the sea. "My father," he said as it dawned on him. "You don't think he should have challenged Per."

Stigr looked taken aback, as if he hadn't been thinking of it directly, then his eye narrowed and he nodded once. "I told him not to, but I think he believed it was best at the time. But that's long done."

"It is," Shard said, surprised and encouraged to hear his uncle letting go of the past, at long last.

Wind drifted, stirring the scent of dust, frost, and all their allies.

Shard felt locked to the earth. He knew there was nothing more to say.

The day of Halflight would soon rise, and with it would come the spring whelping. Shard knew that Kjorn wanted nothing more now than to be present for the birth of his heir. Shard knew that. He too wanted nothing but to ease the strong tugging in his breast that still insisted he must be home, that now felt like a hot claw in his chest.

But he could not move.

"It's time, Shard." Stigr backed away from him, bowing his head. "It's time."

Taking a long breath, Shard turned, extending his wing toward Stigr's good side. With soft surprise, Stigr opened his wing to eclipse it.

"Fair winds, Uncle."

"Fair winds, my prince." Stigr gave him a long, quiet look, and a rueful laugh. "My friend."

Shard met the sharp, green eye one last time, turned, and hoarsely shouted the order to fly.

THE FIRST TWO DAYS passed in excited chatter, with fair skies the first day that took them across the Winderost to the dawnward shore. A brisk tailwind gusted them the second day, ushering the air toward spring, and the exiled Vanir toward their home.

A band of over a hundred warriors from the Dawn Spire, the Ostral Shore, and the Vanheim flew at their backs.

Taking Shard's dire suspicions about the wyrms to heart, Kjorn had assembled an eager army to escort them home. Misgiving shifted in Shard's heart to have them, though he didn't dare tell Kjorn he didn't want them. He hoped he could speak to Rhydda if she truly was there, could make her see reason.

"I made the mistake of not trusting you about them leaving the Winderost," Kjorn had said when Shard commented on the size of the force. "I won't make such a mistake again."

There was iron in his expression, and Shard knew his golden friend thought only of Thyra, now, and what might await them at home. He said nothing about not wanting to antagonize the wyrms further, for he could see that having the warriors made all the rest of his pride feel more secure.

They flew in compact units, some as large as ten, most smaller than five. Each had a responsibility to know those in their group, to keep an eye on each other, to pause or slow if needed.

Nilsine, flying with Kjorn and Shard, had surprised them both by wanting to come. As a leader of the sentry warriors of the Vanhar, she insisted, said she wanted to see the Silver Isles, to meet the gryfons who she was certain had descended from the Vanhar in the Second Age. So she, Rok, Asvander, and Dagny formed an honor guard for Kjorn.

In Shard's unit flew Brynja, Ketil, Keta, and Toskil, and they all flew close to Kjorn's group at the head of the great company. Keta's nest-sister, Ilse, flew just behind with three of the elder Vanir, and it took everything in Shard's will not to constantly check back over his wing that everyone was still there.

Keta and Ilse had already proven their mettle by diving in and out of the sea for fish, and others of the younger generation followed, bringing small fare to the eldest and the middle-aged who led the groups.

When Shard did look back and see the clusters of Vanir with him, and the mass of warrior gryfons behind, he thought both of his ancestor Jaarl, one of the first gryfon kings of the Silver Isles, and of Per the Red, leading his loyal and cursed and blessed Aesir over the sea.

Were you running, or were you trying to help the Dawn Spire, or your son? Shard supposed he would never truly know.

That first long flight, alone, Shard had fallen Nameless, had followed an albatross and his instincts. Now, there was too much to pay attention to. It had felt so long, the sea endless, fathomless, the sky both ally and enemy.

Now the sea lay still, rippled only by little, bumpy waves. The sky glowed with sunset. Shard spied a clear horizon, and the air filled with the stirrings of gryfon wings and voices.

The winds calmed in the evening and they flew high and straight, following the line of stars that Shard believed would lead them to the Silver Isles. Ketil agreed, recalling the way.

As night fell, he thought again of Hikaru as the great dragon band of stars blazed across the night sky.

The third day passed in surprising laughter, with the Vanir showing off in the water, with Brynja impressing even Ketil by managing to snare fish from the waves. Warriors who flew with them but had not practiced sea flight remained on higher winds, tense, alert, and growing weary.

Shard directed the Vanir to fly to them, to teach them how to better use the sea air for more dynamic, long-range flying, as an albatross had once shown him.

When Shard looked at Kjorn, he appeared to be constantly counting heads. Occasionally his wingbrother would glance around, find Shard as if to reassure himself, then look forward again. They shared an understanding, a tension, both trying to focus on the journey at hand, but worried for those at home. Shard didn't dare try to reach out to Rhydda while he flew over the sea. It would take too much effort, pose too much risk.

That night, it rained. The slow, freezing drizzle was miserable, but not the kind of dangerous storm that Shard had faced when making the flight windward last autumn.

Dagny managed to keep spirits light by reminding everyone they would soon be home, they would soon build warm fires and taste the fish of their homeland and see their family and friends.

Shard was grateful for her. He knew he should be the one bolstering everyone, encouraging them, keeping spirits light, but he let others do it. The closer they flew, the heavier, rather than lighter, his heart became. His wings felt strained.

A darkness crept into his heart as he watched Kjorn's face, growing tense, Shard thought, at the idea of perhaps seeing his father again, nervous over his unborn kit, and Thyra, and the pride while they'd been away. Shard knew the source of his own worry—fear that he had led Rhydda and her horde to the Silver Isles.

At last when he'd lost count of the nights, under a star-swept sky, Shard looked up at the sparkling band of Midragur, felt the arc of the curving earth.

In a dreamlike way, he almost thought he could see his islands laid out in the sky, islands like the pad of a gryfon's hind paw.

The great Sun Isle, where he'd been born to a king and queen, where great, white mountains towered over broad fields of peat and birch forest. The Star Isle, where he'd met his friend and guide, Catori, and the boar, Lapu, and the dead wolf king, Helaku.

The stars seemed to raise their shining heads like wolves to call him, call him home, and a great pack raced along the dragon's back across the sky.

Shard felt he could soar to Talon's Reach, where the birds dwelled, Crow Wing, where wild horses ran, an island he'd never explored. At the far end lay Black Rock, where the dead were laid to rest.

Nothing moved, nothing breathed. Everything was hiding. The trees themselves seemed as if they would close in on the earth and hide. Flat. Still. Dead.

Then he beheld Pebble's Throw, where the lava ran.

And clustered on Pebble's Throw, Shard felt them. He felt them with a seizing thread of terror. He felt their anger, their pulsing, Voiceless rage.

Rhydda—

Amidst the unnatural stillness, ravens burst suddenly from all corners of the islands and swirled into the black sky, and formed a laughing, cawing storm. They clustered into a giant, wiggling mass and became Munin, laughing, but when Shard looked down, Munin's shadow was not a raven's shadow on the snow. The shadow of a horned head bellowed, a spade tail lashed.

Down on the pale, muddy earth in the shadow of the wyrm, a flame flicked, ran, singing across the snow, and he knew it was Catori.

She cried out toward the ravens, and their great shadow bled toward her across the ground. *Oh, what days have we lived to see?*

Seeing that, Shard's heart swelled, but not with joy. His blood and wings and heart expanded into a great, hot, beating heart of fury and anger and confusion.

But it was not *his* fury, or his heart. It was Rhydda.

He struggled to control the dream once he realized he was dreaming, to show her images of peace, rolling green fields and woods. Taking memories from her own dreams, he showed her waves of silver and gold.

Her blaring roar sucked the breath and the fight from him.

He dove, trying to outpace the surge of Nameless rage, and someone shouted his name.

"SHARD!"

He woke just before he hit the ocean like a rock.

Seawater filled his beak and his eyes. Flailing, Shard sputtered, realized he had fallen asleep, dreamed, and dropped right out of the sky. Night sky and clustering wings and shouts surrounded him.

"I'm fine!" he managed, flexing his wings against the waves which were not wild, but had only shocked him.

"Give him room," ordered Brynja from above. "Give him air! Shard, can you fly out?"

"I can." So saying, Shard flexed his wings again, coughed out more saltwater, and kicked. Gaining momentum, he was able to force himself from the waves.

"What happened?" Brynja winged around him as Shard tried to shake off freezing seawater.

Kjorn circled back to them, his eyes enormous in the starlight, his voice hard with worry. "All well, Shard? You fancy a midnight swim?"

"Yes, next time join me," Shard said, shuddering, pumping his wings to get away from the water and cold drafts near it. Brynja called out to reassure the rest, and they silently formed back into their groups. Shard looked around at the sky and saw familiar living stars, not the warped, eerie, vision of his dream.

"I..." He realized he'd been about to lie. It was so easy, so tempting to keep his fears and his failures from them. He thought of saying he'd seen a fish, had dived on purpose. "I dreamed," he said, clearly enough for all to hear. "And she's there. Rhydda. She's in the Silver Isles."

"No," whispered Kjorn.

"Shard," Asvander growled from above him, "are you *certain?*"

Shard looked sharply at his friend. "Yes." He worked his wings, and raised his voice, clear, hard, for all to hear. "Friends, hear me! The wyrms have flown to the Silver Isles. I'm certain of it now." He circled, winding up to fly above them all. His voice rang out in the cold, cloudless night, and wary gryfon eyes watched him. "They have flown, and we must be ready."

39

A QUIET WELCOME

THE LAST DAYS OF THE FLIGHT wore heavily on the eldest of their number, especially after Shard's grim announcement. Old Frar flew slower and slower, and Shard often glided back to him to encourage him personally. It seemed to be the only thing keeping him aloft.

Meanwhile, Shard felt the pace like an ache. The whole group worked to keep him awake, present, alert, but a sickening, familiar sense stalked at the edge of his awareness. Alone, he was certain he could have reached the islands much faster. But he could not leave his pride, his friends. Stigr's last words to him beat a steady rhythm in his heart.

Kjorn kept him present by working out their plan. "If all's not well at the nesting cliffs, we'll fly straight away to the wolf caves and see what's happening. I'm certain they would have sheltered there, and they'll be safe below ground."

"Unless the wyrms dig," Asvander said, having been listening from Kjorn's other flank.

Shard recalled the images in silver and gold relief in the halls of the Sunland dragons, of wyrms mining gold and gems. "I think they do. They dug out the gold and stones the dragons used to make their crafts."

Kjorn's feathers pricked in alarm and Asvander eyed Shard with growing wariness. "Let's hope they haven't figured out where your pride has fled, then."

Shard didn't answer.

They all fell into a long routine of keeping each other awake, floating on the waves to rest briefly, slowing, and slowing more for the oldest of them who'd grown tired. Shard's determination grew, and his sense of anger at the idea that somehow he himself might have led Rhydda to the Silver Isles.

Stigr's warning rang truer, that everything he'd tried to communicate to the wyrm might have been misunderstood.

If that is so, Shard wondered, and met Toskil's gaze across the waves to let him know he was well awake, *then how am I to tell her anything or learn anything from her at all?*

In the blur of travel with companions, Shard did not fall Nameless, but he didn't track the days. He thought it might have been a fortnight of flying, which would put their arrival almost straight on the Halflight. The days grew longer, the nights shorter, and the stars shifted toward their spring and summer stories.

Then one morning, like a vision, a dream, in the soft dark before sunrise, Shard realized the clouds he'd been watching on the horizon were not clouds. They were islands.

His heart soared to his ears, to the sky, to the wind.

The last time he'd seen his home from this angle was the last time he'd glanced back over his wing when he left the islands, following a starfire. For a moment, he thought it was still only longing, and blinked hard.

Then Frar, old Frar, cried out, and Shard knew they saw the Silver Isles.

"Steady my friend," Shard said, circling back to glide just under and to the side of the elder. "We're almost there."

"Yes, my king," breathed Frar, his gaze locked on the little bumps in the distance.

His heart pounded hot. Silence clenched the flock of them and they all strained into the morning breeze, which flicked of ice and snow, but also that touch of spring that marked the Halflight coming.

The Sun Isle loomed first, jutting up from the water, crowned with the White Mountains that looked gray before sunrise. Behind and starward of it he saw the humped mass of the Star Island, dark with forest. They flew too low to see the rest, but the Sun Isle stood hard and gray and real in the morning shadow, and as the wind picked up, he discerned the first scent of pine in the wind.

"Shard!" Brynja's bright voice called him back.

Shard wheeled, not realizing he'd pulled nearly a league ahead of the main group. He soared back to them, his heart light. Then, it grew heavier with each wing beat.

"Welcome home," he said grimly to Brynja, swooping once around her. She laughed harshly, her eyes bright with a hunting light. They both knew danger lurked there, that it was not to be the homecoming either of them ever imagined.

Shard straightened into a glide beside her, raking his gaze over the distant islands. From there, everything looked as he remembered, but heaviness clenched his heart, and a shadow hulked and shifted in the back of his mind, the familiar shadow of Rhydda that lurked through his dreams in the Winderost.

"I wish I could have brought you here on a fairer wind," he said quietly to Brynja.

She shook her head. "I would rather fly rough winds with you than fair winds alone."

"Eyes forward," Asvander said, not just to them, but to all the gryfons who were whispering and fidgeting. "Keep alert."

"Remember the plan." Shard raised his voice so all could hear. "If there is danger at the nesting cliffs, don't stop to fight. *No one,*" he repeated, "will stop to fight yet. You flee. Flee to the forest near the river. If the enemy comes, Kjorn's warriors will distract them until the eldest and youngest have time to escape."

He looked to Kjorn, who had been to the caves, and the gold prince described the place again. "You'll find a wide cluster of birch by the river, and a long stretch of bank with slabs of black stone. A cave entrance there marks our sanctuary."

"My plan," Rok called wryly from the back, where he flew with Nilsine and three Vanir, "is just to follow you, my lord."

Others murmured amused agreement.

Shard nodded, and he and Kjorn turned their faces forward, watching the islands. Tension crept across Shard's muscles, and he forced himself to look back at his pride, to make sure none were struggling. All flew straight, ears alert, eyes bright. No one pulled recklessly ahead as he had done.

No gulls stirred the air near the shore, which sent prickles down Shard's back. No sound came from the islands, no tiny spring bird song drifting out on the ocean breezes.

Then, movement. An avian shape lifted from the nesting cliffs to the sky.

Asvander barked an order and four of his sentinels whipped forward to flank Shard and Kjorn.

Shard squinted, but in the half-light before true dawn he couldn't tell if it was gryfon, eagle, or gull. All he could tell, with relief, was that it was much too small to be a wyrm.

The shape flew right at them. Shard loosened his talons from their clenched bunches against his chest, ready for a fight.

Then . . .

"Hail, gryfons! Hail Vanir!"

Shard didn't know the voice, but at last he discerned a gryfess, flying fast at them over the waves.

"Hail!" Shard called, pulling ahead of the whole group. Asvander hissed at him to stay back, but Shard feared no gryfon in the Silver Isles, especially not one who would call out specifically to the Vanir. "I am Rashard, son-of-Baldr."

"My lord!" cried the gryfess. She looked about Shard's age, pale dove brown with soft rosy highlights on her head. He didn't recognize her, which meant she was an exile.

Shard's heart quickened, wondering how many of the exiled Vanir might have already returned home. "I am Istra, daughter-of-Norin." Her gaze flicked over the mass of gryfons, hardening at the sight of so many Aesir, then brightening with joy at the sight of Frar and the other Vanir. "Welcome home!" she called to them. Then, "Welcome home, my prince."

"Well met," Shard said, his heart glowing to see this young, healthy Vanir flying out to greet him. He gave a swift round of introductions for Kjorn, Brynja, Nilsine, Asvander, and Dagny. "What news?" he asked quietly.

"The queen posted sentries to watch for your return." Her pale gray eyes seemed to darken, and she clenched her talons. "I'm afraid you return home to grim tidings. But this will make her glad."

"The wyrms?" Kjorn asked tightly.

Her gaze flicked to him and she nodded once, stiffly. "We fought. I will tell you everything on the way back. We haven't much time." She dropped her voice as alarm grew in the faces of some elders, who hovered with difficulty behind them. "The wyrms often fly a mark or so after sunrise, once their wings are warm. I have orders from the queen," she said, looking between Shard and Kjorn. "Things you need to know, and what Queen Ragna and Thyra wish you to do."

"Let us land," Shard said, with a glance behind him to see the elder Vanir struggling to hover in the cold, still air.

Istra nodded, and winged about with the neat precision of a Vanir to fly just under Shard. He noted with sudden gratitude and humility that she didn't presume to fly ahead and lead the way.

That was his duty.

He glided about, found the first warm current of the morning and rose above all the others to call out, "A little further, my friends!" He dropped down near Frar and the elders. "Let's go home."

AS IN SHARD'S DREAM, everything was eerily quiet.

Wind moved the waves and shuddered along the cliffs, but there were no birds, no smaller creatures scuffling about, no gryfons along the cliffs. The familiar scent of snow and frozen, wet peat and ocean all blended together, and the warring joy and worry in Shard's heart threatened to rupture him.

He flew nearest to Frar, who struggled the last league, as if seeing his goal finally threatened to unravel him.

The host of gryfons landed on the Copper Cliff, near the King's Rocks.

Shard landed with Frar, in the slush snow that remained, and the old gryfon sank to the ground and buried his beak in the mushy peat as if he might devour the island from joy. Shard brushed a wingtip over his back, relieved the elder had made it home again. Raising his head, he saw the exhausted gryfons all flop to the cold ground, squeezing the earth in their talons, laughing, talking mutely, their eyes warily on the sky.

The fields that stretched out and inland from the cliffs ranged between melted pocks of snow and rich, muddy earth.

Spring.

Shard realized by some strange turn of Tor's wings he had left the Silver Isles during the Halfnight, when the year turned toward autumn and winter, and return exactly half a year later, when all winds brought spring.

He was home. It was home, and yet...

Shard felt strange, as if he had cast off an old skin for a new one underneath, as Hikaru told him the dragons did. A new skin, like a snake, a new color, in the dragon's case, for every season. If Shard had been one thing when he'd left, he was certainly another thing now, though he couldn't say what that thing was.

Istra trotted up to him, followed by Kjorn, Nilsine, and Brynja. Dagny and Asvander made rounds, making sure all gryfons were hale.

"Prince Kjorn," Istra said with a slight dip of her head. "Your mate demanded that we send you to her at once. And, my lord prince," she said to Shard, more warmly, "you are called to the Star Isle." Istra glanced behind at their massive army, and Shard thought she looked both reassured and uncertain. "As for the rest..."

She obviously had not expected there to be "the rest," which meant Ragna and Thyra hadn't either.

Shard saved her from her bafflement by speaking quickly. "Kjorn, go to Thyra. Take the warriors and let them join Ragna's sentries for now. Brynja, lead the Vanir to safety."

"No." Brynja's feathers ruffed, her tail twitching as her gaze darted to the dark, forested hump of Star Isle. Shard blinked at her, lifting his talons uncertainly. "No, Shard," she repeated. "I will stay with you. Ketil can lead the Vanir. If there are wyrms here, you're not going anywhere alone."

Kjorn and Shard exchanged a look, and Kjorn tilted his head as if to agree with her.

"We should move quickly," Nilsine murmured, her voice quiet and reasonable.

"Yes," said Istra, eyeing the Vanhar curiously. "The wyrms will stir soon. They will fly, and we must be under cover by then, and my lord, you must be to Star Isle."

Burning with curiosity, Shard turned to her. "Where on the Star Isle?"

She looked briefly baffled, then bowed her head. "I'm sorry, my lord. The queen said she would meet you there, and that you would know the place."

"How should I know . . ." Shard cut himself off, not wanting to look doubtful with so many eyes suddenly on him. "Of course. I'll go to her. We'll go to her," he corrected, looking at Brynja.

Asvander trotted up to them. "All well, my lords?"

"All's well," Kjorn said. He looked distracted, strained. "Gather the Vanir and all our warriors. We go to the river."

"And you?" Asvander looked at Shard, and Shard recalled Asvander's doubts about him.

Well, I'm home now. This is my land, my kingdom, and I will do what I see fit. "I have business on the Star Isle."

Asvander inclined his head, though doubt sparked in his gaze. Without a word, he turned about and roused the weary gryfons, forming them into orderly clumps to fly to the river.

"Why Star Isle?" Kjorn demanded suddenly, looking from Shard to Istra.

The Vanir gryfess straightened, her beak clamped shut, and her gaze flicked to Shard.

Shard lifted his wings a little. "Kjorn, if my mother wishes to meet me there, I'm sure there's good reason. I'll see you after. Go to Thyra, find Caj, and find out about your father. Reassure the pride I'm well, and we'll all be together soon. Here." He tugged the pouch that held his fire stones from around his neck and passed it to Kjorn. "Take these, in case the caves are cold."

Kjorn ducked his head, letting Shard slip the leather thong over his neck, but said nothing.

"And Kjorn . . ." Shard hesitated, but knowing the wyrms were at large in his home, and seeing the army of gryfons at Kjorn's back, he quietly added, "Don't do anything stupid."

"Funny," the golden prince said, "I was just about to say the same thing to you."

"My lord," Istra said tensely. "You must fly now, or not at all. I will lead Prince Kjorn to the others."

"Thank you, Istra," Shard said. Then, since he knew she must have only recently arrived said, "And welcome home to you, too."

She brightened, her feathers fluffing with pleasure, and mantled low.

"Fair winds," Kjorn said to Shard, opening his wing.

Shard stretched his to cover Kjorn's. "I'll see you soon."

They broke, Kjorn calling out to the larger force to follow, and Shard with Brynja loping off to dive from the nesting cliffs as golden dawn at last broke over the sea.

As they soared across the long sea channel between the islands, Brynja broke the silence. "Not that I doubt you, but do you actually know where the queen wants to meet you?"

"I have an idea," Shard said.

Before he could say more, a distant, familiar, horrifying scream shattered the morning from the direction of Pebble's Throw. It bounded across the lapping waves in rolling echo, fracturing Shard's calm.

"Race you," he said to Brynja, and she laughed grimly as they stroked hard toward the dark, sheltering forests of Star Island.

40

QUEEN OF THE AESIR

STILL VAGUELY FAMILIAR WITH THE RIVER tunnel, Kjorn wormed his way forward like an eel, barely heeding the Vanir and the rest behind him. The way narrowed in some places so he had to contort his wings and limbs to crawl through, and he heard surprised and worried exclamations behind him.

Once Istra had led them to the place, he remembered well how to get where the larger cavern would make more room for all of his company, and took the lead. The Vanir gryfess seemed content to fall in with the others, helping the elders and catching up on the stories of their exile.

"Don't worry," Kjorn called back, still bellying forward, "it widens ahead."

And so it did. It also grew less frighteningly murky. Though Kjorn's vision was dim from morning light, he made out the pale, off-green fungus that laced the tunnel walls ahead and cast an unearthly light.

Ahead the tunnel widened, branched into three, and the labyrinth began. The wolves and gryfons had placed stone markers at tunnels that led to other islands, and at tunnels that led to larger caverns where it was more comfortable to dwell. Kjorn recalled the cave under Star Island where the wolves had turned him around and gotten him lost, and he'd finally met the seer Catori. He shook himself of the memory.

"Thyra!" Wedging himself through the narrowest turn in the tunnel, he at last shoved through to the wider way and bounded ahead, his talons scraping stone and earth. "Caj! We've returned! Shard and I ..."

He stopped, remembering he was not alone, feeling breathless with anticipation. If the wyrms had come, as Shard feared, then anything could have happened. Anyone could be injured, or dead. But no, Istra had said specifically that Thyra was alive, and wanted to see him. He hurried forward.

"Thyra!"

Ketil trotted up alongside him, wincing at his shout as the echo rebounded along the damp, cold stone. "Where did they shelter, before? If the caves extend under all the isles, they could be anywhere."

"Just ahead!" Istra called from behind. "Keep going!"

Kjorn could have burst. His tail lashed. He forced his ears forward, hearing the last echo of his own voice fade in the distant caves.

An echo answered Istra's call.

Here! Here, here.

But he couldn't tell which way the voice had come from. Ketil turned slowly, ears twitching back and forth, a surprised look on her face, as if she'd recognized the voice.

"Son of Sverin," said a female gryfon's voice, closer than the echo had been, and vaguely familiar to Kjorn. They turned, blinking at the strange shadows and light of the middle tunnel as a feline figure emerged. "I must say, this isn't how I imagined seeing . . ." Before Kjorn could even think of her name, Ketil said it for him.

"Maja!"

"Ket? Ketil!" Maja, Halvden's mother, who had left a fish outside Sverin's den that summer past as a final insult before exiling herself to serve Shard, seemed to materialize from the tunnel. She stopped, stared at the Vanir who clustered forward around the cave, the mass of gryfons behind, then squarely at Ketil.

With a shriek, both gryfesses lunged at each other, wrestling for a moment like fledges before they pressed their brows together, then extended their wings, Maja's eclipsing Ketil's like a wingsister's. Kjorn watched them first with a pang of guilt, then impatience, for Maja surely blocked the way to Thyra. There would be plenty of time for everyone's reunions later.

"I didn't think you'd survived," Maja said.

"I did, and better." Ketil stepped away, flapping a wing to gesture toward the group. "Meet my daughter, and my nest-daughter. Keta, Ilse, come and meet my wingsister, Maja."

Dagny stepped up beside Kjorn quietly, then Nilsine, who watched the gryfesses in bemusement as Keta and Ilse nudged forward through the gryfons to meet Maja.

"There will be a lot of this in the coming days," the Vanhar remarked, her red eyes strangely lit by the green fungus on the walls.

"I hope so," Kjorn said. "I hope there will be many happy reunions. Including my own. Ketil . . ."

"Yes, of course," she said airily. "For Rashard's sake I will speak for you. Maja, dear one, where is Kjorn's mate?"

"This way," said Maja, and the way from which she'd come was wide enough for two gryfons to walk abreast, and they did, chattering the whole way. Maja answered Ketil's questions. Kjorn listened to enough of their conversation to confirm Istra's report that wyrms had attacked, some gryfons had been slain, no females had whelped, but none had suffered ill from fleeing the wyrms either.

"And the War King is prisoner of Queen Ragna," Maja said, raising her voice, Kjorn thought, for his benefit. "And as Sverin cowered like a grouse, she stood her ground, and then, Sverin fled. He fled to the Star Isle and Ragna pursued. And there they stay, telling us very little. Perhaps the wolves are holding the War King prisoner, or he is afraid to come underground."

Frustration at the lack of information about his father pricked Kjorn's skin. "But he's well? Caj found him, then, and he's remembered who he is?"

"Yes," said Maja. "Well enough." Then, because she apparently didn't feel a need to answer to Kjorn any more, she returned her attention to Ketil, lowering her voice again, but loud enough that Kjorn heard. "I am proud to say that at least my son Halvden matured into a better gryfon, and proved himself a true warrior against the foe, though he paid a heavy price."

Kjorn clenched down on his frustration, knowing that truly, these gryfesses didn't owe him anything. They didn't owe him allegiance, or respect he had not yet earned, or even any more information. He knew enough. His father was alive and sane. He had fled his enemy again, like a coward.

Then Kjorn could think of nothing but Thyra, who had endured all of these things without him, while carrying his heir. His heart thundered, and he said nothing.

A warm wing pressed to his. Kjorn had expected Shard, then remembered his wingbrother had business elsewhere.

"Steady, my lord," Nilsine murmured, watching him.

"Why do you call me that?" Kjorn wondered abruptly, though he had wondered it for awhile and hadn't had a chance to speak with her. "Why did you come with me, in the Winderost, why do you follow me here, and help me, and serve me as if you were born to my pride?"

Nilsine's ears flicked, and she fluffed her wings in a shrug, looking forward. Maja and Ketil had dropped their voices again, and Kjorn thought they must be speaking of more private things. The great band of gryfons trailed behind them in tense silence.

"The first time I saw you in the Winderost, the sun broke from a cloud and shined on your face, and ever since then you have not stopped shining. You seem to me a king, and also seem that you need friends. I always like to go where I am needed."

Kjorn would have stopped walking in surprise if a number of Vanir and Dagny wouldn't have bumped into him. He slowed, then continued apace, and dipped his head low to her. "You honor me."

She chuckled, a rare sound, and tilted her head to eye the fungus along the wall. "I think it best for kindred spirits to stay close, and through their bonds, different clans are not so separate from each other. I think the Vanhar needed me to be your friend more than they needed me to be a border guard. In the coming years I hope the Dawn Spire and the Vanheim will continue to enjoy friendship."

Kjorn had no answer for that but, "Thank you."

They emerged into a small cavern about the size of a gryfon den, with two tunnels branching from there. Maja gestured with her talons, speaking to Kjorn.

"The pregnant gryfesses are nesting in a warren of nooks and crannies this way. The rest are to be found down these tunnels." Her gaze brightened and she looked beyond him, lifting her voice. "Any Vanir seeking family and friends should come with me this way."

"Thank you." Kjorn inclined his head to her, then turned to behold the Vanir, who had all heard the statement. "I wish you had returned home to better circumstances. I know Shard will return soon with tidings for you, and he and I both believe you're safe here." Hard, curious, judging gazes watched him. Many had traveled with Shard and him in the Winderost, some had fought beside him at the Battle of Torches. "Thank you for granting me your trust," he added softly. "It has been my honor to fly with you on your journey home."

He mantled to the host of them, and straightened to see Maja observing him with an approving gleam in her eye.

"Breezy," Dagny exclaimed. "Now for the sake of Tyr's bright talons, go find your mate!"

Kjorn laughed, hoarsely, and lunged down the tunnel.

Despite all reassurances that Thyra had been protected and was whole and fine, Kjorn burst through the tunnels like a falcon, dodging stunned gryfons who shouted after him. He caught Thyra's scent and followed it like a wolf on a hare. He wove through the tunnels, past exclamations and greetings and the other pregnant gryfesses, until he found the niche in the tunnel where Thyra rested.

He stopped short, gazing at her.

"Kjorn," Thyra breathed, rolling herself to her feet. The sight of him didn't appear to surprise her. "My mate. I knew you would be home by the Halfflight." Relief, joy, and sternness each flicked through her voice in turn.

Kjorn rushed to her and mantled his wings around her as they nuzzled their necks together, breathing in each other's scents and releasing the last days in a long, mutual sigh.

"I promised," he said. "How do you fare? Are you well? Are you eating enough? Is everyone well? I heard that Sverin was—"

"Oh, just let me sit with you a moment." Her tone was tight.

They were both thinking of Sverin. *How could we not?*

Kjorn clamped his beak, content in just seeing her again, but she must know he was wondering. He hadn't even meant to mention his father, and he leaned back to preen around her ears, thinking fondly that she looked like a plump wild hen, and knowing much better than to say so.

"I hear you have the pride well in wing," he said instead.

"Ragna and I, yes. There is much to tell you. But where's Shard?" She tilted her head, peering past him into the tunnel for her nest-brother. "He's—he's not . . .?" She pulled back with a pained, questioning look.

"No, he's fine," Kjorn said quickly. "Istra met us, and said Ragna needed to see him straight away."

"Yes, that's right. I thought he might have come to see me, but I suppose he is a prince now." Thyra looked placid, and nodded. "He's home. He's gone to treat with the wolves, to see Ragna and . . ." Her gaze flicked down.

"And my father," Kjorn said tightly. "He's with Ragna?" She nodded once, and the mention didn't seem to upset her.

He had never seen her so relaxed, and wondered if that was an effect of the late stage of the pregnancy. "I should have told him to come see you first." But all he'd been able to think of was seeing her himself.

"Perhaps, but here *you* are," she said warmly. "We are lucky to have two princes among us. He'll come. Don't fret, it upsets me."

Not for a moment did he believe she was upset, but looked rather amused, and so instead of talking about Shard, he asked of all that had passed in his absence, and told her his dealings in the Winderost.

She told him of Caj's loyal hunt for Sverin, of the tense but settling relations in the pride, of Sverin's new, sane demeanor. She would not tell him all that Sverin had told the pride when he'd returned, his outright confession of all he'd done wrong, and why.

"That's for him to tell you." Her voice fell low. "I'm sorry, my love. It's for him to tell you." Before he could ask again she said, "So, now we are exiled to the windward land?"

"Hardly exile," Kjorn murmured. "You will be queen of the Dawn Spire. It's our home. Our birthright, as Aesir."

Her gaze strayed to the cavern wall, and Kjorn could have bitten himself for the foolish statement. She was half Vanir. This land was her birthright as much as the Dawn Spire. He himself had lived nearly his whole life in the Silver Isles.

Surprised voices and gasps echoed to them from down the earthy halls as more Vanir reunited. He realized he'd had half a season to grow into the idea of leaving, and Thyra had just heard that he expected her to pick up and follow him with their kit.

"It's a beautiful place," he added, murmuring against her feathered ear, closing his wing around her more warmly. "Rugged, rocky, but vast. And it's much warmer. The hunting is more abundant than you could imagine. You can fly for days and days and not see the ocean. There are amazing things. Beautiful things. I believe it will suit you. I know you'll love it there. You can see your father's homeland."

Her gaze refocused on him, her eyes a soft brown like Sigrun's, but sparking with fire. "If you love it, so will I. It's where you came from, so it must be a good place. I'll go because I know it's the best thing. But I'll miss the Silver Isles."

"I will too," Kjorn said quietly. "I will."

"And I will miss my family." She squirmed under his wing.

Kjorn realized she was hot, and pulled his wings away, stepping back to give her air. "Caj and Sigrun will be welcome at the Dawn Spire. Sigrun would be an asset to the healers there, and she, I think, would enjoy the company of so many."

Her low, rueful laugh surprised him. "My love, I don't think my father will ever leave the Silver Isles now."

Kjorn ruffled his feathers, dismayed. "You said his wing would heal fully."

"His wing will fly true." She watched him with a curious, searching expression. "But I can see his heart is here, now, even if he can't see it yet. This place suits him—the freezing streams, the high mountains, the sea. He's happy here. I can't see him leaving, even if my mother agreed."

Feeling stubborn and surprised, for the thought had never occurred to Kjorn that some full-blooded Aesir would choose to stay in the Silver Isles, he stood and paced away. "And if Shard exiles the Aesir?"

Thyra's head rose to a hunting angle, cool, haughty, the confident look that had first snared his interest when they came of age. Her flat, unimpressed expression and her silence shamed him, and he knew her unspoken answer.

Unless a crime was too great to forgive, Shard, who had lived most of his life in fear of exile, would never banish someone if they didn't wish to go.

"That was a stupid thing to say," Kjorn murmured. "Please don't tell Shard I even thought it."

"Yes, it was," Thyra said, but relaxed her fierce expression. "I won't tell him."

"My lord." Caj's warm, burred voice was a relief.

Kjorn tilted his head at Thyra to acknowledge her sentiment, and turned to see the large, cobalt gryfon standing a few paces away from the niche.

Having been now to the Ostral Shores, Kjorn could see the breeding in his mentor that matched the Lakelanders. A strapping build, wide shoulders, tall. It was such a relief to see another old, familiar face that Kjorn nearly buckled, finally realizing how weary he was.

"Caj. You have no idea how good it is to see you. Thyra said my father..."

"He's alive. He knows himself." Caj eyed Kjorn up and down, and seemed to disapprove. Kjorn knew he'd lost weight over the sea, and was probably muddy and in need of preening. He didn't care. "The wolves and their companion have taken possession of him, and refuse to release him to us until Shard returns."

"Their... companion?" Kjorn asked.

Caj looked wary, and amused. "You'll see. Anyway I thought you would want to know Sverin is on the Star Isle."

Kjorn couldn't say he was sorry to hear that, and he was too tired to ask about the wolves' mysterious companion. The thought of walking around a bend in the tunnels and running into Sverin was not pleasant. The last time Kjorn had seen his father, he'd still been half-mad, denied Kjorn, and flown away, Nameless.

The unspoken thing settled between them like a stone.

"He'll want to see me," Kjorn said, when Caj would not.

"Of course he will." Caj ruffled his feathers, but his expression remained neutral.

Kjorn wanted to ask so much more, to know everything Caj knew, to know the things Thyra wouldn't tell him, but suddenly the journey caught him, he sat abruptly, and shook his head. "Soon. I need to rest, to think. I'll wait for Shard to come back. But not now. Is—is there anything to eat?"

"Of course," Caj said. "I'll fetch you something."

"Thank you," Kjorn said gratefully, and stretched on his belly. It was certainly not Caj's duty to bring him food, but Kjorn thought he did it for Thyra's sake.

Caj retreated, and without looking back said drily, "I hope you like fish."

Kjorn groaned, then, struck with a thought, called, "Caj!" The blue gryfon paused, looking back over his wing. "In the Winderost, did you and my father ever lose a fight to a lion?"

A moment of quiet, then, "Well. We were practically fledges." He left without further explanation. Kjorn felt his own beak slip open to hear that Mbari's wild tale was true after all, and he shook his head. Perhaps Caj would tell his version of it some day.

Thyra nudged Kjorn. "There's a story in that."

"Oh yes," he said, and began to tell her.

41

MANY GREETINGS

WITH AN EYE NIGHTWARD TOWARD PEBBLE'S Throw, Shard led Brynja in a low, fast flight over the endless pine forest. Now and then he spied the gnarled, twisting branches of a rowan, and he followed the trails of them over the woods.

A dark bird appeared out of the woods and glided under them for a time, then flapped up to Shard's level.

"Could this be? Do my weary old black eyes deceive?" The quorking, clattering voice was all too familiar.

"Ravens," Brynja said dismissively.

"You'll find different ravens here," Shard said, eyeing the single, circling black bird.

When he realized who it was, fresh exhaustion washed over Shard. He would have welcomed anyone but the trickster and riddler, the dream king, Munin, whom he hadn't seen in the flesh since he'd left. Still, he forced friendliness into his voice and called out.

"Your eyes see fine, I've returned. Hello, friend."

"Ha! Friends, indeed, and such a lovely, lovely gryfess at your side, un-cursed Aesir!"

"What is he saying?" Brynja glided closer to Shard, ears perked. She tried, but could not always understand other creatures as clearly as Shard and the Vanir could.

"Nothing," Shard muttered. "He likes the sound of his voice. Clever Munin," Shard called, "I know it's you, for you fly faster than your brother."

"Such flattery. Such a sweet prince. Or . . ." He closed the last distance between them and looped around Shard twice, studying him with bright, fathomless eyes. "Or, or, do I spy a king? A silver king? If you were dragon-cursed, I think you'd be as bright as the son of the Red Scourge. Ha!"

Shard knew it would do no good to get frustrated, but he also knew that Munin made it his business to know important matters, portents, and patterns, and so while Brynja stared, Shard dipped his head in respect. "Munin. How good to see you in the waking world. Tell me, where does my mother wish to meet me? Will you tell us the tidings here?"

"Tidings? Tidings? The tide is in, the tide is in, but fire is in the water."

Shard began to wish they'd taken one more meal at sea, but he hadn't reckoned on untangling riddles upon first arriving home. "What fire?"

"The fire that buried Per!" he laughed. "The fire on Pebble's Throw. Fire burns in the sea, snakes fly in the air while gryfons live under the river, under the stone. What days have I lived to see?"

"Great Tyr's talon," Brynja muttered, and Shard silently agreed, though he was happy she seemed to be understanding more now.

Still, he kept his voice neutral. "Is Catori about?"

"Is Catori about what? About the height of the shortest Vanir." Munin flipped about in the wind, laughing. "Such dreams I saw over the sea, your band of war. Why don't you weave them dreams of peace? Such dreams of war. They may yet come true."

Never, in all his longing, had Shard imagined he would come home to this. Empty nesting cliffs, silent songbirds, no movement at all on the islands, except the creature which most liked to confound and frustrate him.

His words chilled Shard, though. Dreams of war. He hoped the raven hadn't seen such dreams from Kjorn, or the other Aesir.

"I hope not," Shard said out loud, then gave an exaggerated sigh. "Well, if you don't know the tidings, I suppose I'll have to find someone more clever. Someone who's been paying attention. A gull, maybe, or—"

Munin guffawed. "Gulls! Speak of tidings, of tides. Gulls know of fish. I know of war. What tidings do you want to know?"

"The gryfons," Shard said, his tail flicking. "How fares the pride? Where is the queen? Where is Ragna, my mother?"

Munin made a garbling noise as if he was in distress. "The silver king thinks I have time to answer all these questions. Oh, poor, lonely me. Only one me, only poor old me. How does the pride fare? The pride fares on fish, under river, under stone."

"Madness," Brynja murmured, amazed at how irritating the raven was. "I think I was better off not understanding."

Munin looked at her, then made a low, crackling noise that Shard interpreted as trying to sound spooky, like tree branches in a storm.

"The queen waits on the king by the First Tree, and they both bend their ear to a serpent in the sky."

"Munin—"

"Mind you look up!" He folded his wings, letting himself fall toward the woods, awking his long, echoing call across the tree tops. "Mind you look up, there are serpents in the sky." He wheeled once, laughed, and left them, dropping into the pines.

Even though Munin had tricked Shard before, he was not so foolish as to ignore him. Especially when he spoke so relatively plain.

So Shard looked up.

Brynja shook herself, flapping steadily. "Serpents in the—"

"Look out!" Shard cried, as a massive silver form shot down from the clear air like skyfire. Shard folded a wing and knocked Brynja aside. She shrieked and fell back out of the way, diving toward the cover of the trees.

Shard halted mid-air, wings stroking to hover, and stared. A serpent in the sky, indeed. A silver dragon, a Sunlander! He'd never seen a dragon such a color in their dwelling, the Mountains of the Sea, though the black wings, stark against the lightening sky, reminded him of Hikaru.

Awed to see a dragon here, Shard ramped as best he could, flapping his wings in greeting, and called out.

"Sunlander! Welcome to the Silver Isles! I am Rashard, son-of-Baldr, prince of—"

A warm, musical laugh met his greeting. The dragon circled back and flew straight at him without slowing, his jaws splayed in wide laughter. Despite his silver color, realization shot through Shard's heart that this dragon was as familiar as the stars.

"Shard! Don't you know me?"

Before Shard could react, the silver dragon bowled into him, plucked him up as easily as a fish, and lunged higher into the sky.

Shard reeled, breathless, but didn't struggle. His heart could've burst.

"Hikaru! Hikaru, my wingbrother!" Joy and confusion danced in his head, then just joy. He grasped his talons around a scaled silver wrist joint.

The dragon spiraled high, with Shard clasped to his breast scales, embracing him tightly. He had grown. He was twice the size he'd been when Shard left him, long enough for twenty gryfons to stand along his length, delicate and sinuous in build. Shard wriggled, desperate to pull away and see his friend.

Below, Brynja cried out in terror, and Shard managed to holler a reassuring call. "It's all right! Brynja, he's a friend!"

Hikaru laughed again, his voice rich and deep with a familiar cadence and the accent he'd picked up by learning to talk from Shard. "You didn't recognize me!"

"No," Shard gasped. "Your spring scales! They're beautiful, Hikaru. You should let go, Brynja's worried."

"Oohh," Hikaru purred. "That's Brynja? I like her. She looks so strong."

"Yes, and she's going to attack you, Hikaru!" Shard wanted to laugh, could have wept, and at last Hikaru released him. Shard dropped, flinging open his wings.

Brynja soared fast toward them, her talons splayed. "Shard!"

"Brynja, this is Hikaru, my nest-son, I mean, my wingbrother."

Brynja veered off from attacking to circle them and stare. "The hatchling? The dragon hatchling you told us about?" Though Shard had told her how swiftly the dragons grew, she looked amazed that the dragon he'd told her hatched over the Long Night was now the size of a fully-grown cedar tree.

"It's an honor to meet you, huntress of the Dawn Spire," Hikaru rumbled. Then his ears flicked. "I mean, of the Silver Isles." He looked mischievously between her and Shard.

Brynja's gaze darted between them in turn, then Shard was relieved to see her awe and fear washed away by breathless amusement. "The honor is mine I'm sure! Shard, should we get under cover?"

Before Shard could answer, Hikaru loosed a playful, challenging rumble, opened his talons in warning, then surged toward Shard as if he meant to spar right there.

Shard let himself drop, diving for two breaths toward the forest. To show off for Hikaru, he shifted his wings delicately against the wind to avoid stalling, and fell, seeming out of control, flashing his wings in an artful spiral dive. He had forgotten about being subtle, forgotten the wyrms might be in his home, hunting, forgotten about his mother and his pride and his fear.

For a moment of wild joy, it was only he and Hikaru again.

A tail-length above the trees Shard whipped out of the dive. Above, Hikaru laughed again and looped in happy circles against the wind. Shard smoothed his flight and stroked the air, regaining height to meet Brynja and the dragon, dazzled by his metallic silver scales.

As Shard turned, Hikaru took the opportunity to show off new things he'd learned—a series of increasingly elaborate spirals, dips, and turns, that looked to Shard like a dance, or as if he was battling and evading an invisible foe.

"Isn't he incredible?" Shard whispered to Brynja.

"He is," she murmured, but Shard looked over to realize she was watching only him, admiring, wondering. "I'm glad he's here. Though I wonder why? And we should get under cover, as Istra said." The words were pointed, and Shard came back to himself. There was danger. There would be a reason Hikaru had come. And Shard still needed to find Ragna.

"I thought I would never see you again!" Shard called across the blue air.

Hikaru slithered out of showing off and winged over beside him. "That was a silly thing to think. The world is so small."

Shard thought maybe the world seemed small to a dragon, but he didn't say that. "Tell me all that's happened. Why you're here, and your scales—"

"We'll go to your mother," Hikaru said briskly, and Shard noticed with a chill that his gaze slipped nightward, toward Pebble's Throw. They had not heard another wyrm scream, which meant the beasts were hunting, in silence. "We should get under cover. We've been waiting for you. And Catori has waited, too, and—"

"We? You and Ragna, and who else? She's met you?" Shard felt he couldn't keep up.

"Let's go!" Without waiting to explain or hear questions, Hikaru circled them once and dove to the nearest clearing. From above, Shard suddenly realized where they were.

"Brynja, this is where Kjorn and I fought the boar! This was our initiation . . ." he realized he had so much to tell her, so many secrets and wonderful places to explore with her in his home, and they had no time at all.

"Well, what are we waiting for?" she laughed at his hesitation and dove first, following Hikaru.

Shard admired the young dragon's landing, how he flared and wound into a tidy coil on the ground.

"It's beautiful," Brynja said as Shard landed beside her, talons squishing in the mud and slushy grass. "I've never seen trees so large." She raised her head to sniff, and Shard realized she was smelling pine for the first time, the sweet, heady scent of wet earth and evergreen needles. "This is the island where the wolves live?"

"Yes."

"Speaking of wolves," Hikaru said, lifting his head.

Sinking his talons into the slush, Shard turned to see a russet blur sprinting at them from the woods. Black feathers flicked from the heavy fur of her neck, amber eyes gleamed, her fangs showed in a wolf grin.

"My friend! Our Star King, our Summer King!" Catori stopped short of bowling into Shard and raised her voice in a howl.

Before Shard could greet her or introduce her to Brynja, hearty wolf voices answered the howl. A long, low song carried through the pine forest. Ravens cackled and called, and shrill bird voices raised a chorus. After the silence, the sudden cacophony sent shivers down his back. Shard had no doubt all the islands would soon know of his return.

"Catori," he said, and they pressed their brows together, sharing a breath. Her fluffy tail waved and she sprang away, then back at him like a pup ready to play. "I want you to meet Brynja. We'll pledge on the Daynight."

Catori's ears perked, then she broke into a panting grin and stretched her long legs out, bowing down. "A gryfess of warrior blood, to match our prophet king. A good match. Fair winds, Brynja of the windland."

"Fair winds, Catori," Brynja said, looking surprised and pleased at the friendly greeting and the honor Catori showed her. "Shard has told me all about you. His friendship with wolves of the Silver Isles helped teach us to befriend the painted hunters of our own lands."

"This makes my heart glad." She snuffled the muddy pine needles, ears twitching, and her gaze traveled behind them, as if seeking someone else. Shard took a deep breath. Meanwhile Hikaru kept an eye on the sky, his ears flicking, and settled his body in a wide coil around them, like a barrier.

"Catori, where is Shard's mother?"

"They've been hunting. They'll return soon."

"Ah, good." Hikaru ran his talons down his breast scales, peering into the forest.

A thought struck Shard at the mention of Ragna. "Catori, I must tell you that Stigr remained in the Winderost."

She sobered, standing tall, and Shard stared at the black feathers she wore, needled through with regret. "I dreamed of Stigr. I feared you would come to tell me of his death, but I feel his love in the wind, still. I feel his dreams of home."

"He lives," Shard said. "But . . ." He told her of the wyrm's attack, of the battle at the Dawn Spire. He told her of how he and Stigr had slain a wyrm together, and then how Rhydda cut him down. He told her that Stigr would never fly home.

Her ears slanted back, then shook herself, hard. "I will miss him. But we have all suffered loss in this fight against an old, old darkness. Stigr knew what risks he faced, but he is a warrior. I'm glad to know he lives."

"He lives," Brynja said firmly, "and has a place of honor at the Dawn Spire."

"And he's found a mate," Shard added quickly, brightening, remembering all the good things about Stigr's new life. "A huntress of the Dawn Spire."

Catori's ears perked. "I would like to hear more, but we should wait for the rest. Your mother will want to hear."

"They'll be here soon," Hikaru said, his gaze roving the dark forest as if he could see much farther than any of them. Perhaps he could. He poked holes idly in the mud with one claw.

Shard took the moment to sit down, and all his muscles seemed to sigh in relief. He opened a wing toward Brynja and the ruddy gryfess gratefully sat next to him. Her gaze remained trained on the sky. Hikaru noticed, and gave her a reassuring flick with the very tip of his tail. At first she winced, as if he might have a deadly sharp spade like the wyrms.

"Don't worry, Brynja," Hikaru said. "They haven't flown over Star Isle yet. They hunt on the Sun Isle, where they last saw gryfons."

Brynja shuddered. "I hope the others made it underground."

"They did," Shard said with certainty. "They had plenty of time." He turned to the she-wolf, who watched them quietly. "Catori." He didn't know how else to say what he needed to, so he simply said it. "I dreamed of the wyrm, who we call Rhydda. I showed her the Silver Isles in my dream and I'm afraid it's my fault she's here."

"That may be," Catori said, walking over to sit beside them. She didn't look surprised at all. Her warm presence and thick, red fur made a good buffer against a chilly breeze, and between her and Brynja, he was as warm as if he had a fire.

Catori continued thoughtfully. "But it may also be not a bad thing that she has come."

"Gryfons have died," Shard said bitterly. "Istra said they fought a battle, and gryfons died." Suddenly chilled, Shard wondered who.

Brynja pressed against him, but remained quiet, looking between them. He was grateful to her for understanding how he needed Catori's counsel. Though the wolf was not much older than he, she was wise in the ways of dreaming, listening, and the earth. Shard hadn't realized how much he'd missed this friend, the first to suggest he was more than he'd ever known, the first to lead him off the path of serving Sverin blindly and of blundering in his own arrogance, and ignorance. Hikaru watched all of them with huge, worried eyes.

Catori lowered her head, ears flattening. "Yes. I know this. But I feel in these wyrms such an ancient fear, an ancient silence. They have No names, no Voices. Yet they feel anger. They came here hunting gryfons. If they can do that, then they can listen, Shard. They can. And they will listen to you."

"Yes," Hikaru said eagerly. "Yes, they will listen to you. I learned more, Shard. I learned more from the chronicler and I came to tell you. But let me wait for the others."

Shard met Hikaru's bright gaze, then Catori's. "You don't understand. I've tried. I've tried and failed—"

"Did you fail?" Catori tilted her head, and he thought of last spring in the woods, when he'd met her for the first time. He'd thought she was infuriating, enigmatic. He still knew her to be those things, and wise, for she listened.

And he also knew that sometimes she repeated his questions back to him not to infuriate him, but to make him ask himself, instead of others.

"I must have. Rhydda hasn't changed at all."

"That doesn't mean she hasn't heard you. *He speaks to all who hear.*" The amber eyes held summer in them, brightness, hope. Shard clung to the hope in Catori's eyes. "It took you a little time to hear me. Remember that it took Kjorn a long time to hear you, too. It took Stigr time to hear beyond his hatred of the Aesir. Now, he will mate with one. Kjorn recognized Ragna, a Vanir, as queen before he left. Now, even the son of Per has spoken to wolves, Shard. If red Sverin will bow his head to my brother and ask forgiveness, I believe that Rhydda can hear you."

Beak opening at that news, Shard searched her face, even as she showed the points of her teeth in amusement. She'd meant to spring that on him, to surprise him.

Sverin, speak to wolves? Sverin, bow to wolves?

Movement turned all their heads to the trees, and Hikaru made a warm, purring noise of greeting.

Happiness swept Shard as the scent of familiar wolves drifted to them and he stood again. He saw Ahanu, Tocho, and then, trotting behind them, was Ragna. He had nearly forgotten what an elegant gryfess she was, fit and lithe and pale as sea foam. She looked keen, wary, her ears fully perked as she stared at him hungrily. Her gaze flicked curiously to Brynja, then returned to him, now reserved. "My son. Welcome home."

"Mother. I'm glad you're well." He noted her look, and extended one wing to drape over Brynja's back. "This is Brynja, daughter-of-Mar, an honored huntress of the Dawn Spire in the windward land. And . . . my chosen mate."

He said it all before he lost his resolve. For him it seemed easy and natural now, but the surprise on Ragna's face looked as if he'd told her he might choose to mate with a dragon. Clearly, Brynja's height, strong build, and ruddy feathers were not of the Vanir, and Shard realized how much Ragna had expected he would choose one.

"Fair winds, my lady," Brynja said, and mantled to the queen of the Vanir. Then she pressed a wing to Shard, as if for reassurance.

Ragna, still looking struck, wavered between a mantle and bow. "Fair winds, Brynja. We'll . . . come to know each other soon." With a hopeful look, she turned back to Shard. "And my brother?"

Again the weight sank onto Shard's shoulders, his wings, his heart. "Stigr cannot fly home."

He told her all of it, and of how bravely Stigr had fought and fallen. Her hopeful look changed to one he knew better, the cool, impassive, regal expression of the Widow Queen that hid every other emotion. "I see," she said softly, and then, nothing more.

Shard stood witlessly, then Brynja nudged him. He knew should do something. It was time, he realized, time to be the son he never yet had the chance to be, to comfort her because her mate was dead, her brother was gone, and she had been waiting for Shard's return.

Suddenly overwhelmed with relief that she was all right, and grief for all she had lost, Shard bound the short distance between them and butted his head against her. She loosed a soft breath and ducked her head, nuzzling his neck feathers.

"Welcome home," she whispered again, with more warmth, genuine relief, and love. "I always knew you would come home."

Any more words would have to wait, for beyond his mother and the wolves drifted another scent, and Shard drew back with a sharp gasp.

Walking slowly forward until he stood beside Ragna, right beside her, dwarfing her with his size, his majesty, his blazing crimson feathers, was Sverin. Shard drew back several steps, taking him in.

Sverin, who had shadowed Shard's life at every turn, Sverin, who had terrorized the Vanir, poached the islands, and killed the wolf king. The gryfon who once had struck awe and giddiness into Shard's heart, a gryfon who should have been his greatest enemy, stood before him silently. He wore no gold. He stood beside Shard's mother like a comrade, stood among wolves with whom he'd clearly just hunted, stood, and waited for Shard to speak. He inclined his head a fraction to Brynja, who offered the slightest bow in acknowledgement.

Once, Shard would have bowed, mantled, groveled. Now he felt nothing at all. It was a strange relief. It was power, it was freedom, to feel nothing at all for the Red King.

Like so many other things, this was not how he'd pictured their next meeting, but here it was happening. He raised his head high, lifting his chest, opening his wings. He was Rashard, son-of-Baldr, prince of the Silver Isles. His last barrier to kingship had already fallen, and now they faced a common foe.

"Sverin."

Eyes as hard as dragon chains met his, searched him, seemed to scour his body and heart, to see who he was now, a different gryfon than when they'd last met, when they'd battled over the sea in a storm. A faint wind whispered through the tops of the pine trees, plucked at their feathers, stirred wolf fur and Hikaru's silver mane.

Then, Sverin spoke.

"Your Highness."

Before Ragna, Catori, Brynja, Hikaru, and all the wolves, the son of Per bent his forelegs, mantled his wings, and bowed to Shard.

42

THE SHAME OF THE SUNLAND

THE SCREAM OF A WYRM jolted them all. Hikaru whipped up and herded the gryfons back under the cover of the trees.

Still gathering his wits after seeing Sverin bow, Shard thought they must look a very odd collection of creatures. Hikaru slipped like a stream through the woods, surprisingly nimble, barely brushing the trees. Catori and Brynja flanked Shard, with Ragna ahead, and Sverin ahead of her.

He probably should have said something when Sverin bowed, but there was nothing to say. It was with burning curiosity that Shard observed how Ragna and Sverin regarded each other, with open respect and quiet deference. Shard thought Ragna might be unaware of how she acted toward the Red King. Her attitude, he thought, showed more proof of how Sverin had changed than anything else.

Partially because he couldn't bear strained silence, and more so because he wanted news, Shard spoke up as they all trailed through the forest.

"We had little time to speak with Istra in detail when we arrived. Ragna—" he paused, corrected himself, "Mother. Will you tell us more?"

So as they walked, Ragna told them of the end of winter, told them frankly of Sverin's penance, of the Vanir's return. She spoke of the wyrms, and in her voice Shard heard shame. He tried to reassure her that almost no gryfon could stand up to them, and couldn't help but look at Sverin. The red gryfon remained in stony, inscrutable silence.

When Ragna had finished, Shard told her their tale, and by the time he was done, they had reached an opening in the woods where the ground was bare, but thousands of branches overhead gave some semblance of color.

Sunlight glanced down through wiry, clutching, rowan branches, and the ground was muddy and all but bare of snow. Best of all, it appeared Hikaru had built a fire earlier, in a large ring of stones. Embers still burned, sending the fragrant scent of smoking pine through the air.

"We will fetch wood for the fire," said Ahanu quietly. He nosed Shard's head fondly and Shard flicked a grateful wingtip against him, then the wolf king drew his pack away into the woods. All but Catori, who remained with them.

"Hikaru," Ragna said as the silver dragon coiled around the fire ring. "You must tell us what you know, now. Shard has returned. Tell us why you've come, and why you've kept Sverin with you."

Shard walked to the ring of stones and sat, relishing the heat as it seeped under his chilled feathers and his aching, exhausted bones.

"It was for your protection," Hikaru said matter-of-factly to Sverin, then to Shard, "I had to keep him close."

With the warmth from the embers, the long flight over the sea dragged at Shard once again. Brynja laid down beside him, and Ragna drew near but remained standing.

Sverin, in his silence, remained at the opposite end of the stone ring, watching Hikaru now.

Shard realized he hadn't yet asked Hikaru why his scales were silver—about his spring shedding. Ragna hadn't told him very much about the returning Vanir. There was so little time, it seemed. He wondered if he would ever enjoy the feeling of peace again, of relaxing, of simply being with friends again and not fearing an enemy attack, or another death.

Hikaru looked around, and the tip of his tail flicked nervously. "Shard, Ume has made me her apprentice. Even though I'm from the warrior class, everyone agreed I was best suited. When she passes on this spring, I will be the chronicler." He fluffed his wings proudly. "So, I had to come and tell you all I know, and to see the Silver Isles for myself. The new emperor has hatched, and I've made sure we're friends, so that he knows the truth like I do.

"I've seen all the histories now. I wish you could have seen the tale of the wyrms and Sunlanders, Shard, it was so intricate. I won't be able to tell it as beautifully as Ume did when she showed me the pillars, so I'll make it short, with the important things."

"That will do nicely," Shard said quietly.

The others remained quiet, deferring to Shard and the dragon. He realized that he was quickly growing used to the respect others showed him, that he enjoyed it, that he felt he had, most of the time, earned it. Certainly when it came to dragons, he knew more than any other gryfon in the world.

Hikaru sat up on his haunches, his neck curved back and head tilted forward like an egret. He seemed suddenly shy of the others, and spoke mostly to Shard. "You know that Rhydda once flew to the Sunland. So wyrms did, once, fly in daylight. Oh, there were so many details ..."

"Just the most important things, Hikaru." Shard lifted his wings in encouragement, and Catori nodded once in agreement.

"The most important things." Hikaru ran a claw down his belly scales, and ruffled his wing feathers. "In the Second Age, the Sunlanders explored the world and met with the wyrms. They discovered many caches of gold and silver, and other places in the world with gems, and when the wyrms brought them gems, they crafted them treasures in return. They gave them rich food, and names."

Shard tilted his head. "The wyrms never spoke?"

"No. They responded to food, to beautiful things, and to kindness. They learned that the names referred to them, responded to them, and seemed proud to have them. Every year, the Sunlanders traveled to the nightland of the wyrms and gave them gifts, and named their new broods with names that seemed to suit their tongue."

Shard thought of the name Rhydda, how it was almost a growl, rich and earthy. He thought of her wild, shrieking brood.

Hikaru seemed to relax to as the others listened respectfully. "Then, one year—"

"The dragons didn't come," Shard said quietly, and Hikaru's gaze grew bright as he nodded in agreement.

"The dragons didn't come. It was the year Kajar spent with them." His gaze slid to Sverin. "It was the year we decided never again to leave the Mountains of the Sea. And when the dragons didn't come, one wyrm came to us. I don't even know how she found us.

"She followed Midragur," Shard said, and Catori glanced to him with a knowing look. He couldn't meet her gaze, feeling a numb and weary.

"She must have," Hikaru said. "She came, but she couldn't speak, and of course the new emperor didn't know her, and was insulted. One elder knew her, knew her name, and she responded to it. Others tried to tell the emperor of the yearly pilgrimage, of the gifts, of the names. He wouldn't hear it. He was still angry with Kajar. He and others chased Rhydda back to the nightland. She'd had a new brood, and she showed them to the dragons, thinking they would give her wyrmlings names and gold. Instead they . . . they . . ."

He paused, lowering his head in shame.

Sverin spoke. "Tell us, Hikaru. We all have things in our past we aren't proud of."

Shard couldn't help but looked at him in amazement. It sounded as if he were counseling a gryfon fledge.

Brynja leaned into Shard, her face grim, and Hikaru went on, his voice pitched just louder than the crackling fire. "Instead, they drove the young wyrms down into the mines and demanded they dig. If they came out with dirt, they were punished. If they came out with gold and jewels, they got food. If they tried to come out during the day, they were punished. The emperor and his guard only allowed them out at night."

"Until they learned never to fly in the day at all," Shard breathed. "Until they thought daylight itself was dangerous."

"In a single generation, they learned to fear the daylight as if it burned?" Brynja sounded incredulous.

There was silence. Hikaru, restless and self-conscious, tossed a few damp twigs on the fire. Smoke and popping sap filled the quiet.

With a low, unconscious growl, Shard looked at Sverin. "It can be done. There once was a time I wouldn't fly at night."

Brynja looked between them, and Sverin did not lower his gaze, but he didn't speak, either.

Hikaru looked between them uncomfortably.

It was Ragna who said, "None of this explains why they hunt a red gryfon, which you promised you would tell."

"Oh, yes. Yes." Hikaru sat up again, regaining his thread. "The emperor was growing old. They remained with the wyrms almost a full season, until they were obedient, until they had learned."

"Until they were slaves," Catori murmured.

"Until they were slaves," Hikaru said darkly, not debating the point. "To our shame. Then, the emperor decided in his old and bitter age that he wanted revenge on Kajar. He had the craft dragons cast a gryfon in ruby and gold, and showed it to Rhydda. He took gryfon

feathers and let her smell them, like a hunting wolf. He pressed it
to her that the wyrms should find these gryfons, contain them, keep
them from leaving their land. He had such powers, and a seer with
them. Shard, she may have been able to dream with Rhydda the way
you do, to tell her things."

All too clearly, Shard remembered Rhydda's dream, her memory
of a gryfon carved in ruby and gold.

"So the wyrms went to the Winderost," Sverin said. His voice,
which had once been so familiar to Shard as ringing in command,
sounded odd when thoughtfully quiet. "And they hunted at night."

"And all we can guess," Hikaru said, "is that they were so angry,
they hunted any gryfon who dared to fly, even though the dragons
showed her a red one."

Sverin stretched out on his belly, his talons flexing against the cold
ground. "Yet now, suddenly this Rhydda remembers that she can fly in
the day, and so she's brought her brood here, where she also suddenly
knows the last red gryfon dwells."

"Yes," said Hikaru, fidgeting with the end of his tail. "Just so."

"And how is it, I wonder, that she remembers she can fly in day,
and she knows where the last red gryfon dwells?"

It was not a question. Shard took his gaze from Hikaru to see
Sverin staring directly at him.

"Because of me," Shard said quietly, and didn't explain any further.
Sverin inclined his head, as if that was all he'd wanted to hear. Shard
could tell nothing from his expression, and felt frustrated that Sverin
wasn't surprised to hear it was Shard's doing.

"So..." Ragna's voice was flat. "All they want here is to kill Sverin?"

Flickers of ash floated up from the tiny fire, and the red gryfon
looked at her, Shard thought, in wry amusement.

"Yes," Hikaru said. "Well, that's what I think anyway. Maybe
they're just still angry. As soon as I figured it out, I came to tell you,
Shard, but you hadn't arrived home yet. I came across a different sea,

a faster way around the bottom of the world. I met your Vanir, Maja, and the others she'd found, when I passed over the starward quarter."

"About my dying," Sverin began, and Hikaru flicked his wings dismissively, patting a paw against the mud in a reassuring gesture. "Of course we won't let that happen."

Sverin's gaze found Shard again, and they stared at each other across the fire.

Hikaru blinked his large eyes, his ears ticking back uncertainly. "Shard, you won't let that happen." His voice strained as he looked between them, as he seemed to remember their history.

"No," Shard said tightly, more to Sverin than to Hikaru.

He had not stopped himself from dragging Sverin into the sea only to hand him over to the enemy now, and it had been an accident that led the wyrms to the Silver Isles, whether Sverin believed it or not. "Of course that's not going to happen. No one else is going to die for these wyrms."

"And we don't know if that's what they want anymore," Brynja said. "You said they came and slew gryfons at will."

Quietly, Ragna spoke. "We attacked first. When they came, we met them combatively. We don't know what they would have done otherwise. But if they are Nameless, they could have only fought back like witless things."

Brynja shifted her feet, looking stubborn. "The lions and eagles believe wyrms are nothing but their anger and their hatred. We don't know if they even remember what they're angry about. They might be hunting Sverin, or they might be here because of Shard's dreams, and remember nothing."

"I think Rhydda remembers," Shard said, still watching Sverin. "But they don't know that all their original enemies are dead."

"So," said Sverin, "who's going to tell them?"

"Shard will," Hikaru said firmly, and all looked to him in surprise. He ducked his head to a stubborn angle. "He will. He's the Summer King. They'll listen to him."

Shard stood, exasperated, loving Hikaru for his faith, frustrated with his innocence. "Why now, Hikaru? Why do you think they'll listen after they have never listened before?"

Hikaru blinked large eyes at him. "Because now, you know! Now you have the truth. Just as you hunted the truth about the Aesir in the Winderost and the dragons in the Sunland. Now you know everything that happened, so you understand why they're angry. You understand them, Shard. They'll listen."

Shard could only gaze at him, and Catori watched Shard's face.

Sverin broke the quiet. "And if he fails?"

Hikaru raised his head again, his silver mane fluttering, and showed off teeth as long as Sverin's wing feathers. "He will *not* fail."

"In the meantime," Ragna said quickly, seeing the young dragon's temper rising, "we should take Sverin underground. Hikaru, thank you for your protection, but he should be underground. Let me take him to Kjorn, let him see his son. And Shard—"

"I need to think." He stood again. "Mother, Brynja…" He looked at Hikaru, at his friends. "I need to think. Take Sverin to safety, and remain safe yourselves. I can't go in those caves yet. I need to be here, in my old winds, in the forest, and smell the sea. And I need to be alone."

He looked around, and all appeared, with grave expressions, to understand.

Brynja stood, and shoved her head under his neck. "Be well, Shard. Come to us soon."

"I will. Thank you. Tell everyone what's passed. I'll come to you in the morning, first light, I promise. Tell the Vanir I will come soon."

His words felt heavy. Soon things would be resolved, one way or another. He would try to dream again, now that he knew the truth of all that had happened. Perhaps, as Hikaru believed, knowing the truth would give Shard more power over Rhydda.

They made their farewells.

Catori paused near Shard. "Where will you go?"

He thought of the high priestess of the Vanhar, and the things she had recommended he try when he needed more strength and clarity. He thought of Ajia, who had helped him remain rooted in himself. A place came to him. A place of power. The first place Stigr had called him prince, bowed to him, the first place he'd been struck by his true birthright, and realized all he wanted in the world was peace.

"To the rowan," he said. "If it won't bother the wolves."

She nodded once. "No. They will understand." She nosed his ear, then trotted to Ragna. "This way, great lady. This way, to the caves."

They left Shard with Hikaru, who bent his head low, nuzzling Shard. "What will you do, brother?"

Shard closed his eyes, grateful for Hikaru's warmth, for his steady, unfailing heart, eternally grateful to see him again. "First, I'll try to dream. I would ask you to come with me, but I need to be alone, Hikaru. Just for a little while. When all this is settled, I'll show you every wondrous place on the islands I know."

Hikaru laughed, and with a farewell, Shard left him, walking deeper and deeper into the ancient forest toward the place the wolves called the First Tree.

43

UNDER RIVER, UNDER STONE

CRAWLING DOWN INTO THE COLD earth only reminded Ragna of earlier in the winter when they'd fled down the wolf tunnels to escape Sverin and his King's Guard. Now, of course, all Aesir were following Thyra—and Kjorn, now that he'd returned with Shard.

With grim hope, Ragna focused her thoughts on Shard. Oh, how he'd looked like Baldr, truly, grown into his final height and strength, though a bit lean from his travel, a bit worn. She saw new wisdom in his eyes, new care in his words.

And Sverin had bowed to him.

One small, hard part of Ragna's heart relaxed, though it seemed that what she'd thought would be her greatest challenge had come and gone, and a new one had risen.

She hadn't slept much in the last days. The wyrm screams at night, the memory of her dead pride members, and the worry over Shard had kept her awake. Now she had her son, they had a dragon on their side, they even had fire. Tyr's own fire, harnessed and brought to earth. She had to believe they would prevail. And if Shard decided to fight, she would fight, too. She would face the wyrms if he asked her to.

All those thoughts kept her moving forward through the frozen, slick tunnel of mud and stone. She realized that in staying with Sverin and Hikaru, she still didn't have all the news. She didn't know all the gryfons who had died, and lived, and who was injured. She thought of Halvden, leaping to her defense, and the blood . . . She had to turn her thoughts away. She would know soon enough.

Catori led them, Ragna next, then Sverin, and lastly the Aesir, Brynja.

Her heart quickened. An Aesir. Not a cursed one, not a conqueror, but nonetheless . . . Shard couldn't have waited, just a little longer, for his own pride, for a Vanir?

Don't be foolish. The heart doesn't wait.

She thought of Sigrun, who loved Caj truly, and others who had found happiness. She also thought of Vidar, and Eyvin.

Brynja would have a chance to prove herself soon enough, and Ragna would see about her quality.

"Brynja." Sverin's voice broke their quiet travel through the tunnels. "I knew Mar, we are distant cousins. I'm glad to know you."

"I . . ." She hesitated, and Ragna could barely hear her voice, muffled in the stone. "I'm glad to know you, my lord. My family has always been loyal to your bloodline."

Sverin remained quiet a moment, then said with a note of regret, "I hope we will live up to that loyalty."

"Kjorn already has, my lord."

Sverin made a low noise of pleased acknowledgement, and they continued in silence after that. Ragna began to notice, with relief, the faint, glowing fungus on the earthy walls that broke up the cold black of the cave.

"It will take us several sunmarks or so," Catori said, ahead of them, "to walk to where the others are. I wish we could fly there."

So much time of crawling, walking, ducking. There were some places so narrow that Sverin barely fit through, and Ragna had to squirm about and claw at dirt and roots to help him pass. Ragna could fly nearly a whole day without weariness, but the darkness and cold wore on her.

For a little while, it seemed it would never end, and she would dwell forever in the dark. Her thoughts grew more and more grim.

It had to be evening by then, and they back beneath the Sun Isle. Ragna feared for Shard, and where he was, and what he was doing. But she took faith the wyrms had so far stayed away from the other islands.

Then, the faint, distant echo of a gryfon's laughter flitted across the stone.

"A little ways more," Catori said.

A little ways more turned out to be a longer way than Ragna supposed, and knew that wolves had greater stamina for running and crawling than she did. An entire day of it wore her to the bone.

They passed one dark tunnel, but to Ragna's surprise, the sweet scent of river water and fresh air came from that direction. She paused, lifting her beak to smell, and Sverin bumped in to her, then Brynja into him.

"What is it?" muttered the big gryfon warily.

"Catori!" Ragna called, for the she-wolf hadn't slowed. "Is there another way out?"

Paws scuffle on dirt and rock and Catori backed up to them, unable to turn around. "Yes. We sealed that tunnel after . . . my father died. It isn't large enough for an Aesir, though."

"I see." Ragna eyed the dark tunnel, then at Sverin and Brynja's urging, they crawled on.

At last, to her relief, a gryfon voice barked out, "Who goes there?"

"Catori," said the wolf amiably. "And with me I have Ragna, Sverin, and Brynja of the Winderost, friend to Shard and Kjorn."

Catori wriggled free of the narrow tunnel, and Ragna climbed out beside her into a larger cavern, one she hadn't yet seen. Sverin emerged after, and Brynja, who moved to stand a respectful distance from Ragna.

The sentry turned out to be Dagr, and he mantled to Ragna. "My lady. It's a relief to see you well."

"And you," she said quietly, thinking of others lost in the fight with the wyrms.

They wouldn't even have been able to bear the dead to Black Rock, though she supposed the Aesir would wish their dead to be burned, later, at Pebble's Throw, if they could ever go there again with the wyrms in residence.

Other gryfons came forward curiously, and Ragna saw that more tunnels branched out from there. She spied Vidar, with relief, and Caj, who stood up at the sight of them. She would let him deal with Sverin.

"Dagr, will you take me to the other Vanir who arrived with Maja? I would very much like to spend time with them. I've waited too long."

Feeling self-conscious that she had been gone from the pride, that she had chosen to remain with Sverin, Ragna peered around to see the survivors. She didn't see Halvden.

Before Dagr could answer, a bright voice rang through the cave.

"Brynja!" A gryfess whom Ragna didn't know, with the height and build of an Aesir but plain, earth-brown feathers, bounded forward from a corner of the cavern. Though Hikaru had explained to her why some Aesir were brightly colored and some were not, it was strange. The new gryfess and Brynja greeted like wingsisters, then Brynja introduced her as Dagny, to Ragna, and then Sverin.

"Oh," Dagny breathed, ogling Sverin up and down, openly, as if he were not a thinking creature and gryfon lord, but a jewel at which to marvel, a legend. Ragna wanted to cuff her ears to stop her from staring like a witless magpie. She seemed to gather herself, and offered him a slight mantle.

He dipped his head. "Dagny. I believe my mate hunted with your mother, before we left the Dawn Spire."

Her beak slipped open. Ragna couldn't watch her silliness anymore. Did she not know Sverin was a warlord, a coward, dangerous, not something to admire? Clearly she didn't care about his history. She glanced at Brynja, and saw admiration in her face too, though more reserved, perhaps, more aware of what had passed. Perhaps their reactions would make Sverin feel better about returning to his homeland.

Dagr opened his wings for her attention, and she gave it gladly. "My lady. I'll take you around to the Vanir. They'll be glad to see you, relieved. We're a bit scattered now, but everyone's holding strong. I think some of the gryfesses are even about to whelp. Astri would be especially glad to see you. I don't know that everyone heard the news about the dragon, yet."

Ragna should have been happier at the news that the gryfesses would begin whelping, but she could only nod once. She glanced sideways to Caj and Sverin, who greeted and spoke quietly.

"My lady," Dagr urged, as if the matters of the Aesir should no longer concern her. "Let me take you."

"Yes," she said, distracted. She turned to her companions. "Catori, thank you for leading us. Brynja, you'll be all right here?"

The russet gryfess nodded once, worried for Shard, Ragna saw, but happy in the company of her wingsister. Dagr touched a respectful wingtip to Ragna's shoulder, and they turned together toward one of the tunnels.

The sight of Halvden, hobbling determinedly down the tunnel, stopped her short and prickled Ragna's feathers in sudden, vast relief. Then when she saw why he was limping, horror turned her belly.

The wyrm had not killed him, but had completely severed a foreleg just beneath the elbow joint. It looked as if it were mending well enough, a clean cut, patched with black moss and bound with sinew twine. His gaze was fixed on Sverin as he hobbled forward. He seemed not even to notice Ragna standing there in his path.

"Halvden," she breathed, then gathered herself, and opened her wings for his attention. "Halvden. Son of Hallr."

The emerald warrior halted with a lurch, still learning his new gait. Yellow eyes bore into Ragna, then he dipped his head a fraction.

She met his gaze, determined not to stare at what remained of his leg. "Thank you," she said quietly, firmly. It was all she could say, all she had to offer him for leaping to her defense, for risking his life and losing a limb on her behalf. "Tyr will surely hold you in the highest regard for your courage."

Surprise twitched across his face and he merely ducked his head. "I fought for the pride."

The pride, Ragna thought. One pride. She had seen all of them fighting as a single, united pride against the enemy, and now even Halvden acknowledged they were one. She lowered her head. "And you fought well. I've never seen a gryfon fight so well, and lead the others as you did."

"Nor I," added Caj from where he stood with Sverin. "Don't you agree?" he asked the red gryfon.

Sverin lifted his gaze to Halvden. He considered the missing leg, Halvden's proud, unyielding posture, and the desperate need for approval in his eyes.

"I do," Sverin said at length. "I have never seen the like in all my days. Well done, Halvden."

Amazement and gratitude warmed Halvden's face, and his beak opened. He surely would have said something to the gryfon he still considered his king, if someone else hadn't spoken first.

"I'm surprised you stayed to see him fight at all, Father."

Ragna turned, surprised at Kjorn's voice, and at his tone. She had never heard such bitterness from him. He looked taller than Ragna remembered, strong, lean and golden, striding from one of the tunnels with a thunderous look, and straight toward his father.

44
RECKONING

"**B**EFORE YOU FLED, I MEAN," Kjorn added. Any talk in the cavern died.

His father's expression warped from surprise and gladness to sudden, unreadable stone. Kjorn hadn't expected to see Sverin yet when he'd come down the tunnel. He'd been looking for Caj. He wasn't ready, and the shock of seeing the gryfon who had put all of Kjorn's loved ones in mortal danger plunged him into icy anger.

"Leave us," Kjorn barked, eyes on his father. Sverin didn't move, and everyone glanced at each other before realizing he'd meant all of them, not Sverin.

"Leave us, please," Kjorn said, more quietly, more respectfully, with a glance around. Halvden began to move away, and a couple of the other gryfons followed. Kjorn met Ragna's gaze across the dim cavern, and offered a low mantle. She and Thyra had taken over the wounded pride when he'd left to find Shard and the truth, and he hadn't meant to shout at her. Brynja and Dagny murmured respectfully, and Dagny led her and others out of the cavern.

Even Catori slipped back into the tunnel he presumed she'd come from.

Ragna, Dagr, and Caj didn't move, however.

"It's all right," Sverin said quietly to Caj, who looked prepared to stop a fight.

Every feather on Kjorn's back prickled in outrage. *Am I not the ruling prince, now? They still wait for Sverin's word to leave?*

Caj's gaze flickered to Kjorn, pained and rueful. He was wrong, he realized. Sverin was speaking to Caj as his wingbrother, not his king, and Caj still honored him as such.

Kjorn struggled against unreasonable anger and pride. He wished he'd had a little more warning, time to prepare, any time to know what to say or think or feel.

The last time he'd seen his father, the king was almost Nameless with his strange madness, and was about to kill another innocent half-blood gryfon for disobeying him. Halvden had told Sverin that Kjorn was an apparition, not his son, in order to protect his own hide. Sverin had fled, flown, shrieking and mad.

He'd thought he would feel glad to see him in his right mind, but all he felt was fury.

"You're still a prisoner," Dagr growled at Sverin. "Don't forget it."

Kjorn startled slightly, staring at him. The last time he had seen Dagr was when Sverin banished him, in front of his mother and his younger brother, Einarr. The day of their initiation. The day Shard had met Catori...

The day everything we were flew apart in the wind.

"Dagr—" Caj began, but the strong, coppery gryfon's ears slicked back and he marched to the entrance where the others had left, pausing there to look at Ragna.

"My lady?"

"Yes," Ragna agreed, her green eyes flicking from him to Caj, then Sverin, and Kjorn. "For Shard's sake, Prince Kjorn, and because you

returned and I believe you are a gryfon of honor, we will leave you
alone. But remember he is still a prisoner of the Vanir."

Kjorn's temper seethed and cooled at once. He managed to smooth
his feathers and offer the Widow Queen another bow. He noted her
odd stance, that she, like Caj, stood at a diagonal to Sverin as if to
partially block Kjorn from him, in an almost unconscious, protective
position. He wondered at it. He wondered what had passed since he'd
left, since Caj had clearly succeeded in bringing Sverin to reason.

"Sverin?" Caj asked again, low.

Apparently, to his mind, being wingbrothers was more important
than following Kjorn or Ragna's command. Perhaps it was. Kjorn
thought of Shard, and couldn't blame his old mentor.

"It's all right," Sverin said again, but his gaze never left Kjorn's
face.

They left. Kjorn wondered. He wondered at it all, wondered if
his father's sanity was so fragile that they were hesitant to leave him,
wondered if Ragna thought seeing Kjorn might drive him back to the
brink.

But it appeared to be having the opposite effect.

"Kjorn." A season of exhaustion seemed to lift from the shining
gold eyes. He stepped forward.

"Don't." Kjorn lifted his wings in warning, half crouching, managing not to hiss in feral anger. "You denied me. You would have
exiled my mate. My mate, Father! Your own wingbrother's daughter.
My kit might have died. I believed in you, I believed in everything
about you, and you nearly destroyed our pride. I see that others have
forgiven you, but it was *me* you harmed above all."

Sverin's eyes flashed as he tilted his head, hissing in a breath.
Perhaps the rest of the pride's anger had cooled. Perhaps begging
forgiveness before Ragna and all the pride had done Sverin some
measure of good, but Kjorn had seen none of that. Sverin came
forward slowly, his head dipping low to a submissive angle. Kjorn

expected him to defend himself, to claim he was mad, to say none of it mattered.

"Yes," he said quietly, in a tone Kjorn hadn't heard since his kithood. "I did all those things. I did, my son. And they broke me. You mother's death broke me, our cowardice in leaving the pride of Dawn Spire destroyed me, but I have no excuse for what I did to Thyra, and to you."

It was satisfying and appalling to see his father grovel, and Kjorn's skin felt tight, hot. He wanted to run. "Thyra told me you confessed something to the pride, but she wouldn't tell me what." Kjorn glanced beyond Sverin to the tunnels, but they were truly alone. "She said it was for you to tell me."

"Oh." Sverin stopped, shifting, his tail lashing. His ears laid back in dismay, as if he'd hoped someone would tell Kjorn his terrible secrets for him.

"Tell me," Kjorn growled. "Tell me what you've told everyone else. Tell me so I can know who you are, like everyone else."

The fallen Red King watched him longingly, as if from a much farther distance, as if they didn't know each other, or would never again be close as they once were.

As we never really were, Kjorn thought bitterly.

The ember of anger that had glowed in his heart at missing his battle in the Winderost breathed to life again, heating his chest. *We were never what I thought we were. He was never who I thought he was.*

"It was about your mother's death. She did drown . . ." His voice was utterly devoid of emotion. "But she flew out at my insistence." Kjorn watched his face, his blank, red mask, the regal mask he'd worn for ten years that Kjorn had always mistaken for strength. "My goading. I drove her out, Kjorn, and I—"

"That's enough," Kjorn whispered. He remembered the night. As a kit, he remembered his father's shrieking, he remembered his years of mourning, of at first not understanding where his mother was, of watching his father slip further away.

He remembered knowing the sea was wicked, was dangerous, was to blame. First the sea. Then the Vanir.

"I might have been able to save her, but I was too afraid." Sverin went on as if he hadn't heard Kjorn, or as if he wasn't even there, as if once he started the story, he couldn't stop saying the whole thing.

The cave pressed in on Kjorn, dark, wet, freezing cold. He should have given them to Brynja to start some fires. The thought of fire made him wish fervently Shard had come back with them.

Why did they need him on Star Isle? Shouldn't they have been done by now?

Sudden worry for Shard eclipsed his anger, but then he realized if something had happened, Brynja or Ragna would have told him immediately.

"I was too afraid," Sverin repeated, drawing his attention back. "But Ragna tried. She tried to save your mother, and she kept the secret that I cowered there, watching, and didn't fly out. And your mother..."

"You..." The news felt as if he'd been plunged into choking, icy water. "You let her die!"

Sverin's ears laid back, his feathers sleeked, he looked like a red serpent in the cave. "Kjorn, I beg you to forgive me. You don't understand how I—"

"I understand." Kjorn's voice scratched, cracked. "I understand that you fled our homeland because of the wyrms, and you lied to me and said we were conquerors, honorable, that we were warriors. My mother died because of your cowardice. And you lied to me and blamed the Vanir so much that I didn't trust my own wingbrother. Then you succumbed to fear and fled. Everything I thought I was is because of who I thought you were, and I was wrong. I understand, Father. I understand everything."

"Kjorn—"

"You are not welcome at the Dawn Spire." Kjorn snarled out the words. He didn't want to hear anymore. "I won back our homeland,

and I did it without you. I did it in *spite* of you. So, when I return home as king, you will not be at my side. Consider yourself an exile."

Sverin gazed at him, then sank down until his belly pressed to the stone. He mantled his wings, and lowered his head.

Kjorn, battling a tempest in his heart, turned without another word. He chose a tunnel at random and walked, hard and fast, shoving past roots and narrow places. Gryfons saw him and quickly backed out of his path.

Caj found him first, and fell in step with him. "What happened? What did you say to him?"

"Ask him yourself," Kjorn growled, and immediately regretted speaking to his old mentor that way. But he didn't want to speak to anyone. He muttered an apology and shoved past Caj, something he wouldn't have dreamed of doing before his time in the Winderost.

"Where are you going?" Caj growled after him. "Sire, you have my respect, but you must listen to me—"

"You listen to me!" Kjorn whirled, wings flaring, bashing the rock walls of the tunnel. He didn't bother to wince. The sharp sting only made him angrier, and his pride flared hot at Caj questioning him. "I'll have nothing to do with him. I cannot forgive him the way you have. The way the Vanir have, I suppose? I can't, Caj. I won't. I rule the Aesir now. Thyra and I will return to rule the Dawn Spire without him. I don't need him. Do you know what Shard learned about Kajar and the dragons?"

"No," Caj said warily. "I haven't seen him yet. No one's told me anything about the dragons."

Kjorn let his gaze travel along the eerie, glowing wall. "We are not cursed, Caj, but blessed with dragon's blood. With the blessing, the dragons told Shard that *everything we are will be more so.* Apparently my father is a coward, a liar, and a killer. And the dragon's blood made him more so."

"Kjorn." The old warrior looked as if Kjorn had physically struck him. "You're angry now, and hurt, and rightfully so, but you must try—"

Commotion, shouting, and scuffling feathers and talons cut him off, then someone came shouting down the tunnel.

"My lord! Kjorn!"

A young Aesir as orange as dragon fire barreled at them from the nearest tunnel, ears flat to his skull.

Caj blocked him from crashing into Kjorn. "Vald? What—"

He was gasping, panting as if he'd run for leagues. "Oh, Caj. The monsters. They found the tunnel. Found a scent. At least six of them. Digging."

"Digging?" Kjorn breathed, and thought of Shard's dark words when Asvander had joked about the wyrms digging.

I believe they do.

"They'll be on the wider tunnels within a sunmark," Vald panted. "They'll find—"

"They won't," Kjorn growled. The heady promise of battle spun the whirling anger in his heart to talon-tip focus. He flicked his tail, drawing a long breath. "They fled the Winderost, and chose the battleground here instead."

All he heard was Shard's voice, warning him not to do anything foolish. Kjorn forced back a flare of misgiving at taking action without consulting the ruler of the Silver Isles. But Shard was not there in the tunnels, with a mate and unborn kit in danger of dying at the claws of tunneling wyrms. There was no time to find Shard, much less consult him.

He had to act.

"Kjorn," Caj said, his voice gravelly and low. Every cobalt feather stood high. "We'll move deeper. We'll get the pregnant—"

"No, Caj." He turned to his old mentor and could think only of Kajar and the dragons, then Per and his own cowardly father, who'd fled his homeland and cast Kjorn's birthright into the winds. "No.

Some gryfesses are already beginning their birthing. I cannot ask them to move. We will not run again. This is where we end it, and now."

Kjorn folded his wings, and strode past Caj, saying, "Vald, find Asvander for me. Find Brynja. Gather all the able-bodied warriors who flew with us from the Winderost, and lead them to largest cavern."

Vald glanced at Caj, who only ducked his head. The orange gryfon lifted his wings. "Yes, my lord."

Turning down a separate tunnel that led to the largest, main cavern, Kjorn realized with grim dismay that he would have his battle after all.

GRYFON BODIES PACKED THE stone cavern that had once seemed huge. Tunnels branched off into the dark, stuffed with gryfon warriors of all ages—Winderost Aesir, Lakelanders, Vanhar, Vanir of the Silver Isles, and half-bloods born of the Conquering. He thought he smelled wolf as well, but it might have been leftover scent.

Kjorn did not see Sverin. But then, he hadn't expected to.

Feathers rustled in the strange, dim gloom of the cavern. In some places around the perimeter, the stone wall sloped down so low that gryfons were forced to sit, crouch, or lie on their bellies. Dark murmuring and thick tension gave the air a moist, stinging scent. Kjorn intended to have them out as soon as possible.

Vald squeezed through the mass to Kjorn, who stood at the center in a small open space. "All who can fit and are able are here, my lord."

"Very good." Without preamble, Kjorn raised his voice. "Prides of the Silver Isles and the Winderost, our enemy is upon us!"

Those nearest him had to flatten their ears against the volume of his shout, but he wanted to make sure all gryfons crammed in the cavern and in the tunnels could hear.

"Even now, the wyrms have scented us, and discovered the entrance to the caverns. We must drive them out, for they'll dig and be on these caverns by the evening mark."

"How?" demanded a Vanir who crouched at the far wall. "We won't fit enough gryfons in the tunnel where they dig to frighten them! They'll kill us one by one!"

"What of Rashard?" called another, Istra. Kjorn sought her out and met her gaze between the ears of other warriors. "He should know." She swiveled to address the other Vanir. "We should not fight unless he wishes it!"

"We have no choice," Brynja argued, shoulder forward through the mass of feathered bodies.

Grateful, Kjorn watched her step into his small circle. "Vanir of the Silver Isles, exiles returned home, know that I am Brynja, daughter-of-Mar. Shard and I have chosen each other to mate at the next Daynight, and I will serve with all my heart as your queen, for I love your prince. We have no time to reach him now, and we're under deadly threat. We cannot ask the pregnant gryfesses to move when even now they've begun whelping. We must fight. Even Shard would know that we must fight."

To Kjorn's surprise, Ketil stepped forward, in silence, and stood beside Brynja. She looked at Ketil gratefully, then turned her gaze in challenge to the rest.

"How?" came the cry again. A half-blood, from within the crowd. "They nearly slaughtered us before."

Kjorn was secretly pleased to see that though there was surprise and muttering at Brynja's announcement, there was no hostility. Down the tunnels echoed a sudden, heart-stopping sound of rock and earth crumbling, following by horrid growls and shrieks. The wyrms.

"We have ten times the number of warriors now," Kjorn declared. "Mighty warriors from my homeland, prepared to stand and fight with you. And we have something else." He slipped his talons through the leather thong about his neck and brandished the leather pouch over his head. "Dragon fire stones from the distant Sunland. My friends, we will fight the enemy with talons and with fire."

Amazed faces exchanged glances, and the tension rippled into something more familiar—the surge of energy before a fight.

A muttering rumbled through the throng and gryfons parted to allow someone through. Kjorn looked to see the gold wolf, Tocho.

"Prince Kjorn, what if you also sent warriors outside? You should send a few warriors out and harry the wyrms from the air while others prepare fire and drive them from underground."

"How?" Kjorn asked.

"There's no other tunnels out," Vald said, eyes narrowing. "And it would take us all day to crawl and emerge on another island."

Tocho opened his muzzle in a mischievous pant. He reminded Kjorn of the painted wolf, Mayka, for a moment. "There is one other opening that we know of on the Sun Isle. But only very lean and small gryfons will fit."

Silence clotted the cave. All had heard. Only smaller gryfons.

Only Vanir.

Drawing in a breath and hopefully some strength, Kjorn dipped his head to Tocho in thanks, and lifted his gaze the gathered gryfons again. They had so very little time.

"Vanir of the Silver Isles. Even now, Rashard your prince, my wingbrother, is trying to communicate with the she-wyrm who leads the horde. But until he succeeds, we must hold them off. You can help us. You can follow Tocho, and harry them. I cannot command you, but I can ask you, for the sake of your pride, to do this thing. Fight beside us. Fight for your home."

No one answered. He'd failed to stir them at all. They looked untrusting of him, of his warriors, of the whole idea of war. They were unmoved even by the sight of Ketil, one of their own, standing at Brynja's side.

Then, gryfons shuffled, exclaiming, parting. In the eerie light of the cave came Ragna, pale and quiet.

"My pride." Her green eyes traveled sadly over the gathering. She didn't look afraid, Kjorn thought, but resigned to the battle ahead. "I will not command you either, but I for one will stand between these beasts and my home until my last breath."

With a glance at Kjorn, she raised her voice. "I will stand, as I hope you will, as one pride. We must not live in fear. It is then that we lose ourselves, our very names. Remember that we are not mere creatures of blood and bone, but daughters and sons of bright Tyr and Tor. I will fly with the Aesir who have come to us. I will distract the wyrms, even I have to do it alone. I will fight."

For a moment, all held perfectly still. Massive Aesir warriors gazed at the middle-aged, wiry, short gryfess with a mix of awe, and fear for her.

"I will go," Ketil said quietly, but no others stepped forward.

For three heartbeats, Kjorn was terrified that those two would be going by themselves.

"My queen!"

Kjorn's heart clutched to see the elder Vanir, Frar, shoving forward through the throng. "You two will not fly alone."

Kjorn could scarcely believe that the old gryfon who'd flown in that very morning, on the last of his strength, on the verge of collapse, would volunteer. It appeared none of the other Vanir could believe it either, and they looked ashamed. His courage broke the dam of fear, and others followed him, thin, short, wiry, strong Vanir clambering to their queen. Big, seasoned Aesir squeezed aside and shifted and pressed to each other to allow the Vanir to flow forward.

"Never alone," said Istra, followed by a gryfon who looked to be her brother.

"We will stand with you," said Keta, coming forward.

"My queen," said Maja. Toskil, Vidar, and the rest of the Vanir pushed through the crowd to the queen.

Ragna's eyes shone. She dipped her head to them, then looked at Tocho. "Show us the way."

45

THE DARKEST DREAM

S HARD MARVELED AT THE SILENCE of the woods. It was almost
spring—the forest should have been overwhelmed with birdsong.
It was as if the isles held their breaths in fear of the wyrms, or in
anticipation. He hadn't heard any more roaring, and took that as a
good sign.

He walked through dense corridors of pine until the afternoon,
breathing in the familiar scents of earth, salt water, and the wispy
smell of wolf on the breeze. His heart drew him, almost instinctively,
along through the forest toward the great rowan tree at its center. The
wolves made their dens in stones beneath the gnarled roots, but if
Catori said they wouldn't mind his coming, then he believed her.

The silence infused him, filled him, relaxed him. It felt good to
walk and to rest his flight muscles. When sun touched the tops of
the trees, pale light filtering at a sharp angle through naked branches,
Shard stopped, and realized he'd reached his destination.

A series of moss-adorned rocks thrust up from the forest floor in
a short cliff, and on it perched the rowan tree. Its branches spanned
as far as Shard could see, black and spindly against the blue sky, its

immense trunk dipping down into gnarled roots that formed entry-ways into the wolf den. Shard saw no wolves, and wondered if some of them remained underground in the network of caves, out of the weather, away from the wyrms.

Stepping forward, Shard breathed in the ancient scent of the tree, and with it, memories.

Stigr, telling him the history of it. *They say its roots touch the heart of the world*...

Helaku, the wolf king, acknowledging him as Baldr's heir.

Catori, howling, calling him the Summer King, the Star King.

Tocho, Ahanu, and Catori standing atop the short cliff and saying they would not fight his family, when the rest of the wolf pack attacked the nesting cliffs.

He walked forward, weaving through thrusting roots and mud, until he found a hollow between two vast roots, lined by a cluster of dead leaves that were relatively dry. There he curled up gratefully, feeling the ancient rowan embrace him in its roots and the soil that had borne it through all the Ages, cool under his body.

As the long flight over the sea, the trials, the Winderost, and his own fears sloughed from him, Shard plunged into sleep.

At first, murky, exhausted dream-things swamped him. Fears and worries. He saw distorted gryfons and wolves swirling through tun-nels in terror, he saw the wyrms, mining through stone and earth.

A thick sense of terror clasped his throat, and he shoved it away, thinking it was only from his tired mind.

The cold earth beneath him kept him anchored, aware of who and where he was. He beheld a vision of the Silver Isles in an odd, still, half-lit day, as if the sun and moon stood evenly in the sky.

Soon it will be Halflight.

He couldn't place the voice. It sounded like the memory of his father.

The seasons will turn toward spring, toward summer. Now it reminded him of Catori, or like the albatross he'd once met over the sea, Windwalker.

A year ago, Ragna named you the Summer King.

The memory of Ume drifted to him, the chronicler of the Sunland. Then, a raven voice, but not Munin.

> *"He is borne aloft by the Silver Wind*
> *He alone flies the highest peak.*
> *When they hear his song at battle's end*
> *The Nameless shall know themselves*
> *And the Voiceless will once again speak."*

Hugin, who called himself the keeper of time, winged by through the strange light of the dream. Munin tried to follow his brother, and Shard flung him away like a water droplet, pleased and surprised that it was so easy to do. Groa had taught him dream weaving, he had practiced, and there, snug in the roots of a familiar tree, his talons dug into the earth of his home, Shard felt more grounded and powerful than ever before.

He felt the dream net in the spiral of ferns around him, in the twisting branches that fractured off from the trunk of the rowan. He felt the spiral of Midragur, and all the dreams in the islands.

Rhydda.

Rhydda.

In his dream, he flew to Pebble's Throw, following the heat of her anger.

He found the wyrm dreams. Blood, gold, and gryfons. She was pleased, pleased with something, and when Shard nudged curiously, she turned her thoughts away, as if hiding something from him.

Blood and gold.

I know your story now. He tried a new tack, not wanting her to shut him out. He wove the wind and rock and lava into the story for her. Afternoon deepened around them, and the sea glowed blue, and the lava glowed bloody red. He layered his words in images so that she would understand.

A dragon has come, Rhydda. A dragon has come to make amends. They will speak to you once more if you relent, they'll name your brood. I speak for them. Rhydda, I understand now.

Hot, heavy anger swirled around him. Great jaws opened, gnashing, a spade tail lashed.

I understand. Believe me, I do.

For her he spun a dream of his life in the Silver Isles. He showed her that he was forbidden to fly at night, forbidden to swim in the sea, fish, or believe in the goddess, Tor. Sverin appeared in his dream. Her own fantasy flashed back at him with relish—Sverin, dead and bleeding on the ground.

With surprise, Shard realized she was truly communicating with him, showing him what she wanted. Shard swept his talons, showing the red gryfon flying through the sky, alive.

No. No. You cannot kill him. He is the son of the son of the gryfon they wanted you to hunt.

He tried to explain the generations, he showed gryfons growing up, showed Kajar, Per, then Sverin. Maybe his own remnants of anger remained, for she seemed unconvinced. Her dream burned through his mind in molten fire. A red gryfon. A gryfon, dead on the ground.

I know. I understand what they told you, but it's wrong.

Her rage slunk into his heart. He did understand. All the fury, the hatred, the anger. She had been a slave. Her children were Nameless and brutish and wild.

Rhydda, I know. You must listen . . .

Blood and stone. She blocked him. As she always did, she turned from him, even in the dream. She was waking. Something stirred and distracted her.

Desperate at the thought of failing again, Shard loosed an eagle cry and dove, dove hard, and fast, toward her horned head. She reared back, enormous wings flaring wide, and opened her jaws. Shard dove,

dove, knowing it was a dream, and let his fear fall behind him. He plunged into her gaping maw, past the razor fangs, down to her heart. There, he spread his wings wide, trying to open her heart to him, then spun and roared.

She remembered everything.

Shard crashed through her memories, all as Hikaru had said, the mining, the dragons forcing her to fly only at night.

Her children, Nameless, scrabbling for scraps of food in the Winderost.

The scent of gryfon was on the wind, and always that scent made her remember the great, bright masters who had once given them beautiful jewels, honor, and Names.

Now it was all gone. It was gone, until the red gryfon died.

No, Rhydda. Shard tried to wrap his wings around her heart, to fill her with his own sense of justice and peace. He thought of Sverin, and small bitterness flickered that the king who had wronged his pride was now among those he sought to protect.

Rhydda's thoughts snared on Shard's bitterness.

Too late, he felt her seething satisfaction. He saw her fantasy again, of Sverin dead.

NO. Shard scoured for an idea, for anything to impart the idea of wrongness and loss.

Then, he remembered battling wyrms in the Winderost.

Your brood? Are they all your sons and daughters?

Rhydda.

He lashed together a memory as he circled in her waking dream. He rebuilt the memory of a huge, muscled, shrieking wyrm, dull of hide and jaws gaping. The wyrm had chased Shard at the Dawn Spire during the first, awful battle when Rhydda had cut Stigr down.

But the wyrm in Shard's memory was dead now. Shard and Stigr had tricked it into flying head-first into the ground.

Clearly, he recalled the awful cracking of bones and thunderous quaking as the wyrm smashed into the mud. He formed the memory for her, in all its wretched detail. Then he showed her Stigr, cut down in the mud. The wyrm and Stigr, fallen.

He tried desperately to impart pain, loss, the wrongness of it all. She went still.

Great, rank breath heaved from her nostrils and her open jaws as Shard showed her this wyrm. Alive, flying fast, a hulking picture of might and death. Then, dead. Unmoving in the red mud.

A low noise reverberated within her armored chest.

Was he your mate? Your son? He died in battle.

Did you grieve?

Did you feel anything at all?

Stigr's voice resounded in his head. *Be careful how you put things to her. She might not understand.*

A gurgling sound grated in her cavernous chest and roiled, building itself into a rolling, metallic shriek that threatened to shatter Shard's skull.

With horror, Shard realized that she understood well enough—but rather than understand that he was trying to show her his own sense of fear and loss, he felt fresh rage licking up in her heart. She thought he was threatening her, or gloating, or—he didn't even know what she thought.

Blood and jagged stone and hatred flung itself around Shard, seizing his spirit and drowning his will, trapping him in the darkest corner of Rhydda's heart.

In the fury of her wrath, his name slipped from him, his heart, his purpose, and all he could smell and see was the walls and pits of her endless, mindless hatred. And there he stayed, shrieking, locked in a raging, Voiceless nightmare.

46

QUEEN OF THE VANIR

THROUGH THE POCKED BIRCH TRUNKS and their bare, whispering branches, Ragna heard the grating and rumbling of the wyrms. The river rolled at her side as she and nearly fifty of the Vanir, young and old, crept through the forest. The underbrush remained naked and spindly from winter, thin and offering little cover.

Still, the wind brushed their scent upstream, away from the wyrms, though that was all the help Tyr seemed able to offer them. The sun glanced down, mottling their feathers in the undergrowth. Mud and dirt from their crawl through the tight wolf tunnel helped disguise their scent and the sight of them in the woods.

Ketil stalked on one side of her, Istren on the other. Tocho had led them to the second entrance, where they'd had to dig out the remainder of brush the wolves had used to stuff the hole, sealing it off after the wolves' attack on the Sun Isle last summer.

Even Ragna had barely fit through the tunnel, and she was glad no Aesir or half-bloods had attempted it. They would've been stuck fast.

Ragna's feet seemed to prickle. She fancied she could feel Kjorn and his army beneath them, wrapping torches in sinew and sap, preparing to surprise the wyrms with fire in their ugly faces.

The squirming, massive bodies of wyrms caught her eye beyond the next stand of trees. Great chunks of earth flew up and dirt scattered the ground. Broken trees formed dangerous splintered spears, thrusting from the ground.

They would have to leap forward into the clearing near the water, then straight into the air, lest the wyrms catch them too quickly.

"On my mark," Ragna breathed.

Her quiet command passed down the line.

She crouched, and in near-silence, the Vanir followed suit.

Hulking wyrms of dusty green and gray tore at the earth and the giant rocks that marked the main entrance to the river tunnel.

With a flash of relief, and worry, Ragna realized she didn't see the great she-wyrm, the one Shard called Rhydda. Perhaps he was speaking with her. Perhaps, even now he was communicating with her . . .

"We wait on your mark," Ketil reminded her softly, her voice tight with determination and fear.

Ragna loosed a breath. They could not wait on Shard. She had waited too long for everything. Even if Shard reached Rhydda, the prides were under attack *now*. They had to stop that, at least.

Ragna flicked up her tail and fanned the white feathers in the briefest signal, then plunged forward with a ringing, bellowing roar.

"By Tor! For the Vanir! For the Silver Isles!"

Vanir streamed after her, shouting a dozen battle cries.

"Tor is the thunder!" shouted Frar, with surprising vigor.

"*For the Vanir!*" cried Maja.

"*For the queen!*"

"*For Rashard, Rashard the true king!*"

Wings filled her vision as they rushed to the sky. Wings, talons, hard, flashing eyes. Istren and Istra, Ketil and Keta side-by-side with

Ilse, Maja, and Toskil. Old Frar, leading four older, seasoned Vanir. Ragna's blood seized for a moment to see them, to see her Vanir home. Home, and fighting hard for it. For her. For Shard.

She prayed bright Tor would see them all through the battle, and knew that would not be so.

The wyrms scrambled back from their digging in wailing, gnashing surprise. Seven of them, she counted, only seven. Surely they could drive them off. They only had to harry them until Kjorn arrived with his fire.

"Form up!" shouted a clear, ringing voice. Vidar. He winged up beside Ragna, and strength flowed into her, hope. She fell into formation with Vidar and Toskil, forming an arrow that drove at the largest, gray wyrm. The beast reared up, slashing with both forefeet. Dirt flew from its massive claws.

Ragna and Toskil split, darting around its great, horned head, while Vidar plunged under the swinging claws, forcing the monster to lumber around, seeking him. Ragna tilted her wings to stay tight with Toskil, and they banked for another pass.

Vidar swooped out from under the wyrm and rejoined them, higher, but the wyrm remained planted on the ground near the broken trees.

Meanwhile, Ketil, Ilse, and Keta formed another triad, and with Frar and two other elders, they harried a smaller green wyrm from the tunnel entrance. All around them, darting wedges of Vanir swooped, banked, and circled the wyrms.

Wildly trying to keep an eye on every single Vanir, Ragna knew she would die trying to keep watch over them all. She stuck close to Vidar, who didn't leave her side, and Toskil, who seemed determined to protect her in Shard's absence.

They re-formed their triad and drove forward as the gray wyrm at last shoved from the ground to the sky, his deadly tail driving a furrow through the forest floor.

Frar's group shot upward to aid Ragna's triad, but the wyrm spun in a circle with shocking speed, flinging his massive wings open to knock the surprised gryfons away. One elder female careened into the splintered tree trunks, and Ragna, diving fast under the wyrm's wings, saw Frar plummet down to her side.

Four smaller, green beasts leaped at the fallen with gleeful, ear-shattering shrieks and massive slashing claws.

The formations that were still flying broke apart, disintegrating into chaos and fear.

"Get clear!" Vidar shouted at Ragna.

Flying higher, Ragna saw Maja on the ground, mantled protectively over Keta, who nursed a twisted foot. Frar and Istren scrambled toward them, even as two green wyrms lumbered after.

"Get up!" Ragna cried. "Fly!"

"Fly, Vanir!" Vidar was there beside her again. His voice boomed with unexpected depth and a thrill shivered through Ragna. "Get up!"

Maja and Frar shouldered Keta up, and pushed her into the air. They followed, springing from the earth just as a green wyrm smashed its talons to ground where they'd stood. Its tail flashed toward Maja's head, but Istren knocked her aside. The flat of the wyrm's tail smacked into him and sent him sprawling to the ground amidst the broken, jagged trees.

Their simple distraction was already costing lives. Ragna forced herself to remember Thyra, Astri, Kenna, and all the other pregnant females, the fledges, the gryfons down in the caverns relying on them.

"Rise!" she shouted. "Fly! Don't try to fight!"

The scent of wood smoke filtered to her.

Not long. Not long now.

The great, gray wyrm swooped about above it all, screaming, but the others didn't heed it the way Ragna had seen them heed Rhydda. They flung themselves into the air haphazardly, snapping at darting, nimble Vanir.

The wind rose, cold and bracing, bringing the scent of the river and of the sea and earth.

For one breath, Ragna felt she breathed in the spirit of every Vanir to walk the Isles, even Baldr, her beloved Baldr, and that strength might be enough to see them through.

"For the Silver Isles!" she cried once more.

"The Vanir never die!" crowed Vidar, and those still flying re-formed their attacks, and plummeted at the wyrms from all sides.

Dizzying acrobatics filled the air over the river. Ragna grimly counted three gryfons on the ground, unmoving, but didn't dare name them to herself yet. Vidar and Toskil stuck fast to her side like burrs.

Smoke poured from the mauled entrance to the cavern.

Thank Tor.

"Vanir to me!" Ragna called.

"Vanir!" Vidar echoed. "Fly high!"

Swooping and diving to avoid the lashing wyrms, the Vanir began to cluster higher, drawing the wyrms higher, far away from the tunnel.

Shrieking and roars thundered across the Sun Isle. The birch trees quivered from the wind and from fierceness of the battle. The wyrms began to close on the ranks of flying Vanir.

Then, with a cry like Tyr himself, golden Kjorn shoved from the tunnel and took to the sky. Behind him poured the fresh, rested war-riors of the Winderost, seeming huge and impossibly strong in the sunlight.

Brynja, Dagny, and others followed, bearing torches.

"Drive them up!" Kjorn bellowed. "Drive them away!"

The wyrms fell back from the clustered flock of Vanir, taking in the new threat with surprised snarls. Not too dull to realize they were outnumbered, they scattered and lashed out at the fresh arrivals with the ferocity of cornered beasts.

But they did not flee.

Warriors from the river tunnel sprinted to open ground or shoved straight up from the forest floor. Wings sliced the air, talons slashing as they formed into groups and sought targets.

"My queen," Vidar said to Ragna over the wind. They had soared off twenty leaps from the main fighting, and Toskil had left them to join Keta and Ilse. "I beg you go to safety now. We've already lost too many, and we don't know if more wyrms will come."

Flapping hard, Ragna let her gaze slash the battle. Her Vanir had peeled off from her, still fighting, falling in with the Aesir, and heeding Kjorn's orders now.

She looked to Vidar. "Send the elders and the young back into the tunnels. And be sure we fetch the dead."

"I'll see it done," Vidar said. His eyes locked on hers, and in them she saw loss the loss of Einarr, again.

Before she could thank him, another sound broke through the chaos. A musical, hard, grating roar.

Hikaru.

Ragna spied the young dragon as he soared fast over the forest several leagues downriver, flashing silver like a serpent in the sky. At first her heart lifted at the sight of him, but behind him flew two more large gray wyrms, fangs open and claws grasping for the kill. Undulating toward the gryfons with impossible, whipping speed, he dove to join the fray.

The new gray wyrms clashed with the ranks of Aesir, and shrieks and battle cries shattered the air.

Vidar gasped at the sight, then snarled. "Please, Ragna, go. For us, and for Shard."

Ragna saw he was right. With Kjorn there, they had a leader. Her presence would only distract and worry the Vanir, and if she fled, it would give others leave to as well—the injured, old, and young.

With a final, grateful look, Ragna left Vidar. She angled wide around the battle and back the way she'd come, to the smaller tunnel entrance farther upstream, so as not to block the last of Kjorn's warriors from joining the battle.

She flew, and by the sound the fighting, thought Kjorn meant to drive the wyrms all the way back to Pebble's Throw.

She didn't realize at first, as she crawled through the narrow, muddy tunnel, that no other gryfons followed.

THE CAVES WERE EERILY quiet and smoky.

Ragna rushed to the tunnels where the pregnant gryfesses had sheltered, trying to put the battle from her mind. She passed others who exclaimed in relief to see her and found Sigrun, who was huddled with Thyra.

Gryfesses with warrior spirits like Thyra, like Kenna, were furious.

"I can't believe Halvden flew again, with me like this!" Kenna snapped at Sigrun, pacing restlessly. "I'll whelp his kit and join him!"

"I wouldn't recommend it," Sigrun said, her voice low and steady. "Keep walking. It will help the cramps."

"I've felt worse," Kenna said, and flicked her tail dismissively before rounding a bend out of their sight.

Astri bemoaned the loss of Dagr at her side, and one of Sigrun's apprentices comforted her and didn't move from her side, assuring her the copper gryfon would return after the battle.

Ragna wished she could make such promises. She and Sigrun switched attention to Thyra.

"My lady," Ragna said. "How fare you?"

"It will be any time," she said tightly, her gaze trained on the entryway to her little niche. Sigrun didn't look at Ragna, but fussed around her daughter, pressing gentle talons to her belly. "Any time now."

Struck, Ragna sat down near the entryway, watching the younger gryfess, and watching Sigrun. "Sigrun, how can I help you?"

The healer barely looked her way. "You can call them all back from this fool's errand. I can't believe you let them go. I can't believe you joined them."

"Let them? What was I to do, stand in the exit tunnel and block the way of dozens of healthy Vanir and half-bloods and Aesir warriors hungry to fight?"

"Yes," Sigrun said shortly. "Maybe you could have stricken some sense into them. But instead, you go off to war. I have only two apprentices, with a dozen gryfesses about to whelp and all their wing-sisters and mates off to battle. This shall be the merriest, bloodiest Halflight of our time. The kits will be battle-born, ill-fated, cursed to war again all their lives."

"Sigrun," Ragna said sharply, wondering how many of the pregnant gryfesses could hear her. She knew the healer was not actually angry with her, but with the situation. "I don't believe that. And you know there was nothing else we could have done. The wyrms were digging in. What were we all to do?"

Sigrun's pale-brown eyes seared her, then, as if Sigrun realized the true target of her own anger, softened. She only shook her head once, and turned back to examining Thyra, who tolerated it because she seemed to know Sigrun needed to keep busy. "I know. But I wish this hadn't happened. And where is Shard?"

Where indeed? Ragna thought, afraid for him, frustrated with herself for always feeling afraid. He was so like Baldr, she saw it clearly. Off in his own dreams, seeing things no one else saw, drawing together purposes no one else perceived. She could not follow him on those winds, but she trusted that he had to fly them.

For the next long, stretch of time, Ragna remained with her wingsister, helping to tend the gryfesses. For a time, they heard the riotous clash of battle outside, muffled by distance and stone, but near enough to send chills down their backs.

Then it fell quieter, but no gryfons returned. Ragna wondered if Kjorn had truly continued the push, pursuing the wyrms to Pebble's

Throw. She distracted herself with Sigrun. She fetched herbs, moss soaked with water for the thirsty. She told any gryfess who would listen the tale of her own whelping, and assured them their kits would be born healthy, fat and strong.

Marks of the sun stretched on, in the dark, and foreboding closed cold wings on her heart.

Kjorn and his warriors should have returned. The Vanir should have returned.

"He's pursued them," Sigrun muttered darkly, coming up on Ragna's side as she stood, staring toward the tunnel entrance. "He didn't just want to drive them off, he wanted to fight them. I guarantee you, he's taken every willing warrior and flown to Pebble's Throw to fight them."

"I should be with them," Ragna whispered. "I shouldn't have left them."

Sigrun touched a wing to hers. "Ragna. My friend. I don't doubt your skill in battle, but this is an enemy like no other. What good would it do the Vanir if you'd been slain?"

With that, she left quietly as the howl of a whelping gryfess cut the cool, smoky air. Ragna stood locked, wanting to stay and help, wanting to rejoin her warriors.

"My lady." Caj's voice relieved Ragna of staring into the dark. She turned to him as he approached down one of the tunnels.

"If you will," Caj said quietly, "he asked to see you. He's where we left him, in the cavern."

She didn't have to ask who *he* was. She drew a bracing breath, and nodding, walking past Caj, along the tunnels, through the great cavern where she and Kjorn had rallied the prides. Passing down another tunnel, at last she found him.

To all appearances, Sverin had not moved from the spot where he'd held his conversation with Kjorn. Through all the preparations, gryfons coming and going to make sturdy, sap torches, rallying whatever gryfons would fight the wyrms, the hours of battle, Sverin had remained in the small cavern, on his belly on the ground.

He looked up when Ragna entered. "You didn't go to the battle."

"I did," she said. "And returned. The Vanir were only to harry the wyrms away from the entrance to give room for Kjorn to attack. Now, they have followed your son on to further glorious war."

Some of Sigrun's bitterness crept into her voice. She didn't know if this battle was what Shard wanted. She didn't think so, but she didn't know if she should care anymore. For so long she had waited for him.

She had waited, waited.

"I see." His gaze was too keen.

He was silent, laying there like a large, red stone, his gaze searching.

"Caj said you asked to see me." Her tail ticked, back and forth, her talons flexed on the cold rock floor.

"Yes."

Slowly, and ominously, Sverin pushed to his feet. He seemed taller to her, impossible in the cave, as if he wouldn't have fit coming in. A trick of the light, the smoke in the air, her own nerves.

"You once told me that you admired the way I love my son."

"I do." She worked not to hold her breath, not to back away or flare her wings. She didn't understand what he wanted from her. "I always will."

"Now, he battles an enemy that I should have defeated in my youth, not fled from and caused a generation of misery."

"Sverin," she said, "speak plainly, and quickly, in this dark hour, I beg you."

He lifted his wings a little, and they caught the faint light, stirred the smoke. "My son has exiled me from the Dawn Spire. I will not live the remainder of my life as a prideless rogue, and so, I ask to serve you. Let me live at the edge of your pride, as you lived at the edge of mine, but let me live, and serve."

Ragna stared at him.

Then she laughed.

It was all she could manage. The bitter, hard sound cascaded up and down the rock, and Ragna barely managed to keep from flinging at him with beak and talon in a wash of angry disbelief. "You're mocking me."

"You saw me bow to Shard. I was not mocking him. I'm not mocking you now. Let me serve. And more, I ask your blessing to go to battle."

"Battle."

"Yes." He spread his wings, and from tip to tip they nearly filled the cavern. He looked like the king he had never, ever been. "What good am I if, in these hours, I cannot practice my single, admirable quality for my queen? Let me go to battle, and protect my son."

The tightness of regret, of anger, and of something else closed her throat for a moment. He watched her face, and for the first time since she had known him, the severity in his eyes was not cold, but hot, like the sun.

"You have my blessing," she said, very softly. She didn't remind him that he had fled the last time he had seen the wyrms. She saw something new and fierce shining through him. She saw love, and she thought it might be enough to help him remember who he was when he faced the wyrms.

Or, at the very least, who he wished to be.

"Severin," she said quietly. "I think, if we had met in another time . . . we might have been friends."

"Oh, if." His expression quirked. He mantled, then folded his great wings, and turned toward the exit tunnel. Ragna moved to follow and he stopped, swiveling his head to see her. "Where are you going?"

She growled low. "I have fled from a fight too many times in my life. I won't do it again. I too will fight this battle."

He watched her, sizing her up, looking as if he might object, and she waited for him to remember he had just pledged to serve her. "If there comes a choice," he said, his voice so low and gravelly she barely heard, "in the battle, of who to help, I will choose Kjorn."

"As it should be," she said, meeting his gaze. "I have always chosen Shard."

Behind them, a cry pierced the cave, another of the gryfesses to begin labor. Sverin's gaze flickered, hardened.

Battle-born, Ragna thought, though she disagreed with Sigrun that they would be ill-fated. *They will be stronger,* she decided, as if she could decide. *All their kits will be stronger than their parents, as we were stronger than ours, committed to peace because they were born in war. They will be better than us all.*

For a moment they stood in the half darkness of the cavern, looking at each other, not saying more, then when another cry echoed their way, Sverin turned to the tunnel, and Ragna followed him up unto the dark.

47

FIRE OVER THE SEA

CLAWING AT HIS DREAM-PRISON, SHARD battered at Rhydda with images of pity, with pleading, and with apology. He should not have reminded her of the wyrm's horrible death in the Winderost. She remained obstinate, spiteful, and silent.

Then, after a stretch of time Shard could not perceive, something flicked at the edge of her awareness.

Something real, something outside of their shared dream.

Shard—also Rhydda—lumbered about, waking, lifting herself from warm black lava stone to stare windward, toward the most massive isle where she knew the gryfons dwelled.

She had been waiting for something, waiting for her brood to return from ...

Horror chilled Shard's blood when he perceived what she'd hidden from him earlier. Her brood had gone to the Sun Isle. They were hunting. *Digging*. Digging out Shard's pride.

Confused at the darkness through which they stared, Shard realized night had fallen. He'd spent his whole afternoon dreaming with her, trapped, useless.

The sun had set.

His own body was nearly frozen to the earth. Still he dreamed with Rhydda as if they were one creature, but she was awake now. She was awake. Something distracted her from Shard, and she forgot about him, and her prison of hate and fear crumbled away.

When she looked windward toward the Sun Isle, Shard saw what she saw.

Stars floated toward them.

Golden stars, waving, bobbing, glittering in the gusty dark. A cluster of stars twinkled toward Rhydda and the lava isle, and she raised up, staring.

Then she roared, flinging open her massive wings, and Shard was shocked from his communion with her, flung back across the sea channels to his own body and awareness.

He woke, sucking in a sharp breath. His muscles locked as he wrenched to his feet and breath fogged the dark, freezing air. He smelled wet frost, night.

Rhydda had left his mind, or he'd left hers. But he already knew what he needed to know.

"Curse it, Kjorn!" He surged forward, nearly falling on his face when his muscles seized and cramped. He had to fly. He had to get to Pebble's Throw, but already he feared he would be too late.

Shard, watching through her eyes, knew what she saw approaching, and it wasn't stars.

It was fire.

DAMP, COLD WIND BATTERED Shard's face and shivered across his back. He soared high and fast, cutting across the sea route starward of the Sun Isle, past the other islands toward Pebble's Throw.

Distantly, flickering gold stars matched what Rhydda had seen when he dreamed with her.

Torches.

"Kjorn!" he bellowed, though he was ridiculously far, too far for the prince to hear him.

They hadn't even discussed it. Kjorn hadn't even asked his wishes, and these were *his* islands. Maybe Kjorn's pride had overcome him, and he wanted the opportunity to have his glorious battle, to redeem whatever he thought he'd lost when the wyrms left the Winderost. Shard didn't know, and didn't care.

Live by war, and you will die by war, he thought grimly.

And now Kjorn kindled war in the Silver Isles.

Again.

Shard couldn't believe it. He pumped his wings, his chest straining, swearing into the night. He wished to glowing Tor that Stigr was with him, that his best allies Ahanu and Catori and the rest of the wolves could come to his aide. But they kept vigil on the Star Isle, some on the Sun Isle near the gryfons, and they could do no good against the wyrms at Pebble's Throw.

Shard was alone.

Then . . .

"Wingbrother!"

He checked behind to see Hikaru speeding toward him, his silver scales washed in starlight. The wind flicked his mane like silver flame. Shard thought he looked like the Silver Wind incarnate, and called to him gratefully. "Hikaru! What's happening? Why is Kjorn flying to Pebble's Throw?"

Hikaru shot through the air until he flew even with Shard, breathless with dismay. "I'm sorry, Shard, I was too slow to tell you. I was helping them drive off the wyrms. They attacked, Shard. You have to know that. They were digging at the tunnels. Kjorn thought he didn't have a choice. Catori ran to tell you, but I'm guessing she was too slow?"

"She was," Shard growled, though he didn't blame Catori. Someone should have flown. Someone should have risked flying, or run faster, or done *something* to tell him what was happening.

"He had no choice," Hikaru said, his voice almost a whimper, as if he couldn't bear knowing that Shard might be angry with Kjorn again.

Aching moments passed as they flew, as hard and as fast as they physically could, and Pebble's Throw felt no closer.

Shouting and roars began to echo distantly to them over the choppy black water. Screams. Wyrm roars shattered the peaceful Silver Isles night.

Torches sparked ahead. Kjorn appeared to be using the same strategy as he had in the Winderost. Surprise, flame, and pure bravado. *As if the wyrms wouldn't have learned from that.* But maybe Kjorn hoped to drive them off with a show of pure strength and courage.

Or maybe, his pride and anger burned hot from the dragon's blessing, and he didn't care about anything but his battle. Shard believed Hikaru, but he also remembered Kjorn's regret that he hadn't gotten to fight the wyrms once and for all. And he couldn't help thinking that desire, partly, had driven him to battle.

Familiar voices clashed with wyrm roars. Shard sought Rhydda in the dark, though he was still too far to make out individual wyrms or gryfons. He only saw wings, torches, flashing spade tails.

As he drew nearer, he discerned the gryfons in their formations.

Trios of gryfons, lined up in wedges of twelve, circled and drove with stunning precision at their chosen targets. The wyrms scattered and flew in wild disarray, lashing at the gryfons while fumbling farther from Pebble's Throw toward the ocean channel.

With a grudging spark of admiration, he saw that Kjorn's strategy was to drive the wyrms away from the warm lava of Pebble's Throw, out over the cold and windy sea channels where they might grow too cold and weary to fly.

However, it didn't seem as if the plan was working, for the monsters appeared to whip around in almost gleeful disorder, refusing to be herded by the force of gryfons. The one thing they appeared to be doing effectively, as far as Shard could tell, was keep any gryfon from breaking loose to confront Rhydda, who circled high above.

Shard heard Asvander, Nilsine, and Rok, shouting orders over the wyrm roars. Emerald wings shot by his field of vision—Halvden, leading a screaming mass of Aesir to aid the gryfons whose formations were scattered.

To his dismay, Shard also heard Frar. Vidar. Ketil. His Vanir, maybe hoping to atone for failing against the Aesir conquerors once, had chosen to go to battle.

"Shard!" Hikaru pointed silver claws. "I see Brynja! We have to help!"

Shard followed his pointing claws in time to see a black wyrm surprise Brynja's triad from above. It dove, slashing the air, knocking one gryfon from the sky and his torch into the sea. Before Shard had time to react, he heard fierce shouting and saw Nilsine driving her own triad to batter at the wyrm and give Brynja time to recover.

Brynja and the other gryfess, a Vanir who'd flown with them from the Silver Isles, broke off and sped toward Asvander's main force.

A heady roar stopped Shard from flying to her. He knew that roar. The other wyrms heeded it, redirecting their flights as if listening to whom they should attack. Shard watched them split away from the triads of gryfons to regroup.

Rhydda gave her brood their only sense of order. Rhydda was their queen. It was Rhydda who must be stopped.

Shard winged a circle around his dragon brother, who watched the battle desperately, unsure of what to do. "Hikaru, go to them. We have to stop Rhydda. *I* have to stop Rhydda. It's the only way. If you can distract the other wyrms, maybe I can reach her."

Hikaru looked at him with huge eyes orange in the torchlight, then flung himself toward the fray. His musical, metallic roar at least got the attention of the wyrms, and they scattered in shrieking surprise.

Ragged gryfon cheers rose and the gryfons regrouped with Hikaru at their head.

Above it all, Rhydda circled, and boomed another angry roar.

A quick, hot fury blazed to life in Shard's chest and gave him new energy. Everything, everything he had flown for the last year was to seek peace, and it had come to this after all.

Shard dove forward, seeking hotter drafts to give his weary wings lift. The warm thermals of Pebble's Throw swelled under his wings and he wheeled tightly, higher and higher, fighting his strained muscles and his short breath.

But then he saw that one gryfon had already slipped the notice of the screaming brood below.

One gryfon soared high and silent toward the she-wyrm, and the reflection of torches below made him look like a lancing bolt of gold.

48

THE DRAGON BLESSED

KJORN'S TRIAD, MADE UP OF Vald and Rok, formed the head of a spear that managed to force at least one wyrm out to sea.

Halvden's group noticed their success and joined Kjorn, managing to drive and force the shrieking monster down, down into the merciless waves. Once it fell, it could not fly out, but thrashed, bawling with horrible cries until its strength gave out and it sank.

Halvden bellowed in triumph, and others raised their voices high. Kjorn tried to join as he winged back toward the fray, but it seemed such a small win.

One wyrm. One drowned. And the rest grew angrier for it. It was like wrangling eels with his talons, or trying to grasp water.

Stupid, stupid strategy. If only we'd had more surprise!

They'd at least driven the digging wyrms away from the Sun Isle. While half the forces refreshed their torches, the rest harried the wyrms starward, back toward Pebble's Throw, until they fought over Kjorn's chosen ground. The sea channel.

He had a hunch, and now his guess was confirmed—the cold weakened them, and they could not swim.

But it was little help so late in the battle, with gryfons falling left and right around him.

"Halvden! Spread the word! The water is their weakness!"

"Yes, sire!" Halvden sped off toward the main knot of fighting, trying to order and inspire the others to redouble their efforts.

"Rok," Kjorn said, for the former rogue flew close by, waiting on his orders. The torch he carried flickered blue, close to guttering—the windy, damp air challenging all the fire they had left.

"My lord." He watched Kjorn steadily. This gryfon, this lanky, mouthy rogue had pledged his loyalty and his life to Kjorn. He owed it to Rok and every other gryfon in the sky not to fail them, not to lose this battle he'd started.

"Help Halvden. If it becomes necessary, call a retreat. We've done what we hoped to, we drew them away from the tunnels for now."

Rok eyed him suspiciously. "Why am I calling retreats, and not you?"

"Because—"

A bright, metallic roar cut him off, and silver shot past Kjorn's amazed eyes and the wind of great wings buffeted his feathers. The dragon Hikaru had rejoined the battle. Asvander and other gryfons raised a cheer. Certainly he looked impressive, but he was no longer than the largest of the wyrms, and then, more delicately built. Kjorn feared for him, feared even this boost would not help win them the day.

"Because," Kjorn growled, his gaze darting high. "I'm going to cut the head off this monster."

"Let me come," Rok said. "You can't do it alone."

"No. Too many of us, and they'll stop us again. I have a chance to slip through now."

Every attempt to fly at the she-wyrm that Shard called Rhydda had ended with a knot of wyrms flying at them, driving them away. But if Kjorn slipped out of the battle *now*, while Hikaru distracted them, there was a chance.

Rok stared at him. "Sire—"

"I have the strength of dragon's blood," Kjorn said, telling himself it was true. "I will end her. And if I don't return, tell Thyra—"

"Tell her yourself," Rok snarled. "You will return. Or you're not the king I thought you were." He tucked a wing and dove to fulfill Kjorn's orders, and Kjorn was briefly alone in the sky.

He spied Rok, speeding toward Hikaru, and with satisfaction saw the dragon change his strategy from mere attack to a dazzling, spiraling display of flight meant to confuse and distract the wyrms.

Every time they dipped in to try catching him, the silver dragon slipped around and away, like water, like fire. It reminded Kjorn of Shard's duel with Asvander. It was a perfect distraction.

With a soft snarl, Kjorn turned and flew at Rhydda.

He would offer no roar, no challenge. He had just a single chance at surprise and a single, deadly blow.

As he beat his wings against the lukewarm air, he remained below and behind her, just out of her line of sight as she watched the battle. The smaller wyrms took no notice of him, too absorbed with Hikaru and the masses of gryfons who rallied to the dragon's side.

Kjorn angled himself to stay even with Rhydda's tail while she circled, staying out of her line of sight. In fighting the wyrms, he hadn't seen any obvious weak points in their leathery hides or their horned, armored heads.

He would take a guess, a desperate guess that her throat, like other reptiles, was flexible and soft.

As she banked to continue her wide circle and observe the fighting, Kjorn shoved with three quiet, powerful wing beats to fly directly under her belly. She did not see him. His head nearly brushed the massive fore-claws that hung relaxed below her chest.

Her horned head swung back and forth, surveying the battle, as if she hunted. She didn't notice him.

With a beat of his wings he was even with the underside of her neck, every muscle tense and every feather working to keep even and coordinated and silent.

Kjorn spied the paler, loose skin of her throat, flexing as she drew great gusts of air. He gathered his courage and timed his wing beats with hers. Then, he plunged forward along her underside, his wings flashing in the torchlight.

In that instant, she heard, or smelled, or saw him, and jerked her head in surprise. Kjorn hurtled under her neck and flipped upside down around to latch talons, beak, and hind-claws onto her throat.

She snapped her head back with a gut-curdling roar.

Kjorn's talons pierced her skin, his beak tore, but he tasted no blood. Her throat was protected by layers and layers of loose, leathery, calloused hide.

He wrenched, latching on like a mountain cat as she whipped her head back and forth. She didn't swipe claws at him—perhaps afraid of ripping her own throat to shreds. Kjorn held fast, certain this was his only chance, certain that letting go would mean death.

Someone was shouting at him.

Shard.

Relief at having backup, and terror for his friend's safety swept him. Then shame. He had launched this losing battle, and now Shard was fighting too. He clenched his talons tighter on the iron hide, scrabbling his hind claws to seek some weak spot.

The wiry Vanir smashed into Rhydda's shoulders and she jerked into a hard roll, and the force of it yanked Kjorn's beak loose. Claws the length of his forelegs closed around him with eerie precision and yanked him loose, clutching him in a single paw like a fish. Kjorn bucked and tried to flare his wings, and she tightened her grip.

"Shard!" Kjorn shouted. "Get away!"

Shard snapped his beak, clinging to the monster's wing joints as she hurtled through the air. "What were you thinking—"

The claws began to squeeze harder. Kjorn swore, gasping for breath. Pinprick pain began in his shoulders and his hind legs. She would crush him, and she would do it slowly.

"Shard—"

Shard scrabbled madly at the she-wyrm's neck, then bounded along the length of her, swiping talons toward her eyes. She flared to a hard stop and flung up her claws, as if to warn Shard that she held Kjorn, and could break him.

She's not stupid, she's . . .

Red pulsed at Kjorn's vision. He saw Shard drop free. Then the wyrm's massive jaws opened before him, blaring hot, acrid breath, and baring bloody fangs.

Kjorn heard Shard shrieking. Begging, as if she could understand him.

She squeezed, and Kjorn coughed. *Live by war…*

A feral, shrieking roar broke through Kjorn's breathless dizziness. For one heartbeat, he thought he saw bright Tyr blazing above him, all blood and fire.

Then he shook his vision clear in time to Sverin slam into the she-wyrm's horned head.

She dropped Kjorn with a thrashing snap of her entire body, trying to throw the red gryfon from her face. Kjorn fell away, gasping. Pain dazzled across his wings, but they were not broken. He flapped hard, righting himself, and Shard was there at his side.

"Kjorn, are you—"

"I'm sorry," Kjorn breathed. "I had to, they attacked—"

"I know."

Sverin's second roar turned the focus of battle.

Gryfon heads raised, some torches dropped, the smaller, screaming wyrms gathered to flock up to their queen, now that they realized she was in danger.

Halvden, Asvander, Ketil, and Brynja screamed orders, and the gryfons formed a flying wall between the wyrms and Rhydda. Kjorn saw Nilsine soaring fast along the ranks of the Aesir, repeating Asvander's orders, and watched as the gryfons flocked to form lines in her wake, a net of gryfons to stop the wyrms from rising any higher.

Fraenir, flying close to Rok, broke formation and launched straight at a wyrm's head.

Shard croaked in horror, and Kjorn whipped his head about to see his father, challenging the she-wyrm alone.

"Rhydda!" bellowed the red gryfon, and his voice had changed—clear, hard, and mighty. Kjorn had never, ever heard his voice sound so clear. "If I am the one you seek, let us end this!"

The stars edged Sverin's wings in silver, and the torchlight shone on him and seemed to turn his scarlet wings to fire.

The dragon blessing, Kjorn thought wildly, stupidly. He beat his wings harder, meaning to join him.

"Kjorn, fly!" Sverin shouted. "Stay back!"

Shard was speaking to him, but Kjorn could only hover, catching his breath, trying to clear his head.

All that you are will be more so.

Rhydda bellowed and Sverin whipped around her, swiping his talons at her eyes. She ducked her head and lurched up over him, swinging her tail. Sverin fell deftly away, avoiding the deadly spade, but too slow to avoid her claws when she stooped and slashed at his wings, once, twice. Red feathers rained down.

Sverin smashed into her shoulders and she wrenched hard, whipping her head around and gnashing her jaws. Her fangs snapped closed just as Sverin jerked back, shoving up and slapping her eyes with his wings.

She screamed and shook her head. Sverin banked tightly to slash at her neck as Kjorn had done, but his talons left long, red marks. Rhydda shrieked and flapped over him again, swinging fore-claws and hind-claws to try knocking Sverin from the sky.

In turn he smashed into her again, again, slashing, his talons scoring her hide and leaving her bleeding as no other gryfon talons had done.

"Leave this place! Your war is done!"

Rhydda swiped her claws through the air as Sverin dove again at her long, muscled neck. He dodged that swipe but she snagged him in her other forepaw just as she had Kjorn.

That brought Kjorn to his senses.

With a battle cry, Kjorn lunged up to help his father. He had lost all other track of the battle raging below. Shard flew up shortly behind him.

Rhydda's tail cut the air in front of them, and they were forced back. Kjorn tried to maneuver around while Shard split from him flew up, as if he might be able to distract her, but her flailing horns made that a dangerous task.

Kjorn dropped below the lashing tail and circled wide, planning to fly up and dive at her head from above.

Sverin thrashed in the clawed grip and shouted his rage. Rhydda squeezed. Kjorn flung caution aside and lunged high, talons raised. Sverin saw him. Then, with a terrible roar and a hard, whipping roll, Sverin shoved Rhydda's claws apart.

As he fell loose, he yelled hoarsely, "Kjorn, no, flee!"

Kjorn hesitated, and spied Shard, circling fast above all of them. Rhydda's jaws snapped forward and Sverin fell under her, wings thrashing and claws scrabbling, to cling to her throat as Kjorn had done. Kjorn's heart crammed up to the back of his throat, and for a moment he thought his father would slay the giant beast.

But then Rhydda's spade coiled up and lashed down, slicing clear from one red ear and down Sverin's neck, under a wing to his hind leg.

His scream halted Kjorn's heart.

His talons lashed up and out one last time, scouring four deep, red trails down Rhydda's face. With a shocked, angry bellow, Rhydda grabbed Sverin in her claws, and flung him toward the sea.

Kjorn gasped a single, hard breath. Blinded to all else in the world, he dove.

49
BATTLE'S END

S VERIN PLUMMETED TOWARD THE WAVES. Kjorn dropped from Shard's sight like a rock, diving after his father.

Enraged, Shard filled his chest and bellowed a lion's roar.

"RHYDDA."

Apparently stunned by Sverin's ability to bloody her, at last her mind cracked open to Shard a fraction. It was enough.

Shard's mind flashed around hers, dreaming together again, awake, as he had with the priestess of the Vanhar. His thoughts slipped over hers as they had in the Winderost, as they had in his dream earlier that evening.

He clung there, clung to her thoughts, to her mind.

She saw gryfons, gryfons, the enemy, all around.

"Rhydda!" His voice saying her name was like a crystal talon piercing through all else in her mind. It pierced through her triumph, through her anger.

Below them, the battle raged, with Hikaru leading Asvander and Kjorn's main force of battle-seasoned Aesir against the largest of the wyrms to block them from coming to her aid.

"You are Named," Shard called to Rhydda, whipping about her head to keep her attention on him. Perhaps, in the dark and the rising cold, he could even wear out the wyrm queen as he had Asvander, what felt like so long ago. *"Answer me!"*

Wrathful, she shook her head as if to fling Shard from her thoughts, and he dodged around, keeping close to her body, keeping just out of reach of her flashing claws and her whipping tail. If he lost her now, he knew he would lose her forever.

He stopped shouting, and flew hard, winging around her head. Focusing on his flight, he tried to see and grasp at the dream net, to weave something to get through to her. Claws swiped a talon's breadth from his tail-feathers, and his focus disintegrated.

He tried again as he fell away, slapping together a dream of her landing peacefully on the shore of Pebble's Throw. Her jaws snapped a single leap from his head. He ducked and soared beneath her long, leathery body, trying to piece together an image of Sverin, to make her regret. Her wings nearly knocked him from the black air, her hot breath rustled his wings, and he had to dodge back.

The dream net slipped away, away. He couldn't craft a dream while dodging her swiping claws and snapping fangs.

At the risk of losing her attention, Shard flew high, higher into the frigid air, and to his amazement she didn't follow. Perhaps she knew the freezing wind would tire her.

Her gaze dipped to the battle which now fell into disarray, gryfons in ragged, desperate clumps, and the wyrms gleefully scattered among them, lashing and fighting without order or apparent purpose.

Clear of physical danger, Shard fashioned dreams. With the cold wind in his face, he was able to focus, to draw strength and hope from the moon and the wind and the stars in the night.

He had one last chance, and he knew what to do, for he realized had shown Rhydda all the wrong things, before. With Kjorn's scream of sorrow and Sverin's blazing, heroic effort, Shard realized he had shown her injustice and death and anger.

He had shown her what they fought against, but hadn't shown her what all of them fought *for*.

So he formed and image of Kjorn and himself as kits, playing under Sverin's watchful eye.

Confusion, blood and stone pressed back at him in her mind. Shard took a long breath, feeling stronger, and dove to be nearer her again.

At the same time he flung memories of Kjorn standing proudly at his father's side. He made up a vision of Sverin looking lovingly at his mate, and showing her death in the sea.

Rhydda lumbered about in the air, seeking him with eyes he knew now were actually weak in the dark. As Shard winged around her, the spade tail coiled and flipped out at him, nearly severing his head.

He drowned her in a vision of Sverin flying, mighty and bold, to protect his son, then showed her flying over her own brood in the same manner.

She slowed.

She did not strike.

Shard realized, panting hard, that he had shown her pain and loss, but not love.

Rhydda . . .

Confusion and anger stopped her from attacking. She tried to feel triumph at Sverin's fall, and Shard swept it away, showing her Kjorn, diving toward the sea after his father.

Call them off.

A memory of one of her dreams came to him, of her brood full and sleeping all together in a warm, satisfied bunch. He painted that over the battle. *We can have this.*

Safety, warmth, love. Full bellies and good hunting.

Or this.

He showed her more gryfons and more wyrms falling and dying in the sea. His own heart clutched at him.

His carefully crafted dream swirled among her chaotic, furious thoughts. He pressed it to her, showing again the years, the dragons, the generations of a grudge that should have been long done. Kajar. Per. Sverin. Sverin, falling to the sea. Her own wyrms drowning in the waves.

Or she could end it, and go home. Home, to those green, green hills that he'd seen in her dreams.

In a single, blazing moment, his offer and his images and his plea seared to comprehension in her mind. After so long of muddy, angry darkness, the sudden, crystal brightness of her understanding knocked Shard from her mind and he fell away in the sky, gasping.

Out of the dream net, under the stars, with fresh wind bringing him clarity, Shard realized that Rhydda was sinking. Her wing beats slowed, but not from cold.

End this.

Land.

Call them off.

He showed healthy wyrms, fleeing to the warm lava of Pebble's Throw. Leaving. Waiting for his word to do anything else, touching nothing, killing nothing, making no noise.

A hot, steady rumbling met his ears, like a chant.

It was Rhydda, thrumming deep in her throat. She snapped her great wings and turned sharply from Shard. Her mind was a rush of understanding, anger and blood and gold.

Shard stabbed at her with feelings of regret, with pain.

But then, hope. Shining hope burned the rest away.

I understand all you lost.

Now you understand.

Wind rushed him, the heady wind of wings rushing all around him. Wyrms. The wyrms broke from the mass of exhausted gryfons and retreated, following their queen.

Shard beat his wings against the air, his mind whirling through Rhydda's, until someone called his name.

Many gryfons called his name.

Ragna called his name. Brynja called to him.

He snapped back into awareness to hear broken cheers, to see that the wyrms were fully retreating toward Pebble's Throw.

Stay there, he thought, wrapping the words in iron in Rhydda's mind. He didn't feel that he held or controlled her, but only that she understood.

She understood that, and agreed, and then she turned her mind from him, and he was too exhausted to pursue any more dreams.

"Shard!" Ragna's voice brought him back to his own surroundings. "Shard, come, they're retreating, we don't know why. Come to safety. It's over."

Then Shard remembered, and his heart skittered. "Sverin—"

"Hikaru has him." Her voice was hollow. "Hikaru caught him, and even now is bearing him to the Sun Isle."

"Mother—"

"Come with me, Shard. It's done. They're fleeing, we don't know why they . . ." She trailed off and her green eyes, glassed and weary, stared at Shard, then the departing wyrms. With a glance at the exhausted ranks of gryfons, a light came into Ragna's face, as if she understood they couldn't possibly have suddenly frightened off the horde. She looked over her wing at Rhydda, then Shard. "You've done this," she breathed. "You called her off."

"I think she understands," Shard said, his voice hoarse in his own ears. "We'll be safe for now."

"Come," she said. "My son, fly with us now."

Shard glanced once more at the fleeing wyrms, then followed Ragna. Rhydda turned her mind from him, blood and stone. He followed his mother, a point of white in the dark.

50

ABSOLUTION

KJORN SPED AFTER THE SILVER dragon, shouting the entire way for him to slow down.

He isn't dead. He isn't dead.

His father had not finally conquered his cowardice and flown against the wyrms and put himself in harm's way to save Kjorn's life . . . only to die.

"Father!" he shouted. The dragon made some sort of musical bird sound that he supposed was meant to be reassuring, and Kjorn shouted again, hoarsely. He didn't know who followed him. He didn't know who lived, or had died. He didn't know where Shard was.

The rage and pride that had swelled to blazing in him had quenched and died at the sight of Rhydda striking Sverin down. Now he was shuddering and hollow. His wings felt like ice, his talons freezing, sticky with blood.

They flew back the same route they had come, and it took too, too long. Much longer than it had taken to fly to Pebble's Throw, surely. His father needed a healer, not to be dragged through the night air by a dragon for unending, agonizing moments.

It took them a full mark of the moon to reach familiar territory again, to reach the birch wood, the Nightrun, and the entrance to the caves.

Hikaru couldn't fly through the dense trees and clearly didn't want to overshoot the entrance to the caves, so he landed in a clearing, and walked. Kjorn landed and loped after him.

The silver dragon carried Sverin the whole way, ignoring Kjorn as he stumbled and followed through the underbrush. Some gryfons still bore torches, and they cast yellow light against the muddy forest.

The river mumbled and rolled ahead, impossibly peaceful.

Gryfons called each other's names through the woods. Some answered. Some didn't.

Kjorn thought he saw wolf ears perk and a shadow dash off into the forest, perhaps to deliver news. He looked up once to see a snowy owl staring at him from a high birch tree, shining under the moon. When he looked again, she was gone.

At last they reached the series of stone slabs that formed a cave, formed the entrance to the caverns. The wyrms had dug out one side of it, throwing up earth in horrifyingly large clumps to create a yawning, jagged entrance. But they hadn't gotten far.

It became quickly clear that it wouldn't do to drag Sverin down into the cave. So there at the entrance where the earth wasn't torn to pieces, Hikaru laid Sverin out on the driest stone. He moved away to make room for Kjorn, though he ringed his serpentine body halfway around the red gryfon like a barrier between him and the river.

Kjorn staggered forward.

It was hard to tell where the red feathers ended and the wounds began. His wing was bent oddly, broken, a long slash from his shoulder under the wing joint to his hindquarters bled onto his golden flank. Kjorn collapsed near his head, and saw his eyes were still open and seeing.

"Ah, Kjorn. Good." His beak opened in a slow pant, the blacks of his eyes pinpointed in the uneven torchlight when they should have been wide in the dark. "Good."

"Healers!" Kjorn shouted, to no one particular, to everyone. But he knew Sigrun was far underground with the whelping gryfesses. The woods were frozen and dead, no herbs or salves available. And where was Shard? He'd been behind Kjorn, he'd fought. With dread, Kjorn wondered if Shard had also fallen. Desperately, he searched the gryfon faces around him, then, when Sverin drew a shuddering breath, focused in on him.

"Father. Don't worry. We have healers coming."

"I'm not worried," Sverin whispered, staring at him. "You're well?"

"I'm well. Well enough." Kjorn didn't feel his own wounds, though he had them, sprains, bruises, cuts. Shame and anger battled and died in him, he had nothing left. It had been a fool's mission, and he knew it now. He had fallen victim to his own pride and arrogance and fear.

Gryfons crept forward and stopped. Kjorn felt eyes on his back. Asvander, Dagr, the Vanir, the half-bloods, the old Aesir who had followed him faithfully to his battle. A small number of torches still flickered, lighting his father's wounds, his face.

"Healers!" Kjorn rasped again.

"A wolf went down," murmured Asvander. "My lord, a runner went. They'll be here as fast as they can."

"No," Sverin said sharply. "No, tell them to stay, to stay with Thyra, with the rest of the . . ."

When he tried to rise, Kjorn pressed talons gently to his shoulder. It took no strength at all to hold him down. *Where is Shard? Does he even care that my father lies bleeding?*

As he thought it he knew it was unfair, but where was Shard? If he was not there at Kjorn's side, Kjorn was terrified what that might mean.

He stretched out along Sverin's side, curling talons over his foreleg, spreading a gold wing to cover the rest of his wounds from sight.

Sverin closed his eyes, breathing slowly, seeming only to be glad that Kjorn was there. For aching moments, Kjorn couldn't think of a single thing to say to his father.

A murmur broke through the onlookers.

A voice, demanding they make room.

Shard.

"Shard," Kjorn pleaded. "Shard." He had nothing else to say. He saw the small, silent, gray Vanir prince shoving through the gryfons, and realized why he'd taken so much longer. He carried moss, herbs, salves. He'd gone to the nesting cliffs, to Sigrun's den, to gather a healer's tools.

Kjorn moved his wing, and Shard worked in silence, his ears flat, his tail sweeping across the stone. Hikaru watched in silence, his eyes enormous, luminous. Torches flickered in the dark, and no one said a word. Shard took in the wounds, then pressed the black moss to the worst of them. Behind him, Kjorn saw Ragna, watching with an expression of stone.

Kjorn touched his father's feathers gently. "Shard, will he—"

"Kjorn," Sverin's ragged voice rattled now, as if water sat in his chest. "Kjorn, you must know that I'm proud of you. I'm so proud of you. You are everything I wanted to be. You are everything I hoped. More than I ever was."

"Save your breath," Shard said softly. "My lord."

Sverin chuckled, a low, coughing sound. "Are you glad, Rashard?"

"Of course not." He stopped, his talons bloody and pressing moss to the worst wound that ran the length of Sverin's body. "No. This isn't what I wanted. It never was."

Kjorn watched them look at each other, and he believed Shard, and knew that Sverin believed him too.

"You dove," Sverin rasped, and both Kjorn and Shard perked their ears, unsure of what he meant. "When we fought. You didn't fall into the sea. You let go. You could have drowned me."

"Save your breath," Shard said again, working quickly, silently.

"Kjorn," Sverin murmured.

He looked at his father. "Forgive me," Kjorn whispered.

"There's nothing to forgive. I would die for you."

Kjorn tightened his talons around Sverin's foreleg. Another scuffle drew his ear and he hated them, all of them, all of them standing witness. They had injuries and friends to tend to, they didn't need to stand staring like this. He and Shard would take care of him.

"Kjorn." A panting wolf approached. Kjorn recalled he was a friend of Caj, one of the swiftest wolves of the pack. "Kjorn, your mate is due. She is whelping—she wants you. You must hurry." Amber eyes flicked to Sverin, widened, and the wolf ducked his head low in apology, his gold coat like a corona in the torch light.

Kjorn looked desperately back to Sverin, whose face lit up at the news. "Kjorn, go. You must be there. You must go."

"No," Kjorn growled. "I'm not leaving."

"There's nothing left for you to do, here. You've done all I—all I ever wished for you. You've lifted our curse, Kjorn."

A thought blazed through him and he lifted his wings, nearly bumping Shard, who he realized had stopped working and was merely sitting, quiet. "Oh, Father. I never told you. Open your eyes, listen to me. We were never cursed. We were *blessed*. Shard told me." He shook Sverin gently, forcing him to focus, to listen, to know. "A dragon so loved Kajar that she blessed him, blessed the Aesir in the Sunland with her blood. She wanted us to know how she saw us, strong and beautiful. Father." His eyes had closed again, and he looked pleased, peaceful. He opened his eyes when Kjorn touched his beak to his ear. "Please. I didn't mean anything I said. Come home with me. Come back to the Dawn Spire. I was angry and foolish. We'll stand together—"

"I love you, Kjorn."

Kjorn choked on the words in his throat.

"My lord," whispered the wolf. "Your mate . . ."

Sverin tilted his head. His talons closed briefly, flexing, as if gripping something Kjorn couldn't see. "Go to her. Kjorn, always go to her."

Kjorn's throat locked, and he looked at Shard, who didn't return his gaze, but gave his head the slightest shake, telling him to stay. With a breath, Kjorn pressed his head to the feathers of Sverin's neck.

"Fair winds," he whispered. "It will always be light in Tyr's land."

"Ah, my son," Sverin said, so softly Kjorn thought he'd imagined it. "I'm no longer afraid."

A great breath lifted his ribs, relaxed. Kjorn pressed his flank to Sverin's, and felt the beats of his heart. Then he felt when the heartbeats stilled.

Torch bearers stepped hesitantly closer, spilling light on them so that he would not pass in the dark, and the fire laid his crimson feathers out in gold.

"He flies with Tyr," Shard said, so simple it cut to Kjorn's marrow.

"What am I to do?" Kjorn whispered, clenching his talons, looking at Shard desperately, at his wingbrother, around at the torchbearers, dozens of gryfons with heads bowed in respect. "Shard, I did this. What am I to do?"

Shard stared at him, but a different voice answered, low but clear.

"You were always his light," said the Widow Queen, stepping forward, her head low. "And you didn't do this. Now, go to Thyra. That is what you must do now. Kjorn, go to your mate. "

Kjorn looked at Sverin. He couldn't fathom that the great, red body was only a body, that he was gone, that the gryfon he had loved, resented, longed for, was gone from the world.

"Kjorn," Shard said. "Go. I'll stay with him. We'll stay. He won't be in the dark."

"Shard..."

"Go to her."

Kjorn managed to stagger up. He hesitated, looking at Sverin's body, just in case. But he was still. With a soft sound he straightened, raised his head, turned to acknowledge the gryfons who stood vigil.

He was a king, and his father had died in battle, as many other gryfons had died before him. Kjorn managed to keep his head up. They bowed to him, and to Sverin, and drew closer, and the dead king was ringed with the silver of Hikaru's body and by flickering fire.

Kjorn turned and followed the wolf down into the caves. He barely remembered the walk or how long it took, only arriving where he knew Thyra to be. Sigrun sat outside her little niche in the stone, her face gentle.

"She won't let anyone in but you."

He inclined his head, walked in, and stood over his mate. She looked especially strong, and beautiful, gazing at him with bright, brown eyes, her nares flushed pink and her face fierce and so, so alive.

"My lord," she murmured. "You have a son."

He looked at the ball of fluff between her talons. It wriggled and squirmed around to peer at Kjorn with huge, hungry eyes. At the sight of those eyes, his world warped, turned on end, and in that moment he understood everything his father had ever done.

51
THE SILVER WIND

A T DAWN, THEY STOOD ON Black Rock, and sang the Song of Last Light.

Shard stood by Kjorn, barely able to raise his voice. With the strongest warriors and Hikaru's help, they had retrieved bodies from the shore around Pebble's Throw. The wyrms laid low on some far side of the broken lava isle, and the gryfons didn't see them at all, not when they returned to the island, and not when they took the bodies from the shore and the sea.

Rhydda's gloomy dreams flickered against Shard's, as if she sought him now, and he pressed the image of dead gryfons against her, which seemed to pin her in place as if he physically held her.

The final tally broke what was left of Shard's heart. He watched as Sigrun, her apprentices, and other warriors laid them out. Istren, his wings spread as if he would leap from the rock and fly into dawnward sky. Orange Vald, who was pureblooded Aesir but born in the Silver Isles.

Other half-bloods had sacrificed their lives, two of the older Aesir, and warriors who had flown from the Winderost. Shard stared at the faces of Vanir who had flown home, who'd fought, and died, whom he'd never even met.

He looked firmly away from their horrid injuries, focusing on their faces, and the memories of those he'd known in life.

Movement in the rows of mourning gryfons made Shard look to see Nilsine, with bad cuts mending, approach Rok, who stood a few gryfons down the line from Kjorn. The former rogue stared in grim silence at Fraenir's body, laid out beside a fallen Lakelander.

"He got what he wanted," Rok said stiffly. "Glory and honor."

"I know you were like brothers," Nilsine said softly. "But he did fight well." Rok jerked his head in agreement, but didn't look at her. "As did you. Warrior of the Dawn Spire."

Rok's gaze switched to her with surprise and wary gratitude. Shard watched them discreetly, glad for any small measure of hope and light in that moment.

Nilsine ducked her head, eyes averting. "I would ... not refuse you entry to the Vanheim Shore, should you visit our borders again."

"I'll be awfully busy now," Rok said, his voice gravelly as he strained for humor. "A Sentinel and all."

Nilsine's eyes glinted like jewels. "I'm sure you'll find your way to the sea. From time to time."

Shard watched as Rok gazed at her a moment, then turned, and raised his voice with the others in the ancient Song of Last Light.

"Which rises first, the night wind, or the stars?
Not even the owl could say,
Whether first comes the song or the dark ..."

Shard glanced sidelong at Kjorn, watching his face as they sang their warriors to rest. Many of the Aesir had chosen to have their dead rest there on Black Rock, rather than burn them at Pebble's Throw.

"Which fades last, the birdsong, or the day?
Not even the sky could tell,
Whether last stills the sun or the jay."

Vanir voices rose, while Aesir unfamiliar with song remained in respectful silence. The wind carried their song to Tyr, to Tor, to the Sunlit Land and their lost family and friends beyond.

> *"Only the long day brings rest*
> *Only the dark of night, dawn.*
> *When the First knew themselves, the wise will say,*
> *They took their names to the Sunlit Land*
> *but their Voice in the wind sings on."*

It fell quiet again, broken only by waves breaking on the distant shore, and seabirds, calling.

Shard touched his wing lightly to Kjorn's.

Sigrun approached them, asking quietly, "Kjorn, what are your wishes for Sverin?"

"He's welcome here," Shard said, turning to his wingbrother. "He's welcome to rest here, Kjorn, with ours."

"No." Kjorn looked around, not seeming as lost as he had before, but still firm, and cool. Shard knew the feeling, and would remain close as long as he could. "No ..."

Sigrun looked dawnward. "Shall we release him to the lava, like Per—"

"No," Kjorn said sharply. "Not at Pebble's Throw."

"Oh, no." Sigrun ground her beak, glancing at Shard with a look of chagrin. "Of course not."

Then, Kjorn stared at the rest of the gryfons laid out on the black stone, almost fifty all told, and seemed at a loss. Shard met Sigrun's eyes over his golden back, and lifted his wings a little, not sure what to do.

Warmth spread over them as Hikaru drew close, his silver scales pulsing with heat like embers. The dragon touched Kjorn very lightly with one claw.

"Prince Kjorn. King ..." He glanced hesitantly at Shard, who nodded encouragingly. "I have an idea."

Kjorn looked at the dragon, surprised, weary, and Shard watched Hikaru gratefully as he explained.

BUILDING HIKARU'S IDEA GAVE them something to do on a day that seemed mockingly beautiful and bright when their spirits felt so muddy and dark. Gryfons dragged through the forest of the Sun Isle, finding whole birch trunks. No one spoke.

It was Sigrun's idea, at last, for the gryfesses to emerge from the tunnels with their new, healthy kits. Once Shard assured her the wyrms would not fly that day, she brought them out into the light.

As Hikaru dragged birch trunks from the woods and gryfons stripped them of the smaller branches, the mewling of the kits sounded like a chorus of pure life and hope to Shard.

He found Thyra, walking slowly among the pride, just as he was. Her kit was nestled at the base of her neck in between her wings, alert and wobbly, staring around with almost unblinking eyes. Thyra and Shard met, bending their heads together, and regret lanced through him at how much he would miss her when she left for the Winderost.

"Big brother," Thyra murmured.

Shard laughed, for she seemed so much older now, so regal, he hardly felt like her big brother any more. "Thyra. It's so good to see you again at last. Let me meet your kit?"

She drew back and turned so Shard could meet the kit's gaze, and the tiny beak opened—in challenge or hunger, Shard wasn't sure. Though Thyra and Shard knew now that they weren't siblings by blood, they had been raised in the same nest, and Shard felt his heart expand to include the new kit in his family.

"My nephew," Shard said, his mood brightening slowly. "What is his name?"

"Kvasir," Thyra said, her eyes bright as she watched Shard's face. "Son-of-Kjorn."

In the sun, the kit's soft gray down held the faintest, promising shimmer of red and gold. Shard bent his head in, touching his beak lightly to the downy head. "Prince Kvasir, you are battle-born, and dragon blessed, and the heir to a great line. May you always reign in peace."

"Don't I get to reign for a bit too, first?" Thyra asked, teasing.

"Of course." Shard chuckled. "And long may that be."

When he drew back, the kit lifted his ungainly forefoot and pawed at Shard's beak, then sneezed.

Thyra broke into the warm laughter Shard remembered. "Don't worry. He'll come to appreciate a blessing from the Summer King as he grows older."

Shard nuzzled his nest-sister once more, and they parted, watching over their pride. With the presence of the kits and healthy gryfesses and the shining sun, Shard saw his pride begin to speak again, lift their wings, raise their heads.

Once, he even saw Ragna laugh, lifting Astri's tiny, pale puffball of a son into the air.

Shard drew up beside the little white gryfess, touching a wing to hers. She bowed to him, and Shard didn't stop her. "What is his name?"

"Eyvindr," she said, her eyes shining as she watched Ragna, chittering like a starling at the amazed kit. "Son-of-Einarr. He'll be one of the finest in your pride, my lord."

"I know it," Shard said quietly, touching his beak to her brow, and continued walking amongst his pride.

They didn't rush the work, but paused to fish and eat, to breathe the fresh, cool air, to talk to those who still lived. Shard walked among them, helping with the work but mostly seeing to spirits, and keeping his thoughts twined with Rhydda's. She would not leave Pebble's Throw that day.

At last, in the later afternoon, they lashed Hikaru's birch trunks together with split saplings, with sinew that Sigrun used to sew wounds. And on that platform, they built a pyre.

On the eve before Halflight under the last orange rays of the setting sun, they laid Sverin's body to rest both at sea, where his mate had died, and with fire, like an Aesir, like a dragon.

Hikaru pulled the birch-plank craft into the water and lit the flames, and they watched the waves tug it out to sea.

Shard stood on the beach below the nesting cliffs with Kjorn, all the pride, even the newly born kits, and Catori and Ahanu, who had come to offer their respect. They watched the smoke swirl up, sparks float high, and the fire kindle hotter until red feathers became red flames.

The scent of smoke and burning flesh drifted around them, then a bright, cold wind pushed it away, and they smelled earth and pine. Shard looked across the faces of his family and his friends, and saw Ragna, watching the burning pyre, he thought, with a strange mix of pride and loss.

"Tomorrow will be spring," he said quietly, to Kjorn. It was all he could say, but he had to say it.

Kjorn nodded, his feathers reflecting Sverin's pyre.

The flames roared in the water, and the rising sparks seemed to become new stars. The sunset faded toward violet, and points of light pricked the blue.

Thyra joined them quietly, with Kvasir still between her wings, sleeping through all of it.

Kjorn's eyes closed. Then, as if reminding himself of Sverin's final words, he turned and nuzzled his mate, then his son. Shard touched his beak to Thyra's cheek, and left them.

He walked to a lone figure, tall and strong against the sunset. Caj gazed after the pyre. Shard stood quietly beside him, and knew there were no words at all to express his sorrow that Caj had lost his wingbrother. But when he looked at his face, he seemed his same stern, peaceful self.

The older warrior tilted his head, and without taking his eyes from the fire, said, "I'm very proud of you, Shard. You will make a good king."

"Caj..."

"When Sverin was Nameless," his warm rumble continued thoughtfully, "he didn't respond to me until I stopped fighting him. Until I trusted him. He almost killed me, but he didn't."

Shard thought of Rhydda, and though she was nothing like a wingbrother to Shard, he knew that was why Caj had told him. They'd been fighting, fighting, fighting. It was time to stop.

"Thank you," Shard whispered. "I hope ... I welcome your guidance and counsel, nest-father. Always."

Caj looked at him then, the gold eyes that had always frightened Shard now seeming tired, but welcomingly familiar and bright. He nodded once, and in that silent gesture, Shard knew he understood that Shard invited him to stay. He was glad that it seemed he would.

Sigrun approached quietly, and Shard dipped his head respectfully before slipping away.

AROUND MIDNIGHT, SHARD VENTURED to the edge of the birch wood, looking out. He closed his eyes.

The pride had sheltered in the caves once more, none feeling secure enough yet to sleep in the nesting cliffs. No dragon gold was left. Nests had been torn apart by gryfons and wyrms searching for it. Some was lost in the sea, some the wyrms had taken. Maybe it would wash up one day, maybe not. Shard hoped to never see it again.

Awake, he stared out across the moonlit plain that led to the nesting cliffs and the sea, and in his mind he followed the dream net to Rhydda.

He showed her Sverin, laid out under the flames.

He crafted a dream of sunrise over the nesting cliffs, of himself standing there, of her, flying to meet him.

A rolling agreement in her chest sounded like tumbling stones.

She would meet him at dawn.

There was a curious sense to her, like a physical pain. She didn't understand it. She tried to turn from Shard, to turn her thoughts to blood and stone, but blood and stone became Sverin, became a gold gryfon screaming anguish into the stars.

That is regret, Shard thought, though he knew she would never understand the words. *Regret. Once our anger and hatred is quenched, it does not stay to keep us strong.*

He wove a dream of a raging forest fire, of powerful, licking flames, consuming everything, killing without sense or remorse, hungry and fueled by the lives it took. Then the fire ran out of things to burn, and he showed her the ashes, and he hoped she understood.

Footsteps crunched frosty leaves behind him. Ragna found him, came up on his side, and didn't speak.

"I saw how you looked at Sverin," Shard said quietly. "You forgave him. I'm glad."

Ragna bowed her head. "In the end, he did more than any of us could have asked."

Realizing how much he craved Stigr's company and advice, Shard was grateful to have his mother there. He turned and touched his beak to her head, gently, respectful.

"I'm meeting the wyrm at dawn," he murmured. "Alone."

Ragna's eyes narrowed and she didn't speak. The cold wind stirred their winter feathers, and Shard was grateful for it.

"I've been thinking," he said quietly, "I would like a council such as the Vanhar have. I've seen too many kings making poor decisions on their own, unchallenged by their subjects who are afraid to speak. I want to hear others, and I want them to know they're free to speak." He gazed at the stars, at the dragon stars of Midragur. "I want to hear the wisdom and desires of others. If I'm away, then Brynja will lead it, then you."

"That sounds very wise, Shard. Very good indeed."

He could tell she didn't like his tone, that he was speaking of *ifs.*

If he was away.

If he didn't come back from his meeting with Rhydda.

For a moment the night was dark and still around them, and Ragna said, "It will be as you desire. But I wish you wouldn't go to the wyrm."

"Every time I've tried to talk to her, I either did the wrong thing, or we were interrupted. This time, I believe she'll listen."

"I wish you wouldn't," Ragna said again quietly.

Shard closed his eyes, taking in the scent of chill wind, the rain-scent of spring on its way. Tomorrow was the Halflight, a time of balance between night and day. Then all things would turn toward the light.

Finally, Shard spoke. "Mother, you sang the Song of the Summer King to me. I learned to speak to wolves, to birds, to lions, and dragons. You put your trust in me. You asked great things of me. I've traveled across two seas in search of the truth. I've only, ever, done what I hope is right." He tilted his head to see her clearly. "Put your trust in me again. If I'm your chosen king, then trust me, one last time."

Ragna gazed at him, then bowed her head. They didn't speak again after that, and before long, took to their rests.

Shard slept aboveground, outside the tunnel. As much as he wanted to and knew he should be with his pride, his heart closed at the sight of the black hole in the ground. He remained with Hikaru outside, curled in the dragon's warm scales.

He woke before first light.

When he crawled out of Hikaru's coils, the young dragon barely stirred.

He stalked through the tall, white birch. An awareness drew his attention, and he looked up to see the white owl, who remained silent. Around her perched other birds, silent, staring at him with bright, expectant eyes.

Shard dipped his head to them and walked on.

Low, purple light lay over the plain between the woods and the sea, and a pale line traced the dawnward sky. He walked, didn't fly, toward the nesting cliffs. He let his talons sink down through the patches of snow to squeeze the frozen peat of the isle, his home. He relished the taste of the wind. If Rhydda didn't listen, he took every moment to savor what might be his last moments.

For Ragna, he'd been confident. In his heart, he wasn't certain he would live. He thought of his father, Baldr, flying out to meet Per, and with a sting of regret, he thought of Stigr's words to him.

A living king.

A step drew his attention.

A glance to one side showed Ragna, walking a respectful distance behind him. Beside her walked Brynja. Shard didn't say anything.

"We won't interfere," Brynja said. "But you're not going alone."

Shard didn't want to argue. "Show her respect. Do whatever I do. Say nothing. She doesn't understand words. I must try to do something she understands."

They murmured agreement. He turned and walked on. The cool morning wind brought him the scent of the river, the mountains. He remembered what the priestess of the Vanhar had said about places giving him strength, and held to the memory of Ajia's paws, holding him to the earth. The mountains and the river at his back made his heart swell with strength.

Then a new sensation, a prickling awareness, made him look back again. More gryfons appeared from the woods, in silence. When they saw him, they inclined their heads, and didn't walk any farther than Brynja or Ragna.

Shard lifted his wings to them before turning to walk on.

Drawing strength from his pride, from the mountains, Shard let his talons sink into the damp peat and soil. The muddy scent of spring and the salt of the sea brushed his mind with every memory of his lifetime in the Silver Isles. He had promised he would return, but not for how long. If Rhydda misunderstood him, or decided on one last piece of Nameless violence and killed him, he would end just like his father.

He could not fail.

The wind shifted and another scent drew him around once more. Behind the ranks of gryfons, from the shadow of the tree line, he saw Catori slipping out to join them. With her came Ahanu, Tocho, and half of their pack, walking in silence behind the gryfon pride.

Shard halted only long enough to raise his beak in acknowledgement of them, as a chill washed his spine. They came to give him strength. To honor him.

To see him, maybe, for the last time.

Drawing a hard breath, Shard turned and continued forward, but a soft sound from Brynja paused him again, and he looked back.

To his surprise, beyond the line of gryfons and wolves he saw a trio of caribou. Old Aodh, who had once advised him, and two other elders emerged from the trees. Their steps were slow, solid, deliberate as the earth.

When you rise, I will be there to honor you. Aodh had said that. Shard remembered.

At the sight of them Shard thought of thundering herds, the power of Tor, the pure, trusting courage of them to come out of the woods and walk near dangerous hunters just to honor him.

His throat closed, his gaze traveling over each face. His talons clenched the earth, his tail lashed into the wind. Gray dawn touched the tops of the mountains and Shard knew it was best that he'd chosen to do this last task under Tyr's first light.

A sound drew his ear, and he opened his wings a little when Hikaru snaked up out of the trees, making wide, silent circles above the woods. After him, a cloud of birds burst up in eerie quiet before settling again into branches, at the edge of the tree line, and on the ground, just letting Shard know of their presence. A few hawks circled. Ravens, crows. Hikaru hovered, sleek wings beating the sweet morning air.

Shard stared. He thought of turning once more, but he couldn't move. He could hardly believe the display, the faces of his pride, the wolves, birds, and hoofed creatures walking, standing, arriving to acknowledge him.

For a moment, he and the creatures who had come to honor him regarded each other in silence. They remained far back as he'd asked, and a good fifty leaps stood between them. But he couldn't turn from them without acknowledging them in turn.

Hikaru settled on the ground at the end of the line of gryfons, and many of the birds lighted on and near him. From the trees, Shard saw smaller animals, bright eyes, the flicking ears and tails of red deer. Watching. Listening.

Shard spoke, and the wind carried his voice to every ear.

"The song said that the Nameless shall know themselves, and Voiceless will once again speak."

He lifted his gaze to the hovering birds, then dipped down to see Catori standing near Ragna, her eyes shining.

"But those of us who looked down on other creatures as Nameless, Voiceless, witless, know better now. Now *we* listen. Now we hear. We honor the hoofed creatures of the isles. We honor the wolves, and all the smaller creatures who burrow and run and hunt. We honor the birds in the winds."

Not a paw or a wing shifted. All listened. All heard, and Shard hoped his voice sounded like hope and summer. He met Brynja's eyes across the field, and her expression burned with pride and with love. Kjorn gazed at him steadily, earnest and hard. Caj. Ragna.

At last, all of them heard, and Shard knew he had been wrong when he'd thought the song meant Rhydda would speak. They'd all been wrong.

Shard went on, pitching his voice low, but they heard.

"As we recognize those truths, let us recognize the wyrms as creatures of a different, darker, harder Age. I believe the wyrms will never speak like us. That doesn't make them evil."

Lifting his ears forward in determination, Shard raised his wings.

"I will be Rhydda's voice, if she'll let me. As we respect the earth and the sea, let us respect them, too. We united in war, so let us unite, now, in compassion. Thank you, all of you. Now you must let me go on alone."

They watched him, dipped their heads, and didn't speak. Shard realized that he was their prince, and they would do whatever he asked.

So he walked on, feeling his feet on the earth, opening his wings to the morning breeze.

He chose the Copper Cliff, the King's Rocks, but he stood at the base of them, not on top. For long moments he stood, and the light gathered, and he felt the silent support of a wall of creatures far behind him.

A wind rushed them and Shard looked up to see Rhydda, enormous wings shadowing the sky. She stooped, landed on the King's Rocks, and clenched her great talons around them. When she saw the great host on the plain beyond, she bellow a challenging roar.

Shard dipped low, like a wolf, bowed his head, and mantled his wings as if to a queen. He didn't say a word. Heart galloping in his ears, he prayed that others would follow his lead. Tilting his head slightly, he saw with amazement that every gryfon and wolf behind him also bowed to Rhydda. He spied even Kjorn, forelegs stretched, head low.

He remembered Hikaru, telling him of the dragons and the wyrms. *They responded to food, beautiful things, and to kindness.*

When she was silent, Shard lifted his head. Rather than speak, he loosed a soft, warm birdcall, like a parent summoning a juvenile. She lowered her horned head, and a rumbling, grating sound answered him.

Kindness.

Shard stepped forward.

She reared back, jaws snapping, her wing beats sending a rush of wind that battered him and brought him low again.

Murmurs and alarm swept the others. Shard whirled. "Stay where you are! Do nothing. Say nothing."

When he was certain that they would obey, he turned back to Rhydda, crouching low.

All the strength and surety he'd gathered on his slow walk answered to his call. Closing his eyes, he felt the bright spiral of the dream net, connecting them, all of them. He felt Rhydda.

She was angry that she didn't understand his speech, so he crafted one last dream. He showed her all Hikaru had told him. He showed her own story of the dragons, of Kajar, his own long journey, his loss. His knowledge, his truth. He showed that he knew what she'd gone through. He showed her Lapu the boar, old and angry, and Helaku the wolf king, almost Nameless with anger by the end, just like her.

She answered with memory of herself and the battle, and roaring at him during a storm, and cutting Stigr down, and her battle with Sverin. A bitter, hot feeling accompanied the images.

Yes. Yes, that's right. Anger, hate. I understand, Rhydda. I understand everything. Come with me. Let me show you one thing more.

Glancing one final time at Ragna, at Brynja, Shard bounded twice, and leaped into the sky. He caught a wind and spiraled up around Rhydda, and with a cheerful, inviting, witless sound, flew higher.

After three pounding heartbeats, she launched from the rocks, and with great, hard, wing beats, followed.

Shard laid a dream over them both. He had to show her one final thing, one thing so she would know what he wished for her.

At last alone together, he tried to show her joy.

The sun peeked over the ocean and pale light glittered across the waves. Shard wove around her, and she whipped about to keep up with him, not attacking, but curious, he thought.

Rise higher, he whispered, in the dream.

He washed them both in the light of sun. Careful not to appear threatening, he followed his instinct, flying with her. He flew, thinking of Caj's words about trust. He stayed close to Rhydda, thinking of the path between all things that the dragons called *sky*. He tucked into the wind, rolled, and she followed, and the sun rose on them.

This is joy, Rhydda.

She showed him a forest of ashes.

That is regret. Anger and hate are powerful, but they don't keep us strong.

To his surprise, she returned the forest image to what it was before. She thought of green, green hills, she thought of her home, her brood.

That is love. Shard spun around her, and she snapped her jaws, but not in threat, he thought.

He showed her Hikaru hatching.

He showed her Stigr, training him over the sea, Brynja laughing, and his mother, who did everything for his sake. He intertwined the green, living forest with the idea of love. Swimming in the sea, fishing, flying with his Vanir—he tried to show her every joyful thing, every reason he had pursued her and tried to understand her. Everything she could have.

In silence, they soared high, and looked down. The sun crept above the sea and spilled light on the water and the islands, and for a moment they did look truly silver.

It was the Halflight, when all things would turn toward the light.

Shard circled around to see her fully. They hovered, as they once had in the Winderost, but this time no one would interrupt them.

This time, she heard.

"Do you understand?" he whispered, and it didn't matter that his words were lost in the wind. Shard finally understood that she was a creature of the First Age. She knew hunting, breeding, blood, and stone. She would never speak the way Shard knew how to speak. Shard at last understood that she had learned of anger, of resentment, of hatred. But in all her long years, she had not learned of joy, or love.

He flew in close, for he knew from his mother, from his wing-brother, from Brynja, and from Hikaru, that love began in one place.

"I trust you," he said softly. He flew in close, stretched out his talons.

Her wings beat hard. Shard drifted closer, wings aching at the sustained hover.

"You don't have to be like us," Shard murmured. "But you can be with us." He offered his talons, offered his trust, knew that with a single swipe, she could kill him and send his body into the sea.

"Rhydda," Shard murmured. He thought of the dragon who had blessed Kajar, and wished he could bless Rhydda.

Her black eyes stared at him. Sunlight touched them with pale gold.

Then, she bowed her head.

Without fear, Shard slipped closer, and pressed his talons to her brow.

A warm, sweeping rush seemed to fill and spill over from him, a sense of the dream he'd crafted for them, and the real sunlight around them, as if he could feel every living thing.

A great sigh heaved in Rhydda's ribs, and as she breathed in, Shard felt a little piece of himself join her. He released it, a little piece of his heart, for her, so she could hold on to this moment when she understood love, and joy.

"You're free," Shard whispered.

Her great, dark, serpent eyes met his, and in them Shard saw himself. For one heartbeat they were one. His mind flashed on the dream of the forest fire, the ashes. Then, she added something. For Shard, she imagined rain.

Shard choked back a soft noise of amazement and gratitude. "Yes. I forgive you."

She tucked a wing and turned, diving low. There, below him, she banked, flared, and ducked her head low, as if imitating a gryfon mantle. For a heartbeat she watched Shard.

"Fair winds," Shard whispered.

She turned then, and soared without looking back at the Sun Isle, toward her brood, and Shard knew without question that from there she would take her family home.

He looked down at his islands, and saw the great host of gryfons, wolves, birds and the rest, and Hikaru, waiting for him below. During his flight, they had drawn close, clustering all along the Cooper Cliff and fanning out into the field beyond.

Spiraling down, he landed in silence on the highest ledge of the King's Rocks.

He landed where he had seen Per and Sverin stand so many times before, and from there he could see almost every face that stared at him in mute awe. His breath felt short, and he left his wings open to the cold morning wind. He thought he should say something, but a deep, clear voice rang out first.

Kjorn.

"Rashard, the king!"

A burred, hard voice declared, "All hail the king!" Shard looked at Caj, and his nest-father met his gaze with fierce pride.

Every Vanir who stood there echoed him in a single, sharp, victorious chorus. "*All hail the king!*"

Hikaru whipped up from his place and spiraled high like a silver snake, declaring, "The Summer King! *Rashard the Summer King!*"

Voices rose. Birds burst from the birch wood around the forest and sang their approval. Gryfons stood tall and shouted his name, the sun brightened over the sea, and it was spring.

For a moment, Shard flashed on his father's vision of the future, and he could see it now. He could see that it had begun.

Ragna, Brynja, Caj and the Aesir, the wolves, the half-bloods, even Halvden, bellowed for all the isles to hear.

"All hail the king!"

"Rashard, the Summer King!"

FOUR MOONS LATER, THE Daynight dawned cloudy and cool.

Shard stood on the King's Rocks, his face to the wind, and thought the clouds might burn off before the celebrations began.

After leaving for the spring, Hikaru had returned with Natsumi and their dragonet, a little springborn hatchling he named Terasu, after his grandmother.

Natsumi had shed into warm, pearly scales of bronze, and she was fascinated with the gryfess huntresses. They swapped fighting and fishing techniques, and some disappeared with the dragoness for long afternoons, exploring the islands. Now, she seemed content to help them preen for the Daynight celebrations.

Hikaru's summer scales shifted in the dawn light, warm, burnished gray. He'd joked that he and Shard truly looked like brothers now, except he being taller. He'd come to celebrate Shard and Brynja's mating, and to learn what the gryfons and wolves did to celebrate the turn of the seasons. The chronicler should pay attention to all creatures, not just dragons, he'd decided.

After this visit, he would fly with Kjorn to the Winderost. Then, he intended to find the wyrms' homeland, and renew their bonds.

Shard turned from the sea to look out over the windswept plain and the White Mountains, watching as gryfons went about their morning.

Gryfesses emerged with their kits, each telling their own favorite Daynight traditions. After the feasting and the songs, the mating flights, and the next sunrise, the Aesir would depart for home.

Shard felt regret, but also knew it was time. Their kits were strong enough to be carried across the sea, and Kjorn had a new kingdom to rule.

Out in the field, the golden king sat with little Kvasir, who wobbled about on uncertain legs, leading a play hunt for grasshoppers. Tumbling around him were Terasu, pale white of scale and already the size of a gryfon fledge, Astri's kit Eyvindr, and Halla, Halvden and Kenna's kit.

Two wolf yearlings gamboled around them, for Ahanu had brought his family to celebrate the Daynight on the Sun Isle. Then they sped off from the slow and apparently boring gryfon kits to pester Frar and group of fledglings, who were listening to the elder's tales of Daynights past. Among the fledglings sat Vanhar, Lakelanders, and gryfons of Shard's own pride.

For a moment, the sight boggled Shard's mind. He wondered what his father would have thought, to see such a thing. He wondered what Sverin would have. Kjorn's pleased and amused expression told him all he needed to know.

They'd rebuilt the nests in the cliffs, cleaned the shore, and mourned their dead.

Shard had traveled to each isle, meeting the horses, the hawks and falcons of Talon's Reach, the snow wolves of the high mountains on the Star Isle. He wanted all to know that the Vanir were home, that he was king, that he welcomed their alliance and their counsel, and that the gryfons would aid them if ever they had need.

Gryfons took to the sky from their nests and soared out to sea to begin the morning fishing. Shard's heart lifted, as it always did, to see them. Ragna led a group, Brynja and Thyra with them.

From the river, he caught a flash of russet.

"Catori!"

The she-wolf raced across the plain, throwing up dew with her paws, tongue lolling in a happy pant. She bounded past gryfons and kits and wolves and the two enormous dragons, so out of place among the smaller creatures.

Shard hopped down from the rocks to meet her at the base, and she padded right up to lick the side of his head. He laughed and shook himself as she trotted a happy circle, her tail high and waving.

"I'm so happy for you, my friend! Time for you to make Brynja a queen, at last. And I see the Vanir's love for her."

"Yes." Shard's heart warmed, and pounded. Above them, even as he'd hoped, the clouds began to drift apart from each other to reveal a summer-blue sky. "She's been patient to wait for me."

"It's right," Catori said, sitting near him. "Right, to honor the tradition of your ancestors."

Shard nodded once. "I also meant to ask you and Ahanu if we might hunt on the Star Isle. This will be the biggest Daynight celebration the pride has ever seen, and we'll need a lot to eat. And I'd like to honor the Aesir with food I know they'll like."

Her tailed waved. "But it's already done. Ahanu thought of that yesterday, and the pack is hunting, so let him surprise you."

Shard inclined his head, grateful. "Thank you." His gaze drifted back to the odd mix of kits, pups, and the dragonet at play.

Catori nosed his feathers. "You seem far too pensive on this day."

"I was just thinking how it's been exactly a year since Ragna sang the song."

"Yes?" Catori's ears flicked away a buzzing fly. "So it has."

"I was just wondering what might've happened, if I hadn't heeded it, if I'd really thought Kjorn was the Summer King, as Sverin said."

"Perhaps he was." She looked at him, her amber eyes bright and mischievous.

Shard flicked his tail, and ruffled his feathers. "You haven't riddled at me in a long time. But you're right. Kjorn could have been. Or Hikaru, or any of the gryfons in the pride."

"I don't think it could have been *any* of them," Catori murmured, watching him fondly.

"But what if it wasn't destiny, but my decision?"

"What if?" Catori echoed, sounding like a raven.

Shard snapped his beak at her playfully.

"But you *did* decide, you did everything you had to, you became the Summer King, and look what it's done for all of us."

Shard watched gryfons flying high above them, some on their way to the birch wood and others to Star Isle for kindling. They would have fires in celebration. "But what if another gryfon heard the song, and thought they were supposed to follow it?"

Catori stood and shook her bright summer coat, nipping the air in a laugh. "And how awful that would be! For a whole generation of young gryfons to hear the song and think it was about them, to believe they must rise higher, see farther, listen to all who speak . . . what a terrible, terrible thing."

Shard eyed her sideways, and laughed. "I suppose you're right."

She bowed before him, stretching her long legs and digging claws into the peat. "I hope you won't think much more about it. Brynja will not appreciate a distracted partner."

"No, no of course." Oh, the mating flights. He had watched them every year as he grew. Since Shard was known for his flight skills, they would probably expect great things. He was glad for the weather.

A shadow rippled over them and Shard looked up to see Brynja banking about to land, with a fish in her talons.

"For you!" she tossed it proudly to the ground in front of him and Shard trotted to her as she landed, butting his head against her chest.

"Thank you."

Brynja nodded to acknowledge Catori, then eyed the cloudy sky. "I've sent extra flights out, for fish, and the Vanhar will help to feed all this rabble."

Shard flicked his ears in amusement. Of course she would already be taking care of things. "Thank you again, my queen."

"I am not queen yet," she said, with a spark in her eyes, challenging him. "We'll see how well you fly today."

Shard laughed. "Yes."

They backed away from each other, tails lashing with excitement. Shard admired her face in the dawn, and the dramatic angle of her as the wind rushed against her feathers.

Her eyes shone. "At least it's such a fair morning, don't you think?"

"Yes," Shard agreed. The wind brought him scents of pine, of saltwater and of his pride.

Something else, elusive, sweet, and silver touched the air, something he knew he would always sense now, something that he would never quite be able to define.

"Very fair," he said, and opened his wings, breathing deeply, and gazed at the blue peeking through the clouds. "I think it will be a good day for flying."

THE END

Acknowledgements

A<small>T LAST THE</small> S<small>UMMER</small> K<small>ING</small> Chronicles are complete. From the first idea to the final volume, there are so many people to thank that I'll inevitably miss a few, but I owe my entire community and family my thanks. A thank you to my editor, Joshua Essoe, for helping me develop and strengthen the story all along the way to an ending with which I am wholly satisfied, and I hope readers will be too. My cover artist Jennifer Miller, who delivered a stunning finale to the quartet of books! TERyvisions for once again laying out all ebooks as well as the paperback and hardback editions with beautiful, classic artistry. I want to offer a special shout out to all the artists involved in the final Kickstarter—.DOLL plushies, Gann Memorials, Emily Coleman, Jennifer Miller as always, and Lindsay Adams! Thanks as well to Eric C. Wilder for my gorgeous website and being a constant support in many ways, my dear friend Kate for always Being There, and Lauren Head for neverending cheerleading and helping finally get my newsletter going!

Finally and always, a huge thank you to my parents, who support me spiritually, mentally and materially in many ways, my sister who is my critique partner forever, and my husband, who is my wingbrother. Without my whole pride, I would never fly so high.

And finally, here is the list of generous backers whose pledges included a listing in the acknowledgements. Many names will look familiar from previous years. Thank you so much; I'm truly humbled by for your continued support!

In no particular order of amazingness:

The Blood Family	FL
Z.A.L. Storm	Renee LeCompte
Maya & Sylvie	Dr. Robert Early
Kellie Riddett	Michael "Tagar" Teinert
Searska GreyRaven	Anna Wentzel
Björn Schneider	Iben Krutt
Justin Strother	Fiona van der Pennen
Thomas Ally	Renee Rathjen
Samantha Sack	Jessica Pawlik
Chad Bowden	K.T. Ivanrest
Dain Eaton	Emily Weichbrod
Anita	David "Draco Cretel" Taylor
Laura Lewis	Shepherd Sinclair
Amanda "Moon Willow" Smith	Camielle Adams
NightEyes DaySpring	Crisaron Schmehl

ABOUT THE AUTHOR

JESS HAS BEEN CREATING WORKS of fantasy art and fiction for over a decade. The Summer King Chronicles is her first foray into the publishing realm, and she plans many more gryfon adventures to come. Her short fiction has appeared in Cricket Magazine for young readers, and various anthologies online. She's a proud member of the Society of Children's Book Writers and Illustrators, the Science Fiction and Fantasy Writers of America, and the Authors of the Flathead. Jess lives with her husband and their dog in the mountains of northwest Montana, which offer daily inspiration for creating worlds of wise, wild creatures, magic, and adventure. Jess can be contacted directly through Facebook, Twitter, and her website, www.jessowen.com.

Books by Jess E. Owen

The Summer King Chronicles
~~
Song of the Summer King
Skyfire
A Shard of Sun
By the Silver Wind

Made in the
USA
Monee, IL

14727772R00286